MIND OF A MADMAN

Jess Van Cleef remembered the Indians whose faces he'd cut off. Just thinking about it made him want to touch his knife, sharp and shiny in a scabbard dangling from his belt, but he didn't. He sat right where he was, hardly moving. He'd made a little noise earlier, and he'd been afraid that the men had heard him. He didn't think they had, however, since they went on talking, and now one of them was asleep.

The other one was sitting up, keeping a watch, but it wouldn't do him any good. He'd get a little drowsy sooner or later and, when he did, Van Cleef would be right behind him with his knife.

It would be a little while longer, Van Cleef knew, but he could wait. He was good at waiting, as long as he knew his patience would be rewarded. . . .

THE
TRAILSMAN

#291

THE
CUTTING
KIND

by

Jon Sharpe

A SIGNET BOOK

SIGNET
Published by New American Library, a division of
Penguin Group (USA) Inc., 375 Hudson Street,
New York, New York 10014, USA
Penguin Group (Canada), 90 Eglinton Avenue East, Suite 700, Toronto,
Ontario M4P 2Y3, Canada (a division of Pearson Penguin Canada Inc.)
Penguin Books Ltd., 80 Strand, London WC2R 0RL, England
Penguin Ireland, 25 St. Stephen's Green, Dublin 2,
Ireland (a division of Penguin Books Ltd.)
Penguin Group (Australia), 250 Camberwell Road, Camberwell, Victoria 3124,
Australia (a division of Pearson Australia Group Pty. Ltd.)
Penguin Books India Pvt. Ltd., 11 Community Centre, Panchsheel Park,
New Delhi - 110 017, India
Penguin Group (NZ), cnr Airborne and Rosedale Roads, Albany,
Auckland 1310, New Zealand (a division of Pearson New Zealand Ltd.)
Penguin Books (South Africa) (Pty.) Ltd., 24 Sturdee Avenue,
Rosebank, Johannesburg 2196, South Africa

Penguin Books Ltd., Registered Offices:
80 Strand, London WC2R 0RL, England

First published by Signet, an imprint of New American Library,
a division of Penguin Group (USA) Inc.

First Printing, January 2006
10   9   8   7   6   5   4   3   2   1

The first chapter of this book previously appeared in *Mountain Mavericks*, the
two hundred ninetieth volume in this series.

PUBLISHER'S NOTE
This is a work of fiction. Names, characters, places, and incidents either are the
product of the author's imagination or are used fictitiously, and any resemblance
to actual persons, living or dead, business establishments, events, or locales is
entirely coincidental.
    The publisher does not have any control over and does not assume any respon-
sibility for author or third-party Web sites or their content.

If you purchased this book without a cover you should be aware that this book
is stolen property. It was reported as "unsold and destroyed" to the publisher
and neither the author nor the publisher has received any payment for this
"stripped book."

The scanning, uploading, and distribution of this book via the Internet or via any
other means without the permission of the publisher is illegal and punishable by
law. Please purchase only authorized electronic editions, and do not participate
in or encourage electronic piracy of copyrighted materials. Your support of the
author's rights is appreciated.

The Trailsman

Beginnings . . . they bend the tree and they mark the man. Skye Fargo was born when he was eighteen. Terror was his midwife, vengeance his first cry. Killing spawned Skye Fargo, ruthless, cold-blooded murder. Out of the acrid smoke of gunpowder still hanging in the air, he rose, cried out a promise never forgotten.

The Trailsman they began to call him all across the West: searcher, scout, hunter, the man who could see where others only looked, his skills for hire but not his soul, the man who lived each day to the fullest, yet trailed each tomorrow. Skye Fargo, the Trailsman, the seeker who could take the wildness of a land and the wanting of a woman and make them his own.

Fort Laramie, 1860—
there's a killer on the loose along the Oregon Trail,
and it looks like no one but Skye Fargo can stop him.

1

Jess Van Cleef had killed three men in Independence, Missouri, then lit out for the West, somewhere along the Oregon Trail. Nobody knew just where exactly he was heading as he'd been in too much of a hurry to tell them.

It wasn't so much that he'd killed the men that made people take notice of what he'd done, though. It was the *way* that he'd killed them.

"Skint 'em, is what he did," John Keller told Skye Fargo. "Not entirely the way you might think. Just the faces. Cut their faces right off 'em, the son of a bitch. And then carved on their chests and arms a little. You know he musta enjoyed it. Nobody does somethin' like that 'less he enjoys it."

Keller was taking it hard, Fargo thought, which was only natural. One of the men Van Cleef had killed was Keller's younger brother.

"Little Sammy never hurt a fly, by God," Keller said. "Sweet and innocent as a child, little Sammy was. Yet Van Cleef showed him no mercy."

The younger Keller's body had been found in an alley behind a whorehouse and, judging from what Fargo had heard from others, Van Cleef and Sammy had gotten into an argument over a soiled dove named Big Nose Rose. They'd left the whorehouse without settling anything because the madam, known as Flower of the West, or just Flower to her friends, of whom there were reputed to be many, had threatened them with the two-shot gun she kept under the bar.

Nobody knew for sure what had happened after that, but most everybody was morally certain that Van Cleef had thrashed Sammy half to death in the alley, then stolen his face and done a little carving on him before running a knife blade between his ribs to finish him.

"I'd like to think he kilt him first," John Keller told Fargo. "But it just ain't in the cards. A man like Van Cleef don't do things that way. He likes hearin' the moanin' and cryin'. Not that Sammy woulda cried. He was a young 'un, but he was too tough for that."

Fargo nodded his agreement, though he'd never met Sammy. He and John Keller had met a couple of days ago and shared a drink or two since then because they were more or less in the same profession. Keller was a guide who took trains of pilgrims out on the Oregon Trail. Fargo was known as the Trailsman because of his ability to get from one place to another throughout the West. He'd led his share of wagon trains, mapped the land for stage lines, and done a hundred other like things to earn his keep.

Keller, who was about forty years old, had a seamed face and lank hair that hung down from beneath his battered felt hat. He hadn't taken a bath for a while, and there was dirt in the creases on his cheeks.

At the moment, both Keller and Fargo were unemployed. The reason in Fargo's case was that it was too far gone in the year for anyone to go much farther west along the Oregon Trail. The first snow had already fallen, and it would take a much more foolhardy man than Skye Fargo to try to push on to Oregon with a bunch of soft pilgrims in his charge. He'd brought one last small group as far as Fort Laramie, where they planned to winter before moving out again in the springtime.

Fargo would be long gone by then as he had no interest in staying in one place for more than a short time—not if he could help it. He was a man for whom being on the move was a necessity of life, and he'd be leaving Fort Laramie soon, heading back east to see if there was some kind of job he could pick up.

John Keller's reason for lacking employment was of a different nature. He was riding the vengeance trail, looking

2

for Jess Van Cleef, and his search had led him to Fort Laramie.

"I don't know as he's around here," Keller said, "but I heard he'd been seen out this way. Thinks the law can't reach him out here, and I guess he's right about that. But I can, by God, and I intend to. A man like him ought not be allowed to run free, and not just because of what he done to little Sammy. He's done it to others, and he'll do it to more if he gets the chance."

Fargo nodded again. He'd found that was all he needed to do to keep a conversation going with Keller, who was more than ready to do enough talking for the both of them.

They were in the Red Dog Saloon, which was, or wasn't, part of Fort Laramie, depending on your point of view.

Unlike a lot of forts, Laramie wasn't enclosed by a stockade or wall, though Fargo had heard that had been the original plan. Because of a shortage of money, or some other reason, the wall had never been built, and Laramie had become an open fort, more like a small town, depending on the troops garrisoned there for its protection.

And anywhere there was a fort, open or not, especially one on a trail that saw so many passing wagon trains full of thirsty Easterners looking for a new home out west, a saloon or two was bound to prosper. The Red Dog was one of them.

It wasn't on the grounds of the fort itself. The soldiers, for the most part, took their drinks in the Soldier's Board. But the Red Dog was located close enough to the grounds to be within the fort's protection. It was frequented by traders, trappers, travelers, renegades, rascals, cardsharpers, and anyone else who happened to be in the vicinity and had a craving for liquor. And who wasn't too particular about its quality.

It was a little after noon, and at the moment the Red Dog was quiet. There was a broken-down upright piano up against one wall, but no one was playing. In the two days he'd been in Laramie, Fargo hadn't heard a single note come from it. Whether it was broken or whether there was no one who could play, Fargo neither knew nor cared.

In a corner of the saloon, a drunk slumped across the table, snoring and occasionally scratching himself in his sleep. Four men gambled with cards, but without any notable enthusiasm a few tables away from where Fargo and Keller sat talking. The bartender was leaning on his elbows, staring out across the chilly room as if he were somewhere warmer and cheerier, maybe down around Galveston, Texas, where the Gulf waves would be washing up on the beach. Fargo didn't much blame him.

"I'll get the son of a bitch Van Cleef," Keller said. "I know for sure I will."

Fargo nodded again, but he didn't really think Keller had much of a chance to find Van Cleef. A man could lose himself in the West without any trouble at all if that's what he wanted to do. Keller might know the country, but that didn't mean he could find Jess Van Cleef, not if Van Cleef didn't want to be found.

Two men came into the saloon, and Fargo's lake blue eyes narrowed at the sight of the snow blowing through the open door. The bigger of the two men pushed the door closed, but not before the blast of air they let inside had increased the room's chill.

The men stood looking around. One stood more than six feet tall, while the other was at least a foot shorter. Both wore beaver hats and buffalo robes against the cold, and both had thick salt-and-pepper beards that obscured their faces. Each carried an old Hawken rifle that had cost between twenty-five and thirty dollars when new, considerably more than any other rifle. They were fine weapons, but Fargo preferred his Henry.

The men brushed snow off their heavy robes. The tall one said, "Which one of you fellas is John Keller?"

His voice was high-pitched and rusty as if he didn't use it often.

Fargo looked at Keller to see if he'd respond. Keller glanced down at his glass, which was almost empty.

"We want to hire John Keller for a guide," the short man said. "Pay's good."

His voice was a deep, rumbling bass. Fargo could have sworn that it vibrated through the floorboards of the saloon.

Keller looked up when the word pay was mentioned.

"I'm Keller," he said, turning to look at the two men. "What can I do for you?"

The two men eyed him silently, then glanced at each

4

other. After the silence had stretched for a while, the tall one said, "He don't look like much."

"Don't matter," his companion said. "He's the one we want."

"Want for what?" Keller asked.

The two men looked at each other again, then turned back to Keller.

"To help me kill a man," the short one said.

2

The big man's name was Tobias Walker, and his shorter friend was Seth Gant.

The man they wanted to kill was Jess Van Cleef.

Naturally, Keller was interested to hear what they had to say.

Fargo wasn't, not particularly, but he didn't see the need to get up and leave. It was a lot colder outside than it was in the saloon.

"Army won't do nothing about Van Cleef," Walker said, his voice not sounding so rusty after having been lubricated with a drink or two of the Red Dog's bad whiskey. "They say it ain't their job."

"They say they're here to protect people from the Injuns, not from some fella that might be back in Independence by now," Gant said, his voice vibrating the table where they sat.

"Somebody's gotta do something, though," Walker said. "And we hear you'd like to."

He was talking to Keller, of course. Both men had pretty much ignored Fargo ever since sitting down.

Their story was simple. They had once been trappers and hunters before leaving the mountains and going back east to find wives.

"Made a pile of money out of those mountains," Walker said. "But it gets mighty lonesome up there after a while. Not a whole lot of women around. Some folks ain't bothered by that, but me and Gant are. So we decided to try the civilized life for a while."

His lip didn't quite curl when he said civilized, but it was a near thing.

Gant's did. "*Civilized,* my ass. A city is a sinkhole of corruption. We should've brought our wives back out here and lived in the mountains. Both of 'em would still be alive now, instead of just yours."

Gant's wife was the one Van Cleef had killed. It seemed that as he was leaving Independence, he stopped off at Gant's house, maybe because he wanted to steal something, or maybe just because he thought he could find a little entertainment before beginning his long trip west.

What he'd found was Gant's wife, who was in the kitchen, baking bread. Van Cleef raped her and killed her, then cut her up—badly.

"Wasn't much left of her face," Walker said. "The bastard was blood crazy. Neighbor woman happened by just as he was leaving, and he raped her, too. Didn't kill her outright, and that was his mistake. She was able to tell what happened to her before she died."

Keller nodded his understanding. He said, "I know about Van Cleef, all right, and I'd like to see him dead. What I don't know is why you two don't just find him and kill him yourselves. You look like you know this country as well as I do. Maybe better."

"Ain't a matter of knowing the country," Gant said.

He looked at Walker, who looked down at his drink as if it had suddenly become the most interesting thing in the room.

"It's a matter of a man who's pussy whipped," Gant continued.

"It ain't that," Walker said.

"If it ain't, what would you call it, then?"

Walker didn't say anything.

"Cat got your tongue?" Gant asked.

Walker remained silent.

"His wife," Keller said. "She don't like the idea of him going out after Van Cleef. Am I right?"

Gant nodded. "She said he could come as far as Laramie.

7

If we hadn't found Van Cleef by then, he'd better get back to his little house and yard."

"And my son," Walker said. "Don't forget Benjamin."

"I ain't forgot him," Gant said, not sounding too happy about admitting it.

"You can't blame a man for wanting to be with his wife and son," Walker said, shaking his head. "You just can't."

Fargo had known plenty of men who wanted nothing more than a house, a wife, and a son, but he'd never had the urge to settle down himself. There was too much to do and see for a man to let himself be tied down like that.

"If we'd found Van Cleef before we got this far," Walker said, "I'd have killed him for you with my bare hands. But I promised Ruth I'd come back if we got to Laramie, and I got to keep that promise."

Fargo could understand promises, all right. They weren't to be made lightly and, if you made one, you kept it. At least Fargo did.

"And I can't get the bastard by myself," Gant said. "But I got to get him some way or other." He looked at Walker. "My wife ain't waitin' for me, thanks to that bastard Van Cleef. If I was twenty years younger, or even ten, I'd do the job on my own, but I'm just too damned old to go it alone."

He looked to Fargo to be a bit over sixty, older than Walker, who was no youngster himself.

"I reckon I'll go with you, then," Keller said. "You mentioned something about pay?"

He'd have gone for nothing, Fargo thought, but there wasn't anything wrong with making a little money to do something you wanted to do anyway.

Gant and Keller talked about the payment while Walker drank in silence and Fargo looked around the saloon. Nothing had changed. The drunk was still snoring, the card game continued, and the bartender still looked like he wished he were somewhere a long way off.

The discussion of money concluded, Keller tapped a finger on the table and looked at Fargo.

"You want to go with us?" he asked. "I'll split the money with you. Half for me, half for you."

The money was tempting, but Fargo didn't think they

had much of a chance to catch Van Cleef. He said, "I'll be heading back east soon. I wish you luck."

"I could use some company," Walker said, "if you're of a mind to go Independence way."

"When are you leaving?"

Walker looked at Gant, who stared back without speaking. Walker gave his head a slight shake and turned back to Fargo.

"I guess I'll be leaving in the morning. Nothing to hold me here, not now that Seth's hooked up with Keller."

"I guess I'll go along, then," Fargo said.

Fargo had done his share of scouting for the army. He was well-known at Fort Laramie and to most of the people who lived around the fort.

He was bunking at a trading post, and he woke up just before the fort's bugler blew reveille. He lay in the cold darkness under a thin blanket, waiting for the crisp bugle notes and for the first dim light of morning to filter through the cracks in the walls. If the weather had been more hospitable, Fargo would have preferred to sleep outside, but because of the cold, he was glad enough to be inside four walls even though the cracks weren't chinked.

When the clear, clean notes of the wake-up call sounded in the morning air, Fargo imagined the soldiers stirring in their bunks, then gettting up, scratching, yawning, farting, cursing, and complaining.

Fargo lay in his bunk and smiled. He didn't have to rise at the bugle's call, even though he was already awake, and it gave him a good feeling to know that he was freer than most men who had regular jobs, military obligations, or families to tie them down.

It didn't take Fargo long to get his things together and go outside. He went directly to the stable without greeting anyone and found that Walker was already there.

The big barn smelled of manure and hay, and the horses were stamping and snorting. Their breath came out like steam and was reflected in the lantern light.

The hostler, a short man with a bristly black beard, saw Fargo and said, "You gonna leave us now?"

Fargo said that he was, and the hostler said, "Colonel

Alexander might be needin' you. I hear the Crows are causin' a little trouble back down the trail."

Alexander was the fort's commanding officer, and Fargo had done some scouting for him in the past.

"Didn't see any sign of Injun trouble when we came along out here," Walker said.

He was holding the reins of his horse, a big bay, already saddled and ready to go.

"Just heard about it last night," the hostler said. "Must be a small band of 'em that dropped down south for the winter, or maybe just a raidin' party out to see what they can scratch up."

That didn't sound right to Fargo. The Crow were a dignified bunch, in his experience, and didn't go out on raids for no good reason.

"The colonel didn't mention anything about Indians to me," Fargo said. He'd seen Alexander the previous evening to let him know that he'd be leaving in the morning. "Seemed like he was more worried about the weather than about the Crow."

"Don't need to worry about the weather," Walker said. "It's due to warm up today."

"How do you know that?" the hostler asked.

"Anybody's lived out here long as I have would know," Walker said. "This old coon got to where he could smell a change comin' on—and I can do it still."

Fargo knew what the old trapper was talking about. If a man lived in the outdoors long enough, he established a connection with the weather that someone who'd lived inside a house all his life couldn't understand. It wasn't just the usual knowledge of the signs in the wind. It was a special kind of sixth sense, and it was something to be trusted.

"Could be the Blackfeet that's causin' the trouble," Walker went on. "They're more likely to be out in this weather than the Crow. Besides, the Liver-Eater's still around here in winter, settin' his traps. The Crow don't want to tangle with that old coon."

"You know John Johnson?"

"Met him at a rendezvous or two. Never spent any time with him, but I know about how the Crow killed his wife and what he done to 'em afterwards. They sent twenty men to kill him, and he got 'em all, one after the other. And every one of 'em knew before he died that his liver was forfeit."

The hostler nodded. The story of Johnson's private war with the Crow was well-known in the territory. He said, "You reckon the Crow might still be lookin' for him?"

"I think they learned their lesson," Walker said. "They've made their peace with the Liver-Eater."

"Must be something else, then," the hostler said.

"Always some kind of danger in this part of the country, all right," Walker said. "But it was worth it just to be out here where a man has room to breathe."

"You sound like you miss it," Fargo said.

"What I miss is my wife and my boy," Walker told him. "You gonna get ready to ride?"

"Soldiers'll be havin' breakfast in a minute," the hostler said. "You might could get you a bite if you asked."

Fargo knew about army breakfasts. Bread and coffee— with the coffee most likely to be cold.

"I can do without that," he said. He went to the stall where his big Ovaro stallion snorted in greeting. Fargo rubbed the horse's nose and told the hostler, "I'll settle up with you and ride out with Walker."

The hostler didn't object, and within a short time Fargo and Walker were riding east from the fort, heading for Independence.

3

They heard the rifle shots around midmorning, sounding quite near in the brisk air.

"Injuns, you reckon?" Walker asked.

"Don't know," Fargo answered. "We should have a look. Maybe we can help out."

Walker appeared reluctant. "Might not be any of our business."

"Might not," Fargo agreed. "But I'm going to find out one way or the other."

He nudged the Ovaro forward. The snow clouds that had filled the sky for days had vanished, and the sun filled the wide blue sky. The day had gotten warmer as Walker had predicted. The snow had already melted off the trail and was beginning to melt even under the trees, though it still hugged the ground in the shadows of the rocks. The Ovaro's hooves made sucking noises as they pulled away from the mud of the trail.

Fargo rode for about a mile. He didn't look back to see if Walker was following because he didn't have to. He could hear the bay coming along.

Topping a low rise, Fargo looked down the trail at a wagon that had pulled off to the side. A body lay not far from the wagon, and someone inside it was firing an occasional shot out the back. Fargo couldn't see who the firing was directed at, but the wagon's canvas covering was studded with arrows.

Walker rode up beside Fargo and reined in.

"They're back in the rocks yonder," Walker said, but by that time Fargo had worked that out for himself.

The Indians had concealed themselves in a pile of boulders, where they appeared to be content to wait until whoever was in the wagon either ran out of ammunition or made some careless mistake that would give them the advantage.

"Reckon we could get behind 'em?" Walker asked.

Fargo wasn't sure, but he figured that if he knew the Indians were behind the rocks, they knew that he was on the trail.

"I'll ride down to the wagon," he said, "and give them something to think about. You can make a loop around and see about getting in back of them."

Walker nodded and turned his horse back down the trail so that he'd be concealed by the rise when he made his move.

Fargo pulled the Henry from its scabbard. He could fire all fifteen shots from its magazine in under a dozen seconds if the situation required it, but he didn't want to waste any shots, not knowing how many Indians there were or how well armed they might be. Clearly most of them were using bows, but one or two might have rifles.

After giving Walker a minute or two to get started, Fargo worked the Henry's lever action and fired a shot that ricocheted off the top of one of the bigger rocks to get the attention of the men concealed behind them.

He got an immediate response—a bullet whizzed by his head. He kneed the Ovaro into action and rode toward the wagon, keeping low in the saddle, and after another near miss he was beside the oxen pulling the wagon and out of sight of the rocks.

"Hello, inside," he said.

"Hello, yourself," a woman's voice answered. "How many of you are there?"

"Two," Fargo said. "One of us is getting behind the rocks."

"What good will that do?"

"We'll have them in a cross fire," Fargo said.

He looked down at the body of the man who lay face-down on the ground. There wasn't much to see except that an arrow in his chest had been driven through his back when he'd fallen out of the wagon.

Fargo glanced at the arrows that stuck in the wagon's canvas. Crow. He wondered what had the tribe stirred up, though it didn't really matter. Something had them upset enough to attack the wagon. It would have been an easy target, Fargo thought.

He slipped off the Ovaro and onto the wagon seat, taking the Henry with him.

Looking inside, he saw a woman lying at full length in the bed. Even the heavy men's clothing she wore couldn't conceal her womanly curves from Fargo's practiced eye. Black hair, thick and lustrous, showed under the hat she wore. It would have made a prize scalp for any Crow, and Fargo wondered what the hell the woman was doing in that place with only one man, now dead, as her companion.

Now wasn't the time to ask, however, as the Henry rifle the woman held roared and belched fire and smoke. Two Crow, who had moved from behind the rocks, ducked back under cover—or tried to. One of them fell backward just as Fargo heard the blast of a Hawken. Walker had gotten behind the rocks.

Fargo moved to the back of the wagon and got off four quick shots as the Crow scattered. They had no intention of staying around now that the odds had shifted too drastically against them.

Fargo didn't hit any of them, mainly because he didn't really try. He didn't see any need for senseless killing now that the fighting was over.

Walker was of a different mind. His Hawken continued to boom until the little band of Crow had ridden out of sight, but the old muzzle loader was much slower than Fargo's Henry.

Even at that, Fargo saw one of the Crow throw up his arms and pitch out of the saddle. The distance was so great that Fargo realized the old mountain man hadn't lost his shooting eye while living in Independence.

"I appreciate your help," the woman said.

She was standing now, facing him. She was younger and prettier than he'd expected. Her mouth was wide, and her lips were full, promising things that polite ladies never talked about.

Fargo wondered if she was polite as she certainly didn't look like a lady. Her turned-up nose gave her a mischievous look, and her dark eyes had a hint of recklessness in them—the kind of recklessness that appealed to Fargo.

"My name's Priscilla Harrison," she said. "Most people call me Pris." She gave him a bold look. "What do they call you?"

"Fargo. Skye Fargo. The other fella's Tobias Walker." He paused. "What about the man on the ground?"

"Isaiah Tolbert," Pris said. "He was my guide. We weren't expecting any trouble. Those Indians attacked us without warning. They came up over that rise and shot Tolbert out of the wagon seat before he could blink. I guess they thought they'd get me, too. They didn't reckon on my being so handy with a rifle."

"Good thing you had that repeater," Fargo said.

Pris nodded. "I bought it back in Missouri. Cost a pretty penny, but well worth it." She paused. "Damn it all."

"Problem with the rifle?" Fargo asked.

"No. A problem with the guide. He's dead, isn't he?"

Fargo glanced down. Tolbert hadn't moved. A dark red stain surrounded the arrow sticking up through his back.

"He's dead, all right. You have a shovel?"

"There's one tied on the side of the wagon, I think."

Fargo climbed down from the wagon seat and turned the dead man over. His features were obscured by mud, but his open eyes stared blankly up at Fargo.

"Are you going to bury him?" Pris asked.

"It's the right thing to do."

"You don't even know him."

Fargo didn't think that statement needed any comment.

"What if those Indians come back?" Pris asked.

"They won't come back. We have them outgunned. Do you know why they jumped you in the first place?"

"I don't have any idea. Like I told you, there wasn't any warning. They just showed up and started shooting. There were eight or ten of them. One or two of them had rifles, and the rest used bows. They got Tolbert and would have killed me, too, if I hadn't had the rifle. They might have come at me again if you and your friend hadn't happened along."

Just as she mentioned Fargo's friend, Walker rode up to them.

"Howdy, ma'am," he said.

Fargo introduced the two and went to where a couple of shovels were tied to the side of the wagon.

"We got us two Crow," Walker said when he saw what Fargo was up to. "What about them?"

Fargo said, "Go see if they're alive or dead."

"What do we care?"

The Trailsman believed in respecting his enemies, and he wasn't even sure that the Crow had been his enemies. They'd attacked a wagon, but Fargo still didn't know the reason why.

"If they're alive, maybe they can tell us something about this."

Walker said he could see the benefit of that and went off to have a look at the Crow who'd fallen near the rocks while Fargo began to dig a grave for Tolbert beside the trail.

In only a couple of minutes, Walker came back.

"The Injun up by the rocks is still alive," he said. "Other one's dead. The one that's alive won't be around for long, but might be able to do some talkin'. You want to go hear what he has to say?"

Fargo handed Walker the shovel and walked up to the rocks where the Crow warrior lay. A bloody froth was on the man's lips and there was a hole in his chest. Hearing the sucking sound as the man breathed, Fargo knew that his lung had been punctured.

The warrior's eyes were closed, and he didn't open them when Fargo approached. Maybe he didn't hear the Trailsman, or maybe he was past caring who might be standing there.

Fargo watched him for a few seconds, then said, "Can you hear me?"

There was only the sucking sound for an answer.

"The Crow are known far and wide as honorable fighters," Fargo said. "They don't usually attack a lone wagon— not without thinking they have a good reason."

The Crow, who still had not opened his eyes, spoke with difficulty.

"A good reason. A white man kills the Crow."

Fargo didn't quite understand. "You were shot because you killed the man driving the wagon."

"Not that white man. White man kills Crow in the night. For no reason." The warrior twitched in pain, then gained control to speak two more words, "Takes face."

"You mean he skins them?" Fargo asked, but the warrior was now beyond hearing him. The sucking sound stopped abruptly, and a vivid red trickle ran from the corner of the man's mouth. His limbs twitched, went rigid, then relaxed in death.

Fargo would have liked to ask a few more questions, especially as the warrior's final words reminded him all too much of what he'd recently heard about Jess Van Cleef.

Fargo looked back down at the wagon where Walker was still digging a grave for Tolbert. He didn't think he'd bury the Crow. He propped the body up against the rocks and left him for his friends to find when they came back as Fargo figured they would—no use offending them by subjecting the dead warrior to some white man's burial that they would neither appreciate nor understand.

The day had gotten progressively warmer, but the ground wasn't easy to dig below the first couple of inches. Fargo figured Walker would be working up quite a sweat digging Tolbert's grave.

As he walked back to the wagon, Fargo wondered why Priscilla Harrison was traveling at this time of year. Of course, there were always people who waited too long to start out on the trail—like the people he'd led to Fort Laramie. They felt they had to make a start, no matter what the weather might be like and, if they got only to Laramie, they'd at least have a head start come spring.

Maybe that was Pris's reason, but she didn't seem to Fargo to be the kind of woman who'd be looking to start a home alone on the frontier. It wasn't any of his business, but he was curious nevertheless.

When Fargo reached the wagon, Walker jammed the point of the shovel in the ground and said, "There's one more Injun to take care of."

Fargo nodded. "We'll set him up by the rocks with the other one."

Walker seemed to understand why. "How 'bout that one? He have anything to say?"

"Yeah," Fargo said. "He said something about a white man who killed the Crow people in the night."

"Sounds like the Liver-Eater," Walker said as they walked toward the fallen Crow. "I thought he was through takin' revenge for them killin' the Swan, though."

Swan had been the name of Johnson's wife. Fargo said, "I don't think it was Johnson. The Crow said something else, something about the white man taking faces."

"Goddamn," Walker said. "It's Van Cleef again."

Fargo had been thinking the same thing, though he'd hoped he was wrong. "Would Van Cleef do something like that?"

Walker shrugged. "Who the hell knows what a crazy man will do?" he said. "Let's take this Injun over by those rocks and get on the road. Those others might come back."

"Not likely," Fargo said. "Not until after we're gone, anyway."

"You want to take that chance?"

Fargo shook his head.

"Me, neither," Walker said.

Fargo bent down and took the dead warrior's feet. Walker got a grip under his armpits. They hefted the man up, carried him to the rocks, and put him beside the other.

"Hate to leave 'em like this," Walker said.

"They won't be here long before somebody comes for them," Fargo said. "And we'd better leave, too."

"Damn right," Walker said.

4

"I don't know what I'm going to do," Pris said when Fargo and Walker returned to where she waited. "I can drive a wagon, but my guide's dead, and I have to get to Fort Laramie."

"I'm sure sorry about your troubles, ma'am," Walker said, not sounding sorry at all to Fargo. "But the trail's pretty plain from here on, and it's not far to Laramie. Just a few hours, even if you're goin' slow. You can make it before night if you get started now."

"What if the Indians are waiting down the trail?" she asked with a little quaver in her voice. "I'm sure I couldn't fight them off again. Couldn't the two of you ride with me to the fort? I can pay."

"I got a wife and boy waitin' for me back in Independence," Walker said. "I got to push on. I can't go back to Laramie."

"What about you, Fargo?" Pris asked, turning her eyes on him.

She was sitting on the wagon seat, the reins in her hands. The Henry rifle was beside her within easy reach, but she wouldn't be any kind of a match for six or eight determined Crow—not if they came on her fast enough.

"If it's the money you're worried about, I can show it to you," she said. "Please. I have to get to the fort."

"Seems like it'd make more sense for you to go to Missouri with us," Walker said. "You could come back to the fort in the spring, when there'd be plenty of other wagons on the trail and the Crow'd be a lot less likely to come after you."

"I have to go now," Pris said. "I'm looking for someone. I have to find him."

"Who is it that you're looking for?" Fargo asked. "We were just at Fort Laramie this morning. Maybe we've seen him."

"You haven't seen him. If you'd seen him, you wouldn't be alive."

"Doesn't sound like anybody this old coon'd care to meet," Walker said. "All the more reason you oughta head back to Missouri, and the sooner, the better."

"Just who are you talking about?" Fargo asked, though he had an uneasy feeling he already knew the answer. It seemed as if one man's name kept coming up over and over lately.

"Jess Van Cleef," Pris said, confirming Fargo's suspicion. Walker didn't seem surprised, either.

"Lots of people looking for him, I reckon," Walker said, "includin' the Crow. I don't know why you want him, but I do believe it'd be for the best just to forget all about him."

"I can't do that," Pris said, her dark eyes flashing. "I have to find him."

"Mind if I ask you why?" Fargo said.

Pris lowered her eyes. "He killed my father. I'm going to make him pay."

"Is that why you brung along that Henry?" Walker asked.

"Yes. I thought I'd need something like that."

"You'll need more than a rifle," Walker told her. "That man's a killer. I don't know why, but it's bred in his bones. He killed my partner's wife back in Missouri, and he'd just as soon kill you, too." Walker gave Pris an appraising look. "But killin' ain't the worst of what he'd do to a woman like you, if you take my meanin'."

"I'm not afraid of him," Pris said. "I'm not afraid of any man."

"Ain't a matter of bein' afraid," Walker said. "It's just that you don't know what you're up against. Van Cleef skins the faces off those he kills. What kind of man does that?"

"A crazy one. I know well enough what he does. Didn't I say he killed my father?"

"That may be true," Fargo put in. "But it's not up to you to get justice for Van Cleef. There are already two men on his trail."

"And my partner's one of 'em," Walker said. "If those two can't find him, nobody can. They'll take care of him in a way that'll satisfy any ideas of gettin' even you might have."

"No, it won't," Pris said. There was a savagery in her voice that surprised Fargo. "This is something I have to do myself. If neither of you two is going to help me, I'll just get started."

She flicked the reins, and the two oxen started to move, giving the wagon a jerky start.

Fargo looked at Walker, who looked away. Fargo knew there wouldn't be any help from that direction. He reached out and took hold of the reins, pulling back on them and bringing the wagon to a stop.

"I'll go with you," he said, "at least as far as Laramie. Walker has to get back to Missouri, and I don't blame him for that. He has family waiting, and that's important to a man who has one."

"I don't," Pris said. "Not anymore. Van Cleef took that away from me."

Fargo could understand her feelings, probably much better than she knew. He'd lost his own family to violence long ago, and it was that event that had started him on the long, wandering trail that had led him all over the West.

"We'll go to the fort and then see what the situation is," Fargo said. "It might be that you'll have to stay there if the Crow are out raiding. It wouldn't be safe for you to go looking for Van Cleef in the first place, but if the Crow are riled, they'd be likely to get you before you went ten miles."

"Not if I had someone like you with me," Pris said. "They wouldn't bother me then."

Fargo laughed. "You put a lot of faith in a man you just met."

"I can tell what a man's made of," Pris said, giving Walker an accusing sidelong glance.

It was intended to be a withering look, but it glanced off Walker without leaving a mark.

"Well," he said, "I guess that's all settled then. I hope you two can find your way to Laramie without losin' your hair. But you better leave findin' Van Cleef to my partner and John Keller."

He turned his horse's head toward the east and rode away. He looked back once or twice, as if a little sorry about his choice, but he didn't return.

"He's a coward," Pris said. Fargo heard the disdain in her voice.

"No," Fargo said. "He's just got good sense. He has a wife and a son, and his place is with them. But he trapped in the mountains around here for a long time with just one other man to watch his back. That's not a life for cowards."

"Maybe not. But he should have helped us."

"A man has to look after his family," Fargo said.

He tied the Ovaro to the back of the wagon and climbed up in the seat with Pris, who handed him the reins.

"It's a man's job," she said by way of explanation. But there was something in the way she said it that caused Fargo to doubt she meant it.

She was no tender blossom, as he knew from the way she'd handled the Henry, but he took the reins without comment and urged the oxen forward.

It was late afternoon when they got to the fort, and Fargo stopped the wagon near the small group of pilgrims that he'd led to Laramie earlier. He introduced Pris to Betty McCallum, a matronly woman who, Fargo hoped, would see that Pris got settled in for the night, and maybe for longer.

"You just plan to be part of our wagon train next spring," Betty told Pris. "We'll be heading out of here to Oregon soon as spring comes along."

"I'm not going to Oregon," Pris said. "I'm looking for someone."

Betty gave Fargo a quizzical look.

"It's a long story," Fargo said. "I'm going to see Colonel Alexander and talk things over with him. I'll be back later. Meanwhile, you two can get acquainted."

Neither woman looked happy at that idea, but Fargo left

them there and led the Ovaro to the stable. Then he headed toward the colonel's headquarters.

He knocked the mud off his boots on the log step, and the corporal at the door announced him.

Alexander was a small man, a full head shorter than Fargo, but he looked trim and stern in his uniform. He stood and leaned over his desk to shake hands with Fargo.

"I didn't think I'd be seeing you again so soon," he said. "You told me yesterday evening that you were leaving for Missouri."

Alexander sat back down and motioned for Fargo to have a seat in one of the straight-backed wooden chairs nearby.

"I did leave," Fargo said, seating himself. "I came back because I came upon a wagon under attack by some Crow warriors."

Alexander leaned forward, resting his forearms on the desk.

"We haven't had any trouble with the Crow lately," he said.

"Seems like they're stirred up about something," Fargo said. "According to one I met today, a white man's been killing some of them."

Alexander raised his eyebrows. "The Liver-Eater?"

"I don't think so," Fargo told him. "A man named Seth Gant came here yesterday looking for a killer named Jess Van Cleef. Priscilla Harrison, the woman I met in the wagon today, is looking for the same man. He's killed members of both their families back in Missouri. From what they say, it seems like he kills people out of meanness as much as anything. And then he skins them."

"My Lord," Alexander said. "What kind of man is he?"

"A crazy one, sounds like. Anyway, both Gant and Harrison think he's out in this part of the country. Could be that he's the one that's killing the Crows."

"And that's got them out raiding?"

"Getting a little revenge," Fargo said. "If you can't find the man you're looking for, maybe anybody will do."

"I'll send out a patrol," Alexander said. "And I'll be sure to keep an eye on things around the fort. What did you do with this woman you mentioned, Miss Harrison?"

Fargo told him that he'd left her with some pilgrims.

23

"But she's not planning to stay with them," he added. "She says she's going after Van Cleef."

Alexander thought it over.

"She can't do that," he said after a few seconds.

"That's what I told her," Fargo said. "She didn't listen."

"Surely she realizes she won't last a day in this country—not alone."

"I told her that, too. It didn't change her mind."

"I'm responsible for her safety. I can't let her go," Alexander said.

"You're going to stop her?"

"I have to."

Fargo thought about Pris. He hadn't known her long, but he had a feeling that when she set her mind to something, nobody was going to stop her.

Fargo gave Alexander a grin.

"Good luck," he said.

5

Fargo didn't want to have to deal with Pris Harrison until he'd had a drink and something to eat, so as soon as he left Alexander's office he went to the saloon.

It wasn't much changed since he'd last been inside. The upright piano still sat silently against the wall. Three men played cards, though Fargo didn't know if they were the same three he'd seen the previous day.

But several men stood at the bar. They had drinks in their hands, but they weren't interested in them. Their attention was focused on a woman who stood in front of them.

It was Pris Harrison. Maybe Fargo should have been surprised, but he wasn't. He hadn't really expected Betty McCallum to be able to handle her.

Pris didn't see Fargo come in.

"Isn't there a man among you with the grit and the nerve to help a woman who's alone and friendless?" she said to the men at the bar.

Fargo thought that was laying it on a little bit thick. He stood just inside the door to see what the reaction would be.

One of the men at the bar was Sid Frazee—slat thin and snake mean. Fargo knew him all too well. He'd been in the wagon train with the McCallums, and he was a constant source of trouble and irritation to Fargo and everybody else. He was never willing to do his share of the work, always blaming someone else for his failings, always looking to get back at people for any kind of slight, real or imagined.

"A woman pretty as you oughta be able to find some help, all right," Frazee said. He turned to wink at the other men nearby. "Just depends on what kind of help you need."

"Not the kind you have in mind," Pris said.

Frazee smirked, and the other men laughed. Fargo knew them, too, though not as well as he knew Frazee. They were brothers, Lee and Chad Tuttle, both of them big, with mean little eyes set too close together. They were oafish and lazy as lizards in the sunshine. They loafed around the fort, doing a little trapping and a little trading, but never working any more than they absolutely had to. They never had much more money than it took to buy liquor and food and otherwise scrape by. They'd attached themselves to Frazee almost as soon as he'd arrived, knowing they'd found a kindred spirit.

"You shouldn't say that before you know exactly what I have in mind," Frazee said, leaning back against the bar. "You might like it."

"I wouldn't like anything you have," Pris told him. "I'm sorry I ever came in here. I should have known that I couldn't find a real man in a saloon."

The cardplayers didn't even look up. They might not even have heard what Pris said.

But the Tuttles heard it. They clenched their fists and looked at Frazee to see what he'd do.

Frazee gave Pris a hangdog look as if his feelings were bruised. Then a sly grin crept over his features, and he lifted his whiskey glass to his mouth for a slow sip. He set the glass down and pushed away from the bar.

"I think it's time you found out what I've got and what kind of man I am," he said.

The Tuttles grinned and nodded at each other. This was more like it. But Lee stopped grinning when he caught sight of Fargo.

"Hey, Sid," he said, inclining his head in Fargo's direction.

Frazee turned to look. That was all the distraction Pris needed. She moved to him as quickly as a cat, sliding across the saloon floor without a sound.

Frazee sensed the movement, but before he could even turn back to look at her, Pris landed a solid kick in his groin.

Frazee's eyes widened, and his mouth opened in a circle of surprise.

"Arrrgggh!" he cried.

He crumpled to the floor, clasping his hands together over the injured area and drawing up his knees almost to his chest.

"Bitch," Chad said.

Lee reached out for Chad's arm, but Chad brushed his hand aside.

"Hold it, Chad," Fargo said.

"You go to hell, Trailsman," Chad said, not taking his eyes off Pris, who had backed away to stand near the card-players. They were eying her warily.

Lee pulled a well-worn Colt and leveled it at Fargo.

"You just stay where you are, Fargo," he said.

Frazee lay on the floor, twitching and moaning. Pris looked at him and smiled as if approving of a job well done.

The smile angered Chad, who almost stumbled over Frazee's curled body.

Again, Pris was quick to take advantage of her opening—so quick that Fargo almost didn't see her movement as she snatched up a poker chip from the table and spun it hard at Chad's face. It hit him just over the eye, opening a small cut before it fell to the floor and rolled for a couple of feet before falling over.

The cardplayers stopped their game, not sure of what had just happened. They gave each other quizzical looks, and one of them looked at the poker chip, but none of them looked at Pris.

Chad stood where he was. He put a hand over his eye, then looked at his dirty palm, which had a small streak of red across it.

"Shit," he said. "You're gonna be sorry you did that."

"I don't think so," Pris said.

"I do," Chad said, and he pulled his pistol. "I'm tired of messing with you already."

Fargo was still under Lee's gun, but he thought it was time to do something about the situation. He fell to the side, drawing his Colt at the same time.

Lee was quick, but not quick enough. He fired at the spot where Fargo had been. The roar seemed to shake the whole saloon, and the cardplayers kicked away from the table, seeking shelter behind their chairs.

The bullet slammed into the wall, and Fargo fired at Lee, whose right arm jerked to the side. The pistol flew from Lee's limp fingers, hit the bar, and slid to the end before falling off and bouncing to the floor.

Chad turned toward Fargo, but before he could trigger off a shot, Fargo's Colt boomed a second time.

Chad's left leg buckled under him. His finger yanked the trigger of his pistol and sent a bullet to plow up the floor in front of him as he fell.

Quiet settled over the saloon, and gun smoke swirled in the air. Fargo stood up and looked around.

Lee clung to the edge of the bar with one hand, holding his shattered hand against his chest.

Frazee still hugged himself on the floor, his own pain rendering him oblivious to the furor going on around him.

Chad lay stretched out by the card table, so shocked by what had happened to his leg that he couldn't move.

The cardplayers remained huddled behind their chairs, and there was no sign at all of the bartender, who had dropped down behind the bar at the first shot and had not yet reappeared.

Fargo's ears rang from the shots. Pris stood with her hands on her hips, her eyes defiant. A faint smile played on her lips.

"I thought I asked you to stay with Miz McCallum?" Fargo said to her.

Pris shook her head. "I don't remember hearing anything like that. And I don't remember asking you for any help."

Fargo holstered the Colt. "I guess you didn't, at that."

"You can't just put me off on some old woman and expect me to stay with her," Pris said. "If you think I'm going to spend the winter at this fort, helping out with somebody's cooking and washing, you have another think coming. I'll find help somewhere around this fort, and then I'm leaving."

"You might consider looking for help in a better class of establishment next time," Fargo said.

"I run a good clean place," said the bartender, who had

reappeared. He surveyed the saloon for damage, but saw nothing significant. He eyed Frazee, who was still where he'd fallen. "I can't help who comes in here."

"I'll leave it to you to clear them out, then," Fargo said. He went over to Pris and offered his arm. "The smell of gun smoke is starting to bother me. May I escort you out of here, Miss Harrison?"

Pris smiled and put a hand on his forearm. "Yes, you may, Mr. Fargo."

They started out of the saloon like two society swells, stepping over the prone bodies of Frazee and Chad.

"You'll be sorry for this, Trailsman," Lee said.

It would have been a more effective threat if he hadn't slid to the floor while he was making it. He wound up leaning against a cuspidor, and the glare in his eyes faded as he passed out. His head fell forward, and his chin rested on his chest.

"They're a pitiful sight, aren't they?" Pris said.

Fargo didn't answer. He could hear the chairs scraping on the floor behind him as the cardplayers got to their feet.

"Do you think they'll try to cause any more trouble?" Pris asked.

They passed through the door and into the clean smell of the winter air.

"I don't think they'll bother anybody for a day or so," Fargo said. "They'll get bandaged up and liquored up and do some loud talking, but that's about all. Sid Frazee'll be walking carefully for a while."

Pris laughed. "You should have seen the look on his face. He thought he could do whatever he wanted with me. The fool."

Fargo thought that was a pretty harsh judgment. Pris wasn't a small woman, but she was slim and pretty and didn't look dangerous in the least. Anybody who hadn't seen her in action might make the same mistake that Frazee had made.

But Fargo had seen her, both in the saloon and in the fight with the Crow, when she hadn't appeared frightened at all. Just determined. He knew even on short acquaintance that she wasn't a woman to be trifled with.

And now Frazee knew it, too.

6

Betty McCallum was apologetic when she met Fargo and Pris at Pris's wagon.

"I tried to tell her to stay here," Betty said, avoiding Pris's eyes. Betty was a comfortably stout woman with a red face and the rough hands of a hardworking frontier wife. "I guess you know that she didn't listen."

"I know, all right," Fargo said. "I thank you for your trouble, but I don't think either one of us will be able to talk any sense into her."

"If you want me to try again, I will," Betty said. But Fargo said no, thanks, and she went back to her own wagon.

"She's a good woman," Fargo said. "You should've taken her advice and stayed here."

"She doesn't know what's best for me, and neither do you," Pris told him. "I came here to find Jess Van Cleef, and that's what I intend to do. You can help me or not, but I don't want you to try putting me off on anybody else that's supposed to take care of me. I can damned well take care of myself."

After what he'd seen, Fargo believed it. "All right, but Colonel Alexander thinks he's responsible for your safety. He's going to try to stop you from leaving the fort."

"Well, he can't. Even if I can't find anybody to help me, I'm going. If it weren't for those Indians, I'd go alone."

Fargo looked around the fort, then beyond it. The sun was going down behind the mountains far off in the west,

30

and their snowy tops blazed under the glow of the fiery sky.

The few pilgrims who were moving around the wagons were getting ready for their evening meal. Some of them still lived in their wagons, while others had built rudimentary houses. A couple of families had been lucky enough to claim abandoned shacks.

They were good people, Fargo thought. With the exception of Frazee, they'd cooperated with him on the journey from Independence, doing their share of the work without complaint. All of them wanted to get on to Oregon and establish homes for themselves in the spring.

They were good people, but they weren't Pris's kind of people. Something about her set her apart. Fargo couldn't quite figure out just how she would ever fit into a regular community. She seemed too combative, too stubborn, too interested in her own welfare to get along well in any organized society.

So in a way, he thought, she wasn't too different from him. He'd never succeeded in staying among any civilized society for too long. The settled feeling of people living in houses and towns stifled him, made him yearn for the trail and the open skies.

"I'll go with you," he told Pris, almost before he was aware of having made the decision.

"I figured you'd come to your senses," she said, as if she'd been expecting his decision. "When can we leave?"

"In the morning, I guess," Fargo said. He didn't have anything tying him to the fort, and certainly Pris didn't. "I'll let Colonel Alexander know. He won't like it, but he won't try to stand in our way."

"Good," Pris said. "Now, I'm hungry. Where can we get something to eat around here?"

They had boiled potatoes and tough steak at the saloon, which also served as the only café at the fort. The cardplayers still sat at their table, playing for small stakes and ignoring Fargo and Pris. A couple of other people were eating, but most people fixed their own meals. There was no sign of the Tuttles and Frazee.

Fargo had beer with his supper, and so did Pris. She not only fought like a man, but she also drank like one, not sipping timidly but knocking it back with gusto. That was something else that set her apart from the women in the wagon train.

When they'd finished their meal, Fargo said that he'd go speak to Alexander and meet Pris early the next morning at her wagon.

"Where will you sleep?" she asked.

"I have a friend at the trading post. I'll stay there."

"I have a better idea," Pris said. "You can stay in my wagon. We might as well get to know each other better if we're going to travel together."

Fargo wondered how well she wanted to get to know him, and he gave her an inquiring look.

Her smile told him all he needed to know.

"I don't know what you're thinking, Fargo," Colonel Alexander said, his disapproval clear in his voice. "You know how treacherous the weather can be out here at this time of year."

Fargo nodded. The day had turned out warm, and most of the snow had melted, but that didn't mean it wouldn't turn cold again within the next twenty-four hours. Even a blizzard was possible, but Fargo didn't sense that anything like that was coming.

"Besides," Alexander went on, "the Crow are stirred up. And this man you're looking for sounds even more dangerous than the Crow." Fargo started to interrupt, but Alexander held up a hand to stop him. "I've known you for a while, Fargo, and I know you're not scared of the Crow. This Jess Van Cleef doesn't scare you, either. But you'll have that woman with you, and she'll be your responsibility. You have to consider that."

"She can take care of herself," Fargo said.

Alexander allowed himself a smile.

"I've already heard about the little dustup at the saloon," he said. "And it does sound as if Miss Harrison can handle herself in some situations. But that doesn't mean she'll do equally well out on the trail."

"Maybe not. But there's no talking her out of it. I tried."

Alexander leaned back in his chair, balancing it on two legs.

"The whole thing's a bad idea, Fargo, and you know it."

Fargo nodded. "But she's going anyway. If I go with her, at least she'll have a little better chance."

"Of doing what? You don't really think you'll find Van Cleef, do you?"

"You never can tell," Fargo said. "A couple of men left here yesterday to look for him. Maybe they'll get to him before we do."

"Yes, or perhaps the Crow will get to them first. Or Van Cleef himself. If he's as dangerous as you say, he might not take kindly to the idea of people coming after him. That's something you should keep in mind."

"I've thought about it some."

"But not enough to discourage you."

"Oh, I'm easy enough to discourage. But I'm not the one who's in charge."

Alexander sat forward, the chair legs thumping on the floor.

"I know you better than that, Fargo. You're always in charge, one way or the other."

Fargo smiled and stood up.

"I'm not so sure of that," he said. He shook his head. "Not this time."

Alexander stood and extended his hand across the desk.

"I wish you'd reconsider, but since you won't, I wish you luck."

"Thanks," Fargo said. "I have a feeling I'm going to need it."

Fargo walked to Pris's wagon through the gathering dark. The dining hall had emptied out, and the soldiers were back in their barracks for the night, writing letters to their families and sweethearts, maybe, or playing a game of cards. Those who were handy with a needle might be taking care of any rips and tears in their uniforms, while others might even be trying to sleep, though the bugle call hadn't yet sounded.

Firelight flickered near some of the wagons, and Fargo could smell wood smoke on the air. The moon was half full, and the black sky was full of stars.

Fargo saw Pris's wagon and wondered if she was waiting for him there. He suspected that it was going to be an interesting night.

7

It was going to be an interesting night for John Keller and Seth Gant, too, though they didn't know it yet.

They were camped among some tall cottonwood trees. The snow had melted off the tree branches and was mostly gone from the ground, which was wet and muddy. Keller cut some limbs from the trees and made a place where he and Gant could sit without getting mud all over their butts, and they had a small fire going. They'd eaten bacon and biscuits for supper, and now they were drinking coffee and talking over their plans for finding Van Cleef.

"You say he's out this-away," Keller said, taking a sip of the scalding coffee, "but you don't know that anymore than a cat knows the alphabet. I don't mind taking your money, but I have to say I think we might as well be chasin' the wind."

"I ain't told you all I know," Gant said.

"Well," Keller said, "don't you reckon it's about time you did?"

Gant thought it over while blowing on his coffee to cool it, and then taking a drink. Finally, he said, "Might as well, I guess. Here's the way it is. I know Van Cleef started out on the Oregon Trail because he'd told people that's what he was gonna do. It's a place where he can lose himself, and he thinks he can make a little money by trappin'. Because he didn't think anybody'd come after him, and if they did, they couldn't find him. Even if they did find him, he figured he could handle 'em. That's just the kind of man he is. He thinks he can handle just about anybody."

Keller worried that Van Cleef might just be right about that. From the little he'd heard about him so far, he sounded as mean as a wounded grizzly and just about as tough.

"Even so," Keller said, "this is a long trail we're on, and Van Cleef don't have to stick to it. He had a head start on you, and he could be just about anywhere by now."

"I think he'll stick to the trail," Gant said. "Or pretty close to it, anyway."

"Why should he?"

"Why not? It's like I said. There's no law out here, not to speak of. So why should he go wanderin' off? He can stick close to the trail and not be in any rush. Try a little trappin' this winter, sell off his hides in the spring, if'n he gets any, and make his way to Oregon or California. Once he's there, he can start doin' his meanness all over again."

If he's not still doing it, Keller thought. The way he'd murdered Sammy proved to Keller that Van Cleef killed for the pure fun of it as much as anything else.

"You say Van Cleef's never wintered out in the mountains, never trapped before?"

Gant drank a gulp of coffee and nodded. "That's what I hear tell."

"Well, neither have I. It ain't no easy life."

"Don't I know it," Gant said.

He was about to take another sip of coffee, but instead he put his tin cup down on the ground beside him and said, "Did you hear somethin' out there?"

Keller hadn't heard a thing, and he didn't think Gant had, either. The old mountain man was just jumpy, thinking about Van Cleef—not that Keller blamed him for that. Van Cleef was one scary son of a bitch.

"Maybe it's a bear," Keller said.

"Bears'll already be holin' up for the winter," Gant said. "It wasn't an animal."

Keller still hadn't heard anything. There was no wind, and sound carried a long way on clear nights. He'd have heard a noise if there'd been one.

"Nobody's out there," he said.

"Maybe you're right," Gant said, though he didn't sound as if he believed it.

Gant took a drink of his coffee, but his face was tense, and Keller could tell he was still straining to hear again whatever it was he thought he'd heard in the first place.

"You're not lettin' Van Cleef spook you, are you?" Keller asked. "He's bound to be miles from here." Keller hoped that was true. He didn't want to meet up with Van Cleef after dark. "I know what he did to your wife, but he's just a man."

Keller added the last part to convince himself as much as to convince Gant. After what Van Cleef had done to Sammy, Keller wondered if Van Cleef wasn't more than human—something worse than human, in fact.

"I'm not spooked," Gant said. "I heard something out there."

"Could be Injuns, I guess."

Keller said it, but he didn't really believe it. The way he figured it, the Crow were like the bears, holed up for the winter.

"You don't know much about this country, do you?" Gant said. It wasn't a question.

Keller was offended. "I've guided pilgrims through this part of the country more times than you can count."

"Maybe you have. But I've lived in it. I've trapped all over it, and I've talked to the people. I know more about it than you ever will."

Gant's tone was mild. He didn't mean what he said as an insult. Just a statement of fact.

"You could be right, at that," Keller said, not taking offense. "But I still didn't hear anything."

They sat in silence for a while after that, both of them listening. Keller heard nothing at all, and apparently neither did Gant.

Five or six minutes went by, and Gant finally said, "I guess maybe you're right, Keller." He shook his head ruefully. "Maybe I was just spooked. Anyway, I ain't heard nothin' else. If there was anything out there, it's gone now."

"Good," Keller said. "I was beginnin' to wonder."

He wasn't really wondering at all. He didn't care how long Gant had lived or trapped in the mountains. He was old and nervous and hearing things that weren't there. No use to get into an argument about it, though.

"I think I'll turn in," Keller said.

He tossed the dregs of his coffee into the fire, which sputtered and sparked.

"I believe I'll just sit up for a while," Gant said. "Keep my ears open. I'll wake you in a few hours, let you take a turn."

Keller thought that was a good idea. Even if there wasn't anything out there, it didn't hurt to keep on your guard. A man never knew what might come up on his camp in the dark. And Keller sure didn't like to think that Van Cleef might come slipping up on them. God knew what might happen if he did.

"I'll take first watch if you want me to," Keller said. "You're the one payin' the freight."

"I'm not sleepy," Gant told him. "You go on to sleep. I'll wake you when the time comes."

Keller said, "Whatever you say."

He curled up in his bedroll and was asleep in minutes. Gant watched him for a moment, then got his rifle and put it across his legs.

He sat by the fire and thought about the old days—when he'd been young, when he'd walked through the winter snow to check his traps along the frozen river, when he'd come into the trading post in the spring with the furs he'd taken, when he'd gone to the rendezvous with the other trappers and traders.

Those had been hard days, he thought, but they'd been good ones. And while Gant missed them in a way, he'd been happy to leave them behind and settle down with his wife in Independence. That had been a good life, too, until Jess Van Cleef had taken it away from him.

It wasn't right, Gant thought, for Van Cleef to be running free after what he'd done and was most likely still doing whenever he got a chance. But that was all over now. Gant and Keller were going to put a stop to it once and for all.

Gant just hoped that after they caught up with Van Cleef, they could keep him alive long enough to give him a taste of his own medicine. That son of a bitch deserved it if anybody ever did.

Gant thought about Fargo then, and wished that he had the Trailsman with him. Keller would be fine, Gant thought, and he had as good a motive as anybody for catching up with Van Cleef. But there was something about Fargo that made Gant think that if it came to a fight, Fargo would be the better man to have beside him.

But that wasn't to be, Gant mused. By now Fargo and Tobias would be well on their way toward Missouri. Gant had been a little upset with Tobias at first, but he didn't really blame him for going back. He had a wife and son to get back to. Hell, Gant could understand that. But he'd have been a good man to have along, too.

Well, it wasn't to be, and that was that. No use in chewing it over. Walker and Fargo were probably camped out on the trail right now, well on their way back to Missouri.

Gant wished them well.

Fargo wasn't camped out anywhere. He was in the wagon with Pris Harrison, who was asking him how his talk with Alexander had gone.

"About the way you'd expect," Fargo said. "He doesn't like the idea of us going after Van Cleef, but he won't try to stop us."

"That's good," Pris said. "I don't like it when people try to stop me from doing what I want to do."

She was a very determined woman, but Fargo had known that almost since they'd first met.

"What is it that you want to do?" Fargo asked.

"Do you mean right now?"

"That's kinda what I was wondering."

"I don't think you were wondering." Pris removed the coat she was wearing and started to undo her shirt. "I think you already know."

"Yeah," Fargo said with a smile. "I think I do."

8

Jess Van Cleef sat with his back against a rock and looked up at the sky. He wasn't really seeing it, just staring blankly. He'd heard the two men talking at their campfire, but he hadn't been able to get close enough to hear what they'd been saying, not that it mattered to him. He'd never been much interested in what anybody else had to say about anything.

All he cared about was how people might be of use to him, and he figured that the men had some supplies he could use. He was running short on a few things, like coffee and bacon—not to mention money. Though he didn't know what good money would do him out here. He wasn't going to stop anywhere that he could use it because by now the word would be spreading about what he'd done back in Missouri, and there were some small-minded people who might hold that against him—which was why he'd given Fort Laramie a wide berth. It wasn't that he was afraid or minded a little trouble. It was just that he'd be a little out-numbered with all the soldiers at the fort. No use in tangling with a bunch like that. Van Cleef preferred to have all the odds on his side, the way it had been in Missouri.

Remembering Missouri and what had happened there gave Van Cleef a good feeling inside. It wasn't like those Indians he'd killed the other day. Hell, they weren't hardly even human, so killing them wasn't much of a thrill. He'd caught them away from their camp, and it had been easy—as easy as killing that young fella at the whorehouse or raping that woman. He'd thought Indians were supposed to be tough, but that hadn't proven to be the case. Van Cleef was a little disappointed in them.

That hadn't stopped him from mutilating them, however. He liked doing that—Indian or not.

Just thinking about it made him want to touch his knife, sharp and shiny in a scabbard dangling from his belt, but he didn't. He sat right where he was, hardly moving. He'd made a little noise earlier, and he'd been afraid that the men had heard him. He didn't think they had, however, since they went on talking, and now one of them was asleep.

The other one was sitting up, keeping a watch, but it wouldn't do him any good. He'd get a little drowsy sooner or later and, when he did, Van Cleef would be right behind him with his knife.

It would be a little while longer, Van Cleef knew, but he could wait. He was good at waiting, as long as he knew his patience would be rewarded.

Fargo didn't mind waiting, either.

Pris was undressing slowly, teasing him a little, but it just added to his pleasure.

When she removed her heavy man's shirt, he could see that he'd been right about her figure. Her breasts were large and firm, tipped with nipples already stiffened and projecting from the dark areolae.

Pris dropped the shirt to the floor of the wagon and ran her hands over her breasts as if she were admiring them, pinching the rigid nipples between her thumb and forefinger, smiling at Fargo as she did so. Then she cupped her hands beneath her breasts and lifted them up for Fargo's admiration.

"You like what you see?" she asked.

Fargo's rod had stiffened in his pants as soon as Pris took off her shirt. It seemed to him that it grew even harder at her words, though he wouldn't have thought that possible.

"I like everything just fine," Fargo said. "Just fine."

"Then why aren't you showing your appreciation?"

Fargo didn't need further encouragement. He closed the short distance to Pris and took her in his arms, laying her

40

gently down in the bed of the wagon. He brushed his palm lightly across the hard tips of her breasts, and Pris sighed.

Fargo took one of the nipples in his mouth, teasing it with his tongue, and Pris arched her back to him, forcing more of her breast into his mouth. At the same time, she ran one hand down the front of his pants until she encountered the bulge that she'd been seeking.

"Ummmm," she said. "I like it when a man enjoys his work."

Fargo lifted his head enough to speak.

"I wouldn't call it work," he said.

"That's good. Now give me a little room."

Fargo did as she requested. Pris moved her hands to her waist, undid her pants, and slithered out of them.

Fargo pulled a bit farther away from her and removed his own clothes as quickly as he could. His shaft stuck out in front of him like a tent pole.

"It's even bigger than I thought," Pris said, taking it in her hand and letting her fingers play with the tip. "I hope you don't hurt me with it."

"I'll be careful," Fargo said. Then he drew a sharp breath as Pris took him into her mouth, which seemed hot as a furnace.

For a second she didn't move, but then she began to torture him with her tongue as she let him slowly in and out of her burning mouth. He put his hands behind her head and twined his fingers in her hair as she eased him from one plateau of pleasure to the next.

Just when he thought he would explode, she stopped, moved away from him, and lay back on the floor. Fargo, breathing raggedly, lay down beside her and let his hands rove over her body. He started with her breasts, but he moved rapidly to the dark nest of hair between her legs. His fingers quickly found her slit, which was slick and hot and ready for him. His middle finger slipped up and down between the sides, rubbing her engorged clitoris, and Pris began to moan and move her hips, slowly at first and then faster.

As she enjoyed the sensations between her legs, Fargo once more took one of her distended nipples in his lips. He tongued it lovingly as his finger moved faster and faster.

Just as Pris had done with him, he stopped when he

judged that she had almost reached the peak of her excitement. She lay there, panting.

"You son of a bitch," she said. "You'd better be ready to give it to me, and give it to me good."

Fargo was ready, all right. He knelt between Pris's widespread legs, and touched the tip of his ivory shaft to her hot, wet opening. She took her lower lip between her teeth and bit down to keep from crying out with pleasure, so Fargo slid the tip up and down over the slick joy-button.

Pris reached behind him and grasped the cheeks of his rear, pulling him into her. She was so slippery and ready that there was no resistance. He went straight in, right up to the root, their pubic hairs meshing into one dark tangle.

Fargo started to slide out, but Pris held him where he was. Rather than letting him control the tempo, she ground her hips against him and forced him even farther inside her. Her head thrashed from side to side, her dark hair flying.

She sighed, and Fargo felt her grip relax after a moment. At that point he started to ride her, giving her long, slow strokes at first, then faster, shorter ones as his own tension grew.

"Now!" Pris said. "Give it to me, Fargo! Hard! Harder!"

Fargo gave it to her, and in seconds she began to moan.

"Aaahhhhhhhhhh, Fargo, ahhhhhhhhhhh."

Fargo could hold back no longer. He ejected a lavalike stream, while Pris wrapped her legs around him and tried to hold him to her as she convulsed beneath him in the throes of her explosive orgasm.

When it was over, they lay side by side in the wagon bed. Pris said, "I hope we didn't wake the neighbors."

"We might have rocked the wagon a little," Fargo said. "Let's hope they're sound sleepers."

"Do you really care?"

"No. Do you?"

"Not one bit."

Pris reached out a hand to touch Fargo.

"Oh, my. You're almost ready to go again."

There was no *almost* about it. Fargo's pole was standing at attention.

Pris took him in hand and said, "How would you like it if I did this?"

She moved her hand slowly up and down his shaft.

Fargo liked it quite a bit.

"And then what if I did this?" she said.

She pushed Fargo to his back and straddled him. Taking the root of his sex, she rubbed the tip of the shaft vigorously in her slit before settling herself on him, taking every inch of him inside her.

Fargo liked that, too, but before he could say so, Pris took his hands and placed them on her breasts. As he stroked her, she moved on him in small circles. He'd never felt anything quite like it before, and it seemed like only seconds before he shot into her a second time as she moaned her appreciation.

She fell forward limply, as if exhausted, but Fargo knew she wasn't. She was almost all appetite. He'd known many women, and she was as voracious as any of them—never happier than when she was feeding her own desire for pleasure and sensation.

She rolled to the side and said, "You're much of a man, Fargo. I think I'm going to like being around you."

"As long as you don't get tired of me," Fargo said, only half joking. She didn't seem the type to be happy very long with any one man.

"I don't think I could ever get tired of what we just did. But I hope you're not thinking it's time to stop."

"Nope," Fargo said. "Not yet."

"I'm glad to hear it. There's something else I'd like to try when you're ready."

"I'm ready."

"You're joking," Pris said, reaching for him. "No. You're not joking. My God, Fargo. Come here!"

Fargo rolled into her embrace.

9

The night had gotten a bit colder, but the cold didn't bother Jess Van Cleef. He seldom thought about things like heat and cold. The weather simply didn't concern him.

He had gotten up from his place against the rock only once, to go and check on his horse, which was hobbled nearly a quarter of a mile away, and to flush his bladder. Then he'd settled down again to wait.

The first man was far too alert to suit Van Cleef. He'd kept his eyes open and hadn't relaxed in the least. More important, he'd kept his hand on that damn rifle he had, and he looked like he knew how to use it.

Van Cleef wasn't scared of any man—rifle or not. He'd heard other people talk about fear and how it could affect a man, but he'd never experienced it.

Although he wasn't afraid, he was practical, and he knew that he wouldn't be able to function very well if a bullet took him in the chest and exploded his heart. So while he wasn't fearful, he was careful.

An hour or so after midnight, the man with the rifle woke the other man. Van Cleef couldn't hear what they were saying, but again he didn't think it mattered.

Nothing they said could change what was going to happen to them.

"You better keep your rifle handy," Gant said. "You never know what might pay you a visit around here."

Keller shook himself, trying to come fully awake. He'd

44

been dreaming about a woman he'd known years ago—a woman who'd been happy to do things for him that no woman since had wanted to try.

"Is there any coffee left?" he asked.

"Yeah," Gant told him. "I'll sit with you while you drink it."

He thinks I'm not awake yet, Keller thought. *Well, hell, he's right about that.*

He found his cup and poured the last of the coffee in it. After a few swallows, he felt better.

"I'm fine now," he said. "Let me get my rifle."

He got it and sat braced against a cottonwood tree with his rifle ready. His back itched, and he rubbed against the tree to scratch it, though he didn't get much relief.

"You can go on to sleep now," he told Gant. "If anybody tries to sneak up on us, I'll take care of him."

Gant nodded, wishing he trusted Keller to do exactly that. It wasn't that Keller wasn't willing. Gant just wasn't sure he had the kind of sixth sense a man needed to survive out in this part of the country. It was one thing to lead a wagon train, where there were always other people around, and plenty of eyes and ears to be on the watch. It was something else to be on your own.

But Gant hadn't heard anything while he watched— nothing but the rustling of the leaves overhead. He knew that nothing light-footed enough to cause that sound would bother them.

So he got his bedroll and lay down, being sure that his rifle was handy and that his pistol was also within reach. It took him a while to go to sleep, but eventually Keller heard his slow, steady breathing.

Keller concentrated on his watch for a half hour or so, but before long, thoughts of the woman he'd dreamed about drifted back. He found himself thinking that it was time he went back to Saint Louis. That was where she'd worked in one of the better whorehouses in town. He could look her up if she was still around.

Thinking of whorehouses reminded him of Sammy, his younger brother, who might still be alive today if he'd stayed away from whores.

Keller thought of the woman in Saint Louis again. Maybe he wouldn't look her up after all, but she could sure do some exciting things. His mind dwelled on that, and then strayed. The next thing he knew, his head had slumped forward on his chest.

He snapped it up with a start.

Damn, he thought. *I better not go to sleep.* Not that anything would happen, but if Gant caught him napping, there'd be hell to pay.

He thought about the woman again and all the things she could do. He heard nothing moving behind him, not even when Van Cleef reached around the tree and clamped his huge hand over Keller's mouth.

Keller hardly had time to struggle before he felt a sharp tingle at his throat as Van Cleef's knife sliced through the arteries and the windpipe. Blood spurted out, and Van Cleef released his grip. Keller wasn't going to be calling out to anybody now, nor would he ever think about the woman in Saint Louis again.

Van Cleef let Keller fall to the side of the tree. He hadn't expected any trouble from Keller, who'd been half asleep within thirty minutes of going on watch. It was the other man that Van Cleef thought might be a problem.

And he was right. Gant was a light sleeper at the best of times, and even the little noise that Keller had made in dying had awakened the former mountain man.

Gant didn't stop to think, which would have been instantly fatal. He simply rolled to one side, grabbing his rifle as he did. Without aiming, without even looking, he instinctively fired the big gun where he thought the trouble was coming from.

His instincts were as good as they'd ever been. The shot went in the right direction, and it even came close to doing some damage. It tore through Van Cleef's coat and took a little chunk of flesh off the top of his left shoulder.

"Shit," Van Cleef said, and put his hand to the wound to convince himself that he'd actually been shot.

There wasn't much pain, no more than an ordinary man would feel from a mosquito bite. But Van Cleef had never felt real pain, anymore than he'd ever felt fear. Pain just wasn't part of his makeup.

The slight pause to check his shoulder almost cost Van Cleef his life.

Gant tossed the Hawken aside and grabbed his pistol, a big Navy Colt. He pulled the trigger and sent a .36 caliber ball toward Van Cleef.

Van Cleef's instincts were working too, however, and he moved quickly to the side just before Gant pulled the trigger. The ball passed by and took a chunk out of a cottonwood tree.

Before Gant could pull the trigger a second time, Van Cleef had dodged behind a tree and drawn his own pistol.

Gant didn't wait around for him to shoot. He got to his feet and ran for the horses.

He didn't quite reach them. Van Cleef stepped around the tree and shot him in the back.

Gant pitched forward on his face. He looked dead enough, but Van Cleef noticed that the old man held onto his pistol. So he was careful as he approached him. When he got within five feet, Gant tried to roll over and shoot him.

Van Cleef had been expecting that little trick, so at Gant's first move, he triggered off a shot of his own, hitting Gant in the elbow before Gant could turn over.

This time Gant dropped his pistol. He remained lying face down.

"You can go ahead and roll over, old man," Van Cleef said. "I like to see a fella's eyes when he dies. I missed out on that with your partner over there." .

"You can go to hell, you son of a bitch," Gant said, not moving from where he lay.

"I don't doubt that I will," Van Cleef said. "But not before you do. Now roll over and look at me."

Gant didn't say anything. He didn't move, either.

"Well, hell," Van Cleef said. "You're an ornery old bastard, aren't you?"

He holstered his pistol and went to Gant. He pulled his knife and knelt down beside the wounded man.

"I could shoot you in the head, but I'm not gonna do that," Van Cleef said. "It would go too easy with you."

Gant lay silently, cursing himself, Keller, and Van Cleef. This wouldn't have happened if the Trailsman had come with them. Or if Tobias hadn't gone back to his wife and son.

But that was selfish thinking. Gant was glad Tobias wasn't there. No use for him to die, too. Because Gant knew he was going to die. Not much doubt about that.

Van Cleef took a handful of Gant's hair and turned his head so that Gant would have to look in his face.

"Now that's a lot better, ain't it?" Van Cleef said.

Gant tried to turn his head away, but Van Cleef had a firm grip on his hair.

"You get a good look at me, old man," Van Cleef said. "Then you can say farewell."

Gant didn't know where the first shot had hit him, but it felt like half his body was paralyzed. His elbow was starting to hurt like hell, too. But, by God, he wasn't going to give in to any son of a bitch like Van Cleef.

"You can kiss my ass," he said.

Van Cleef grinned. "I like a man with a little gumption. But I don't like to be trifled with. So I'm gonna make you sorry for the way you've talked to me."

Gant said nothing. He'd be damned if he'd give Van Cleef the satisfaction.

"See, I was gonna kill you before I did anything else," Van Cleef said. "But now I'm not. I'm gonna skin you alive."

It was some gratification for him to see the old man's eyes widen, but still Gant didn't speak.

"You are a tough old bird," Van Cleef said. "But I got me a feeling you'll be talking before I get through with you. I believe you'll be begging me to stop."

Gant just looked at him. Then he hawked up a gob of phlegm and spat it at Van Cleef's face.

It didn't even come close.

"That was a mean thing to do," Van Cleef said, a little surprised at the old man's courage. "I'm glad I didn't kill you because I'm gonna enjoy taking your damned old face."

He put the point of his knife to Gant's neck.

Gant closed his eyes and told himself that no matter what happened, he wasn't going to scream.

Eventually, of course, he did.

10

The next morning, Fargo and Pris rode away from Fort Laramie. Not too early because Fargo had slept a bit longer than usual, thanks to the night's activities. As far as he could tell, Pris was unaffected. She was as fresh as if she'd slept for days.

It was a cool, clear day, and the sky was a bowl of blue. But Fargo could tell that the weather was going to change, and fairly soon. He couldn't have explained how he knew if anyone had asked him. It was just a sense he had, a feeling in the air, and because of it, he made sure that he and Pris had plenty of supplies and warm clothing.

He was atop the Ovaro, and Pris straddled a roan that she'd bought from one of the pilgrims. Fargo had persuaded her that the wagon was no way to travel, not if they were looking for someone like Van Cleef.

"He won't be sticking to the trail," Fargo said. "We'll have to travel places where a wagon couldn't go, and it's too slow, anyway."

Fargo didn't really hold out much hope of finding Van Cleef. The only clue to his whereabouts would come from the Crow, and Fargo wasn't too sure about how easy it would be to talk to any of that bunch. They didn't seem to be in the mood for conversation.

Pris had given in to his urging, but she insisted that Van Cleef would be easy to track.

"I don't believe he'll stray far from the trail," she said, as she had when Fargo had broached the topic earlier. "He doesn't know the country, and he won't want to wander off into it on his own, not before he has some idea about how to get by out here."

Fargo wasn't so sure. Van Cleef had already killed some of the Crow, apparently just for the fun of it. He didn't sound like someone who'd need to know anything about the territory before he made himself at home in it.

As they rode along, Fargo told Pris again that he thought she was making a mistake going after Van Cleef.

"I know you think you have a good reason," he said. "But those two men I told you about, Keller and Gant, they have a lot better chance of catching up to him than we do."

"You're supposed to be good at tracking, aren't you?" Pris asked.

Fargo admitted that he was.

"Then we have as good a chance as they do. Maybe better."

"We have to find a track to follow before we can find anybody," Fargo reminded her.

"We'll find one. I promise you that."

Fargo didn't understand her confidence.

"You can follow the tracks those other two left, can't you?"

He had been seeing the tracks ever since they'd left Fort Laramie. The hoofprints of the horses were still clear in the wet ground because nobody else had gone in that direction since Keller and Gant had headed out.

When he told that to Pris, she said, "Then we'll find Van Cleef because he'll find your friends."

Fargo didn't see how she could know that.

"Do you think he's looking for them?" he asked.

"Not necessarily. But he's looking for somebody."

"Who?" Fargo said.

"Nobody special. Just somebody to kill. He'll prey on whoever's on the trail. That's the way he operates."

She seemed to know a lot about Van Cleef. Fargo asked her how she'd found it out.

"I talked to people back in Missouri," she said after a little hesitation. "He has a reputation."

Fargo couldn't argue with that.

"Considering the things he's done, you'd think the law would have him by now."

"He's too smart for that," Pris said. "He never stays in one place very long."

"I don't doubt it, with those bad habits of his," Fargo said.

"He's worse than you think," Pris said, though she didn't sound to Fargo as if it bothered her much.

When he asked what she meant, she wouldn't explain.

"Your job's to find him, not to understand him," she said.

"If that's the way you want it."

"That's the way I want it. Do you think we can catch up to those friends of yours before he finds them?"

"You sound mighty sure that he will," Fargo said.

"If they're out here, he'll find them. That's the way he is."

She sounded awfully certain of it. Fargo wondered why, but she wouldn't say any more.

"I don't blame you for wanting to get him. It's a natural thing. It's just that I don't think we'll find him out here."

"We'll find him," Pris said. "Or he'll find us. You'll see."

The way she said it sounded a bit ominous to Fargo.

"What about the Crow?" Pris said, changing the subject. "Do we have to worry about them?"

Fargo liked the Crow, for the most part. He had friends among them.

"We wouldn't have to worry about them in the ordinary way of things," he said. "But now that Van Cleef has them stirred up, we might."

"So we'll have to keep a good watch."

"We sure will," Fargo said.

Sid Frazee sat in the saloon looking into his nearly empty beer glass.

Lee and Chad Tuttle sat at the table with him, but they didn't have anything to say, and in fact they were half afraid to make any comments. Sid had been in a black mood ever since that woman had kicked him in the stones.

For that matter, neither Lee nor Chad were feeling exactly chipper.

51

Lee's right arm was bandaged because Fargo's bullet had taken a big chunk of it out and even nipped the bone. The army surgeon told Lee he'd been lucky the bullet hadn't broken the bone.

"Might've had to take half your arm off in that case," the surgeon had said, spitting tobacco juice on the floor.

Lee didn't like to hear that kind of thing at all, but even if he'd lost the arm he'd have been better off than Chad would've been if he'd lost his leg. He'd gotten one of Fargo's bullets through the calf. Another inch or so, and he'd have had a shattered bone, and maybe no leg below the knee.

So both of them were in a mood at least as foul as that of Sid Frazee. When he made them his proposition, they were more than ready to go along with it.

"I say we ride after that son of a bitch," Frazee told them. "For what he done to us, he deserves killin'."

Chad looked at Lee. They didn't disagree with what Sid had said, but neither of them wanted to be the one to mention that Fargo hadn't done anything to him. It was the woman who'd taken him down, and that was a little too embarrassing to bring up with Frazee as mad as he was about it.

After a second, Lee looked away from Chad. There just wasn't any way around it, but he thought he could put it so it wouldn't bother Frazee too much. He said, "What about that woman? We gonna kill her, too?"

Frazee smiled, revealing crooked yellow teeth.

"We can find something better to do with her," he said. He took a drink of beer. "And after that, we'll kill her."

Lee wasn't too sure about that idea. He could see killing Fargo, but killing a woman was different. It just didn't seem right, somehow.

Chad didn't like it, either. He said, "That might not be very smart, Sid. Maybe we could just leave her out there, let her try to get back on her own."

"And if she did," Sid said, "she'd tell every son of a bitch in the territory what happened to her and who done it. Is that what you want?"

Chad guessed he didn't, and neither did Lee.

"All right, then. Are you in this with me or not?"

The Tuttle brothers thought it over. Then Chad nodded.

"We'll do it," he said. "But we might ought to wait a day or so before we leave. Me and Lee, we ain't quite up to snuff yet."

"You can ride, can't you?"

Lee held up his right arm for Frazee to have a look. It hurt him when he did it.

"I'm mighty sore," he said.

"And I can't walk worth a damn," Chad said. "Those crutches the sawbones gave me ain't much help."

He gestured to the crutches that stood against the wall behind his chair.

"I'm sorry, boys, that you're all stove up," Frazee said, not meaning a word of it. "But I didn't ask about your goddamned ailments. I asked, could you ride? How about it?"

First Lee and then Chad said that well, yes, maybe he could ride, but it would be painful.

"And what if you were sitting on a pair of balls that was bruised black-and-blue?" Frazee said. "You think you could ride then?"

Lee and Chad allowed as to how they didn't know about that, but they expected it would be mighty painful.

"You're goddamned right it would," Frazee told them. "But you don't hear me whinin' about it, now do you? A man don't let something like that hold him back when he's got to set things right."

Lee and Chad nodded their agreement, eyes downcast, ashamed that Frazee was so much tougher than they were.

Sid stood and shoved his chair back. It scraped across the floor and hit the neighboring table. The drunk asleep there snorted, opened one eye, and closed it again.

"Let's get goin'," Frazee said. "Maybe we can catch up to 'em by dark."

"What if we don't?" Lee asked.

"Then we'll catch 'em tomorrow. If we ever get started, that is. Come on."

Lee and Chad stood up. Chad hopped around on one foot until he could get his crutches set under his armpits, and then they followed Frazee outside into the sunlight. Chad clumped along slowly, so Lee walked along with him. They were far enough behind Frazee to have a few private words together.

"You reckon he'll really kill that woman?".Lee said.

"Sure he will. Frazee's a mean one."

"You sure we oughta be goin' along with him, then?"

"What else you gonna do? Sit around the saloon pickin' your nose?"

"But we ain't never killed nobody," Lee said. "Much less a woman. We done some bad things now and then, sure, but we ain't killers."

Chad snorted. "You don't have to go if you're so damn worried."

"You ain't never steered me wrong before, Chad. If you say it's all right, I'll go along."

"I'm not sayin' it's all right. I'm just sayin' we ain't got nothing better to do. Might as well stick with Frazee and see how it turns out. Is that good enough for you?"

"Yeah," Lee said. "I guess it is."

He gave his brother a crooked grin to let him know he meant it. But he was still worried about killing the woman.

11

Van Cleef didn't bother burying what was left of Keller and Gant. He simply left the bodies where they lay. He figured animals and buzzards would get to them soon, and that was good enough for him. Besides, his shoulder hurt. It wasn't much of a wound, and he'd doctored it up. Still, there wasn't any use to bury men who'd shot him, by God.

He'd skinned their faces and stretched the skin out over a couple of rocks. The distorted visages might have looked spooky to some people, but Van Cleef thought they looked downright nice—certainly better than they'd looked when the two men had worn them. If he'd had time, he might have tried drying out the skins and taking them with him, but he couldn't afford to wait around that long.

He took all the food that the men had with them and loaded it on their horses. He took their weapons, too. He never knew when a little extra armament might come in handy.

After he had everything loaded up, he led the horses to where his own mount waited. He needed to look for a little better hiding place because he didn't want the damn redskins finding him. He knew they were looking.

He also knew that someone else would be coming along after him sooner or later, and he wanted to be ready. He couldn't always be sure of sneaking up on people during the night. He had to have another plan or two, and he didn't want anyone to find him until he was good and ready.

He figured he had a pretty good head start and that he could find a good place to hole up on the way to the Divide, or somewhere in the mountains beyond it.

The more he thought about it, the better he liked the idea of the mountains. He didn't plan to stay around this part of the country any longer than he had to. He knew nothing about trapping and hunting, and he was going on to California or Oregon just as quick as he could. As soon as he was ready, anyway. He had some unfinished business, thanks to leaving Missouri in such a hurry, so he had to stay around the Fort Laramie area for a little while.

But when the time came, he'd just get on out to the Tetons, not stopping there, but finding somewhere to stay, if he had to, until the springtime thaw came and the mountain passes cleared. If the weather warmed up again, hell, maybe he could cross the Divide right away and put the East and everything that had happened there behind him.

Nobody knew him out West, and he could start all over. He'd try to live like everyone else. It would be hard to give up the things he liked, he knew that, but he thought he could do it. And if he couldn't, he'd get by some way. He always had.

He hoped nothing would happen to slow him down. The weather was good and, if it held, he'd have no trouble. He'd keep an eye out for the redskins, and he'd get where he was going without anybody there being the wiser.

He smiled. Everything was going to work out just fine.

The wind picked up not long after Fargo and Pris left Fort Laramie, and the clouds moved in, gradually blotting out all the blue in the sky. In the middle of the afternoon, snow began to fall.

The wind was out of the northwest, not strong but steady, and the day had grown sharply colder from noon onward. Fargo wasn't sure how cold it would get, but he knew the weather could be treacherous at that time of year. He wished more than ever that he'd been able to talk Pris out of her ill-advised idea of revenge, but he couldn't change her mind. When he brought the subject up again, she was, if anything, more determined than ever to find Van Cleef. And she didn't like the way the weather seemed about to slow them down.

"The snow's going to cover the tracks, isn't it?" she asked.

Fargo told her that it might, but that it didn't seem to matter because Keller and Gant had stuck right to the trail, and Fargo could follow that in his sleep.

"They'll have to get off it sooner or later," she said. "At least for a little while, to camp."

"Plenty of places for that, right along the trail," Fargo said. "They won't get too far away, not unless they know more about where they're going than I do. Which I doubt."

The wind swirled the snow. The big flakes were thick in the air, and the clouds now covered the entire sky.

"How could they know anything?" Pris asked.

Fargo didn't know. "Maybe Gant had something to go on," he said. "Something he didn't want to tell anybody about until he got on the way."

Pris laughed. "He won't know anything. Van Cleef doesn't leave any clues."

Once again she spoke as if she knew more about Van Cleef than she was telling, but Fargo didn't press her. He figured she'd let him know sooner or later.

The clouds thickened throughout the afternoon, shutting out the light. There was sleet mixed in with the snow now, and it stung Fargo's face when the wind whipped it into him.

He suggested that they stop for the night before it became too dark to see. He spotted a place not far off the trail that looked good. There were a couple of big rocks that would shelter them from the wind, and they could build a fire with sticks from the cottonwood trees.

Fargo took care of the horses first, rubbing them down, graining them, and being sure that they were sheltered from the wind.

Meanwhile Pris gathered up some limbs for the fire. She had a blaze going by the time Fargo finished with the horses.

"Beans, bacon, and coffee sound all right?" she said.

It sounded fine to Fargo, who was a little surprised that she was offering to cook. For some reason, he found it hard to imagine her at work in a kitchen, or even over a campfire.

But she knew what she was doing, and before too long

Fargo could hear the bacon sizzling and smell the coffee in the pot.

Since he had some time, he rigged a covering with a blanket and some sticks. They'd be able to sleep comfortably there if they kept the fire going, which he intended to do, even if he had to be the one to keep watch all night long.

With a good meal and a warm fire, he thought, they'd be just fine. They were lucky to have found a good spot to camp on such a night.

Frazee and the Tuttles weren't so fortunate. The snow had started only an hour or so after they'd left Laramie, and they hadn't taken the time to think things through. They had food, but the weather had fooled them. They'd noticed the change in the wind and the gathering clouds, but they'd expected that the day would remain warm.

Lee was thinking they shouldn't have been in such a hurry. If they'd waited a few hours, they'd have seen that it wasn't a fit time to be leaving, and maybe they'd have waited until the next day. Better yet, they might not have left at all.

But that didn't figure into Frazee's plans. He had rushed them, making fun of Chad's problems with the crutches.

Chad hadn't liked it, but he didn't do anything about it. He didn't even say anything. Lee couldn't blame him. Frazee had turned downright mean. He'd been bad enough before, but now he was different—worse in some way that Lee couldn't quite put his finger on.

He'd even laughed when Lee had to help Chad get mounted on his horse.

"Hell," Frazee had said, "you're as awkward as a kid gettin' his first piece."

Lee hadn't thought that was funny, and neither had Chad, but they'd laughed, or tried to. It had seemed like the thing to do.

They hadn't laughed anymore after that, though. The weather was nothing to laugh about, and night came sooner than they'd thought it would. They were caught off guard by the suddenness of the dark.

"You ever been in anything like this?" Frazee asked.

"Hell," Lee said, "we ain't been out in this part of the country that long. We been around the fort for a month or two, that's all."

"Goddamn," Frazee said. "And here I thought I was hooking up with a pair of real mountain men."

"If you thought that, you was wrong," Chad said. "Fargo, now, he's a Trailsman. He could've told you what the weather would do. But the two of us are just a couple of rowdies lookin' for a new start. What was it that set you out on the Oregon Trail, Frazee?"

Frazee's story had to do with a gang of men who'd badly bungled a bank robbery. He'd gotten away, but some of the others hadn't. He didn't see any need to tell that to the Tuttles, and he didn't like them asking.

"Same as anybody," he said. "Looking for a better life out west."

"Shit," Chad said, waving an arm to indicate the snow and the darkness. "You call this better? Better'n what?"

Frazee didn't think it was any better than anything else, but he knew that if they didn't find a place to camp, they'd be in big trouble.

He couldn't see more than a few feet to either side of his horse, and he wondered if he hadn't made a mistake going out after Fargo and the woman. Sure, his balls hurt, and his pride, too, but that had been hurt plenty of times before. Because it had happened too often, he'd let his feelings get the best of his common sense.

He wondered if it was too late to turn back to the fort. He couldn't do that, though. It would make him look bad to the Tuttles, and by God he wasn't going to be made to look bad to a couple of idiots like them. He'd keep on going even if they all froze to death.

"Look over there," Lee said, pointing into the dark. "Is that some trees?"

Frazee couldn't tell, but it did look like a blacker area in the darkness. It could be trees. Not much of a shelter, but better than nothing.

"Let's go have a look," he said.

Van Cleef was luckier than them all.

He hadn't gone far from the place he'd killed Keller and

Gant, but he hadn't wanted to stay around there with them. Best to let the bodies keep each other company without him.

A little way down the trail and off to one side, he found an abandoned wagon. It was missing its canvas and all its wheels, which didn't matter to him in the least. It was tipped over on its side in just the right direction to block the wind. He could even use part of the wood from the bed to make a good fire.

The horses wouldn't be sheltered, and that worried Van Cleef. He liked horses a lot better than he liked people, and he was never cruel to one if he could help it. He decided to bring them behind the wagon bed with him, where they'd at least have some kind of windbreak, and maybe they'd survive the night without too much trouble. Van Cleef hoped so.

When he had the horses situated, Van Cleef built a little fire and congratulated himself on the way his luck was running. Things were working out just fine, he thought, even better than he'd thought they would. He snuggled into Gant's buffalo robe and settled in for the night, not worried about a thing.

12

The wind blew hard through the little stand of trees, but a couple of them were close enough together for Lee and Frazee to tie up a blanket between them. It wasn't much, but it helped to keep off the wind and the biting sleet.

It wasn't easy for Lee to help because of his arm, which the cold was making hurt even more than before. As for Chad, all he could do was sit and shiver in his sheepskin-lined coat. His crutches were just about useless on the wet, snow-covered ground.

After they had the blanket up, Frazee was able to get a fire going, but it wasn't much of one. It would barely keep them warm.

Lee thought that he and Chad were damn fools for being out in a snowstorm with somebody like Frazee. Yeah, Fargo had hurt them, and it was right to get back at a man when he did something like that, but there were other, easier ways to do it. You could just wait till he came back to the fort and then poison his horse or something. Shoot him in the back, maybe, if you felt like you had to kill him. Catch him in the dark somewhere and beat the hell out of him. But this chasing him along the Oregon Trail in a damn snowstorm was just plain crazy.

Frazee must've known that, too. Lee figured that it was the woman. Frazee had plans for her that couldn't have been carried out back at the fort—not without serious problems. That didn't mean Lee and Chad had to be mixed up in it, though. They should've had enough sense to tell

Frazee to go on by himself if he was bound and determined to get revenge on anybody.

Lee wished he could talk to Chad, maybe suggest that they go back to the fort come morning. But they were all huddled behind the one blanket, and Frazee would hear every word. Besides, it didn't look like Chad would be interested. He had his eyes closed and might even have been asleep.

This is one hell of a mess me and Chad have got ourselves into, Lee thought. He looked at Frazee, who was getting a skillet out of his gear.

"You plannin' to eat?" Lee asked.

"Damn right. We need something in our bellies if we're gonna get through a night as cold as this one's likely to be."

That sounded about right to Lee. He said, "We didn't bring nothing but beans."

"Beans'll get us through rougher nights than this," Frazee said. "Beans and coffee. Perk you right up. You'll see."

Lee didn't believe a word of it. He looked at Chad, but his brother still had his eyes closed.

"Shit," Lee said aloud.

"You got a problem?" Frazee said.

He hefted the heavy iron skillet in his hand like a weapon.

"No. Hell, no," Lee said. "I'm just cold, and my arm hurts, that's all."

"Yeah. Well, we're all cold. But we'll be fine in the morning."

Shit, Lee thought, but this time he didn't say it aloud.

The wind whistled around the rocks, but Fargo and Pris were well protected. They'd eaten bacon and beans, and Fargo had cleaned the plates with snow. They were wrapped up in blankets, and they sat with their backs to the rocks, drinking hot coffee that helped a little to warm them.

"You never told me why Jess Van Cleef killed your father," Fargo said. "You want to talk about that?"

Pris looked into the tin cup that held her coffee as if thinking about what Fargo had said.

"Was it in Independence?" Fargo asked. "That's where

Gant was from. Seems like Van Cleef went on some kind of killing spree there."

"That's where it happened," Pris said. She looked up at Fargo. "It was awful."

Considering what Gant had said and what had happened to the Crow, Fargo wasn't surprised. But there was one thing he wondered about.

"How could one man kill three people, nearly kill another one, and still get away? Everybody in Independence should be on his trail by now."

"And do what?" Pris said. "Come all the way out here? There might be a warrant on him, so maybe a marshal will show up one of these days, but it'll be too late when he does. And maybe there's a bounty hunter or two who will get on the trail if the reward money's good. But I didn't want to wait for a judge to issue a warrant or for a bounty hunter to come along. I guess Mr. Gant didn't, either. Some things you have to do for yourself."

It made sense, Fargo thought, but it still seemed strange to him that a woman would come this far into a country she didn't know anything about to look for a man she had no idea how to find.

On the other hand, Pris Harrison was strong willed and tough, and she didn't seem to be afraid of anything.

Fargo had known women like that before, self-sufficient and strong, but there was something that set her apart from the others, though he couldn't quite figure out what it was. It was something about her attitude and her confidence in herself, he guessed.

He realized that she still hadn't told him about her father's death, so he asked her again.

Pris didn't say anything for a good while. Fargo waited, listening to the whining of the wind and watching the flurries of snow in the firelight.

"My father was a farrier," Pris said. "I suppose that Van Cleef was on his way out of town when he killed him. He might have killed Mr. Gant's wife already, but I don't know about that. Van Cleef was in a hurry, and he didn't have a horse. He stopped at my father's shop to steal one, and my father tried to stop him. Nobody stops Van Cleef. When he wants something, he takes it."

As before, she sounded as if she had considerably more information about Van Cleef than she was telling, and Fargo tried to get some of it out of her.

"I told you before," she said, avoiding his eyes and his question. "I talked to some people. They told me about him."

"What people?" Fargo wanted to know.

"A marshal. Well, he's not a marshal now. But he used to be, and he told me about Van Cleef. He'd heard of him. Not by that name, but by others. Van Cleef started off back east, stealing and moving from place to place. He could never stay anywhere for long because he'd always get into arguments and fights. But he wouldn't just fight back. He'd kill whoever crossed him, and then he'd cut them up."

"Take their faces," Fargo said.

"No, not then." Pris paused. "At least that's what I heard. That came later."

"And your father? What about him?"

"Van Cleef was in a hurry. He didn't have time to use his knife. So he just threw my father headfirst in the furnace and burned him."

She said it in a matter-of-fact voice, and Fargo marveled at her self-control.

"He was already dead," Pris said. "So it didn't hurt him. But it was still a terrible thing to do."

"Seems to me that Van Cleef does a lot of terrible things."

"He does. That's why we have to find him."

Fargo wished he knew how they were going to do that. He'd been thinking that it would be best if they could join up with Gant and Keller. That way, if Gant did have some kind of plan or some information that would lead them to Van Cleef, he could share it with Fargo. And when you got right down to it, four against one might be just about the right odds when you were going up against a man like Van Cleef.

He asked Pris what she thought about joining forces with the others.

She nodded. "If you think so. We know they came this way. Do you think we can find them, now that their tracks are covered with snow?"

"All we have to do is pick up their trail. Tracking is easy in the snow—if it stops."

"Do you think it will?"

Fargo listened to the sound of the wind. It wasn't as shrill as it had been earlier, and the snow flurries had just about stopped. He could no longer hear any sleet bouncing off the rocks.

"Wouldn't be surprised if it cleared off in an hour or so," he said. "We might even see the stars."

"That would be nice," Pris said. "Now, I told you about my father. Tell me a little about yourself."

"Not much to tell," Fargo said.

"I'd like to hear whatever there is."

Fargo wasn't comfortable talking about himself, but he told her a few stories about his adventures on the trail, and one or two of them even brought a smile to her face.

He was about to launch into another story when Pris said, "There's the moon."

The clouds were breaking up, and a sliver of the moon was visible behind them, edging the black with silvery light.

"You were right about the stars," Pris said. "We'll see them any minute now."

"Won't be long," Fargo agreed.

"Good," Pris said, and she threw off the blanket she was wrapped in and began to unbutton her shirt.

13

Fargo couldn't believe what he was seeing. He thought that Pris might have suddenly gone crazy.

"What are you doing?" he said.

Pris removed her shirt and threw it on the discarded blanket.

"What does it look like?"

The cold air put gooseflesh on her breasts and made her nipples hard as stone.

"I know what it looks like," Fargo said. "But—"

"But, what? Haven't you ever wanted to do it in the snow?"

Fargo, to tell the truth, had never even considered it. But now that she mentioned it, he had to say that the idea had a certain appeal—especially when she kicked off her boots and shucked off her pants. The dark tangle of curls at the base of her flat stomach was so powerfully attractive that it lured his eyes away from her breasts.

"Are you afraid you'll get cold?" Pris asked. "If you are, you don't have to worry. You can wrap us both up in the blanket. I think I can keep you warm."

Fargo didn't doubt it. He put the blanket aside long enough to get out of his clothes. The cold air puckered his own nipples, and he was afraid at first that it might have some effect on his pole.

It didn't. He was so hard and erect that he had difficulty removing his britches.

As soon as he was nude, he pulled the blanket up to his

shoulders, and Pris came to him pressing herself to him so that he could enclose both of them.

She'd been right about keeping him warm. Her body was like a brand from the fire, and the tips of her breasts against him were like two tiny hot coals in spite of their exposure to the cold air.

She opened her mouth for a kiss, which he was happy to give her. Their tongues tangled for what seemed like a long time. Fargo's shaft burned against her stomach.

"Ummmm," Pris murmured when they broke apart.

The breath steamed from her mouth, and Fargo tucked his head down into the blanket to tease her excited nipples, taking first one and then the other into his mouth and caressing them with his tongue.

As he was doing this, Pris's hand was busy at his root, rubbing it against her stomach. The heat of it was almost enough to start a small blaze. Neither of them noticed the weather any longer.

Pris left off her handling of Fargo's shaft to raise his head out of the blanket and then to push him gently toward the ground. He lay back on the blanket, and she slid down his torso until her breasts were above his erect penis. With her hands, she closed them together and enfolded him in their warm softness.

"Move a little," she said.

Fargo didn't need any encouragement. He moved his hips, and his steely pole slipped back and forth between her breasts while she pinched the stiff nipples between her finger and thumb.

Before Fargo went too far and lost control, she stopped him with a touch and straddled him. She seemed to hang above the tip of his penis for a long while, moving only a little, grazing him with the wiry hairs.

Then she lowered herself onto him, gasping as he penetrated the fiery entrance. Fargo seized her engorged breasts as she started to rise and fall on him, priming him and then pumping him until he could no longer hold back.

As he spurted into her she cried out, throwing back her head and whipping her dark hair around her.

Exhausted then, she fell forward on him, her breasts as soft as down pillows.

Fargo pulled the blanket over them, and they lay like

that, sharing the heat of their bodies until Pris sat up. She got off Fargo and moved away from him to where the snow lay thicker on the ground. She reached down with both hands and took snow in them.

While Fargo watched from where he was wrapped in the blanket, she rubbed the snow on her breasts. The intense cold hardened her nipples in less than an instant. When she came back over to Fargo, she still held a bit of snow.

"Are you watching, Fargo?" she said, but of course she knew that he was. He couldn't take his eyes off her, and beneath the blanket his shaft had stiffened and become harder than a wagon spring.

Pris cupped her right hand over her left breast. With the other hand, she traced a line of snow from her navel down to the crisp black triangle of hair, shivering as she did. She was so far gone in pleasure that Fargo thought she might have an orgasm at that very moment.

Instead, she steadied herself, and let her frigid finger find the spot she'd been wanting to touch. As soon as it made contact, a tremor shook her body and she cried out.

Fargo couldn't stand it any longer. He tossed the blanket aside and reached for her. She came to him eagerly, taking his penis in her mouth and working at it with her lips and tongue. Then she took it so deeply that Fargo cried out in surprise just before she made a low humming in her throat. The vibrations encircled the tip of his shaft with sensations unlike anything he'd ever felt. He was so close to release that he thought he wouldn't be able to hold back.

But hold back he did. Pris knew what was happening, and she loosed him with an impish smile before turning her back to him and inviting him to enter her from behind.

Fargo reached around her and rubbed her breasts while tantalizing her hot clitoris with his tumid shaft. She squirmed with pleasure, and then he entered her, shoving himself hard against her buttocks. Her squirming increased and she moaned. "Ahhhh, Fargo. Ahhhhhhhhh!"

She quivered all over, and Fargo shot into her again and again.

They were slicked with sweat when they were done. Fargo got them back into the blanket and as close to the fire as they could without being burned.

The sky over them was almost clear now, the white moon

throwing the shadows of the rocks over the glistening snow. The stars glittered in the black sky.

"I hope you don't think I'm doing this just to repay you for helping me," Pris said after a while. "That's not it, not at all."

Fargo knew she was telling the truth because she had clearly enjoyed their fun as much as he had, if not more. She was satisfying herself as much as she was satisfying him. And that was the way it should be, he thought.

Knowing they'd need more than a single blanket for the night, Fargo, being better prepared than Frazee and the Tuttles, got a buffalo robe to cover Pris. He sat near the fire in the blanket to keep watch.

"Wake me in four hours," Pris said. "I want to do my share."

"If you really want to," Fargo said.

"I really do."

"Fine," Fargo said. If she wanted to do her share, he wasn't going to discourage her. "I'll wake you."

The next day was bright with only a few high, thin clouds to obscure the sun. The snow glistened white and clean, but it wasn't going to melt this time. The day was far too cold. Fargo and Pris wrapped themselves in heavy buffalo robes before they left their camp.

"How are we going to find anything out here?" Pris asked, staring across the level expanse of white.

"The main trail's easy enough to find," Fargo told her. "And I can follow that even with the snow. If Gant and Keller aren't too far ahead of us, we'll catch up with them."

He wasn't as certain as he tried to sound. He wished they'd gotten off to an earlier start, but Pris had slept so soundly after Fargo took his second watch that he'd let her sleep longer than he'd planned.

Traveling in the snow would be harder on the horses than the going had been the day before. They'd have to go more slowly and rest now and then, even though the snow wasn't more than eight or ten inches deep.

"I'm glad you came along," Pris said. "I'd never have managed this on my own." She smiled. "And I'm glad for other reasons, too."

Fargo thought about the way she'd been last night—as

69

free and wild as any woman he'd ever known. Yet there was something that bothered him about her. He couldn't quite figure out what it was. Maybe it was the way she seemed to be holding back on what she knew about Van Cleef, or how she knew it. She sure didn't hold anything else back.

"It's not too late for us to go back to Laramie," he said. "I'm not sure it's a good idea to keep going in this kind of weather."

"I have to find Van Cleef," Pris said, and her tone left no room for doubt that she'd go on without him even now.

"Then I guess we'd better move on," Fargo said, and he urged the Ovaro forward through the snow.

The Tuttles and Frazee had already been on the trail for nearly two hours. Frazee didn't let Lee and Chad linger after he woke them just before dawn. He hadn't even let them fix breakfast, but that was all right with Lee. He didn't think beans were worth a damn in the morning, and Chad didn't seem to care about anything. To Lee, he looked half asleep in the saddle as they struggled along through the snow.

"We could go back," Lee said. "All this out here looks alike now. We're not ever gonna find Fargo and that woman."

"The hell we're not," Frazee said. Each word sent a white cloud out of his mouth. "You just keep up."

Lee hoped Chad didn't fall off his horse. He didn't think Frazee would even stop and let Lee help him back on. That might not be so bad, though. If Frazee went off and left them, they'd just go back to Laramie on their own.

"And don't get the idea you can go back to Laramie," Frazee said. "By God, you're going with me."

"Sure," Lee said with a vigorous nod. "We know that."

14

Van Cleef had a feeling things were going his way again. It just seemed that he couldn't do anything wrong, and when he woke up and saw the snow, he smiled a big smile, rolled out of the buffalo robe, and got ready to boil some coffee.

He didn't know where he was, and he didn't know how he'd find his way in the vast whiteness, but he didn't care. Something good was going to happen—the way it always did. All he had to do was follow his luck, and nothing could go wrong.

Van Cleef checked the horses and, to prove how his luck was holding, all of them seemed fine in spite of his lack of care. He knew then that they'd last him at least as far as the Divide, and probably farther than that.

While he drank his coffee, he leaned back against the overturned wagon, perfectly content and relaxed. There was nothing that could go wrong with his plans because that was just the way it was. Nobody could stop him because nobody had ever been able to. Slow him down, maybe, but not stop him.

He didn't know how things would work themselves out, just that they would. They always had.

He smiled as he thought about that and, as he did, he knew what he was going to do next.

It was a little after noon when Fargo and Pris came to the spot where Van Cleef had killed Keller and Gant.

"There's something in those trees over there," Fargo said. "I'd better have a look."

"I'm going, too," Pris said.

Fargo didn't bother telling her not to. It wouldn't have done any good.

They rode to where the bodies of Keller and Gant lay, three-quarters buried in the snow. Fargo dismounted and brushed the snow away from Gant's face—or at least from where Gant's face should have been. Instead there was a frozen mask of blood and tissue from which two dead eyes stared up at the Trailsman like black marbles.

Fargo moved to hide the sight from Pris, but she didn't seem bothered at all.

"It was him," she said, looking down at the body. "Van Cleef did that."

"Most likely," Fargo said.

"Where's the rest of his face?" Pris asked.

"Maybe Van Cleef took it with him," Fargo said, hoping he was right. But as he looked around he saw two rocks, from which some of the snow had melted. He also saw part of the skin that was stretched over the rocks.

"He didn't," Pris said, having followed Fargo's gaze.

Fargo went to the rocks and brushed away the snow from one of them. Something like a brutal caricature of Gant appeared from under the snow. The face was distorted, the eyeholes and mouth cruelly stretched.

Fargo brushed the snow from the other rock. There was nothing there he wanted to see, but he had to do it. He tried to remove the skin, but it was frozen to the rock.

"I'll do something about the bodies," Fargo said, wondering if he should bother, even though he knew it was the right thing. Keller and Gant wouldn't know or care. He would, though.

"Do you think Van Cleef's around here?" Pris asked.

Fargo didn't think so. The way he saw it, the two men had been dead for about a day. Van Cleef had moved on, taking their horses and their gear.

"Can you follow him?" Pris wanted to know when he told her.

"We'll see," Fargo said.

Any thought of returning to Laramie was gone now. Van Cleef, or whoever had killed Keller and Gant, didn't deserve to go on living, and Fargo would do what he could to see that he didn't.

"I'll take care of things here first," Fargo said. "Then we'll see about Van Cleef."

He moved the bodies to the trees and put some rocks over them. He wasn't able to cover them completely, but it was the best he could do under the circumstances.

Pris didn't offer to help. She sat astride the horse and watched as if she might be waiting for something—or someone.

When Fargo had done all he could, he went back to the Ovaro. Before he mounted, he looked down the trail and saw the three men riding along it.

"That's them, by God," Frazee said. "Just act natural. Don't let them know what we have in mind."

That would be easy for Lee, who didn't have any idea himself what Frazee had in mind. All he could think about was how cold he was and how Chad hadn't said a word all morning. He was just sitting on his horse with his eyes closed, looking like he'd fall off at the next step. He never did, though. Lee had the reins of Chad's horse in his left hand, leading the horse along because Chad wasn't capable of doing anything.

Frazee rode up until he was opposite Fargo and Pris. Lee and Chad trailed along. When they stopped their horses, Frazee gave a little wave.

"How you doin'?" Frazee asked.

"Better than the two men who were camped here," Fargo said.

"What happened to 'em?" Frazee said.

"They're dead."

"You kill 'em?"

"Jess Van Cleef did," Pris told him. "Did you come to help us find him?"

Frazee grinned. "Well, now, I hadn't thought about that."

"What had you thought about?" Fargo asked.

73

As he spoke, there was a noise back in the trees, but no one else seemed to hear it, and Fargo wasn't going to turn his back on Frazee to see what was causing it.

"Well," Frazee said, "I thought about a lot of things, let me tell you. I thought about how you shot Lee and Chad, there." He looked at Pris. "And I thought about how she near crippled me."

"And you decided you'd do something about it?" Fargo asked.

Frazee nodded. "I might."

"You'll need more help than those two," Fargo said. "They don't look up to doing much."

Frazee didn't bother looking at the Tuttles. He said, "Maybe not. But I am."

His hand started for his pistol, but before he could complete the move, a Hawken rifle roared from the trees behind Fargo. The ball hit Frazee squarely in the middle of his forehead and took a chunk of his skull off the back as it made its exit.

Frazee fell backward off his horse and hit the ground without ever having drawn his gun.

Fargo didn't turn. He had a feeling he knew who was back there.

Lee looked down at Frazee, lying in the snow with his mouth and eyes open, a red hole in his head. Red stains splattered the snow, too.

Van Cleef walked out of the woods. He'd set the Hawken aside and was holding a Colt in his big fist.

"Hello, sis," he said. "I figured you'd be showing up around here sooner or later."

For just a second, Fargo thought Van Cleef had said *Pris,* but then he realized his mistake. He looked over at Pris. "He's your brother?"

"That's right," Pris said. "He's a mean one, but he's all the family I have. We Van Cleefs stick together."

"Sorry I ran out on you back there in Missouri, sis," Van Cleef said. "I was in kind of a rush."

Pris smiled at him over Fargo's shoulder.

"I know," she said, shaking her head. "You always were a rascal, Jess."

She nudged her horse to the side so that Fargo wasn't

between her and Van Cleef. Fargo didn't take that as a good sign.

Lee Tuttle spoke up about that time.

"Me and my brother'll just be leaving you folks alone," he said. "This ain't none of our fight. Hell, Chad's half dead, and I sure as hell don't even know what's goin' on."

"I don't think you should leave," Pris said. "I don't think that would be a good idea. Do you, Jess?"

"Nope. Wouldn't be a good idea at all."

Van Cleef fired one shot, and Lee pitched out of the saddle.

"You want one of 'em?" Van Cleef asked Pris. "Only one left's a sitting duck."

Pris drew the Henry rifle from its scabbard and cocked it. Half turning in the saddle, she put it to her shoulder and fired.

Chad jerked in the saddle, but his eyes didn't open. He slumped forward and then slid to the ground.

"Didn't even know what hit him," Van Cleef said. "Not much fun, but you take what you can get, I guess."

Pris slid the Henry back into the scabbard, as unaffected by what she'd done as if she'd merely swatted a fly.

Van Cleef walked around where Fargo could see him. He was a big man, taller than Fargo and wider—wide as a door.

"What're we gonna do with this one, sis?" he asked.

Fargo had an idea what Pris would say. She didn't seem to be the sentimental type. He looked over to where the Ovaro stood. The horse was at least three steps away, maybe four. He didn't think he could get there before Van Cleef shot him. And even if he got to the Ovaro, he couldn't escape.

"Don't go thinking you can get away from us," Van Cleef said. "It just ain't in the cards."

"No," Pris said. "It's not. I'm sorry, Fargo. I really am. Nothing against you. You were fun, but this is about family. Jess and I, we stick together."

Fargo believed the part about family. Somehow, though, he didn't think that she was sorry.

"I'll say one thing for you," he told her. "You're one hell of a storyteller."

Pris laughed as if they were two old friends recalling some favorite joke.

"Sis always was a stem-winder of a tale spinner," Van Cleef said.

He had a happy smile on his face and looked like a man who was having a fine time. Maybe, Fargo thought, he was just glad to see his sister. Or maybe killing two men while his sister had shot another one was what had made him feel so good.

"Jess and I had decided to stay around Independence for a while," Pris said. "It was a nice town, and we had an idea of how to make ourselves a little money there. But Jess put a crimp in our plans. He just can't help himself sometimes."

"Now we're gonna start over," Van Cleef said. "Out west somewhere. California, Oregon, somewhere like that."

Fargo didn't think it would work out, given Van Cleef's bad habits. And considering neither Van Cleef nor Pris knew a damned thing about the country they'd be traveling through.

"You'll never get there this winter," he said.

"Don't matter. If we can't, we'll get by out here till spring, then cross the Divide. It'll be just fine, long as we're together. Ain't that right, sis?"

"That's right, Jess. Now are we going to talk all day, or are we going to do something about Fargo?"

Fargo had kept them talking as long as he could, hoping that some way to escape would occur to him. But he hadn't come up with anything.

"Maybe I could just go with you," he said to draw things out a little longer. "You'll be needing a guide."

Pris smiled. "That sounds good, Fargo, but you know better than that. We'll just have to find our way without you."

"You can bet we'll do it, too," Van Cleef said.

Fargo shook his head and started to edge toward the Ovaro.

Van Cleef had relaxed while they talked, but his eyes narrowed, and the smile left his face.

"Watch it, Fargo," he said.

Fargo couldn't draw on him. Van Cleef already had his

pistol out. So the Trailsman did the only thing he could do. He tried to get to the Ovaro.

He managed to take one full step before Van Cleef shot him.

A red blossom bloomed on the back of Fargo's buffalo robe, but he didn't go down, and he didn't stop.

So Van Cleef shot him again.

15

Fargo pitched forward as the second bullet struck. He couldn't mount the Ovaro, but he managed to get hold of the stirrup as the big horse bolted forward.

Fargo's grip tightened just in time, and he managed to hang on as the horse ran into the trees, dragging Fargo along beside him.

Van Cleef let off another shot, but it went wide and chipped a limb on one of the frozen cottonwoods.

"Damnation," Van Cleef said as Fargo and the Ovaro disappeared from sight. "We better go after him. No telling where he'll get to."

Pris didn't agree. "Let him go, Jess. You hit him twice. How long can he last in weather like this? He's wounded and, if he doesn't bleed out, he'll freeze tonight. Let's think about us. How are we going to survive out here? I hope you have some kind of plan."

"Sure, I have a plan. Just what I told Fargo. We find us a place to stay until we can go west. That's it."

"That's not much of a plan," Pris said, despite her comment when he'd told it to Fargo. "You'll have to do better than that, or I'll just go back to Fort Laramie alone and tell them that the Crow killed Fargo. They'll take me in if I behave myself."

"Aw, sis," Van Cleef said. "You wouldn't go off without me like that."

He was right. Pris wouldn't leave him. She hadn't lied when she'd told Fargo that she and Jess stuck together. It had been that way since they were kids. They'd been different from anybody else they knew, and they'd often gotten in trouble for their tendency to beat up the other children, or in some cases, kill their pets. There had been more than one beating that Pris still remembered. So as soon as she and Jess were able, they ran away from home.

From that time on, they'd made their way together. There had been plenty of tough times because Jess had so much trouble controlling himself, but things had always worked out in the end, mainly because Pris never let her impulses get the best of her—except where it came to men. She enjoyed sex, and Fargo had provided some of the best she'd ever experienced. It was really too bad that they'd had to kill him. It would have been fun to keep him around, but Pris knew he'd never have approved of Jess. Or of her, for that matter, not when he found out what she was really like.

While she'd never enjoyed killing as much as Jess, she'd certainly never minded it. The deaths of others left her completely unaffected. Whether someone lived or died simply made no difference at all to her—except in the case of Jess. Other than herself, he was the only person she'd ever cared about, and Jess knew it.

"No, Jess," she said. "I'd never go back to Laramie without you. But we have to have some kind of plan to survive the winter out here."

"I know the Divide's a ways down the trail," Jess said. "But we can get there, all right. If the weather warms up enough, we can even get through the mountains this winter, traveling light like we are."

"And if the weather stays like this?"

"There's bound to be a trading post or something along the way. I hear there's one on up the trail where some fella's built a toll bridge across the river. We'll just show up, tell 'em that we started out late on the trail, and need a place to stay for the winter. Somebody'll put us up. Or, hell, there's trappers out in the mountains. They've all got cabins. We can take one of 'em for ourselves."

Pris didn't have to ask what would happen to the trapper whose cabin they took.

"All right," she said. She remembered something about a cabin in that area, herself. She wasn't quite sure what it was that she'd heard, but she knew it would come to her. "We'll give it a try. We sure can't go back to Missouri."

"I'm sorry about that, sis, but that son of a bitch was giving me a hard time. He's the one who wanted to fight, not me."

Pris started to ask about the women, but she didn't say anything. Jess would try to make some excuse, but she knew there wasn't one.

Van Cleef looked around at the three fresh corpses. He said, "What're we gonna do about these fellas?"

Pris couldn't help but smile.

"What is it that you want to do?" she asked.

Jess grinned at her and fingered the handle of his knife. "Well," he said. "You know."

"Go ahead then." Pris got off her horse. "I'll help."

Fargo lost consciousness before the Ovaro had run a quarter mile, but he maintained his grip on the stirrup. Struggling through the snow while dragging a man the size of Fargo had taken its toll on the big horse, but it kept going, snorting clouds of moisture in the cold air. There was blood on the snow behind them, the streaks showing starkly red against the whiteness.

After passing through the cottonwoods and traveling a distance of about a mile over mostly open ground, the Ovaro found itself in a stand of fir trees, their green branches covered with snow.

The horse stopped just inside the shelter of the trees, and Fargo's fingers slipped from the stirrup.

The man lay still on the ground, and the Ovaro leaned down to nudge him gently with its nose.

Fargo didn't move. The Ovaro walked a couple of paces farther into the trees and stopped as if to wait for Fargo to awaken.

There was a fire, bright and hot. All around it was darkness.

Fargo was lying close to the fire, and he wondered if he'd gone to hell because he knew for damned sure he was dead—just about had to be.

Or maybe not. Hell didn't have horses in it, and he heard a horse somewhere nearby. He lay on his back, his face turned toward the fire, and felt its warmth on his cheeks. He tried to turn his head to see the horse.

"Don't be stirrin' around too much, Fargo," someone said.

Fargo knew that voice. It didn't belong to the Devil.

"Walker?" Fargo said.

His voice wasn't much more than a croak, and he realized then how much he was hurting. His whole body was a lump of pain. Being dead might have been better.

"You got yourself shot," Walker said, and Fargo remembered what had happened.

He tried to tell Walker about Pris and Van Cleef, but he found that he couldn't.

"No use tryin' to talk," Walker said. "You're in a hell of a mess, no other way to put it. You got two bullets in you, one in the shoulder, and one in the side. I expect you'd be dead now if it hadn't been so cold and if you hadn't been wearin' that buffalo robe. Thing is, I'm gonna have to get them bullets out of you. It's damn sure gonna hurt."

Fargo croaked a response.

"I saw what happened to Gant and Keller," Walker said, as if he understood what Fargo had tried to say. "Three other fellas, too. It was Van Cleef that got 'em. Couldn't have been nobody else, not considerin' what was done to 'em. Somebody was with Van Cleef. I saw the tracks. Was it that woman?"

"Yes," Fargo said, or tried to say. The pain that gripped him wouldn't let the word past his teeth.

"I figgered it was her," Walker said.

He walked into Fargo's view and hunkered down by the fire.

"You'll be needin' a drink," he said. "I carry a little something in case of emergencies."

He raised Fargo's head. Even that slight movement sent shocks of pain through his back and chest.

"Hurts, don't it?" Walker said. "Drink this."

He tilted a long-necked bottle to Fargo's mouth, and the Trailsman managed to take a couple of swallows of bad whiskey. It burned going down his throat, but Fargo never felt it hit his stomach.

"Now we have to get to the hard work," Walker said.

He disappeared for a second, then came back and knelt down by the fire. He reached into it and pulled out a knife with a blade that was glowing as hot and as red as the flames. Walker held up the knife and looked at it.

"Guess that oughta do it," he said. "You're a pretty strong fella, Fargo. I hope you're up to this. Come to that, I hope I'm up to it. I ain't dug a bullet out of anybody in near-about twenty years."

He uncovered Fargo and said, "Gonna have to roll you over. If that don't kill you, we'll see what I can do about those bullets."

With one hand, he turned the Trailsman over onto his stomach. Fargo's pain, which had seemed to be as intense as it could ever be, doubled. He passed out.

When Fargo came to again, he was still lying by a fire, but it was daylight. His pain had lessened, but not by much.

Fargo turned his head. Tobias Walker was still there, sitting with his back against a tree, drinking coffee from a tin cup.

"I was wonderin' if you'd wake up again," Walker said. "Diggin' those bullets was more trouble than I thought. You're pretty much stove up. Might've been better off if I hadn't found you."

Fargo didn't agree. Being alive beat being dead anytime. He hurt, damned right he hurt, but there was always a chance he'd get better.

"I should never have let Seth go after Van Cleef," Walker said. He drank some of his coffee. "I felt bad about it, and the more I thought how I'd let him go off without me, the worse I felt. Let me tell you something, Fargo, I never had a brother, but Seth Gant was like a brother to me. He was as much family as my wife and son." Walker smiled and swirled the coffee in his cup. "I guess when it came right down to it, I couldn't leave him. So I turned around and came back. Not in time to help him, though, goddamn it."

Fargo wanted to thank Walker for coming back, but he still wasn't up to talking.

"I don't know what the hell I'll do now," Walker said. "Seth's dead, along with four other fellas, and all their faces are gone. It was an awful sight, Fargo, one of the worst this old coon's ever seen, by God, and I've seen a few."

Fargo knew what it must have been like to come up on those bodies. He wondered if Pris had helped Van Cleef with his grisly work. He wouldn't have been surprised if she had.

Walker seemed to be wavering like the smoke above his coffee cup. His face dimmed and then disappeared, and that was the last thing Fargo knew for a while.

Night. A fire.

Fargo was getting used to having time go by without him, but at least the fire was a constant. He turned his head.

Walker was still there, too, but he was asleep with his back against the tree, almost as if he hadn't moved since the last time Fargo had awakened. Maybe he hadn't. Fargo had no way of knowing.

When Fargo awoke again it was daylight. Walker was over by the fire.

"You got to eat something," Walker said. "And drink some water. We'll give that a try first."

Fargo surprised himself by raising his own head, and Walker gave him some water out of a tin cup. Fargo swallowed it eagerly.

"By the great horn spoon, Fargo," Walker said. "I believe you're gonna live."

"You can count on it," Fargo said.

16

The cabin was warm, and chinked tight against the weather. Fargo was buried under a mound of buffalo robes near the fire that roared in a stone fireplace.

"Mighty nice place, ain't it?" Walker said. "I was a mite surprised it was still here, or at least that nobody was livin' in it. Been a good many years since Seth and I built it, and I'd have thought somebody would be usin' it, for sure. Maybe nobody could find it. Had to chase a few varmints out and dust it up some, but it's near-about good as new."

The cabin was located somewhere on a little branch of the Platte. Fargo wasn't sure just where. He hadn't been awake for much of the trip there—a trip that had taken most of a day. Walker had rigged a travois, and the Ovaro had pulled it through the snow. Fargo felt he owed the big horse an extra ration or two of oats for that job.

"I'm gonna leave you here by yourself this mornin'," Walker said. "Can't be helped. You'll be all right, and I need to trap us something to eat. Rabbit, maybe. Cook us up a little stew. We're gonna need it, 'cause we'll be here for a while, till you get healed back up and can ride again."

Fargo wondered how long that would be. He was still in considerable pain. It hurt to twitch, much less to move an arm or a leg to a different position.

"Don't worry about a thing," Walker said. "You don't need me here. You're healin' up just fine, far's I can tell.

Not any mortifyin' of the flesh. You just rest up, and I'll take care of ever'thing."

"None of this was your fault," Fargo said.

He found he could talk now, thanks to drinking water, and a little whiskey.

"I can't help blamin' myself a little," Walker said. The fire threw the big man's flickering shadow on the wall. "If I'd've stuck with my partner, he'd be alive now, and you wouldn't be all shot up like you are."

"You couldn't have stopped Van Cleef. I'm not sure anybody can stop him."

"I don't want to hear no more of that kind of talk. Somebody's gotta stop him, and I figger it's gonna have to be me and you. Not right now, mind you. After you get to feelin' better, I mean."

Fargo hadn't really thought about it, but now that Walker had brought it up, he agreed with him. The Van Cleefs had to be stopped. People like Pris and her brother offended Fargo's sense of justice. Fargo knew that when he was able to ride, he'd be heading out after Van Cleef and Pris. And he'd be glad to have Walker for company if the old mountain man wanted to go along. But Walker had other obligations.

"What about your family?" Fargo asked.

"I left word at Fort Laramie where I was headed," Walker said. "Somebody'll get the word to 'em, and they'll understand. My wife's a mighty patient woman. She'd have to be to put up with the likes of me. She'll be a mite upset, but I'll make it all right with her when I get back."

"No guarantee you'll get back."

"Yeah, I know that. If I don't, she'll understand that, too."

"What about your son?"

"He's a good boy," Walker said, smiling. "Takes after his mother more than me, and that's all to the good, I think. Likes schoolin' and books. All that's fine, too. I wouldn't want him to be like me, have to live his life rough, the way I did for so long. He'll be all right if I don't come back. His ma'll see to that."

"No guarantee we'll find Van Cleef, either."

"Oh, we'll find that son of a bitch, all right. He's not

gonna get too far in this country, not in the kind of weather we've got now."

"It could change before I'm able to leave this cabin," Fargo said.

"Nope. That ain't gonna happen. We're in for some genuine cold. Maybe no more snow for a while, but that's comin', too. Mr. Van Cleef's gonna have a hard time gettin' very far down the trail."

"The woman's with him," Fargo said. "She's his sister."

"Well, I figgered she was with him, judgin' from the signs I read back where I found you and Seth and them others. She's likely to slow him down some. I thought he might've taken her along to keep him warm, though. Sure didn't figger her to be his sister. She had me fooled."

Fargo hadn't figured it, either. Pris had fooled him as badly as she'd fooled Walker, and he didn't like that. He didn't like being used by anybody—especially by a killer.

And there wasn't any doubt that Pris was a killer. Fargo thought about the way she'd shot Chad Tuttle out of the saddle, cool as you please. There hadn't been any need for her to kill him. Chad had looked more than half dead already.

As far as that went, Fargo supposed he should have been grateful that Pris hadn't turned the Henry on him. He might not have been around now if she had. The big rifle had a lot more punch to it than Van Cleef's pistol.

"She's his sister, all right," Fargo said. "And she's more like him than you'd ever guess by looking at her."

"Must be," Walker said. "Considerin' what the two of 'em did to those fellas back there, she's mighty damn bad. But I reckon we two are man enough to handle her."

Fargo wasn't so sure. Well, he could handle her in one way. He'd proved that, right enough, but of course that wasn't what Walker meant.

"Don't forget her brother," he said. "We'll have to handle him, too."

"I ain't forgettin' him. We'll do what has to be done. You think I don't know you, Fargo, but I've heard tell of you and some of the things you've done. If even half of 'em are true, you and this old coon don't have a lot to fear from Van Cleef."

Fargo wished he had as much confidence in himself as Walker seemed to have.

"I'm the one that's been shot," Fargo reminded the mountain man. "And there's five men dead back in those cottonwoods you saw before you tracked me down. Van Cleef doesn't have a scratch on him anywhere, far as we know."

"He will after we finish with him, by God. Now I better get out there and set some traps, or we'll starve to death while we're talkin'."

Walker left the cabin, and Fargo lay quietly under the robes. Even the short time of talking had tired him out, used up most of the energy he had. It was going to be a while before he was up to going after Pris and Van Cleef— a long while if he was any judge.

And who knew what might happen to the Van Cleefs in the meantime? Maybe the Crow would get them if they were still after the man who'd mutilated some of their tribesmen.

Or the cold might do them in. If Van Cleef and Pris didn't know how to deal with the weather, it could easily kill them.

For that matter, they could get lost and wander so far off the trail that they'd never get back on it. There were too many possibilities. Fargo drifted off to sleep while he was thinking about them.

Fargo didn't count the days. They all seemed to run together, and they were all the same. He got all too familiar with the cabin's walls, ceiling, and floor.

As he began to feel better, he was able to sit up, then get around a little, and finally sit in one of the crude chairs that Walker and Gant had made years before.

Walker liked to talk, and he regaled Fargo with tales of the things he and Gant had done, of the money they'd made as trappers, of the people they'd known, and the things they'd seen. One day he told the story of how Liver-Eater Johnson had been attacked by a man in the dead of winter and how Johnson survived by killing his assailant, cutting off his haunch, and feeding on it as he made his way back to civilization.

"But don't you go thinkin' that the Liver-Eater was anything like Van Cleef," Walker said. "He never killed no-body for the fun of it, nor skint 'em. That fella he et had tried to kill him first, and he only et him to keep himself alive. I know he et those Crows' livers after he killed 'em, too, but he had a reason for that. They'd killed his wife, you see, so he had to show them that they were gonna suffer for it. He wanted them to be afraid of him and, by God, they were."

Fargo didn't argue the point. He wasn't sure if those things truly excused the Liver-Eater's actions, but at least they were reasons, of a sort, for his behavior. Van Cleef didn't have any reasons. He did what he did because that's what he wanted to do. It was as simple as that. And Pris went along with him, not just because she was his sister, but because she really didn't care what he did. Maybe she even liked it.

Fargo didn't care how it was. He intended to stop both of them, one way or another. All he needed was the chance.

By the time Fargo was strong enough to get around the cabin without any help from Walker, the winter had set in for good. While it wasn't cold enough to crack stones, it was plenty cold to freeze a fella if he wasn't careful. Or so Walker said. Fargo hadn't yet ventured outside the cabin.

"Snow's not too deep, though," Walker said. "Some folks say it can get too cold to snow. Maybe that's what's happened. All I know is that we're lucky we're not snowed in. I want to be able to get out of here and get after that Van Cleef son of a bitch soon's you're able. How're you feelin', by the way?"

Fargo was feeling weak and soft. He'd been walking some in the cabin, and he could do that well enough. He was getting stronger by the day. But he wasn't sure how he'd feel if he had to ride, or whether he'd be able to do any traveling for a while.

"I wouldn't be much of a threat to Van Cleef yet," he said, thinking that he wouldn't be much of a threat even to a rabbit. "What about the horses?"

There was a lean-to built onto the south side of the cabin and covered with fir branches. The horses were stabled there. Walker had fed them as best he could, but they were going to run short of food before too many more days.

"They're doin' fine as of right now," Walker said. "By the time you're able to travel, though, we'll be needin' to look for something to fill their bellies."

Fargo didn't know where anything like that was to be found, but he'd leave that up to Walker, who didn't seem worried. Walker, however, never seemed worried about anything.

So Fargo tried not to worry, either, and mostly he was successful, until one day Walker went out to check his traps and didn't come back.

Sometimes Walker would be gone for several hours at a stretch, so at first Fargo wasn't concerned about the length of the mountain man's absence. He figured Walker was just taking his time, maybe looking over the countryside, thinking about the old days, when he and Gant had pretty much been the only people in this whole part of the territory.

But after a while it became obvious that something was wrong. Or at least something was different. Walker always went out in the mornings, and he always returned by noon, at which time he'd fix up something for the two of them to eat. Fargo had gotten a little tired of rabbit and rabbit stew, but that was about the only thing Walker had to offer. He didn't want to go too far from the cabin and leave Fargo alone for too long at a time, which is what he'd have had to do if he wanted to find larger game. And even Fargo had to admit that rabbit stew was better than nothing.

But now it was long after noon, well over an hour, and there was still no sign of Walker. Fargo was sure the old man hadn't gone hunting big game, and he was sure he hadn't wandered off and gotten himself lost. That was one thing Walker would never do. But he could have had some kind of accident—fallen, maybe, or turned an ankle.

Fargo wondered if he was up to strapping on a gun and going to see about Walker. Hell, he had to do it. He owed it to him. The only question was—how long would he wait before he did it? Well, there was another question, too. Would Fargo hold up to the strain of walking through the snow and the cold?

He thought he would. His wounds had knit up pretty well, leaving behind a couple more scars that added to the collection that he had already accumulated. He still had a little bit of pain, but that was disappearing day by day. Fargo wondered if it would come back when he put a little strain on his body.

He guessed he'd find out.

17

Fargo strapped on his Colt and put on a sheepskin jacket. Then he put on gloves and tried bending over to the floor a couple of times. The effort didn't seem to bother him overly much, so he went on outside.

The cabin was in thick woods, mostly fir trees, and Fargo could see why nobody had found it for the last twenty years. It was a place you'd have to be looking for. Nobody was likely to come on it by accident.

Fargo pulled the cabin door closed behind him, and the cold air almost took his breath away when he inhaled. He stood where he was for a minute, looking around at the thick woods, and the chill from the air started seeping in under his clothes. He figured he'd better get moving before he froze to the spot.

Walker was a smart man, and even though the cabin was well hidden, he'd taken care not to leave any tracks if he could help it. So he'd taken different routes to his traps every day, and he'd rigged a pair of snowshoes so as not to wear a path in the hard-packed snow. Of course, that was going to make it a lot harder for Fargo to track him.

Fargo had talked to Walker about their location, and he knew that the creek was to the north of them about a quarter of a mile.

But that was the extent of his knowledge about their location. He walked around the cabin to search for some trace that Walker might have left.

The movement didn't bother him much. Now and then

he'd feel a sharp pain, but only when he made an awkward step. The pain quickly subsided, and Fargo figured he was pretty much healed up.

He found a couple of places where the crust of the snow was broken. Walker wouldn't have been as careful near the cabin as he would have later on.

Fargo was able to pick up a direction, and he decided to go that way. It was as good a chance as any.

The walk through the trees was good exercise, and it helped Fargo keep warm. He occasionally spotted something that kept him on track: a limb with some snow knocked off to expose a green fir branch, or a trace of a print where there was no snow under the trees. In about twenty minutes, he came to the creek that flowed to the Platte—or at least did when it was flowing. At the moment, it was frozen and covered with snow.

A few minutes later, Fargo found one of Walker's traps. It was empty, and there were signs of a struggle. The snow crust was broken, as if Walker might have fallen, and there were signs that at least three more men had been there. Fargo could see that they'd followed the creek to the spot where they'd come upon Walker, probably having found one of his traps.

Indians, Fargo thought. He had no idea which tribe they might be: Arapaho, Shoshone, Crow, Cheyenne. They all moved around, and Fargo wasn't sure where they wintered. He'd been surprised to find the Crow near Laramie, but it could be that they were here, too.

It looked as if they'd gone back the way they came, taking Walker with them. Fargo hoped they hadn't gone too far.

Fargo was tired, but not as tired or as sore as he'd feared he'd be after walking for nearly a mile along the bank of the frozen creek. From where he stood behind the shelter of a big fir tree, he could see the Crow camp, for it was indeed the Crow who had found Walker.

Fargo counted six of them, and he wondered if they could be the same ones who'd attacked Pris's wagon. The number was right. Fargo was sorry that he'd ever interfered in that little episode.

Walker was tied to a tree near the creek. The Crow had built a shelter for themselves and had a fire, but Walker wasn't anywhere near it.

He thought about what he might do. There were two or three choices.

He could try to slip around the trees and cut Walker loose. He could do that and maybe not be seen, but he didn't think he and Walker would be able to get away. If Walker had been tied there for long, he wouldn't be able to walk easily.

Fargo could walk right into the camp and open up with his Colt. If he was lucky, he might kill all the Crow before they could get him. But he didn't think he was that lucky, and he didn't want to kill anybody who didn't need killing.

He could even walk into the camp and try to reason with the Crow. At first that seemed the least likely of the possibilities, but the more he thought about it, the more sensible it started to look to him. The Crow wouldn't kill him out of hand, or he didn't think they would. They hadn't killed Walker, after all, and Fargo thought he knew why.

They wanted information, and they thought Walker might be able to help them. For all they knew, he might even be the man they were looking for. If he was, they'd find that out sooner or later. The Crow had ways of doing that.

So Fargo kept his pistol in its holster and walked out of the trees.

Walker saw him first, and his eyes got wide. He opened his mouth as if he were going to warn Fargo away, but then he closed it. The Crow had seen Fargo by then, and it was too late for any kind of warning.

Fargo held his hands with the palms up and out. He knew enough Crow to say, "Ka-hay Sho-o Dah Chi," which meant something like, "Hello. How are you?" It wasn't the best greeting under the circumstances, but it would have to do.

The Crow warriors were at least as surprised to see him as Walker had been, and they were even more surprised at his greeting. Two of them had Hawken rifles that they pointed straight at Fargo, who stood where he was and waited to see what would happen next.

The Crow talked among themselves, too fast for Fargo

to follow. Then one of them stepped forward. He was a little taller than the others, but not by much, and he was wrapped in a buffalo robe.

Speaking slowly so that Fargo could follow, he said, "You are the other one from the wagon."

Fargo wondered if they'd identified Walker. Now he knew, so he said, "Yes." He nodded toward Walker. "That man and I are the two who set your dead for you to find and to deal with in a proper manner."

The warrior turned and spoke rapidly to the others. Then he turned back to Fargo.

"My name is Two Ponies," he said.

Fargo said his own name.

"You and the old man killed Sky Dancer and Running Fox," Two Ponies said.

"You were trying to kill a couple of innocent people," Fargo said, stretching the truth a little. "We stepped in to help. After that, we honored your dead. We are looking for the same man you are, and for the same reason. Let the old man go. He doesn't know where the man you're looking for has gone, but together we will find him and kill him for you."

Two Ponies looked over at Walker. "That is what the old one said."

"You should believe him," Fargo said.

Two Ponies turned to the other men and spoke to them again. Fargo could tell that a couple of them weren't any too happy with what he had to say, and a full-scale argument broke out.

Two of the Crow didn't take part in it, however. The two with the rifles stood with their eyes on Fargo and paid no attention to the talk of the others.

The talk got louder, and for a second Fargo considered going for his pistol. He was pretty sure he could get both the men with the rifles. They hadn't shown themselves to be especially good shots in the earlier encounter.

After those two were down, there wouldn't be any trouble taking care of the rest of them. But Fargo didn't want to do that. It wasn't the kind of thing Van Cleef went around doing, but it was close enough to make Fargo uncomfortable with the idea.

So he waited until the argument ran down, standing as easy as he could in the cold.

When Two Ponies turned back, his eyes were troubled.

"White Bear says that you are a liar and that we should kill you now. He believes you are the one who took the faces of our friends."

"I will say it again," Fargo told him. "We honored your dead. We left them for you to find, and we did not cut their faces. You have seen it for yourself."

"Yes," Two Ponies said. "I have. But sometimes a man can do things to save himself that he would not do otherwise."

"We never thought we'd see you again. We did what we did because we are not like the one you're looking for."

Two Ponies nodded. "I believe you. Not just for what you have said here, but because I have heard your name spoken with honor among the Crow."

Fargo was glad his dealings with the Crow in the past had worked out for the best.

"Because you are a friend of the Crow," Two Ponies went on, "I am going to give you your friend and let you leave."

At those words, one of the men gave an angry snort. He was stocky and tall, with a scar on his forehead that might have been made by a knife or an ax. Fargo figured he must be White Bear, but he ignored him because he wasn't one of the two who had rifles.

"What about the face taker?" Fargo asked. "Are you still going after him?"

"We have little food left. We are going back to join our tribe. We had promised to get revenge, but we have failed. We will suffer the shame of that."

"We'll get the revenge for you," Fargo said. "I'll make you that promise."

Again, there was an angry sound of disbelief from White Bear.

"White Bear does not believe in your promise," Two Ponies said. "But we have little choice. What is spoken of you among my people tells me that you will keep your word. Take your friend and go."

Fargo didn't wait for further talk. He walked over to

where Walker was tied to the tree, took his Arkansas tooth-pick from the scabbard on his belt, and cut the rawhide thongs that bound Walker to the trunk.

Walker tried to stand up, but he didn't quite make it. Fargo took his arm and helped him. When he was steady, Walker stomped around and flapped his arms to bring some blood back to his cold and stiff limbs.

"We'd better be moving along," Fargo said. "Soon as you're able."

"I'm able right now," Walker told him. "Let's get ourselves outta here."

They walked away without looking back, but Fargo could feel White Bear's eyes on them until they were out of sight.

"I didn't think you'd show up," Walker said when they were back in the cabin, warming themselves in front of the fire. It had almost gone out, but they'd built it back up as soon as they'd come inside. "Wasn't even sure you'd be able to."

"I owed you," Fargo said. "And I was able."

"I'm mighty glad you were. They were about to start to work on me to find out where my camp was. I think I might've told 'em."

"I'm not so sure of that," Fargo said.

"Me, neither, but I'm glad I didn't have to find out. You reckon they're really gonna go on back home?"

"I think Two Ponies is, and I think the others will follow him."

"You really believe that, or are you just hopin'?"

"Just hoping," Fargo said.

"That White Bear, he didn't look any too happy about the way things turned out."

"No. I'm not so sure he's going anywhere. He didn't act satisfied with the proceedings."

They were silent for a few minutes, rubbing their hands and enjoying the warmth of the fire.

"You know the thing I hated the most about all that?" Walker said after a while.

"Being tied to the tree?" Fargo asked.

"Nope, that wasn't it. Want to guess again?"

"No," Fargo said, "I get the feeling you're going to tell me sooner or later."

"Damn right. What I hated the most was when they called me an old man."

Fargo smiled.

"You know something else?" Walker said.

Fargo shook his head and waited to hear what Walker had to tell him.

"You called me an old man, too."

"I don't remember doing that," Fargo said.

"Well, you did, by God. Hurt my feelings, is what it did."

Fargo tried not to smile. He said, "Well, I won't do it again."

"See that you don't," Walker said.

18

Walker was asleep, snoring the way he did every night. He made a sound that reminded Fargo a little bit of a hog rooting around for food that had fallen under a trough.

Fargo was used to the sound, and it didn't bother him, much less keep him awake. What kept him awake was his feeling that White Bear might have decided to do something about his disagreement with Two Ponies—something that might lead him to try to find the cabin.

The place would be easy enough to find now, Fargo thought. He and Walker hadn't been any too careful as they made their way back, and White Bear would have no trouble following their trail. Judging by White Bear's reaction, Fargo figured that one of the men Van Cleef had killed had been White Bear's friend or relation. Like anybody else, the Crow wasn't going to take something like that lightly, and nothing Two Ponies could say or do would discourage him from trying to get his own brand of justice.

So Fargo was awake, listening to Walker's snores and to the sounds outside the cabin—the wind in the trees, the shuffling and occasional snorts of the horses in the lean-to, and once even the call of an owl.

Or was it an owl? That was the only thing he'd heard so far that bothered him because it seemed a little out of place. He didn't recall having heard any owls the whole time he'd been in the cabin.

Fargo thought it might be a good idea to have a look outside and see if there was any sign of an owl, or if the call had been made by something else. Or someone. White Bear, for instance.

The Trailsman strapped on his gun belt and went outside. He made no special effort to be quiet, but Walker slept on, undisturbed.

It was dark under the firs. The sky was clear, but the moon was on the wane, and only a little of its light filtered through the thick tree branches. Fargo stood outside the door and waited for his eyes to become accustomed to the dark.

After a short time, he could see well enough to distinguish trees from their shadows. He looked straight ahead, hoping to catch any movement out of the corners of his eyes. Seeing nothing suspicious, he turned his head first to the left, then to the right. Still, there was nothing to see but the unmoving trees.

Fargo made a circuit of the cabin, keeping as much to the shadows as he could. He stopped at the lean-to and checked on the horses, but nothing had disturbed them.

When he got back to the door, he went inside. He'd seen and heard nothing, but his suspicions weren't quieted.

So he sat watching the fire and waited.

It was about an hour later when Fargo heard something else. It wasn't much of a noise, and in fact it was almost drowned out by the sound of Walker's snores. If Fargo had been poking up the fire, as he'd been just about to do, he wouldn't have heard it at all.

It was the scuff of a foot on the snow crust, and it wasn't far from the cabin.

There was only one window in the cabin, and it was covered by a beaver skin. Fargo stepped to the window and moved the skin just enough to allow him to peek outside. He saw nothing unusual.

Then he heard the horses stir in the lean-to, and he thought he knew what White Bear was up to—if indeed it was White Bear he'd heard. He figured it just about had to be. Nobody else was likely to be sneaking around the cabin at that time of the night.

Another sound came, this time from the roof, and Fargo knew he was right. White Bear had taken advantage of the lean-to and climbed up onto the roof. Most likely he intended to cover the chimney and smoke Fargo and Walker out. By the time they left the cabin, White Bear would be waiting for them.

It would take a while for the smoke to build up in the cabin, and for White Bear to get ready for them, so Fargo decided to surprise him and go outside at once.

He went to the door, but stopped before opening it. White Bear might not be alone. Someone might be watching to see if anybody came outside early.

Fargo eased the door open, but no shot was fired. No arrow buried itself in the wood.

He opened a crack wide enough to slip through and went out, leaving the door open a bit behind him to give the smoke an outlet.

Slipping along the side of the cabin, Colt in hand, Fargo went to the lean-to just as White Bear was climbing back down. Fargo let the Crow get his feet on the ground before speaking.

"You should have gone with Two Ponies," he said.

An ordinary man would have shown surprise, maybe even panic. Evidently, White Bear was no ordinary man.

"Two Ponies is an old woman," he said, his voice level. "I could not leave without doing something to set right the deaths of my friends."

"Your friends were killed in a fair fight," Fargo said.

"I am not speaking of the two at the wagon."

Fargo wondered how White Bear could take things so calmly. After all, Fargo plainly had the drop on him.

"The others weren't my doing," Fargo said.

"So you say."

"My word is good. You should have believed Two Ponies. Now you're going to be trouble for me. I have to decide what to do with you."

White Bear shrugged. "Kill me."

"If I was who you think I am, that's just what I'd do. But you're wrong about me."

"You, too, are wrong, Trailsman."

"About what?"

"You thought that I was alone."

When he'd encountered no one outside the cabin door, Fargo had believed White Bear had no one with him. Now he heard a rustling behind a fir tree, and a shadow moved.

100

Fargo dropped to one knee and fired the Colt. There was a yell and the sound of someone falling as Fargo tried to turn back to White Bear.

But White Bear was fast, and had moved as soon as Fargo did. Almost as the shot was fired, White Bear jumped for Fargo. He struck him hard, and the two of them fell to the snow-covered ground.

The fall jarred Fargo and sent a jolt of pain from his wound down to his feet and up to the top of his head. He dropped his pistol, but White Bear didn't try to get it. He put his fingers on Fargo's face and gouged at his eyes.

Fargo brought his hands up and knocked White Bear's arms away. The Crow fell backward and jumped to his feet.

Fargo sat up. He couldn't see his pistol, but he had his Arkansas toothpick in his hand.

White Bear kicked Fargo's wrist, and the knife went flying. The Crow leapt forward, but Fargo rolled aside before White Bear landed on top of him.

White Bear slid a couple of feet and came to a stop near Fargo's knife. He grabbed hold of it and came up with it gripped in his hand.

Fargo was standing as well by then, but he still hadn't been able to find his pistol.

"Now," White Bear said, moving the knife with a menacing underhand motion.

Fargo didn't find out what would have come after the *now* because he was distracted by the coughing and hacking of Walker, who had emerged from the smoke-filled cabin and was stumbling around outside.

White Bear turned at the sound, too, and Fargo started toward him.

The Crow turned back and slashed at Fargo with the big knife. Fargo moved back quickly.

"Goddamn it, a man can't even sleep in peace around here," Walker said, coming around the corner of the cabin, coughing theatrically. "What the hell's goin' on?"

White Bear was frozen with indecision. Forced to keep his eyes on Fargo, he couldn't turn again to see if Walker posed any threat to him.

Which the mountain man certainly did—when he came into sight, he was holding his heavy Hawken. The barrel rested lightly in the crook of his left arm.

Seeing that Walker was armed, White Bear made his decision. He whirled to throw the knife.

But he wasn't fast enough. Walker flipped the Hawken into position and pulled the trigger. The heavy ball hit White Bear squarely in the center of his chest, knocking him a couple of steps backward. Fargo's knife dropped from his fingers, and he fell to the ground.

"Looks like we've killed another Crow," Walker said, his voice raspy with the smoke.

"Two," Fargo said. "There's another one over in the trees."

"Damn," Walker said. "Well, I guess they didn't give us much of a choice. What'll we do with 'em?"

"Leave them here," Fargo said. "When they don't show up, maybe Two Ponies will send somebody for them."

"What if he don't?"

Fargo shrugged. "Not our problem. We won't be here."

"Might not be a good idea to stick around," Walker agreed. "Where you plannin' on goin'?"

"Away," Fargo said. "But not until morning."

"Take that long to clear the danged smoke out of the cabin. You shoulda woke me up. What's the matter? You think I was too old to be any help to you?"

"No. I was just careless. I thought White Bear might be alone and, when nobody shot at me when I went outside, I was convinced he was." Fargo picked up his knife and then located his pistol. "I'm glad you woke up and came out in time to save me."

"Made plenty of noise, didn't I?" Walker asked. "I bet you thought I was plumb indisposed."

"You fooled me, all right," Fargo said.

"Fooled that Injun, too. I'll teach those sons of bitches to call me old."

"They should've known better," Fargo said.

"Yeah. So should you."

"I told you I wouldn't make that mistake again."

"Glad to hear it. Now let's see you climb up there and pull that blanket or whatever it is off the chimney."

"Youngster like you ought to be able to make that climb faster than I can. My wounds are paining me."

Walker laughed. "I can outclimb you any day. But since

I saved your skin, I'll let you do the climbin'. I'm goin' back inside. It's too damn cold out here."

Fargo watched him go. Then he went to the lean-to and started to climb.

19

Just after dawn, Fargo and Walker moved the bodies of White Bear and his companion up to the cabin. The man Fargo had shot had been carrying one of the Henry rifles, and Fargo elected to take that along.

"Good idea, I guess," Walker said. "Never know when you'll need an extra gun."

Though it delayed them, Fargo cleaned and oiled the Henry. It hadn't been well taken care of, and he didn't want any problems with it if he had to use it.

It had taken them a while to clear most of the smoke out of the cabin after they returned to it, and even then it had made for uncomfortable sleeping.

Fargo dreamed of Pris. She was in the cabin, nude, her breasts standing out proudly. With one hand she fondled a firm nipple. The other hand rested on the mossy curls below her navel, and the fingers played happily between her legs. She seemed to be calling out to Fargo, who awoke with a start, his pole stiff in his britches.

After that he'd sat up for a few minutes, wondering how somebody so pretty, somebody who could enjoy life so much, could be a coldhearted killer. It was a good while before he got back to sleep.

"What kind of plan you got for us?" Walker asked when they finally got on their way the next day. His voice was raspy from the smoke he'd inhaled in the cabin. "Any idea where Van Cleef and his sister might be headin'?"

"West," Fargo said. They hadn't been able to clear the smoke out completely, and his voice rasped as well. "You know this country better than I do. Is there any place close to where you found me that they might have been able to hole up?"

"There's always places like that," Walker said. "But you'd have to know how to find 'em. Those two wouldn't know. They ain't never been here before."

"There must be some place they might have heard of," Fargo said.

Walker gave it some thought. "Well, there's one. But it would take 'em a few days to get to it, and even at that they might not find it. It's a ways off the main trail. Hell, how could they even know about it?"

"You do," Fargo pointed out.

"Sure as hell do. That don't mean anybody else would."

The horses crunched along, breaking through the crust and sinking into the snow. Wherever they went, Fargo thought, it was going to take a while.

"What's the place?" he asked.

"Ain't got no name. It's a kind of a natural bridge. Solid rock, with a creek running under it and then right into a mountain gorge. It's a sight to see. Not right on the trail, though, so not too many pilgrims pay it a visit."

Fargo had heard of the place, though he'd never been there. He asked Walker why anyone would go there in the winter.

"Come to think of it," Walker said, "some of the pilgrims talked it up, and there was even something about it in the newspaper in Independence a month or so back, so it's some place them Van Cleefs might know about, after all. That story said it was just about as fine a sight as the bridge that's so famous in Virginny. I wouldn't know about that, not ever havin' seen that one."

Neither had Fargo, not that it mattered. He thought about the location of the bridge Walker was talking about. If it was off the trail, then it was enough out of the way to be attractive to Van Cleef. However, there was still one problem.

"Where would anybody stay around there?" Fargo asked. "Some cave in the mountains?"

"Ain't no caves, far as I know. But there was a fella who

trapped on that creek for a few years. Don't know exactly what happened to him. Some folks say he died, some say he went back east. There's even some say he married a Crow woman and went to live with the tribe. I don't know about any of that, myself. Didn't figger it was any business of mine."

Fargo thought that Walker had gotten off the track somehow, but if he had, he brought himself back.

"Anyway, it don't matter what happened to him. The thing is, that cabin he built is still there. It was even brought up in that newspaper story. It's about a quarter mile from the bridge, and those pilgrims spent the night in it. It ain't easy to get to. Quite a little climb down a steep bank, and there's a lot of trees. Far's I know, other than that there ain't been anybody usin' his cabin any more than there was somebody usin' mine and Gant's. It's just about as hard to find. Hell, maybe harder. Speakin' of Gant, if it'd be all right with you, I'd like to stop by and pay my respects."

"Might as well," Fargo said. "We're going that way anyway. Now what about this cabin?"

"It'd make a good enough shelter. Wasn't as good as mine and Gant's, but it'd hold up to the weather. If them Van Cleefs knew about it, they might go there. If they could find it."

They'd been in Independence for a while, Fargo recalled, and one or both of them might have seen the story. The question was whether they'd remembered it. Van Cleef hadn't mentioned it, and neither had Pris.

"Could be they're both lyin' by the trail, froze stiffer'n a board," Walker said. "I'd just as soon that was the way of it. Make our job easier."

Fargo said that would suit him just fine. But he didn't think it was the case. Things like that never happened to people like Van Cleef and Pris. They always seemed to find a way to get by.

"I think we'll take a look at that cabin," he said.

Jess Van Cleef wasn't much of a hunter, and he was even less of a trapper. Killing people was one thing, but being able to track an animal was different. He was just plain no good at it. So he and Pris hadn't eaten too well for the

106

past few days. Pris had started to complain about it, and Jess didn't like it.

He hadn't done anything about it, not yet, but he'd started to think about it.

He was also starting to think that maybe it hadn't been such a good idea for them to come to the West. Jess was the one who'd suggested it, but Pris had thought the idea was a good one. She'd gone along with it without any argument because they'd about played out the string east of the Mississippi. Too many people had heard of them, or him, mainly, and it had been time to make a change.

It was Jess's own fault that they had to leave, he guessed. He knew that he should do better about controlling his temper and not allowing himself to do the things that he liked so much, but he'd never been caught and that made him more reckless than he should have been.

Pris had tried to tell him, but he'd never listened. Now he wished he had because they were trapped in a dinky cabin all to hell and gone away from the rest of the world, and it didn't look like they'd be getting away from it any time soon. The weather had been cold when they'd arrived, and it hadn't changed the whole time they'd been there. The only good thing was that it hadn't snowed much, but it was enough to make travel hard, and Jess was sure there would be no way they could get across the Divide.

He was down by the creek that ran swiftly between its banks. The creek was another good thing. It moved so fast that it hadn't frozen over, and Jess could always get water without having to melt snow or break ice. He wished it was that easy to get something to eat. He'd tried fishing, but he hadn't had any luck, so far.

At first, things at the cabin had been all right. They'd had a little food of their own, and they'd found a good bit more in the supplies the men they'd killed had brought along.

The thought of killing the men warmed Van Cleef with pleasure, and he remembered exactly how he'd felt when he slid the sharp point of his knife into them and made the slices just before ripping the skin away from their faces. He thought of the sound the ripping had made, and of how he'd had to be careful not to damage the skin too much so that the mask, when he held it in his hand, still resembled something human. Thinking about it made him smile with pleasure.

The smile faded as Van Cleef was reminded that the food hadn't lasted long enough, not nearly long enough, even though they'd tried to stretch it out. He really hadn't thought about how he'd supply himself and Pris with food, which he knew was a mistake. How in the hell were he and Pris ever going to last until spring? He'd killed a rabbit or two, but he hadn't seen anything bigger than that the whole time they'd been at the cabin.

It was lucky that Pris had remembered about the cabin. Getting to it hadn't been easy, and more than once Jess had thought she'd been imagining things. They'd finally had to go down the creek bank at the rock bridge and then walk along beside the creek to find the cabin. But Pris had been right all along.

Jess had never heard of either the bridge or the cabin, but Pris said she'd read about it somewhere or other. That was the advantage of having an education. Jess himself had never learned to read, and he admired Pris for having done so. It hadn't been easy. She hadn't had much schooling, but in their traveling around, she'd spent some time with a couple of schoolteachers who'd been glad to help her with her reading. And well they should have, considering how she'd paid them.

Jess looked at the rushing water of the creek. He liked the sound it made as it surged and splashed along over the rocks. He just wished a deer would come along, or, hell, even a goddamned rabbit.

Pris was in the cabin, which was where she spent most of her time. She didn't like the cold, and she tried to stay close to the fire. She never let it burn too low, and she was glad there were plenty of trees nearby to provide the wood they needed to keep the fire burning. Sometimes at night it burned down almost to the coals, and in the morning the water she kept in a bucket for washing would have a thin skin of ice on top if she didn't remember to put the bucket by the fireplace before she went to sleep.

Pris knew that it had been a mistake to follow Jess after the trouble in Independence. She should have gone her own way, but she just couldn't think of life without Jess. They'd been together for too long, and for most of that time they'd had to depend on each other for just about everything.

Not *everything*. Pris had certain needs that Jess couldn't satisfy, or that Pris had never thought about letting him satisfy.

And Jess would never have thought about it, either. As far as Pris knew, sex never entered Jess's mind—at least not in any usual way. He might have sex with a woman, but only if he was planning to kill her afterward.

Pris wasn't built like that. She liked sex, and plenty of it. That was one reason she hated being in the cabin for so long without a man in sight, or even the prospect of a man.

She'd thought about Fargo more than once, and that was unusual for her. When she was done with a man, that was it. He never entered her mind again, or at least never before.

But Fargo was different. There was something about him. Pris didn't know what it was. The way it had ended? She didn't know.

As she thought of him now, she felt a warmth in her belly, and her nipples hardened under her shirt. She squirmed a little to rub them against the rough fabric, and they got even harder. She thought about sliding her hand into her britches and pleasuring herself, but she didn't want Jess to come in and catch her doing that. So she resisted the impulse and tried to get Fargo out of her mind.

It wasn't easy. At times she wondered if he had even died, though there couldn't be much doubt about that. He'd been shot at least twice and dragged by a horse. How many men could survive that kind of treatment? And even if Fargo hadn't died immediately, he couldn't have survived the weather—not for long. She and Jess almost hadn't survived, and they'd been very much alive.

Pris wondered if they'd survive the rest of the winter, however. Things weren't going well. The food situation, for one thing. That was bad enough by itself, and she knew she was starting to aggravate Jess when she complained about it. She tried not to say anything, but she couldn't help herself. The whole situation was becoming difficult. Even two normal people would have trouble surviving a winter trapped together in a tiny cabin, and she and Jess weren't exactly normal. Pris knew that. She didn't know what they could do about it, however.

She hoped that Jess would find them something to eat.

She also hoped that she wouldn't complain if he failed because she was no longer sure how he might react if she did. She looked at the wall of the cabin by the door where Jess had hung his trophies after he'd dried the skin. The grotesque faces leered back at her. She imagined her own hanging there beside them. But it would never come to that, she told herself.

She wished she could make herself believe it.

20

Fargo and Walker found travel hard going.

They stopped and paid their respects to Gant and Keller, whose bodies remained undisturbed. Fargo's rough burial of them had served well enough.

The ravaged bodies of Frazee and the Tuttles were still there as well, lying where they'd fallen. Animals had been at them and there wasn't enough left to be recognizable. They might not have been recognizable anyway, Fargo thought, because he was pretty sure Van Cleef had removed their faces.

"Think we oughta to do something for 'em?" Walker asked.

Fargo believed in respecting the dead, but Frazee and the Tuttles had intended to kill him, and there wasn't much of them left to bury, anyway.

"We'll leave them," he said. Walker didn't have any objections.

When they pushed on, Walker said he was sorry that Gant wouldn't have any kind of marker.

"That was one reason he wanted to leave this country in the first place. He said he'd like to die in a place where they'd plant him in a little cemetery with a fence around it and put up some kind of stone with his name cut on it. That way, there'd be something to remember him by."

"You'll remember him," Fargo said.

"Yeah, but what's that worth to a man? After I'm gone, there won't be nobody left to tell who he was or what he done in his life. He'll be plumb forgotten, and I reckon when that happens, a man's gone for good. There just ain't nothing left of him, not even his name."

"You sure do know how to cheer a fella up," Fargo said.

"That's one of my good qualities, always has been. You reckon that Van Cleef has any good qualities, Fargo?"

"I couldn't name one."

"Nor could I. How come a fella like that's still takin' in air, while Seth Gant's lyin' back there dead?"

Fargo didn't have a good answer for that question. So he said, "Van Cleef won't be around much longer, not if we catch up with him."

"Even if we do, there won't be much satisfaction in it. We can't bring Seth back, no matter what we do to Van Cleef."

"I thought you were the one who wanted to put a stop to Van Cleef."

"I am. Don't get me wrong. I know that stoppin' him would be a good thing and keep him from killin' anybody else. It's something we got to do. But Seth's still gonna be dead, just like his wife. Where's the justice in that?"

Fargo couldn't answer that one, either.

They camped that night among some aspens near the trail. The trees were bare and didn't give much shelter, but the grove was the best place they could find. Their supper was beans and coffee. Walker had somehow managed to save some beans while they were in the cabin, and that was all they had left to eat. The coffee was running low, too.

"I'll get us a rabbit tomorrow," Walker promised.

"I could do with something besides rabbit," Fargo said.

"So could I, but you gotta take what you can get. A deer would just be a waste even if I could find one, which I can't, not without spendin' too much time at it. Besides, I can trap a rabbit right easy, and that's what I'm gonna do. You'll eat rabbit and like it, or else you'll just have an empty belly."

"I'll eat the rabbit," Fargo said.

"Damn right, you will," Walker said.

The wind had been light all day, and after sundown it was entirely gone. The stillness gathered under the aspens, and after nightfall the temperature dropped fast. They wrapped themselves in their bedrolls and slept close to the fire, and the dry air made Walker's snoring even louder. It took Fargo some time to go to sleep.

While he lay awake, he thought of what Walker had said about a man's name being remembered. Fargo had traveled all over the West, had walked a lot of trails that other men had never seen, had helped a lot of men out of trouble, and had loved a lot of women. But would any of them remember him after he was gone?

He looked up at the hard, cold glitter of the stars. They'd been there long before he ever walked any trail at all, and they'd be there long after he was gone. They were the only markers Gant and Keller had, Fargo thought, and that was just fine. They were good enough for him, too.

After that, Fargo went right on to sleep. Walker's snoring didn't bother him at all.

They got going early the next day, a little after dawn, but not until Walker had checked the trap he'd set out. It had a scrawny rabbit in it, but Walker said that was as good as they could expect.

"Cold as this weather is, we're lucky even this pitiful creature limped into a trap," Walker said as he dressed out the rabbit. He held it up for Fargo's inspection.

The skinned carcass reminded Fargo uncomfortably of Van Cleef and his bad habits, but the Trailsman didn't mention that to Walker.

"Won't be much meat on these bones," Walker said, and Fargo nodded his agreement.

"We'll make do," Fargo said. "Put it in the stew pot. Maybe the Van Cleefs are running a little short of food by now, too."

"Goin' hungry might make 'em a little testy," Walker said. "It works on some people that way. Don't see what good that does us, though."

"If they get testy, maybe they'll do each other in."

"Nope. That kind never does. They might argue and fuss at each other, but they'll keep on goin' long after anybody else'd quit. You can bet on that."

Fargo figured Walker was right. Jess and Pris had been

through a lot together, and they'd stuck it out ever since they were youngsters. That wasn't likely to change now, no matter how tough things got for them.

"We'd better ride," Fargo said. "We need to put a few miles behind us today."

Walker finished up with the rabbit and they rode away through the heavy snow.

"How long will it take us to get to this natural bridge?" Fargo asked after they were well on their way.

"At the rate we're goin', I'd say a week," Walker told him. "That might be too long. Don't know if the horses can take it. Don't know if we can take it."

"We'll do what we have to. We won't push the horses, though. We can't take any chances with them."

"Might have to eat 'em, worse comes to worst."

"It won't come to that," Fargo said.

"What about the horses?" Pris said. "We have seven of them. Why not butcher one?"

Jess hadn't thought of that. It would never have entered his head. He was tenderhearted when it came to horses. Killing people didn't bother him in the least, and in fact he enjoyed it. Dogs and cats were just pests as far as he was concerned. Doing away with one of them was like swatting a fly.

But he'd never harmed a horse. Horses had never let him down. When he'd needed to get away from a place fast, it was always a horse that had carried him, and they had a look about them that he liked. Long and lean and muscled. He didn't think he could eat one.

He was the one who'd insisted that they bring all the horses with them. Pris had wanted to leave them, or at least most of them, but Jess had worried about how they'd get along without someone to take care of them.

"I don't know about eating a horse, sis," he said. "I'd sure enough hate to do it."

"Two of them are half dead already," Pris said. "And the others are going to starve or die of the cold if we don't get out of here, and it's looking like we might not. We might as well get some good out of them before it's too late."

Jess still didn't like it.

"I wouldn't know how to butcher one," he said.

"Just like you'd butcher a cow."

Jess had come in empty-handed again, and he realized that they had to eat something. But he wasn't ready to give in.

"A horse and a cow ain't built the same. Anyway, I never butchered a cow, either."

"You don't mind taking the face off a man or a woman. I think you can figure out how to butcher a horse."

Jess couldn't argue with that point.

"Well, yeah, maybe I could do it. That don't mean I'd like it."

"Nobody asked you to like it," Pris said. "Would you rather have us starve to death?"

Jess shook his head. Pris always seemed to get the better of him whenever they disagreed.

"I don't want us to starve," he said.

"Then it has to be done," Pris said. "If you're too soft-hearted to kill one of the horses, I'll do it. I don't see how you could have gotten attached to them. They're not even ours."

"One of them's mine. Been a damn good horse, too."

"Then we'll kill one of the others."

Pris walked to the door where her Henry rifle was propped against the wall.

"Take him out away from the house," Jess said.

He'd cut some trees, built a little corral on the south side of the house, and put the horses there.

"I'll try not to scare them," Pris said with heavy sarcasm.

Jess didn't notice. He said, "I'll be out right after you put him down. I'll take care of things."

"I'm sure you will," Pris said.

She picked up her rifle and left the cabin. Five minutes later, Jess heard one shot rip the silence. It hurt him to think about the horse dying, but he didn't think he'd mind cutting it up.

Hell, it might even be fun.

It wasn't fun. At first sight of the dead horse in the snow stained red with its blood, Jess felt something he'd never felt before. He didn't even know what it was, though someone else might have called it pity.

All Jess knew was that his throat burned and that if he'd tried to talk, he wouldn't have been able to. No one's death had ever affected him that way, neither had the death of any animal, so he had no idea why he felt that way about the death of a horse.

He told himself that if he'd spent more time outside of cities, he'd have seen plenty of horses die, and he wouldn't be taking it so hard.

But what did it matter? The horse was dead, and he and Pris had to eat. He took out his knife and walked to the carcass. He swallowed hard a couple of times and bent to his bloody work.

21

Fargo and Walker stopped at the place where the trail crossed the rushing creek. The sky was a leaden gray, solid with clouds. It had been that way ever since they'd started out, and Fargo didn't think it was likely to change.

The country had become steadily rockier and more mountainous as they went west, and this place, while not as wild as the Tetons that lay ahead, was certainly un- tamed enough.

The creek went through a gorge with sides that were a hundred feet high and right through a mountain that rose at least four hundred feet above the plain. The bridge across the creek looked sturdy enough, but it was covered with snow, so Fargo wasn't entirely sure how safe it was.

"Well," Fargo said, looking down into the gorge, "here we are. Just how far's that cabin you told me about?"

"I'd say it was a good two miles from here to that natural bridge," Walker told him. "And then another quarter mile from there to the cabin. It's rough goin' even in the good weather, so we'll have to take it easy."

They'd traveled for four days. The trail hadn't been quite as snowed under as they got farther west, and the cold had moderated a little. Not much, but enough so that they didn't feel it just about every minute of the day.

"What are the chances that we can sneak up on the cabin without anybody seeing us?"

"Depends."

"On what?"

"Well, I ain't been there in years, so you can't expect me to know exactly how things are laid out, now, can you?"

Fargo admitted the truth of that and asked what the place had been like the last time Walker saw it.

"It's at the bottom of the gorge and set back from the creek a little ways. You'd have to climb down some from the cabin to get to the water, but you could see it from the creek if you looked in the right place. Lots of trees all around it."

"So unless somebody's cleared the land, we can get pretty close without anybody seeing us."

"Yeah, that's right. But you never know about trees. They can die off if they're not cleared. In this weather, lots of 'em will've lost their leaves. We'll just have to see how clear it is when we get there."

"And what's the best way to do that?"

"I'd say we go down into the gorge right there. That's what the pilgrims did before somebody built this bridge. Some places the sides are sheer, but there's a little slope, and maybe even a trail if we can locate it. We're not likely to find a better place. After we get down, if we don't break our necks, we just follow along the side of the creek till we come to the big rock bridge. We can stop when we get there and figger out what to do next."

It was getting on toward the middle of the afternoon. Fargo didn't want to be traveling after dark, not in country he didn't know, and Walker hadn't traveled in years. There was no telling what they might run into.

"We'll go on down to the creek and camp there for the night," he said.

Walker allowed as how he thought that was a good idea.

"What if them Van Cleefs ain't at the cabin?" he said. "What do we do then?"

Fargo hadn't thought that far ahead, mainly because he didn't want to think that the Van Cleefs had pushed on to Fort Bridger or even beyond. If they had, it would be hard to ever catch up with them. And if they got across the Divide, Fargo would never see them again.

He didn't want that.

"Well?" Walker said. "What if they ain't there?"

"They will be," Fargo said.

"Sure they will," Walker agreed.

Fargo climbed down off the Ovaro. Twisting around still gave his back a twinge or two, but he was getting so that he hardly noticed. He was just about good as new, or that was what he told himself.

He walked along the rim of the gorge until he came to a place that looked as if the lip had broken away. He looked down among the rocks and, after a minute or two, he convinced himself that he could see the outlines of what might have been a trail.

"Don't look like no trail to me," Walker said. "Just looks like snow and rocks."

"And trees," Fargo said. "Don't forget the trees."

The trees were mostly aspens, tall, thin, and bare, their white bark looking a little gray under the heavily overcast sky.

"My eyes are just as good as yours. I can see the trees. Don't mean a thing."

"Yeah, they do. If you look, you can tell that there's a trail that goes through them."

"Maybe you can. I sure as hell can't."

Fargo thought it was obvious that the trail was there and that it wound among the trees as if someone had removed some of them to make way for it.

"You've been here before," he said to Walker. "You should know where the trail is."

"Been a damn long time for me, and I can't remember ever'thing, much less where one trail out of a thousand is."

"I've never been down in the gorge," Fargo said. "But this looks to me like the way to go. We might as well give it a try."

"If you say so." Walker dismounted. "You were plannin' to walk, I hope."

Fargo nodded. The rocks were too icy and the slope was too treacherous to try any other kind of descent. Even at that it was risky going on the ice-and snow-covered trail. If he or Walker broke a leg, or even sprained an ankle, the rest of the trip would be next to impossible. If one of the horses broke a leg, it would be even worse.

"We'll walk," Fargo said. "And be careful."

"I was travelin' this country when you were suckin' a sugar tit," Walker said. "I know how to be careful. You're the one better watch his step."

"You want to go first?"

"Might be a good idea. That way, if you fall, you can slide right into me 'stead of goin' all the way down. You ready?"

Fargo said that he was and got out of the way so that Walker could start his descent.

"You're right sure this is a trail?" Walker asked, looking back at Fargo after he'd led his horse over the edge.

"Looks like the best bet to me," Fargo told him. "You got a better idea?"

"Not a damn one."

"Then this is the trail."

"Here we go, then," Walker said, and started down.

They made it halfway with no trouble at all. After they'd begun, it became clear that there was indeed a trail below the snow, and following it was easy enough as long as they stayed on the track.

But just past the halfway point, Walker made a misstep. Fargo saw it happen. Walker was going along just fine, but he put his foot on something, maybe a rock under the snow, and the next thing Fargo knew, Walker was falling.

He tumbled to the right, pulling his horse's head sharply toward him. He let go of the reins, and the horse staggered back, snorting, and luckily staying on its feet.

Walker landed on his right shoulder and rolled up against an aspen tree.

Fargo let go of the Ovaro's reins and went over to where Walker lay unmoving, his face buried in the snow. Fargo bent down and put a hand on the old man's shoulder.

"Walker?" he said.

"Goddamn it," Walker said.

His voice was muffled and the word sounded more like *gahhmn it.*

Fargo figured that Walker was all right if he could still cuss. He said, "Can you sit up?"

Walker raised his face out of the snow.

"Might need a little help," he said.

"Turn over, then."

"Might need a little help with that, too."

Fargo straightened Walker out and rolled him over.

"That hurt?" Fargo asked.

"Not enough so's I could tell it." Walker struggled into a sitting position and moved around as if checking to see that all his parts still worked. It seemed that they did, and he put up his hands. "Give me a pull."

Fargo did as he asked, and with his help Walker managed to get to his feet, wincing as he did so.

"You going to be able to walk?" Fargo said.

"I can walk just fine. It's my damn shoulder that's hurt. I did something to it when I hit that tree."

Fargo looked at the tree. It was so slim that it didn't seem strong enough to hurt anyone. Then he looked at the spot where Walker had first hit the ground. The black top of a rock stuck out of the snow.

"There's what got you," Fargo said, pointing to it with a gloved finger.

"Goddamn it. I'll be bruised up like ever'thing." Walker made a circular movement with his shoulder. "Gonna be stiff and sore, too. But I'll be all right quick enough, don't you worry. And I didn't fall because I was old. The damn horse tripped me up." He looked at Fargo. "You believe that, don't you?"

"You know I do," Fargo said.

"Then let's get on down the trail. I'm tired of standin' here talkin' to you."

Walker didn't want to start a fire.

"Them Van Cleefs might get wind of it," he said. "I'd sure hate it if Van Cleef came up here and killed me in my sleep."

"They'll have a fire of their own," Fargo pointed out. "They won't get wind of ours. And didn't you say the cabin was more than two miles from here?"

"Yeah. I guess I'm gettin' a little skittish thinkin' about Van Cleef bein' so close. 'Course we could be wrong about where he is. He could be all the way out to Californy by now."

He moved his right arm around, trying to get comfortable. When he noticed that Fargo was watching him, he said, "Don't you worry about my shoulder. I'll be all right."

Fargo ignored the shoulder. He said, "Van Cleef's close

by," trying to make himself believe it. "But he won't smell our fire, and he won't see it. So you don't have to worry about that."

"Go ahead and make a fire, then. I'll see about cookin' us a supper when you get done."

Fargo built the fire, and Walker fried up the last of a rabbit he'd trapped the day before.

"I'll swear I'm thinkin' I might be growin' long ears," Walker said when he'd finished eating. He reached up under the muffler he had tied around his head as if checking to be sure his ears were still normal sized. Then he patted his behind. "And a little white tail, too. I might start hoppin' instead of walkin' any day now."

"Don't count on that last part," Fargo said. "You're too old to be hopping."

"There you go again," Walker said. "I wish you wouldn't say things like that. It's because I fell down. That's what it is. You wouldn't talk like that to some youngster like yourself. You wait till you get my age and see how you like it when people talk about you."

Fargo grinned. "Maybe I won't live to be your age. Maybe Van Cleef will get wind of our fire and sneak up here tonight and slit my throat."

"Damn. It's cold enough without you makin' me feel like an icicle is bein' dragged down my spine. Sometimes, I think you're just tryin' to get my goat."

"You ought to keep it tied up somewhere that I can't find it," Fargo said. "You get your feelings hurt too easy."

"Yeah, well, you would too if people were always tellin' you how old you are. You and them Injuns both. Makes a man feel damn near useless."

"Any man who can save my life when I've been shot, get me through the healing, and then lead me to this place couldn't be called useless," Fargo said. "Not by me."

"Well, 'course you'd say that, even if you didn't mean it."

"I mean it, and I'll prove it."

"How's that?"

"I'll take care of you now that you're all busted up and can't move your shoulder."

"You just don't ever let up, do you?" Walker said.

"Just passing the time," Fargo told him.

"Yeah. Well, we better get some sleep. Likely to be a

rough day tomorrow if them Van Cleefs are where you think they are."

"You think they're there, too," Fargo said. "Don't you?"

"Yeah," Walker said, moving his shoulder. "Yeah, I do."

22

Jess Van Cleef woke up before dawn, sat straight up out of his bedroll as if someone had stuck him with a pin, and looked around the cabin.

Pris was still sleeping undisturbed and unmoving, only the top of her head showing above the covers.

There was still a little bit of a fire in the fireplace, but it had about burned down to the coals. Jess got up and put a couple of logs on, then found the poker and punched the coals around until the fire was blazing again. He stood the poker by the fireplace and lay back down on his bedroll to stare at the ceiling.

He couldn't say what had wakened him. It could have been a noise outside the cabin or some critter in his bedroll, but he didn't think so. It was something else—something he couldn't explain, something from some part of him that had always been a mystery to him. It was a kind of sense an animal might have that warned him when danger was near.

The thing was, he couldn't figure out what kind of danger could be anywhere close. Nobody knew where the hell he was. He and Pris hadn't seen another human soul for weeks, or any sign of one. And they damn sure hadn't seen any animals lately, except for the horses.

The thought of the horses made Jess sit up again. He felt something thick and wet and hot rise in his throat, and he forced it back down. He'd puked the first time they'd eaten horse meat, gone outside and puked in the snow like a sickly little brat. But he couldn't help himself. He'd tried to hold it down, but it had forced its way out, and he'd gone outside and let it come out of him and make a steaming hole in the snow. It had been mighty damn embarrassing.

But by God, it wasn't going to happen again. The look Pris gave him when he came back in the cabin had shamed him. She hadn't said a word. The look had been enough. It said everything.

Eating the horse hadn't bothered her one bit, or so she claimed. She even said she thought the meat tasted good, but Jess wasn't sure he believed her. Didn't matter, anyhow.

He could just barely choke it down the next time he tried it, but he managed some way or other, and he kept it down, too. He didn't think he was ever going to get used to it, but if it would keep him from starving, then he'd eat it. He could do that much.

But it wasn't the horse meat coming back up that had wakened him. He knew that. It was something deeper. Something had affected him the same way in the past. One time in Saint Louis, he'd gotten up, put on his clothes, and gone out the window of his hotel room just before the law came crashing through the door. He'd gotten away by the skin of his teeth that time, and he knew he'd never ignore that warning feeling when it came to him.

It was coming to him strong now, a sort of tingling at the back of his neck, like somebody was watching him from far off. There wasn't any way somebody could see him, though, except Pris, and she was still sleeping like nothing had ever bothered her in her whole life.

But something was bothering Jess. He got up and poked Pris with his toe.

"Wake up," he said. "We need to have us a talk."

Pris didn't want to wake up. She grunted something and rolled over.

Jess poked her again. "You gotta get up, sis. Something's about to happen."

She sat up, stretched, rubbed her eyes, and yawned. Jess watched impatiently, but kept quiet until she looked at him and said, "Why did you wake me up?"

He gestured to the window. "I think somebody's out there."

Pris looked at the window, but nothing was visible other than the heavy low clouds and the snow.

"There's nobody out there, Jess," Pris said, snuggling back down in the blankets. "Now go back to sleep."

"There's somebody out there, all right. I can feel it."

Pris had started to get comfortable again, but now she sat up, alert and straight.

"You mean like before?"

Jess had told her about the time in Saint Louis, and a couple of other times, too.

Jess nodded, glad that she understood. "Yeah, like that. We got to get ourselves ready."

"Who do you think it is?"

"I couldn't say. Might be those Injuns. They're probably still after me. They don't give up easy."

"Sometimes I think you don't even care what happens to us," Pris said. "You've almost gotten me killed once because of what you did to those Indians."

Jess hung his head. He knew he should do better, but he just couldn't help himself.

"Well?" Pris said. "Do you have any kind of a plan?"

Jess's head snapped up. When it came to self-protection, he could come up with a plan quickly enough.

"First thing, I think we oughta get out of the cabin. That's where they'll expect to find us, and if we're not here, maybe they'll leave."

"They'll see the horses. And there's plenty to let them know we've been here." Pris looked at the fire. "That right there will be enough. Even if you clear it all out, the hearth will still be warm."

"We won't leave, then. We'll just put ourselves where we can pick 'em off when they get here."

"There might be too many of them."

"How many came up on you and that wagon?"

"There must have been eight or ten. We killed two. If it's the same bunch, there'd be six or eight of them left."

"We can handle that many without any trouble if we get in the right spot. We can pick 'em off before they even know where the shots are coming from."

"You're sure about this?"

"Sure as I can be without seeing anybody."

"Let's get out there and find a spot, then," Pris said.

She and Jess bundled up against the cold, and put cartridges in the pockets of their coats. They got their rifles and went outside.

The sun always came a little late to the bottom of the gorge. The overcast sky and a cold mist that hung in the air made it hard to see clearly for more than a few yards in any direction.

"How are we supposed to see anybody?" Pris asked. "They'll be right on top of us before we know they're here."

"It'll lighten up before long," Jess told her.

"Maybe. Until it does, how are we supposed to find a place to wait?"

"I know my way around here," Jess said, glad for the first time that he'd walked all over the damn place looking for some kind of game to kill. "What we'll do is get over by the bridge. It's not too far, and there's a spot there that'll be just right."

"I hope it's warm," Pris said.

"It won't be. And we can't risk a fire. We'll just have to hope they come before we freeze."

"I'm starting to worry, Jess."

"We'll be in some rocks, out of the wind, and we'll be all right."

"Let's go then," Pris said.

"Better take a gun belt," Jess said. He put on his own gun belt with an old Colt in the holster. "Never know when you'll need one."

It was a little after dawn when Fargo kicked some dirt on the fire and said, "Time to get started."

"I reckon so," Walker said. "We gonna walk or ride?"

"We can ride for the first mile or so," Fargo said. "Then we'll find somewhere to leave the horses until we come back for them."

"If we come back," Walker said. He took off his left glove and stuck his hand up in the air. "Does it seem to you like it's gettin' warmer?"

Fargo hadn't given it any thought, but now that Walker mentioned it, there did seem to be a change in the air.

"Down here below the big mountains, it don't stay cold and frozen all winter," Walker said. "We might be in for a thaw. Seems like it's about time."

"If it comes, how long will it last?"

"Might last a day, might last a week or two. Hard to say. Be good to see a little sun, though."

Fargo had the impression that there had been some days of sun while he was recuperating in the cabin. He mentioned that to Walker, who said, "One or two. Damn few, though, and still mighty cold. I got a feeling this is goin' to be different."

"Right now the weather's in our favor," Fargo pointed out. "We should be able to get right up to the cabin without anybody seeing us."

Walker sniffed the air. "Won't stay like this for long. Might be some sun breakin' through by the time we get to the bridge. You better hope for trees and brush to cover you if you're plannin' to get close to that cabin."

"We'll see about that when we get there, then."

"I reckon we will. Now, are we gonna stand around here jawin' all day, or are we gonna go after them Van Cleefs?"

"One more thing. You ought to take the Henry we picked up. It's lighter than your Hawken, and it's a repeater."

"I don't know about that. I'm not used to it. Might not be able to hit anything."

"You'd have a lot more chances, though."

"Hell, could be you're right. Hand it over."

Fargo gave Walker the Henry and swung himself up into the saddle. In spite of the cold, his wounds hardly twinged at all.

Walker sighted down the barrel of the Henry.

"Too bad I can't try it out."

"Not worth taking the chance," Fargo said.

"Yeah. Well, I expect I can use it well enough if I have to."

"You'd better," Fargo said.

23

The rocks that Jess had told Pris about were positioned a little way up the side of the gorge and about a hundred yards from the bridge. Two of them were more than six feet tall and appeared to have rolled down from the top of the gorge at some time in the distant past. They were positioned about two feet apart, which meant that they offered both excellent cover and a good place to watch for, and fire on, anybody who came under the bridge.

"What if they come from the other way?" Pris asked.

"They'll be coming from the trail," Jess told her. "That's about the only way to get here."

Pris thought of the other possibilities.

"And what if they come along the rim of the gorge?"

"Not likely," Jess said. "They could get to somewhere up above us, but they couldn't get down to where we are."

"They could shoot us from up there."

"Maybe, but only if they could see us. Which they couldn't."

Pris supposed he was right. Thick bushes grew just under the rim of the gorge, and many of them hadn't lost their leaves. They were covered with snow, which would make it even more difficult for anyone up there to see Pris and Jess behind the rocks.

What Jess had told her should have been reassuring, but something about the situation still bothered Pris. She didn't doubt that Jess's intuition was correct. Someone might well be headed for the cabin. But who could it be? She couldn't believe that the Crow would be so persistent. They might be vengeful, but why would it take them so long to arrive?

"We should have made sure that Fargo was dead," she said.

Jess looked at her. "You're the one who said to let him go. You said he'd die from the bullets or he'd freeze."

"I'm not discussing who's to blame. I'm just saying that we should have made sure of him."

"You think he's the one we're waitin' for?"

"I don't know that. But I think he could be."

"Damn. He's one tough son of a bitch if it is him."

"He's not like most men," Pris said.

"You think he's comin' by himself, or do you think he's got some soldiers with him?"

"If it's him, he'll be alone. He wouldn't even consider bringing the soldiers."

Jess patted his Henry rifle and smiled.

"That's where he made his mistake, then."

Pris looked around again. She still didn't like the spot they were in, though she couldn't really explain why. After all, Jess had answered all her objections, and he sounded plenty confident about their chances.

"I think we should go up on top of the bridge," she said.

"Why? We're fine right here."

"If someone's coming from the trail like you say, we can see him better from up there. And sooner, too, since the sun's coming out. And look down there. There's not enough of a trail for someone to get under that overhang."

Jess looked down at the base of the bridge. He'd never gone up the creek past that point, so he hadn't really noticed before that the trail petered out there. But it did.

"Might be a tough climb to the bridge," he said.

"No, it wouldn't," Pris said. "Look at all the rocks sticking out of the snow. It's almost like having steps."

Jess looked up the slope and considered the climb.

"I guess we could do it. It might be a better spot, at that. We don't want to take any chances."

"No," Pris said. "We certainly don't."

Fargo and Walker had gone no more than a quarter mile when the sky began to grow lighter. By the time they decided to dismount and tie the horses, an occasional gap in the clouds gave them a glimpse of sunshine that gave a golden haze to the mist and the clouds.

The creek rushed along beside them, breaking over large rocks and throwing spray. Its sound covered any noise they might make, which might prove to be an advantage, but Fargo wasn't sure he was happy to see the sun.

"You oughta see that creek in the springtime," Walker said. "It's about twice as rough as it is now, and this is right pretty country down here."

Fargo could imagine the pink and gray rocks along the side of the gorge, the green of the trees, the clear water. And no snow. It was a nice enough place now, but in the spring it would be even better.

"Too bad somebody like Van Cleef has to come along and spoil it," Walker said.

"This place will be around a lot longer than Van Cleef will," Fargo said. "And maybe he's not even here."

"I wish to hell you'd make up your mind about that," Walker said.

Fargo dismounted and tied the Ovaro's reins to an aspen limb.

"We'll walk from here," he said.

The walking was easy enough in some places, but in others the walls of the gorge rose up straight beside the creek, leaving only a narrow path of slippery and sometimes icy stones.

"Damn good thing we left those horses," Walker said. "They'd never have made it along here."

"I'm not sure we're going to make it," Fargo said, putting his foot on a rock and testing it before trusting it with all his weight. "You be careful not to slide off into the creek."

"I swear, you're just like an old dog with a favorite bone," Walker said. "You get hold of something, and you just won't let go of it. You could make me slip yourself, talkin' to me like that, you know."

Fargo didn't reply. He was too busy keeping himself steady. The trail widened out in another twenty yards, and he told himself that he'd get there safely. Occasionally, the spray from the creek would splash him, reminding him how cold the water was. He wouldn't last long if he fell in, he thought. And Walker wouldn't last as long as he would.

When he got to the point where there was more room, he turned to give Walker a hand, but the mountain man just gave him a disdainful look and came right on past him.

"Gotta be watchful from here on," he said. "The bridge is just around this next little bend."

They went past the gentle curve, and Fargo saw the bridge for the first time. He had to stop and look at it for a minute, just to take it in. In all his travels, he'd never seen anything quite like it.

The stone bridge formed a perfect arch about a hundred feet long over the creek. It was probably twenty feet across, and at each end of it a tall column of stone rose a hundred feet into the air.

"Kinda gets you, don't it?" Walker said, his voice low. Fargo could hardly hear him over the rush of the water.

Fargo nodded his reply. A few trees grew on top of the bridge, and there were some bushes poking out of the side, but other than that it looked as if someone had carved it out of the natural rock with a gigantic knife.

"Just one little problem," Walker said, pointing. "I didn't know about that part there."

The problem was that the trail virtually disappeared right at the bridge. To get under it, they'd have to go into the creek. And that, as Walker pointed out, would likely freeze their feet off.

"Or," he said, "if the water's deep enough, it might freeze off some other part of me that I'd a whole lot rather hang onto. Or have hangin' off of me, however you want to think about it. So what're we gonna do?"

"We'll have to go over the top," Fargo said.

"You reckon we can do that?" Walker said. Then he clamped his mouth shut as if he wished he hadn't said it.

Fargo grinned. "One of us can go over it. I don't know about you."

"I can do any damn thing you can do."

"Then let's give it a try," Fargo said.

"Hold on," Walker said. "Let's get a little closer. I think there's enough of a path there for us to get by. We'll sure as hell have to hunker down to do it."

Fargo looked to see if he could make out any sign of a path. Sure enough, there was one, but it wasn't more than a foot wide, and the bridge made a very low roof over it.

"You'd have to slither on your belly like a snake to get under there," Fargo said. "It would be mighty slippery. Besides, a fella as big as you is going to hang over the edge. Be a good chance of going into the creek and freezing off that hanger you're so worried about."

Fargo looked up along the side of the gorge. It was steep, all right, but there were enough rocks and bushes to provide foot and handholds.

"I'm going up," he said. "You can slide along under that bridge if you want to, but if Van Cleef's waiting on the other side, he'll put a bullet in your head as soon as you poke it out."

"That's the damn truth. Maybe I'll see about climbin' up the side with you."

"You sure you can make it?"

"I got down didn't I?"

Fargo nodded. "I was thinking about your shoulder."

Walker rotated his arm. "Shoulder's fine. You want me to go first?"

"Go ahead. Just don't fall on me."

Walker gave Fargo a look. "You just try to keep up. I don't want to be all by myself when I get to the top."

"You don't have to worry about me," Fargo said, and Walker started to climb.

24

Almost as soon as he raised himself above the level of the bridge, Walker saw Jess Van Cleef.

Van Cleef smiled and shot him.

The bullet hit Walker just under the left shoulder and blew out the back of his coat. Walker, who'd been precariously balanced in the first place, fell backward. Fargo barely had time to move out of the way as Walker slid past him while the sound of the rifle shot still echoed in the gorge.

Fargo ducked behind a nearby rock and waited. Whoever had shot Walker, and Fargo was certain it was Van Cleef, wouldn't know who else might be with him. So he might take a look.

Fargo turned to see what had happened to Walker. The mountain man had come to a stop against a puny bush about ten yards down the slope. He was already in a sitting position by the time Fargo had turned.

As Fargo watched, Walker spit into his hand and held it up so that Fargo could see there was no blood on it, which meant that the bullet most likely had missed his lung.

When he fell, Walker had lost his grip on the Henry. It had slid down past him a couple of feet, and he inched over to pick it up.

Fargo saw all this within a couple of seconds and returned his gaze to the top of the bridge, where there was still no sign of Van Cleef.

Fargo glanced back at Walker, who was trying to stand up. Fargo motioned for him to stay where he was and looked around for some kind of cover at the top of the bridge, which was about twenty yards above where he crouched behind the rock. All he saw was some scruffy brush that didn't appear likely to stop a bullet.

Still, the brush would hide him if he could get to it, and maybe Van Cleef wouldn't be able to get off an accurate shot once Fargo was partially hidden.

Fargo decided to give it a try. He turned to Walker and indicated that he was going on up. Walker nodded and put the Henry to his right shoulder.

That was the one he'd fallen on, Fargo thought, and he'd been shot in the other one. There wasn't much doubt that his marksmanship would be affected, but Fargo didn't have anybody else to cover him.

The Trailsman put his own rifle down. His Colt would be better for close quarters work. He pulled it from the holster and held it in his right hand. Then he jumped forward, heading up the steep slope at a shambling run, hoping that his feet didn't skid out from under him before he got to the top.

He'd gone about halfway when he saw movement above him. Jess Van Cleef was leaning out over the edge of the bridge with his rifle, but before he could get off a shot, Walker fired from below. The bullet missed Van Cleef and pinged off the rock column that towered above him.

Fargo covered the rest of the distance and dived for the brush. He hit the ground and rolled over twice, winding up behind one of the thicker bushes.

A rifle shot cracked, and a bullet dug up some dirt, but it was a good five feet away from where Fargo lay. He was well enough hidden that Van Cleef couldn't quite see where he was lying and probably wouldn't risk coming out of hiding to look for him.

But that meant that Fargo couldn't see Van Cleef, either. He glanced back down the slope and saw that Walker was coming up. There was a bright stain of red on his coat, but it wasn't large, and Fargo thought that Walker would be all right if he got a chance to clean the wound.

Van Cleef must have seen or sensed that Walker was on his way. Fargo heard him moving up on the bridge, and then he saw him through an opening in the snow-covered leaves.

Fargo fired a shot at him. It went wide, but Van Cleef ducked back out of sight, and Walker was able to get to the cover of the rock where Fargo had been only a minute before.

They were both closer to Van Cleef than they had been, Fargo thought, but that wasn't doing them much good. As soon as they showed themselves, Van Cleef would shoot them, and he wasn't likely to let them have another glimpse of him.

Fargo looked the situation over. A big cedar stood right at the edge of the bridge near where it began to emerge from the wall of the gorge. Van Cleef wasn't behind the cedar, or he hadn't been. He'd come from somewhere near the column of rock. If Fargo could get to the tree, he might be able to slip around the column and come up on Van Cleef from behind. It wasn't likely, but it was the only thing that offered itself.

Getting to the tree wouldn't be easy. It was a good ten yards away. Covering that much ground without making a sound, or without Van Cleef getting a glimpse of him, just wasn't in the cards.

The sun made shadows under the brush where Fargo lay. It had come through the clouds in full force sometime within the last few minutes, but Fargo had been too occupied to notice. An occasional drop of melted snow dripped off the brush. Let that keep up, and he would be even more exposed than he already was. Might as well go for the cedar tree, he thought.

He rolled out from under the bushes, rose to his knees, and looked toward where he thought Van Cleef might be. He wasn't there, and Fargo jumped to his feet.

As he did, Van Cleef appeared from behind the column. Fargo made a flat dive for the cedar tree, landing on his chest and rolling into a ball behind the trunk, his knees pulled to his chest. A bullet whacked into the tree and Fargo got a strong whiff of cedar bark as the bullet ripped a chunk of it away.

Fargo didn't move. He stayed hunched into himself, but there was no following shot. Van Cleef wasn't going to waste his ammunition or come after him.

When he reckoned Van Cleef was behind the column again, Fargo straightened himself out and got as comfortable as he could. He took a look back down the slope, but couldn't see Walker who was still crouched behind the rock.

There was nothing to do now except wait, Fargo thought, and see who made the first mistake.

Fargo knew one thing for certain. It wasn't going to be him.

Pris sat with her back to the rock and stared across the bridge at the column on the other side. It looked red in the sun, and there were rivulets of water making darker streaks down the sides as the snow melted on top.

She and Jess were in a real fix, Pris thought, and she didn't see how they were going to get out of it short of killing Fargo, and that had turned out to be a lot harder than she'd ever thought it would. He should have been dead a long time ago, but there he was, at least according to Jess, and he had someone with him—someone who looked like the friend of the old mountain man Jess had killed. Pris had no idea where he could have come from. The last time she'd seen him, he'd been on his way back to Missouri. If Jess had only killed him, that would have made things a little easier, though she wasn't sure how much. And Jess hadn't killed him, anyway.

Jess stood in front of her and a little to one side. The rock column hid him from Fargo, and the man he'd shot was somewhere on down the slope and couldn't possibly see him even if he was alive.

Jess looked upset. Pris knew he couldn't figure out what to do any better than she could, and he was angry that he hadn't killed the old man. He was even angrier that Fargo had managed to get so close to him and Pris.

"Well?" Pris said, keeping her voice low so that it wouldn't carry to where Fargo was hiding. "What are we going to do?"

"I don't know, goddamn it," Jess said in a rough whisper. "It's a good thing we came up here, though." He looked down to where they'd been hidden earlier. "If we'd stayed there, they'd have shot us where we sat as soon as they got up here."

Pris didn't mention that it had been her idea to move. She said, "Well, they didn't shoot us, not yet anyway.

Maybe they can't get at us, which is fine, but we can't get at them, which isn't. Something has to be done."

"I know that." Jess rubbed his face. "I just can't think of anything."

His indecision worried Pris. She'd never seen him like that. Whenever they'd been in tight spots before, he'd always come up with some kind of plan, even if it wasn't a very good one.

"We could go back to the cabin," Pris said. "We could stand them off from there for a long time."

"We'd never get there," Jess said. "They'd hear us going down the slope, and they'd pick us off before we got halfway there."

"We could cross the bridge. Maybe once we got on the other side we'd be able to get away from them."

That wouldn't work either, and Jess knew it. There was hardly any cover on the bridge. A few trees grew from the rock, but they were small and scrawny and wouldn't be much help. He and Pris would never make it to the other side. And where would they go if they did get there? Jess didn't have any idea. When he pointed this out to Pris, she said, "At least we'd have some kind of chance."

"We've got a better chance right here. We can't go running away."

"Then we'll have to trick them," Pris said.

Tricking people wasn't Jess's strong point. He relied on surprise, strength, and animal cunning, but not outright trickery. Working out a plan that would fool somebody was pretty much beyond him.

"How can we do that?" he asked.

"You just watch for Fargo," Pris told him. "I'll think of something."

Waiting was something that Fargo did well. His experiences had taught him that a patient man had the advantage in nearly any situation, whether it was at a card table, with a woman, on the track of an animal or man, or in a standoff with someone like Van Cleef.

There had been no movement behind the rock below since Walker had hidden himself there, and Fargo was sure that Walker was also patient. Anyone who'd made a living as a trapper would have to know how to pass the long

138

hours of a winter's day or night without getting in a hurry for darkness or dawn.

Fargo wondered how patient Van Cleef would be. He hoped Van Cleef would get nervous and make some kind of move. It was when a man got in a hurry that he made blunders.

A noise from behind the rock column made Fargo perk up. He took a quick glance from behind the tree trunk, but he saw nothing before he ducked back.

Then someone called his name.

It was Pris. He recognized her voice easily enough, and there could have been no other woman around anyway.

"Fargo," she said. "Help me."

25

Fargo took a cautious peek around the trunk of the cedar. The low-hanging branches obscured his view, but he could see Pris hobbling toward him. Her hands appeared to be tied behind her back, and part of a leather belt dragged along beside her right foot. It looked as if her feet had been bound together and she had somehow gotten free.

Fargo didn't believe it for a second. He'd heard it said that seeing was believing, but in some cases what you saw could be not only misleading but dangerous.

If he hadn't heard Pris talk about the importance of family and her devotion to Jess Van Cleef, if he hadn't seen her kill Chad Tuttle, he might have believed his eyes. But he'd heard and seen those things, so he knew that what he saw was some kind of trick.

"He's going to kill me, Fargo!" Pris said, and then she fell.

Fargo knew that he was supposed to come rushing to her aid. Maybe she thought that the things they'd shared together would make him careless, but everything she'd told him had been a lie. The physical pleasure had been as much hers as his, and he owed her nothing.

But this might be his chance to get Van Cleef, who no doubt was waiting behind the column of rock for Fargo to show himself. Except that he wouldn't know that Fargo was onto him.

Instead of being surprised when he emerged, Fargo

would be ready, and Van Cleef would be the one caught off guard.

Fargo shook the branches on one side of the cedar tree, then turned and came out from the other side, his pistol ready.

But Van Cleef didn't appear, and it was only then that Fargo noticed that Pris had fallen on her side, in order to conceal her hands. He now saw they hadn't been tied at all because Pris was rising to her knees and bringing Jess's Colt from behind her back. She gripped it with both hands and pointed it at Fargo.

At that exact moment, Jess came from behind the column, his rifle cocked.

Three weapons fired almost as one.

Fargo felt something tear into his calf, and his right leg collapsed beneath him. He hit the ground and rolled over, bringing up his pistol to fire again at Van Cleef, who was leaning against the rock with a stunned look on his face. But before he could pull the trigger, Pris kicked the pistol out of his hand. It skittered away, out of reach.

"If you've killed Jess, you'll pay, Fargo," she said.

She held the pistol in her right hand, and her finger was tight on the trigger as she glared down at the Trailsman, who had a feeling he was going to pay even if Jess didn't have a scratch on him.

A sound came from off to the right, and Pris looked away from Fargo, who grabbed her foot and twisted, throwing her to one side.

In doing so, he probably saved her life because a rifle cracked and Fargo knew that Walker was there.

Pris fell heavily and Fargo crawled over to where his pistol lay. By the time he reached it, Van Cleef was gone.

"Watch her," Fargo said to Walker, who had reached the top of the bridge. He was a little unsteady, so he might have missed Pris even if Fargo hadn't tripped her up.

"I'll shoot her if she moves," Walker said.

The bloodstain on the front of his jacket had gotten a little bigger, but not much, and Fargo noticed that his scarf was missing—stuffed inside his shirt to stop the bleeding.

Fargo stood up. His leg held him, but it was a near thing, and when he put much pressure on it, the pain ran all the way up to his head. He gave Pris a quick look. She appeared to be unconscious, but again he didn't believe what he was seeing. Her arms were spread out above her shoulders. Her pistol was nowhere in sight.

"She's treacherous as a snake," Fargo warned Walker. "Be careful."

"This old coon's been bein' careful for a lot longer than you, Fargo," Walker said. He looked at Fargo's bloody calf. "I ain't the one she shot in the leg."

"Nope," Fargo said. "Van Cleef's the one shot you. In the shoulder."

"Where is that turd, anyway?" Walker asked.

"Behind that rock. He's been hit, but I don't know how bad."

"You goin' after him?"

"Thinking about it," Fargo said, testing his leg again. It would do, he decided. "But I don't trust him any more than I trust his sister."

"We can both go after 'em, you from one side, me from the other. He can't get both of us."

It could work, Fargo thought, but he wasn't going to leave Pris unattended. When he started to hobble toward her, she rolled over. Grabbing the pistol from where it had lain beneath her, she snapped two quick shots in Fargo's general direction. She didn't come close to hitting him, but she did make him move back, which gave her just enough time to jump up and run back behind the rock.

"Why didn't you shoot her?" Fargo asked Walker.

"Hell, why didn't you?" Walker said.

His voice came from the cedar tree where he'd taken cover when Pris had started to shoot.

Fargo grinned. Walker could move pretty well for a man with a wounded shoulder.

But Fargo's grin changed to a frown. He hadn't thought he'd let himself get fooled by Pris, but he had. Twice. Give her credit, he thought. She was as smart as she was pretty, and just as dangerous as she was smart. Even more dangerous than her brother.

"What do we do now?" Walker said.

"That idea you had about going around both sides of the rock might work."

"And if it don't, then I'll be to blame, I guess."

Fargo grinned again. "You're the one who thought of it. How are your shoulders?"

"Bullet went right through it, clean as a whistle. I got the bleedin' stopped, I think. Hurts like hell, though. Sort of takes my mind off the other one."

"You got behind that tree pretty fast. Can you hold up for a few more minutes?"

"I can hold up long as you can. It's my shoulders that're hurt, not my leg."

"I think you could outrun me, all right," Fargo said.

"Damn right I could."

Fargo grinned again. Walker was tough as saddle leather.

"We gonna go after 'em?" Walker said.

"You keep an eye on that rock while I put some more cartridges in this Colt," Fargo said.

"They ain't comin' out from behind there," Walker said, but he watched just the same.

When Fargo had reloaded, he rolled the cylinder with the heel of his hand and said, "I'm ready. You go to the right. I'll take the left."

Walker took one step, then stopped and turned his head so he could see Fargo.

"What about the woman?"

"Shoot her same as you would a rattler. She's just as bad as any snake you ever saw, and she'll sure as hell shoot you if you give her the chance."

Walker looked a little doubtful. "Don't seem right, killin' a woman."

"If you get the chance, do it," Fargo said. "If you don't, you'll be a dead man."

"All right, then. You know her better'n I do. You ready?"

"Ready," Fargo said, and they started toward the column, Walker walking with a slight wobble, Fargo limping only a little.

Jess wasn't hurt much more seriously than Walker was, but he'd seldom been shot before. During the course of his long criminal career, he'd killed many a man and woman, but he'd given few of them a chance to harm him. Gant and Fargo were the only two who'd done it, and it worried him to think that he was as easily hurt as his victims. The thought made him whimper.

Pris was upset with him.

"Don't be a baby," she said. "You have to buck up now. They'll be coming for us."

"Sons of bitches," Jess said, wiping his nose with the back of his hand. "That goddamned Fargo shot me."

Fargo's bullet had taken a little piece of flesh off Van Cleef's leg, chipping a bit off the bone as well. Jess was feeling the pain.

"I heard them talking when they thought I was knocked out," Pris said, trying to get Jess to concentrate on their immediate problem of survival. "They're going to come from both sides. We have to be ready."

Jess took a deep breath and leaned against the rock. He turned his face to the left.

"I'm ready," he said. "Let the sons of bitches come."

As they approached the stone column, Fargo stopped. He motioned for Walker to do the same. When the mountain man stopped, Fargo picked up a rock.

Walker grinned and shook his head as if to say that even Van Cleef wouldn't fall for that old ploy. But Fargo didn't care if anybody fell for anything. He just wanted a second's distraction. He wasn't counting on anything more than that.

Van Cleef felt something warning him. It was almost exactly the same feeling he'd had earlier that morning in the cabin. It told him that Fargo and Walker were coming, and that he wouldn't be able to stop them. He was already hurt, and he'd seen how hard it was to kill Fargo. That other old bastard was just about as bad.

"I'm leaving," he said to Pris.

"What? Where are you going?"

"Across," Van Cleef said, and he started moving.

He couldn't walk normally, and he almost seemed to be skipping as he brought his right leg down heavily while barely touching the ground with his left. But he was covering the ground fairly rapidly.

Pris went after him. Maybe he was right. If they could reach the other side, they could get behind the column there. Fargo and the old man wouldn't have a chance if they tried to cross the bridge to get to them.

The wind was blowing pretty hard down the gorge, but going across the bridge wasn't as treacherous as Pris had thought it might be. A lot of the ice had melted, and the stone surface, while slippery, wasn't covered with a lot of small rocks that might slide out from underfoot. Little bushes grew here and there, and the few stunted trees gave the illusion of cover.

They were less than halfway across when something hit the ground not far behind them. Pris turned to see what it was, but Jess kept right on going.

A rock rolled to a stop against a little bush. Pris knew right away what it meant.

"They're coming," she said.

Jess stopped and turned around. "Let 'em. They don't know where we are."

Fargo and Walker came around the column at almost the same time. Both were surprised that the Van Cleefs weren't there, but both turned immediately toward the bridge.

It was too late. Jess and Pris were already shooting.

Bullets pinged off the stone column as Fargo and Walker dodged back behind it. Now the Van Cleefs found themselves in the position where they'd hoped to catch Fargo and Walker. They turned and started for the opposite side of the bridge, Pris running, Jess skipping.

They almost made it. Fargo had a natural inclination against shooting anybody, even a Van Cleef, in the back, and Walker felt the same.

So if Jess hadn't set a foot wrong, he might not have fallen.

It was likely his wounded leg that caused the problem. He was favoring it so much that it threw him off balance. He landed halfway over the edge of the bridge.

There was nothing to hold onto. Jess's fingers scrabbled at the rock as he slipped farther down, looking for something, anything to grab.

Pris knelt beside him and the wind whipped her hat from her head. She reached for Jess's hand, but she was a fraction too slow. She missed by inches, and Jess was gone.

Fargo saw him fall. He didn't land in the creek, but on

one of the rocks that stuck out of the water. He hit it hard and lay spread-eagled on it, unmoving.

Pris looked at him, then back to where Fargo stood as he came out onto the bridge.

She screamed something at the Trailsman, her hair blowing around her face, but though Fargo saw her mouth twist with hate, he couldn't make out the words.

"You gonna shoot her?" Walker asked. "Or you want me to do it?"

But neither one of them had to. She screamed some more incomprehensible words. Fargo figured they weren't flattering to him or to Walker.

Then she looked down at her brother, and jumped.

26

"Don't go tryin' to help her," Walker said, putting out a hand to hold Fargo back. "Wouldn't be no use."

Fargo nodded. He hadn't planned on helping anybody. He just wanted to have a look and see what had happened. Pris had missed the rock and disappeared under the water of the creek. Fargo wondered if she would pop up anywhere.

"Water's pretty shallow," Walker said. "But I don't see any sign of her."

Fargo didn't, either, and that was what worried him. She should have come to the surface somewhere, but he could see nothing in either direction.

"Might be stuck between some rocks under the water," Walker said. "Foot might be caught. We wouldn't be able to see her under there."

The water was a brownish color, and froth skimmed along the top.

"I guess you're right," Fargo said. "I'd feel better about things if I knew for sure where she was. And whether she was alive."

"Speakin' of that, we better go down there and see about her brother. He might not be as dead as he looks."

"Good idea," Fargo said, but he didn't think there was much doubt about Jess's condition. As far as the Trailsman could tell, Jess hadn't budged since hitting the rock.

Fargo wrapped his scarf around his leg and tied it, though

the calf had already stopped bleeding. The day was getting warmer, and he didn't need the scarf to keep off the cold.

He and Walker made their way down the slope to the edge of the creek and looked at Van Cleef. Jess still hadn't moved, and when they got closer, they could see that he'd struck his face in falling. In fact, there wasn't much face left. It was more like a bloody mask.

"I'll be, go to hell," Walker said. "His whole damn face is gone. It's like a judgment on him. Whatever a man sows, that's what he reaps. Book of Galatians."

Fargo smiled. He hadn't thought of Walker as a Bible reader.

"Sometimes a son of a bitch gets what he deserves," he said. "Book of Fargo."

"Don't believe I've read that one," Walker said. "But I like the idea. We gonna leave him on that rock?"

"Nothing's going to bother him out there."

"You got a point. No use riskin' drownin' to get him. We oughta check that cabin, though."

"How far did you say it was?"

" 'Bout a quarter of a mile. Might be something there we could use. Might be some horses."

"We'll go have a look," Fargo said.

Pris let the water take her under and downstream toward the cabin. She held her breath as long as she could, and when she broke the surface, she was well beyond the bridge. She took a deep breath and went under again.

The cold of the water struck through her clothing and straight to her bones, but she refused to give in to it. She had no doubt that she was going to die, but she didn't give a damn, not as long as it didn't happen until Fargo and his friend paid for killing Jess.

The thought of Jess's death racked her in ways that the cold never could, and for the first time in her life she realized that she was completely alone. Without Jess, it didn't matter in the least if she died, but she was going to see Fargo dead first.

When the current slowed at a small bend, Pris managed to pull herself out onto the bank. The wind struck her like a hammer, and she was so cold that she wasn't sure she could move any farther. She thought that she'd be better off just to lie there and freeze.

But she struggled to her feet and walked in the direction of the cabin. She still had the pistol in her hand, though she couldn't feel it. There was more ammunition in the cabin, if she could just get there. Her feet were like blocks of ice, and it was hard to tell when they touched the ground. But she kept walking.

One thought that kept her going, other than the revenge she'd have on Fargo, was that a fire still burned in the cabin's fireplace. She and Jess had thought they'd be coming back to its warmth together.

She walked woodenly but doggedly along, ignoring the fact that she was already half dead.

Luckily, she didn't have far to go. She reached the cabin and pushed open the door. Shutting it behind her, she went directly to the fire and poked it up into a blaze. When the flames were hopping, she stripped off her sodden clothing and let it fall on the floor. She took a blanket and began to rub herself as briskly as she could, standing as near to the fire as she dared.

When her blood finally started flowing again, it was so painful that she almost screamed. But she held the scream inside, though her face twisted in agony and tears flowed from her eyes.

After a while, she realized that she might live. But she kept rubbing herself, and she didn't move away from the fire.

She knew that Fargo would be coming, and she knew that it wouldn't take him long to get there. After another few minutes, her skin was rubbed red, and though she still wasn't entirely warm, she stopped rubbing herself. She dried the pistol carefully and found the cartridges that had been left behind.

After she loaded the pistol, she dragged the room's only rickety chair over by the fire and sat down facing the door and the distorted faces nailed to the wall beside it. She pulled a dry blanket around herself until she was completely wrapped in it.

Then she waited.

*　　*　　*

"Still got smoke comin' out of the chimney," Walker said when he and Fargo came in sight of the cabin.

Too much smoke, Fargo thought, for a fire that had been burning since Van Cleef and Pris had left the place.

He and Walker went on, and when they got within a few yards of the building, Fargo said, "Somebody's in there."

"How do you know that?" Walker asked.

"You can see the tracks. Looks like they came from the creek."

"God a'mighty. You think that woman could've made it all the way here without dyin'?"

Fargo said he wasn't sure. "But I don't know who else it could be. It sure as hell isn't Jess."

"We gonna find out who it is?"

"I am," Fargo said. "You stand aside."

"The hell you say. You just gonna walk in there and let her shoot you?"

"Maybe I'll shoot her first," Fargo said, pulling the Colt from its holster.

"She might surprise you."

"I don't see how she could. I know she's in there."

"If it's her."

"It's her, all right. Who the hell else could it be? Liver-Eater Johnson?"

"Not likely he'd be down from the mountains this time of year," Walker said with a thoughtful look.

"I didn't really mean it," Fargo said. "It's Pris Van Cleef. She came out of the creek and walked up here. Now she's waiting for us."

"And you're goin' in after her."

"You have a better idea?"

"Well, you remember what those Crows did to us, or tried to?"

"Damn," Fargo said. "You're smarter than I thought."

"Smarter'n you," Walker said. "Question is, how're you gonna get up on that cabin?"

"Easy enough," Fargo said, looking over at the corral Van Cleef had built. "If that fence will hold me."

"You go making a lot of noise, and she'll shoot you through the roof."

"I can be quiet as a Crow," Fargo said.

"I guess we'll find out, won't we?" Walker said, moving away.

Fargo went to the corral and climbed the fence. The horses whinnied and stamped the ground, but that was probably nothing unusual. Nothing Pris would take notice of, or so Fargo hoped. He stood on the top rail of the fence and pulled himself to the roof. The snow was still packed there, though it was beginning to melt around the edges. Fargo padded through it to the chimney, then took off his coat and laid it across the opening. He had nothing to hold it down, so he took a few handfuls of snow to lay around the sides. When he was satisfied, he climbed back down.

"Pretty good job," Walker said when Fargo joined him. "How long you reckon she can stay in there?"

"Not long," Fargo said.

He drew his pistol and thumbed back the hammer.

When the smoke started pouring in from the fireplace, Pris thought she knew what had happened. She remembered the noise the horses had made a few minutes earlier, and wondered how Fargo had managed to be so quiet on the roof. Maybe the snow had absorbed the sound of his footsteps.

Pris cocked the pistol she held and walked to the door, still wrapped in the blanket. She took a last look around the cabin, her eyes coming to rest at last on the skin faces that now seemed to be smiling.

Pris smiled back at them and opened the door.

27

When Pris stepped outside, about all Fargo could see of her was her face and her feet. The blanket that was draped over her, along with the smoke that followed her out of the door and swirled around in the wind, hid the rest of her from his sight.

There was still a little snow in front of the cabin door, and Pris stood in it barefoot, seemingly unconcerned about the cold.

Her face showed no emotion at all. The rage that suffused it as she stood atop the natural bridge had disappeared as if it had never been. It was hard to say what she was looking at. Whatever it was, it seemed a thousand miles away.

"I seen folks like that before," Walker said. "She ain't really there anymore."

Fargo agreed. But he still didn't trust Pris. He called her name, but she didn't respond.

"See what I'm tellin' you?" Walker said. "Gone."

"Maybe. Don't get cocky, though."

"Hell, I ain't cocky. I just think . . . Goddamn!"

Walker's exclamation came as Pris flung her arms wide, throwing aside the blanket and revealing that she was totally nude. Her breasts stood high and firm, the nipples pointing straight out. The black hair at the joining of her legs stood out in stark relief against her white skin.

And she had a pistol in her right hand.

"Sweet Jesus," Walker said reverently. "I ain't never seen anything like it."

Neither had Fargo, and he was momentarily paralyzed by the sight, a fact that almost cost him his life. Pris swung the pistol barrel around and brought it to bear on him. She pulled the trigger a little too quickly, and the bullet clipped the side of Fargo's hat.

She was about to shoot again, but Fargo fired his own Colt first. The bullet struck Pris just above the left breast, and a bright spray of blood spattered on the snow as she fell backward, landing on the blanket. Her right foot kicked twice, then was still.

"Goddamn," Walker said in a low voice no less reverently than before.

Fargo walked to where Pris lay, staring sightlessly up at him. Seeing that she was dead, he holstered his pistol. He bent down, took hold of the sides of the blanket, and pulled it over her, covering her completely.

When he straightened back up, Walker was standing beside him.

"I like to have got us killed," he said. "I forgot ever'thing you said about not gettin' cocky. I never woulda thought to pull a trigger on her, not seein' her buck naked the way she was."

"Don't feel too bad," Fargo said. "I didn't do much better."

"Hell, you got her, didn't you?"

"I didn't mean to," Fargo said. "I was trying to hit her arm."

"Her fault," Walker told him. "Don't you be worryin' about it. A man can't be held responsible for what happens when she looks like that and has a gun in her hand."

Fargo felt a hollow sadness, not so much because of what had happened, but because of the waste of Pris's life and all the others'. Frazee and the Tuttles. Gant and Keller. White Bear and all the other Crow. Who knew how far back the line of dead extended? Pris had been involved in all of them, one way or the other, so Fargo shouldn't have felt bad about killing her. But he did.

"Reckon there's a shovel inside?" Walker said.

Fargo said he didn't know. "You stay here with her. I'll

go back and get our horses, and we can spend the night in the cabin. We'll leave for Laramie tomorrow."

"Better get your coat."

Fargo climbed back up on the cabin and retrieved his smoky coat. When he came back down, Walker said, "You oughta have a look in the cabin."

Smoke was still eddying out the door of the cabin as Fargo followed Walker inside. Walker pointed to the wall, showing Fargo the twisted skins.

"Shit," Fargo said.

"Yeah. That Van Cleef was crazier'n a bedbug. The world's a lot better off without him."

Fargo had to agree. The thought made him feel a little better.

Walker rummaged around the cabin and found a half-empty bottle of whiskey. He didn't drink any. He said, "We better use this on our wounds."

"Good idea."

Fargo was first, and the whiskey burned like a hot poker on his leg. It must have been even worse for Walker when his turn came, but neither of them cried out.

"I'll be going for the horses now," Fargo said when they'd bound up their wounds again.

"How you gonna get 'em here?"

"Walk them in the creek. They can get under the bridge without getting into deep water."

"You gonna be all right about the woman?"

"I'll be fine," Fargo said.

When Fargo reached the bridge, he looked under the arch.

Van Cleef's body was gone.

At first, Fargo thought that the water might have rushed over the rocks and taken him away, but that just wasn't possible. The water wasn't moving fast enough to carry someone as big as Van Cleef, and it wasn't running high enough, either.

With a sinking feeling, Fargo thought that Van Cleef must still be alive. Had to be, even though his face was gone. Otherwise, how could he have gotten off the rock?

Instead of climbing up to the top of the bridge and going over, Fargo got down on his belly and slithered along the ledge of rock beneath the overhang. It was slippery wet, but Fargo was under and on the other side in seconds.

There were bloodstains on the rock. But no Van Cleef.

Fargo stood up, wondering what the hell could have happened. Then he heard a horse snort way above him. He looked up and saw a line of horses along the edge of the gorge.

Two Ponies rode one of them.

After they rounded up White Bear's body, they stuck around, Fargo thought. They'd waited to see if he'd get Van Cleef as he'd promised. He saw that Jess's body was thrown across the back of one of the horses. Fargo didn't know what the Crow would do with it. He didn't want to know.

Two Ponies raised a hand, whether in greeting or dismissal Fargo couldn't tell, and the Crow turned their horses and rode away.

Fargo went on down the gorge to get his own horse, and Walker's. They'd been a long time finding Van Cleef and Pris, and Fargo wanted to get on the move again, away from this place, and on to other places where he'd never been.

Tomorrow he'd be on the trail again, back where he belonged.

LOOKING FORWARD!
The following is the opening
section of the next novel in the exciting
Trailsman series from Signet:

THE TRAILSMAN #292

SAN FRANCISCO SHOWDOWN

*California, 1858—where the land of gold runs red
with blood, and Skye Fargo is marked for hard
death.*

Many hard trails, and many rough scrapes, had taught Skye
Fargo that sudden danger often left a warning tingle in the
air. Right now he and his pinto stallion felt it simultaneously.

"Easy, old campaigner." Fargo soothed the nervous
Ovaro, patting his neck to calm him. "Hell, you know trouble never leaves us alone for long."

The tall, crop-bearded, buckskin-clad rider reined in
among some sand dunes and wind-twisted Joshua trees. At
first, the Trailsman's lake blue eyes, closed to slits against
a grueling sun, detected nothing that didn't belong to the
area.

He was traversing the vast desert just east of the Mor-
mon settlement of San Bernardino, California. As far as

the eye could see, there was only that nameless desert color.

"There's room out here to swing a cat in, all right," Fargo remarked softly, mostly so his voice would calm his sidestepping mount. "Wide open with no good place to mount an ambush. And I don't see any trouble brewing."

The Ovaro nickered, sternly disagreeing with his master.

"I trust your nose better than my eyes," Fargo said, sliding his brass-framed Henry rifle from its saddle boot. He levered a round into the chamber.

Despite the endless risks, once again Fargo's needle pointed west—always west. Following the urge to push over the next ridge, he'd come nearly as far west as a man could get without swimming in the Pacific. This time with lucrative trail work waiting for him the moment he reached a dusty little pueblo just north of Los Angeles. The preferred route to California was the well-established westward trail from Saint Joseph, Missouri. Fargo had followed it at first, counting as many as seventeen pioneer graves to the mile.

Then, tired of the traffic and the ruined water holes, he had opted for the less popular route through the old Spanish land grant country of the Southwest. He had found little growth besides scrub cottonwood and mesquite. Even so, the route somehow grew more desolate as he followed the Gila River of southern Arizona Territory. Bone-dry expanses of salt sage produced alkali dust, galling his eyes to tears and rawing his throat like harsh tobacco.

Ever since crossing the Colorado River into southeastern California, however, water had become Fargo's chief concern. The vast Salton Sea was too saline, but luckily he had come across the occasional saguaro cactus just bulging with water.

Now, spotting dust puffs beyond the next line of wind-sculpted, rippled dunes, Fargo suspected he had bigger problems than a parched throat.

"Looks like you were right, old warhorse," Fargo told his stallion. "I'm too tired to run, so let's take it by the horns."

He thumped the Ovaro's ribs with his boot heels, holding

his Henry straight up with the butt plate resting on his thigh.

Fargo rarely consulted calendars or timepieces. He reckoned it was some time in early fall—cool down on the coastal plain and cold up in the mountains at night. But this daytime desert sun had weight as well as fierce heat. He felt it on his shoulders and back now as he crossed a landscape sparsely dotted with prickly pear, creosote, and cholla.

A female voice jolted Fargo like a slap.

"Newt! Newt, look! Those men are charging at us, and their guns are—oh!"

The whip-crack sound of a rifle cut her short. Fargo, his vision blocked by the line of dunes, smacked the Ovaro's rump hard.

"No, Newt!" the woman cried again while the Ovaro tried gamely to reach a gallop in deep and sloping sand. "God, no, they'll kill you!"

More gunshots, rifle and pistol, hammered Fargo's ears. Damn sure *sounded* like killing was imminent, he decided. With the Ovaro making poor time up the steep, almost liquid surface of the dunes, Fargo figured he'd best send in his card, and quick.

He swung the Henry's stock up into his shoulder socket. Unexpected gunshots might take some vinegar out of those attackers, whoever they were. Vicious road gangs, sometimes Mexican, were common in lower California. But Fargo had never heard of them preferring the merciless desert with its scant traffic.

He pulled the Henry's trigger and the hammer clicked uselessly.

Just ahead and out of sight, a conveyance of some sort was trying to gain speed. Fargo could hear iron tires scraping the desert hardpan. The gunfire was an unrelenting crackle now. The woman screamed.

Cursing the Henry's hang fire, Fargo cleared the faulty bullet, jacked a new one into the chamber, and heard the firing pin again click uselessly.

This time Fargo swore with real heat, making up a few

words of his own. The ammunition of his day was notoriously unreliable, especially the new self-contained cartridges. He'd found that as many as half the bullets, in any given box, might malfunction. That was definitely a deterrent to spontaneous showdowns—but left a man vulnerable at times like this.

More gunfire, more female screams, and Fargo's Colt was to hand when he and the Ovaro finally crested the line of dunes.

"Newt! Oh, good heart of God! We're stuck in the sand—oh!"

The woman flinched hard when a bullet knocked a chunk off the seat of their rugged Dougherty wagon, a passenger conveyance favored for its strong steel springs. Fargo saw only a young couple in the wagon—the woman and a man in a plug hat and clergy black suit. He was aiming a long Jennings rifle at four riders, who were bearing down on them with guns blazing. He, too, seemed to be having rifle troubles.

Fargo never fooled himself—with only his Colt, he could never defeat four mounted men armed with repeating rifles. Then again, he reasoned, very few of these California bully-boys had much stomach for a hard fight.

A bullet sent the woman's bonnet twirling even as Fargo, bracing himself against a bag of oats tied to his cantle, shot the front rider's horse out from under him.

The sorrel gelding dropped like a sash weight, trapping the surprised rider's legs. Fargo, loathe to hurt a horse, realized the two travelers had only one chance, and that was if he could put all four attackers on foot, quick. Especially since it was clear the man in the wagon was having trouble with his rifle—or his nerve. He had yet to fire a shot.

The Colt leaped in his fist when Fargo tagged a second horse, a buckskin with a roached mane. By now, the other two mounted men had spotted Fargo's position and opened up on him with a vengeance.

Geysers of sand spat upward as rounds thumped in nineteen to the dozen. Fargo's hat went spinning off his head and a round raked a shallow furrow along the Ovaro's right flank. Still, man and horse stood steady as a granite mountain. The moment Fargo had a decent chance to score a hit at handgun range, he knocked a rider out of his saddle.

The fourth rider, seeing all this and losing his fighting fettle, wheeled his black stallion to flee. Fargo, who looked the other way on many crimes, never gave quarter to murderers. Determined to finish this right, he dropped the stallion with two shots.

"Do it," he shouted when the fourth rider slapped for his short gun, "and I'll drill an air shaft through you!"

That fourth rider, Fargo saw as he walked carefully forward, was an Apache, his long black hair restrained by a rawhide thong. He had the powerful legs and chest typical of his tribe.

"Coyote," Fargo said, recognizing one of the most notorious bandits in the Far West. "Why don't you stay down south in Apacheria?"

"Skye Fargo," the Apache responded, still sitting in the sand. "The famous Trailsman, white do-gooder. I was educated by the mission padres, remember? I am not welcome in Apacheria."

"A murdering scut like you ain't even welcome to his mother. Taking them scalps from your own clan and selling them for bounty in Mexico . . . I always wondered how you sleep at night."

"On my back," Coyote responded with his quick, goading grin. "Or on a white man's woman."

Fargo was worried about those other riders catching him off guard. One was still pinned and bawling like a bay steer. The black-suited man in the wagon had the other men covered. But did that damn rifle even work?

"Unbuckle that short iron and toss it toward me," Fargo ordered Coyote. "That knife in your moccasin, too—but slide it, don't throw it."

Fargo moved quickly around, gathering all of the attackers' weapons. The West might be big, but he recognized one more face: Joaquin Robles, a road bandit and smuggler from the tiny Mexican village of San Luis. He wore a straw Sonora hat and the white cotton of a Mexican peasant. All four desperadoes wore clothing squirming with beggar's-lice.

"*El famoso* Fargo," Robles said, for he was the one pinned under his horse. "You make the big mistake, *verdad*? You did not kill us."

"I'll consider requests," Fargo assured him, aiming the Colt at his head.

"Wait!" The bandit's copper skin paled. "My little joke, eh?"

Fargo whistled when he spotted Robles's rifle in the sand: a fifteen-pound Sharp's equipped with a telescopic sight. This wasn't the usual outlaw's gun—somebody was damn eager to assure hits.

The other two prisoners, strangers to Fargo, were both white men. He assumed the names they readily gave him were "summer names." The one calling himself Rick Cully was tall and beanpole thin, with only a slight wound where Fargo's bullet had raked his rib cage. Stone Lofley, the fourth man, was silent and brooding. He had a broad, blunt, expressionless face that lived up to his first name. Fargo feared him and Coyote most of all.

"A thousand thanks, sir," the young man with the rifle said. He was strong limbed, and his dark hair was slicked back with axle grease. "You just saved our lives. My name is Newt Helzer, of Troy Grove, Illinois, and that's my sister Lindy in the wagon."

Fargo nodded curtly, ignoring the hand Newt offered. With those cunning killers still unsecured, this was no time for parlor manners.

"Name's Skye Fargo," he told the evident greenhorn. "Gather up the ropes off their horses, Newt. We need to get these boys' hands trussed up good before they make a fox play."

"You killed our horses, Fargo, you idiotic bastard!" the beanpole calling himself Rick Cully spat out. "The hell we s'posed to do now, *walk*?"

Fargo's strong white teeth flashed through his beard when he grinned. "Congratulations. You guessed it in one."

"Shit! I'm wounded, you heartless son of a bitch! I need doctorin'!"

Fargo, who had once set his own broken arm with a

canteen strap, gazed in contempt at the slight wound. How could it have knocked Cully out of the saddle?

"What you *need*," Fargo retorted, "is a set of oysters on you. That bullet barely creased you."

"Like hell! Christ, this wound could mortify."

Fargo nodded. "It might," he agreed cheerfully, "if there's a God."

"All tied up, Mr. Fargo," Newt reported. "All their weapons are loaded in our wagon."

Fargo spoke low in the kid's ear. "Is that rifle of yours even loaded? I didn't see you fire it."

"I tried," Newt said, looking embarrassed. "But nothing happened."

Fargo took the piece and thumbed the hammer to full cock. He pointed at the obviously cracked firing pin. "Hell, this rifle is brand new, yet it ain't worth an old underwear button. You been dry firing it?"

"Dry firing?"

"Snapping the hammer down when the gun's unloaded."

"Oh." Newt flushed. "Hundreds of times. I thought I should practice."

"Practice with a loaded gun. Well, this one's past shooting until it's repaired. Replace it with one we just confiscated."

Both men fell in step to go check on Newt's sister, Fargo leading the Ovaro and sending plenty of cross-shoulder glances toward the captives.

"Essence of lockjaw?" Newt offered Fargo a bottle of Kentucky bourbon.

Fargo cut the dust and wiped his mouth on his sleeve.

"Ain't my way," he told Newt, "to nose a man's back trail. But just where the hell are you and your sister headed? Right now you're on the trail to Los Angeles. That's not a 'destination,' just a stepping-off place for men outfitting for the gold mines. And that trade has dwindled lately."

Newt looked like he'd been sucker punched. "Los Angeles? But we're headed farther north for San Francisco. Aren't those the Tehachapi Mountains?" he asked, pointing ahead at some scant-grown hills.

"The Tehachapi range is a couple hundred miles north of here," Fargo replied.

"We're darn lucky we even got this far," Newt admitted. "We fell for John Fremont's lie about the 'shortcut' from Great Salt Lake to California. It's clearly marked on his map."

Fargo shook his head in silent disgust. It was downright sad how few pilgrims spent much time in the map files back home—assuming maps were available, which they often weren't. It was also downright appalling how many pilgrims accepted any map thrust into their hands as reliable.

But Fargo's disgust quickly gave way to sudden pleasure as they drew nearer the wagon and the waiting woman. Despite the heat, she wore a black calico skirt, a knitted shawl, and the ubiquitous coal-shovel bonnet. She was slender and wasp-waisted with a straining bodice, her wheat blonde hair in sausage curls. Big, fetching eyes of liquid green set off a sensuous mouth and startling white teeth.

Newt quickly introduced them.

"Thank you, Mr. Fargo," Malinda Lindy Helzer said effusively. "You were so brave. You saved our lives."

"This time," Fargo said. "But despite eight years in the Union, this entire state is still overrun with kill-crazy marauders. And the most dangerous place of all is San Francisco. That's starting to change, but frankly, it's no place for a decent woman—not yet. Any chance you could change your plans?"

Lindy cooled herself with a grass fan, watching Fargo from big, appealing eyes. "Newt and I have already made an initial payment on a boardinghouse. Today's October fifteenth. If we aren't there by the first of November, we lose both the boardinghouse and our money."

"Fifteen days? Lady, that's not likely."

Fargo hooked a thumb over his shoulder toward the four hardcases. These were common frontier thugs who murdered from ambush, not men who had mastered the art of draw-shoot killing. However, they had cohorts, plenty of them.

"Just curious," he told Lindy. "Usually these road gangs

just rob their victims, shooting over their heads. Nor do they waste a comely female. But look there.''

He pointed at the space where a chunk of seat was missing, only inches from Lindy. "Why do I get the distinct impression they were trying to kill you?"

Her eyes fled from his. "How can *I* explain the criminal mind?"

"I wonder . . . anyhow, there's murdering trash like that packed into the hills and mountains. Men of no church conscience who kill with enjoyment," he warned.

Lindy batted long lashes at Fargo. "Then . . . won't you guide us? We can pay you well."

Temptation sent a little heat squiggle into Fargo's groin—it had been some time since he'd enjoyed the "mazy waltz" with a female.

"Can't," he said reluctantly. "I'm reporting near Los Angeles to ride security for a surveying crew sighting through a railroad to San Francisco."

He glanced into the wagon. "No water?" he asked.

"This morning we licked the dew from our gear," Newt admitted. "That's all we've had today."

Fargo looked at both of them and realized they were suffering hard. He also realized they stood damn little chance of reaching San Francisco alive. Of all the decent places in the country to open a boardinghouse, why pick a wide-open hellhole like San Francisco? Fargo was skeptical of the whole story.

"We'll pay you ten dollars a day," Lindy said, reading Fargo's indecisive face.

"Tell you what," Fargo replied. "That's damn good money. I'll ride with you folks as far as Los Angeles and find you a good man. We'll take these four sage rats with us and turn them over to the law."

A disappointed frown creased Lindy's face. "I'd say we've found a good man in you, Mr. Fargo."

Her eyes took his full measure as she said this. She added a come-hither smile in case he didn't take her meaning. Fargo, feeling that smile in his hip pocket, feared he was on the verge yet again of doing something stupid.

No other series has this much historical action!

THE TRAILSMAN

Available wherever books are sold or at
penguin.com

Praise for
DONNA GRANT

THE DARK WARRIORS SERIES

"Paranormal elements and scorching romance are cleverly intertwined in this tale of a damaged hero and a resilient heroine."
—*Publishers Weekly* on *Midnight's Lover*

THE DARK SWORD SERIES

5 Tombstones! "Another fantastic series that melds the paranormal with the historical life of the Scottish highlander in this arousing and exciting adventure. The men of MacLeod Castle are a delicious combination of devoted brother, loyal highlander, Lord and demonic God that ooze sex appeal and inspire some very erotic daydreams as they face their faults and accept their fate." —*Bitten By Books*

4 Stars! "Grant creates a vivid picture of Britain centuries after the Celts and Druids tried to expel the Romans, deftly merging magic and history. The result is a wonderfully dark, delightfully well-written tale. Readers will eagerly await the next Dark Sword book." —*Romantic Times BOOKreviews*

4 Hoots! "These are some of the hottest brothers around in paranormal fiction." —*Nocturne Romance Reads*

5! Top Pick! "An absolutely must read! From beginning to end, it's an incredible ride." —*Night Owl Romance*

5 Hearts! "I definitely recommend *Dangerous Highlander*, even to skeptics of paranormal romance—you just may fall in love with the MacLeods." —*The Romance Reader*

MIDNIGHT'S SEDUCTION

DONNA GRANT

St. Martin's Paperbacks

This is a work of fiction. All of the characters, organizations, and events portrayed in this novel are either products of the author's imagination or are used fictitiously.

MIDNIGHT'S SEDUCTION

Copyright © 2012 by Donna Grant.
Excerpt from *Midnight's Warrior* copyright © 2012 by Donna Grant.

For information address St. Martin's Press, 175 Fifth Avenue, New York, NY 10010.

ISBN: 978-0-312-55250-3

Printed in the United States of America

St. Martin's Paperbacks edition / November 2012

St. Martin's Paperbacks are published by St. Martin's Press, 175 Fifth Avenue, New York, NY 10010.

10 9 8 7 6 5 4 3 2 1

ACKNOWLEDGMENTS

As always my thanks goes first to my fabulous editor, Monique Patterson. I'm so very blessed to be working with such a wonderful person, and talented editor.

To Holly Blanck, Paul Hochman, Anne Marie Tallberg, and everyone at St. Martin's who helped get this book ready, thank you. Also a shout-out to the awesome gals at Heroes & Heartbreakers—Liz, Megan, and Heather.

To my extraordinary agent, Amy Moore-Benson. Thank you!

A special note to Syd Gill. Thanks for everything you do. You make my life easier, and for that, I owe you so very much.

To my kiddos, parents, and brother—A writer makes sacrifices when writing, but so does the writer's family. Thanks for picking up the slack, knowing when I'm on deadline that I might not remember conversations, and for not minding having to repeat things.

And to my husband, Steve, my real-life hero. Thank you for the love you've given me, for the laughter you brought into my life, our beautiful children, and the happily ever after I always dreamed of. I love you, Sexy!

CHAPTER ONE

Saffron sucked in a harsh breath as she came instantly awake. But she kept her eyes closed tight, afraid to open them and see nothing but darkness. Again.

She heard the crackle of the fire in the hearth, and the wind as it rattled against the window from the fierce winter storm that had raged for days.

Three years of being blind, of fighting the darkness she had been confined to, and she was too frightened to open her eyes and see if the spell had truly been broken.

A spell that had been put on her by Declan Wallace, a Druid with unimaginable black magic. A Druid who had wanted to use her abilities as a Seer to his advantage.

Even now, just thinking of the power of his magic sent a cold chill snaking down Saffron's spine.

But it wasn't just his magic. It was the evil inside Declan, the malice and the spiteful soul that was as black as pitch. And owned by Satan himself.

Saffron had discovered all too painfully how extensive Declan's magic was. He had used her fear of spiders to torment her. To torture her endlessly, incessantly.

Ruthlessly.

She inhaled deeply as the fear that had been with her for three years began to take over once more. Saffron struggled to remember the glorious feel of Declan's magic snapping as Danielle found his spell deep in Saffron's mind. And broke it.

Relief had poured through Saffron. Relief and . . . calm. She relaxed as the same mixture of emotions soothed her once more. The reversal spell, however, had affected Saffron in a way that even now made her stomach clench in terror.

She shouldn't have passed out. She shouldn't have felt the tug of Declan's magic as it struggled to keep a hold on her.

Yet she did. She felt all of it keenly.

"Stop being a ninny, and open your eyes," she whispered to herself.

Saffron swallowed past the lump in her throat and clutched the heavy blanket that was atop her. Her heart pounded with a sickingly slow beat that echoed in her ears.

And before she could change her mind, she opened her eyes.

There was no half measure for her. No cracking open a lid to see if she saw any light. It was all or nothing.

Instantly, she raised her hand to shield her eyes as the light from a table beside her made her turn her head away quickly. Her heart missed a beat as she blinked against the bright light.

Saffron sat up and swung her legs over the bed so that her back was to the light and she let her eyes wander the room. She had been in MacLeod Castle for several weeks. She'd gotten to know the room as any blind person would. By touch and learning how many steps from any given point to another.

But now she was able to look at the castle as everyone else did.

A wall of gray stone rose before her, broken by the window and a medieval tapestry with rich hues of burgundy, green, and gold. Saffron had to blink several times to allow her eyes time to adjust to the brightness that seemed so foreign to her.

She scrunched her toes on the rug and looked down at her

feet. There had been a time in her life when she wouldn't have let a month go by without a pedicure. Her once impeccably polished toes needed trimming, and a good soak.

If her feet had changed so much, what would the rest of her look like? Even before her trip to Britain, she had gone to the gym regularly to keep fit. It wasn't just about staying trim, it was about being healthy, especially after her father's death due to heart disease.

Saffron promptly pushed thoughts of her father out of her mind. If she thought of him, she'd have to think of her mother and stepfather, and she couldn't deal with that and her new sight at the same time.

Slowly, Saffron rose from the bed and walked to the window. She knew it was exactly eight steps from the bed to the window, but this time she didn't count. Or at least she tried not to. It was so ingrained in her she couldn't help it.

When she reached the window, she pressed her face to the glass and sighed as the cold touched her. The movement of the water outside her window made her breath catch in her throat. She'd had no idea her room faced the sea. After a few more moments watching the dark, rolling water, she straightened.

Then she turned to face the rest of the room.

She had to shield her eyes from the light, and it took several tries before she was able to see past the glare. Her eyes roamed from the chest of drawers to her left to the small door that led to a private bathroom. Then on to a chair in the corner next to the door that led into the corridor. Beside the door were hooks that Saffron knew had been there since the castle was built.

Farther along was a dressing table where her brush and other belongings were laid out. Next came the bedside table with the lamp, the bed, and then the hearth.

Saffron stared at the flames, amazed at the hues of orange, yellow, red, and even blue that she saw. It had been so long since she had seen color that she found herself mesmerized. Completely enthralled.

She could easily allow herself to become lost in the fire-light. The urge was so overwhelming that Saffron took a step toward the hearth, intent on doing just that.

It was the sound of footsteps approaching her chamber that pulled her attention from the fire to the door a heartbeat before the knock sounded.

The door opened a crack, and a woman poked her head in. Her gaze went to the bed first. She frowned slightly before her eyes moved about the room. When she found Saffron, she smiled and stepped into the chamber.

Saffron had no idea who she was. She knew voices and the cadence of a person's footsteps, but she didn't know anyone's face. Panic began to set in. She dug her fingers into the stone behind her and tried to control her breathing.

"You're awake."

Saffron let out a sigh as she recognized Cara's soft brogue. She had been the first Druid at the castle, the one who had brought the MacLeods into the world. "Cara."

"Aye," said the petite brunette with kind mahogany eyes. Her curly chestnut hair was pulled back in a low, loose pony-tail with curls framing her face. "Forgive me. I should have told you who I was."

Saffron waved away her words. "I knew as soon as you spoke."

"It doesn't matter. I should've thought of that. But I'm glad to see you up. How is your eyesight?"

"As if Declan's spell never was." Of course Saffron knew that to be the lie that it was. Declan's evil presence had been inside her for three long years. And her eyes were sensitive to light.

"That's wonderful news. Dani has been so worried about you."

"How is Danielle?" Saffron asked, knowing what a risk Dani had taken to go into her mind to break the spell. "I need to thank her."

Saffron knew just how awful it had been for Dani to go into her mind and feel the slick, cloying mass that was Declan's magic. Saffron had been so concerned it would harm Dani that she almost didn't let her try this last time to break the spell.

"Dani and Ian have been in their chamber," Cara said with a chuckle.

Saffron shifted her feet on the cold stones. Ian just returned to the castle, with Dani's help, after four centuries of being gone. But his disappearance hadn't been his doing. It had been Declan's. And Deirdre's.

The thought of the other *drough* made Saffron shiver. Deirdre and Declan were *droughs,* Druids who gave up their pure magic to have black magic. And with it, their souls to the Devil.

Saffron learned about Deirdre through the other *mies,* or good Druids, at the castle. Deirdre had been alive for over a millennium, and she was the one who had unbound the gods in the MacLeods, thereby beginning the war they were waging. A war that the rest of the world had no idea was taking place.

But Dani and Ian had found each other. Dani, another Druid, had needed Ian's help to reach the castle. And Ian, struggling to control the god inside him, needed Dani to get the upper hand over his god.

Gods. Saffron inwardly laughed. That's who she lived with. Druids and Warriors with primeval gods locked inside them. These Warriors were able to detect magic, but more than that, they were immortal and had amazing powers.

Or at least she had been told about the powers. She hadn't actually seen them herself.

But she had heard the roars of the Warriors. She knew their strength, like the feel of Camdyn's thick muscles beneath her hand.

Just thinking about Camdyn made her stomach flutter. Saffron swallowed and shoved thoughts of him out of her mind. She told herself she was only drawn to him because he'd been the one to free her from Declan's prison.

There was no doubt in her mind that if she'd been told the Warriors had the power to control fire or teleport, it was true. But she couldn't wait to see it for herself.

"Saffron?" Cara asked.

She shook herself and blinked as she looked at Cara. Saffron began to wonder what everyone else looked like. She especially wanted to see the couples together, like Cara and her husband, Lucan MacLeod. "Apologies. I'm—"

"No need," Cara interrupted her with a wink. "I understand. Are you hungry?"

"Starving. How long did I sleep?"

"Just through the night. Dawn broke an hour ago."

Saffron glanced down at her clothes from the day before and grimaced. "Let me change first."

"We'll be waiting." With one last smile, Cara was gone.

Saffron walked to the chest and opened a drawer. She looked at the socks inside, all white, and all folded neatly so she would know what she grabbed. She took a set, determined to buy every color imaginable now that she could see again.

She hurriedly pulled the socks over her icy feet and jerked off her jeans and sweatshirt. She smiled as she thought of how offended her mother would be to see her not only in jeans, but a sweatshirt as well.

Her smile grew as she dug out another pair of jeans and a soft yellow sweater. She took a look at her clothes and noticed they were all solid colors that could easily intermingle with each other so she wouldn't mix anything up.

All the clothes she had were given to her by the other Druids in the castle. Nothing in the drawers was hers alone, except for her panties and bras. Reaghan had brought a bag full of lingerie to her, and to Saffron's delight, they were all lacy and sexy. And all different colors.

There was so much she needed to take care of. First and foremost, she needed to call her lawyer. If what Gwynn had told Saffron the other day was true and her mother was trying to claim her legally dead, then her mother and the son of a bitch that was her stepfather would get all her money. Money her father had refused to give her mother.

"Over my dead body, Mother," Saffron said as she stuffed her feet into black boots.

She ran a brush through her hair, unable to look at herself in the mirror. One thing at a time. It was going to take much more courage than she had right now to see herself in the mirror after three years.

Saffron walked out of her chamber and turned right. She paused a moment, listening to the sound of voices below her in the great hall. The castle was huge, but her hearing had improved when her eyesight had been taken.

There was laughter and conversation. Meals in the castle were almost always an entertaining affair. There were so many couples in the castle, from the three MacLeod brothers, Fallon, Lucan, and Quinn, and their wives, Larena, Cara, and Marcail, to Hayden and Isla, Galen and Reaghan, Broc and Sonya, Logan and Gwynn, and now Ian and Dani.

She wasn't the only single person at the castle, however. There was Marcail and Quinn's son, Aiden. Fiona, and her grown son Braden, and the newest Druid to the castle, Kirstin. Then there were the other Warriors, Ramsey, Arran, and Camdyn.

Saffron ignored the way her heart raced when she thought of Camdyn. She had sensed a gnawing inside Camdyn, a vise-like grip on him that refused to relent. Yet, when he dealt with her, he was always gentle, if not silent.

What did he look like? She rubbed the pads of her fingers over her thumb as she remembered the silky, cool texture of his hair against her palm when he had caught her from falling the last time she'd had a vision.

Camdyn always seemed to be near her. Even when he didn't say anything, she knew he was there. And oddly, that comforted her. Everyone looked out for her at the castle, but with Camdyn it was different. He had a different undertone in his voice when he spoke to her, and there was a distinctive gentleness mixed with power when he touched her.

She'd touched his face once. It had been the only way to know what he looked like with her eyesight gone. Her palms still felt the prickle of his whiskered cheek, the sharp angles of his face, and the full, wide lips.

He hadn't known what she'd done because she'd been

quick, but the need to know him had been tantalizing. She'd gotten a peek at his face using her hands, and it had been enough for her to mentally draw an image of him.

And it was a glorious image.

The question now, however, was whether he would live up to what her mind had created.

Something akin to excitement ran through her at the idea of seeing everyone for the first time. She was at the stairs leading to the great hall when she realized she wished she had washed her hair and maybe put on a bit of makeup first.

"Saffron!"

Her head swung in the direction of the voice as a woman with long silver-blond hair jumped up from her spot at the table and raced over to her.

Saffron recognized the cadence of the walk and couldn't help but smile as Danielle Buchanan's arms wrapped around her. She returned Dani's embrace and squeezed, realizing then that she had missed Dani and Ian's wedding the night before.

"It worked," Dani whispered.

For the first time since waking, Saffron found herself blinking back tears. "Yes. You did it, Dani. Your magic let me see again."

CHAPTER
TWO

Orkney Islands
Ring of Brodgar standing stones

Camdyn MacKenna stood in the silence of the coming dawn with fellow Warriors Arran and Fallon. Lucan, with his ability to command darkness and shadows, was patrolling the area to see if Deirdre was already there.

They were spread around the area, hunkered down and waiting on the windswept expanse of land with only the stones to shield them. To Camdyn's exasperation he found his thoughts wandering. But not just to any time. To a time when he had been happy.

A time with Allison.

He squeezed his eyes closed as he thought of his wife, of her smiling hazel eyes. Of the life they had shared together.

A life she hadn't turned away from despite the god inside him. She had known he was a Warrior. She had known of his power to manipulate the earth, his incredible speed and enhanced senses. And his immortality.

Despite it all, she had stayed with him.

His Allison.

Camdyn opened his eyes and focused on the ring of standing stones that were most likely as ancient as the gods inside the Warriors. No one knew where the standing stones had come from, or why they had been built.

The Celts had used them, revered them. The stones were seen all over Britain, their origins a mystery. Few realized it was the magic contained within them that drew people.

But a Warrior knew. A Warrior had the ability to sense magic—good and evil. Camdyn dug the heel of his black boot into the earth, thankful the magic he felt wasn't doused in evil as a *drough's* magic was.

Droughs. How he hated them. Or one in particular. Deirdre.

Just thinking about her made the bile rise in his stomach. He'd had a good life before Deirdre had found him and unbound his god, turning him into the monster he was.

Camdyn had survived her cursed mountain and managed to escape. He'd found refuge in the deep forests and the mountains. Until he had come across Allison. She had been like a light in the darkness.

As soon as Camdyn saw her he knew she was the one for him. She hadn't batted an eye when he told her how the Celts of old had allowed the *droughs* to call up primeval gods locked in Hell. The strongest warriors in each family stepped forward and allowed those gods into their bodies, creating the first Warriors.

It was those first Warriors who rid Britain of Rome. But it came at a price—the death of many Celts before the *droughs* and *mies* combined their magic to bind the gods inside the men since they couldn't make the gods leave.

The gods traveled through the bloodline of these warriors, waiting for a day when they could have control once again. Deirdre gave them that wish when she found the hidden scroll and learned the MacLeods held a god.

Three brothers, in fact, shared one of the most powerful gods between them. Once Deirdre unbound their god, she set about finding the rest.

Camdyn snorted, the claws of his god lengthening from his fingers as hatred rolled inside him. He drew in a long, deep breath until he had himself back under control and his claws had disappeared.

Allison had believed every word of his tale, but even then it had taken Camdyn nearly five years before he allowed her to see what he changed into when he called up his god. The times before, he would make sure he was far from her and their cottage before he changed.

Yet, not even his transition could make her cower in fear. Camdyn had rarely left her. He'd stayed by her side, living the life they had been granted.

And when she began to age, he saw the sadness in her eyes.

A shift in the air drew Camdyn's gaze to the left and his thoughts to the present. He turned his head to find Arran watching him closely. Arran had already called up his god, and his white skin, claws, and eyes stood still in the darkness.

Arran cocked his head to the side, a silent question.

Camdyn gave a quick shake of his head before he looked back at the stones. They had come to make sure they were alone, because somewhere below the stones rested Deirdre's twin sister, Laria.

The answer to ending Deirdre's life once and for all.

Moments ticked by before a cloud of darkness began to dissipate and Lucan MacLeod stepped out and looked at each of them.

"Well?" Fallon, the eldest MacLeod and leader of the Warriors at their castle, asked.

Lucan lifted a brow. "I doona sense Deirdre or any of her wyrran."

Camdyn spat at the mention of the wyrran. They were Deirdre's pets, created by her to be commanded only by her. They were small in stature, hairless and thin, but deadly with their talons on their hands and feet. Their yellow eyes were sinister looking, but it was their mouthful of teeth that their lips couldn't fit over that made them truly ugly.

"I agree," Lucan muttered to Camdyn.

Arran moved toward Lucan from his hiding place, the white skin of his god disappearing once more. "Has the ground been disturbed?"

"Nay," Camdyn answered. Since his power was to command the earth, he could also tell when it had been dislocated and how. "Nothing has touched the stones, especially inside the circle, in quite some time."

"Camdyn's right," Lucan said.

Fallon crossed his arms over his thick chest as he looked at the stones. "The magic is heady here."

The other three nodded silently.

Camdyn rubbed his hands together. "Finally, after two hundred and fifty years, I'm going to help end Deirdre."

"Six hundred and fifty," Arran corrected with a grin. "Remember, we allowed the Druids to toss us into the future."

How could Camdyn keep forgetting he lost four centuries of his life? Not that he minded. He was getting used to this modern world fairly well, and with the aid of his god he'd learned to understand their language swiftly.

"Aye," Camdyn said.

Lucan moved to stand by his brother Fallon. "Regardless, it's about to end."

"It almost seems too good to be true," Fallon said softly.

The four of them stood together as the sun crested the horizon, lighting the Ring of Brodgar in its golden glow.

Camdyn had to admit the sight was glorious. The stones themselves stood in a huge circular pattern on a thin strip of land on an eastern-sloping plateau separating two lochs.

Twenty-seven stones remained upright in the circle, and even more interesting was the area where the stones themselves were. It was as if it had been hollowed out. No weeds or wildflowers grew where the stones were. The grass was greener, leaving a distinct circle that could be seen from any angle.

There was no doubt in Camdyn's mind it was magic.

The shadows began to fade as the sun continued its ascent into the sky, and even though Camdyn knew how dangerous it was to stand in the open with Deirdre likely to appear any moment, he couldn't make himself leave.

There was something so appealing, so . . . comforting about the stones that made him crave to stay.

Camdyn looked at Arran, Lucan, and Fallon, and one by one, the Warriors pulled their gazes from the stones.

"It's time to return to the castle and tell the others what we've learned," Fallon said.

Arran grinned, his eyes flashing with excitement. "And get ready for a battle."

Camdyn didn't have time to say anything as Fallon put his hand on his shoulder, and in the time it took him to blink, they were standing in the bailey of MacLeod Castle. Fallon called it jumping; its more modern term was teleporting, and Camdyn rather liked the speed with which they could travel.

"Lucan!" Cara shouted and raced to her husband as they walked into the castle.

Fallon hurried to his wife, and lone female Warrior, Larena, and wrapped his arms around her. Camdyn and Arran continued past them to the two long tables that had been put together.

As Camdyn walked by his fellow Warriors, he noticed just how many had found their women. He, Ramsey, and Arran were the only Warriors left without mates at the castle.

At least they weren't the only single men. There was Aiden, Quinn's son, and Braden.

That thought had no sooner gone through his mind than he felt a wave of forceful, brilliant, and all too pleasing magic move over him.

Camdyn didn't need to look up to know it was Saffron. Her magic had had a distinct feel for him ever since he lifted her in his arms in Declan's prison.

He found his gaze rising to the top of the stairs where Saffron stood in a pale yellow sweater and jeans that fit her long lean legs to perfection. Her walnut-colored hair hung freely about her face as her eyes moved leisurely over the hall.

He released a breath he hadn't known he held. When Danielle raced to Saffron, and Saffron's eyes followed her, Camdyn knew Declan's spell to blind Saffron was truly gone.

Everyone worried that the spell wouldn't release Saffron, but the simple fact that no nightmares had plagued her the previous night, as they had in the past, told Camdyn she would be all right.

He'd been the one to go to her every night and calm her, though she never knew of it. No one did, and that's how he wanted it kept.

Camdyn had been unable to stay away from her this past night, however. He'd checked in on her several times. And each time she had been sleeping peacefully.

Still, it was good to see for himself that Declan's spell was truly gone.

He kept silent, trying to hear what Saffron and Dani said to each other, but everyone was so excited to see Saffron that they began talking at once.

Cara disengaged herself from Lucan's arms and waited at the bottom of the stairs for Saffron and Dani. Saffron whispered something to Cara who gave a nod and a soft smile.

Saffron walked with slow, measured steps that were graceful and elegant. Her posture was impeccable, but the smile on her face was forced.

Camdyn wondered if anyone else noticed. She passed him with nary a look, and then suddenly halted. Their eyes met, clashed. Held.

For several heartbeats they said nothing, but he saw her shoulders relax a fraction before she walked around the table to sit next to Fiona and Braden.

Camdyn wanted her to know who he was, but how could she? She only knew his voice, not his face. Why he'd wanted her to recognize him, Camdyn couldn't begin to fathom. But it made him uncomfortable.

He surreptitiously glanced at Saffron to find Fiona and Braden both talking to her.

It was because of Isla's magic of shielding the castle from view, as well as keeping the mortals from aging, that the

Druids, including Fiona and Braden, who had been at the castle over four hundred years, hadn't grown older.

Camdyn didn't blame Fiona and Braden from staying at the castle. The world had changed drastically since they took refuge in the castle in the seventeenth century, and with Deirdre still out there hunting Druids, it was better to stay hidden.

But he couldn't help but wonder what they would do when Deirdre was gone. There was still Declan to consider, but Declan didn't hunt Druids for their magic as Deirdre did.

Once Deirdre was gone, Declan was next on their list.

The thought of Declan reminded Camdyn of Saffron. He'd never forget how he'd first found her, chained and half starved, how she had quivered in his arms when he'd broken the chains and lifted her.

She'd been frightened by him, but despite the horror Declan had put her through, she had gathered her courage and wrapped her arms around Camdyn's neck.

He'd been the only one who could gain access to Saffron's prison because of his power to move the earth, and that was how he'd become her rescuer. Or so he told himself.

The truth was, once he saw her, he'd wanted to be the one to free her, the one to bring her out of the darkness. Camdyn wasn't sure why, nor did he understand this yearning he had to be near her in case she needed him.

Saffron had proved to be adept and courageous. Yet, regardless—or maybe in spite of that—Camdyn kept a close eye on her at all times.

Out of the corner of his eye he watched as she tucked a strand of hair behind her ear. It was a nervous gesture she probably didn't even know about. But her anxiety caught his attention.

"How do you feel, Saffron?" Quinn asked.

Saffron's tawny eyes shifted to the youngest MacLeod. "Better now that Declan's magic is gone, Quinn."

Quinn chuckled. "How did you know who I was?"

"Your voice," she answered.

One by one Camdyn watched her call out each person's

name after they spoke to her. Her shoulders relaxed each time, and her smile grew more genuine.

Inwardly he nodded as realization dawned. She had been afraid.

That was something Camdyn hadn't expected. As long as Saffron had been at the castle she'd had an iron will, an unbreakable attitude.

However, it wasn't the first time Camdyn had seen a chink in her armor. No one but he knew of the nightmares she suffered, and he only knew because he heard her in the lonely hours of the night when he walked the corridors of the castle.

He'd been unable to stay away from her strangled cry that first night. Every night since then he had gone to her. He did nothing but lay a hand on her forehead, but that seemed to calm her.

Until the next night.

At first it had been just to quiet her, and then he'd needed to touch her, to see her. He dared only to touch her forehead, but he'd come to love the feel of her thick hair and the way it fell against the pillow. He'd come to need the sound of her soft breath as she fell into a dreamless sleep.

Camdyn had tried not to see her bare legs that had kicked at the covers, or see the dusky nipple that poked through her white tank.

He'd tried and failed.

A flood of heat seared through his body as the memory of her lithe body flashed in his mind.

He cocked his head to the side as he studied her. Would she have more nightmares now that Declan's black magic was gone? More importantly, could he keep away from her?

Suddenly, her tawny eyes moved to him and held him captive. She stared at him for numerous silent moments. Camdyn took that time to drink in the stunning sight of her, from her oval face and slim neck to her wide lips and high cheekbones.

Thick locks of her rich brown hair fell over her shoulder to lie artfully above her breast. He wanted to reach out and touch her hair because he knew just how soft it was.

There was a poise about her that spoke of refinement and

class, yet in her gaze he saw a wildness, a recklessness that nearly matched his own. It was so unexpected and startling that it made his balls tighten in a desire so fierce, so intense, he had to grip the bench he sat on to keep from going to her.

"Camdyn."

Her voice, soft and gentle, fanned the flames of desire that was already out of control. He gave a slight bow of his head, and smiled inwardly. It hadn't been a question but a statement. Another testament to her confidence. "Aye."

For several minutes her beautiful tawny gaze held his before she looked away. But Camdyn couldn't stop looking at her. Couldn't stop the way her magic enveloped him, covered him.

Seduced him.

CHAPTER THREE

Saffron inhaled deeply and found herself relaxing as the breath left her lungs. Everyone treated her no different than they had before, and that was saying something.

Most people handled the blind with kid gloves, but not the residents of MacLeod Castle.

At least now she knew not only everyone's voice, but also their faces. Lucan, the middle MacLeod brother, with the small braids at his temples and griffin-head torc.

Fallon, the eldest MacLeod and leader, with his boar-head torc and dark green eyes. Quinn MacLeod, with his wolf-head torc and alert attitude. Hayden, the tallest of the men, stood like a blond giant. Galen had kind indigo eyes that seemed to see right into her soul.

Broc, who stood guard over all of them; Logan, who had a mischievous grin; Ian, who had eyes only for Danielle; Ramsey, who was the quiet one with silver eyes; Arran, who was the one eager for a fight; and Camdyn . . .

Saffron refused to look at the Warrior again because in the depths of his dark eyes she saw the same loneliness and anger that was within herself. The same sadness, the same hunger for something more.

She'd known it was him as she passed him in the hall. He'd not spoken, not moved, but she'd known who he was simply by the feel of the man himself.

It had sent a shiver of delight through her, a shiver that had made her stomach flutter and her heart skip a beat.

After just one look at him, his face was branded in her mind. From his long, straight black hair that he let fall freely around his sculpted face, to the dark shadow of a beard on his hollowed cheeks that only made him sexier.

It could also be his dark eyes and the thick brows that slanted over them. She swallowed as she recalled the hard line of his jaw and his full lips, lips she knew could probably make any woman swoon. All of which she had felt with her hand, but she hadn't been prepared to see just how devilishly handsome he was.

But it wasn't just his face. She had felt the thickness of his muscles, but feeling and seeing were two different things, especially when it came to Camdyn.

His meaty shoulders were made visible by the black tee stretched taut over his arms and chest as he braced his forearms on the table and listened to something Ramsey said.

She'd caught a glimpse of his bum and the way the dark denim hugged him. With one glance, she'd taken in all that was Camdyn. And she wanted more.

"What happened on the isle?" Broc asked Fallon, bringing Saffron out of her thoughts and back to the war that raged.

She shifted her gaze to Fallon, who sat at the head of the table, his hands folded over his tight stomach as he leaned back in his chair.

"Deirdre hadna arrived," Fallon answered.

Arran snorted. "Yet. We need to get there before she does."

"Did you sense her nearby?" Hayden asked.

Lucan shook his head. "Nay. The Ring of Brodgar is huge, and I walked it several times searching for the smell of her foul magic."

"The area is devoid of trees," Camdyn said. "There was nowhere for her to hide. The peninsula where the stones are located is long and skinny with lochs on each side."

Reaghan, one of the Druids with powerful magic and wife to Galen, leaned her elbows on the table and nodded. "It's just as I remember it described to me."

Saffron still had a hard time believing that Reaghan, beautiful, soft-spoken Reaghan, had put a spell on herself that wiped her memories every ten years to hide the location of Laria from Deirdre.

It was difficult to tell who was the oldest of the Druids, Reaghan or Isla. Both of them had gone through several more centuries of being immortal than any of the Warriors had.

"What are we waiting for then?" Sonya, the healer, asked as she looked around the table.

It was Ian who raised a dark brow and said, "It seems too easy."

"My thoughts exactly," Logan said.

"Easy or no', we need to get to Laria," Quinn stated.

Broc shrugged. "I can always locate Deirdre with the use of my power."

Galen drummed his fingers on the table and said, "We'll need you to do just that, my friend."

There was a crackle of tension as Fallon focused his gaze on Ramsey. Saffron glanced at Ramsey who sat to her left a little ways from her. He returned Fallon's stare with nonchalance, as if he were testing Fallon in some way.

"I think it's time you told us who the male Druid from Torrachilty Forest is," Fallon said.

Ramsey slowly sat up from his reclining position. "You said you trusted me."

"And we do. I'd feel much better if I knew who the Druid was."

"He'll be there," Ramsey vowed.

Saffron had been witness to enough tension between her parents while her father had still been alive to become uncomfortable in the silence that followed.

It was Camdyn who broke the quiet. "We all know Deirdre put Charlie here as a spy. We've no idea how much information she obtained before Arran killed him, but the simple fact of the matter is, we've waited centuries to kill this bitch."

"I agree," Logan said with a gleam in his eye.

Ian nodded. "I'm eager to end her once and for all."

Larena, her hand atop Fallon's, said, "It won't be over then. We'll have Declan."

"One villain is better than two," Quinn stated with a shrug.

Marcail worried her bottom lip with her teeth a moment before she said, "We need to find the spell to bind the gods inside you Warriors. If I had remembered it all before Deirdre tried to kill me then—"

"Shh," Quinn said as he took her in his arms and kissed the top of his wife's head. "We'll find a way."

"And if not, my magic will keep all those mortal immortal inside this shield," Isla said as Hayden took her hand.

Aiden slammed his hand on the table. "And what if we doona want to stay in the castle? What if we want to see the world?"

Saffron looked from Aiden to his parents, Quinn and Marcail. Saffron could see the apprehension in Marcail's turquoise eyes and the resignation in Quinn's green ones.

"I've only asked that you wait until Deirdre, and now Declan, are ended before you leave," Quinn said.

Aiden's jaw clenched, the muscle ticking. "I'll wait. But as soon as they're dead I'm leaving. I doona care what evil suddenly springs up. I'm tired of being caged."

Saffron looked down at her hands to find they were clasped together tightly. A similar conversation between her and her parents had occurred years ago when she had wanted to see the world while her parents wanted her to begin college in Colorado immediately.

"Saffron?" called a male voice she recognized as Galen's.

Her head snapped up to find every eye on her. "Yes?"

"Are you all right?" Galen asked.

She swallowed and forced a smile, a smile she had learned early on in her life to call up when necessary. "I'm fine."

One of Lucan's dark brows rose in response. "We've been calling your name for quite some time, lass."

Saffron licked her lips as embarrassment washed over her. "Apologies. I was . . . somewhere else for a moment. What is it that you need?"

"Have you had any visions?" Fallon asked.

She cleared her throat softly and found an interesting spot on the table to stare at as she said, "No."

Using her thumbnail, Saffron outlined the knot in the wood over and over as she listened to everyone speak of the stone circle. She had been unconscious when they'd learned they needed to go to the Orkney Islands to find Laria. So she sat and listened, blending into the background.

Her stomach grumbled, reminding her it had been hours since she had last eaten. Saffron rose and quietly walked to the kitchen and got some eggs, sausage, and biscuits out of the refrigerator. She had turned on the stove and was cracking the eggs when Fiona walked into the kitchen.

"Would you like some help?" the Druid asked.

Saffron smiled. "That would be nice."

They worked in silence for several moments before Saffron asked, "Do you regret spending all these centuries in the castle as you watched the world change around you?"

"Nay," Fiona said without looking up from cooking the sausage. "My priority was keeping Braden alive at all costs. With Deirdre out there, our only chance was here in the castle where everyone welcomed us. Thanks to Isla's magic, Braden was able to mature while I didn't age. It was more than I could have hoped for, especially since I have very little magic."

"And now Braden isn't aging."

Fiona glanced at Saffron and grinned. "Aye. There are times I see him staring from the battlements. He's been out in the world several times with Aiden, and I know both of them want to see what else is out there. They want to visit the places they see on the Telly. And they want their own women and families."

"But you've kept him here."

"Never. I was made to stay in our village near Loch Awe. Reaghan was also kept there, though for a different reason.

Still, she will attest to how the elders manipulated us into stay-ing when all we wanted to do was leave. Braden has stayed here because he wants to help."

Saffron poured the eggs into the pan, remembering her own desires to see the world. After college she had done just that. She'd had the time of her life until Declan found her.

"Do you think we can really end Deirdre?" Fiona asked.

Saffron began to scramble the eggs. "Everyone has worked tirelessly to attain the artifacts needed to awaken Laria. Some have even lost their lives. So, yes, I do think they can awaken Deirdre's sister." She paused and looked at Fiona. "Then it'll be up to Laria to kill Deirdre."

"Aye," Fiona said with a sigh. "What about Declan? I've heard so many things about him."

Saffron found herself squeezing the handle of the spatula. "Declan is mine to kill."

Out of the corner of her eye she saw the way Fiona's head jerked toward her, but Saffron didn't care. After what Declan did, after the life he had taken from her, she would make him pay.

"That smells delicious," Gwynn said as she checked the biscuits in the oven. "Reaghan said Galen already raided the kitchen this morning, but he's hungry again."

Fiona laughed as the sausage began to sizzle in the skil-let. "Galen is always hungry."

It didn't take long to finish cooking the meal and the others to take it out to the great hall. Saffron felt something in her head shift, a warning that a vision was on its way.

She leaned her hands against the counter and took a deep breath as she closed her eyes. Throughout her life she'd al-ways had visions. Some were so horrific they would leave her with nightmares, and some brought a smile to her face.

Always the visions were about someone other than her-self. Not once had she had a vision about her own future. Nor could she call up the visions on her own.

They came and went like the wind. And normally they came to her when she least expected them.

But more than that, she was tired of people wanting her because she was a Seer. It was the reason Declan had sought her out. The MacLeods might have saved her, but they had seen the wisdom of having a Seer on their side.

Until her blindness had been reversed, Saffron had been powerless to leave. Now she could, but in order to kill Declan she would need the help of those at the castle. So while they were using her, she was using them.

Just when she thought the vision would wait, it slammed into her mind. She heard screams echoing in her head and blood coated the walls. A woman fought against a man who held her back against his chest.

"*Where is she?*"

Saffron's eyes flew open as Declan's voice reverberated in her mind: The images faded, and she felt herself falling.

Suddenly, strong arms were around her and she inhaled the scent of cedar, sizzling power, and man.

Camdyn.

She knew it was him without opening her eyes. His scent, the way he held her. There wasn't another man in all the world who could come close to Camdyn MacKenna.

"I've got you," he whispered close to her ear so no one else could hear.

He alone knew how her body shook after a vision, and how weak she became. He knew because he was always there, always ready to catch her should she fall.

A girl could certainly get used to that, and Saffron feared she'd already become used to it. The thought frightened her. Yet, instead of pulling away, she clung to him as much as her shaky arms allowed.

With one of his hands splayed on her back holding her close against his rock-hard chest, Saffron rested her face in the crook of his neck as his other hand held the back of her head.

She might feel weak, but in Camdyn's arms she knew nothing could harm her. And after all she'd endured with Declan, she was amazed that she could feel that way.

"What was the vision?" Gwynn asked, her Texas accent coming through thick with emotion.

Saffron's heart pounded as she lifted her head to look at Gwynn. "It was Declan."

Without a word Gwynn walked to her and put her hand on Saffron's arm. Gwynn and Logan had had their own run-in with Declan that had nearly cost both of them their lives. Gwynn's father had also been recruited by Declan to translate a magical book, and he hadn't survived.

Saffron held on to Camdyn long after she should have released him. Camdyn didn't move, he simply held her as footsteps approached the kitchen and Danielle appeared. Dani paused, and then rushed to her.

The three of them were the only ones from the U.S. Gwynn was from Texas, Danielle from Florida before she came to live in Scotland after her parents' death, and Saffron from Colorado.

"What did you see?" Dani urged.

Saffron shivered as she recalled the hard sound of Declan's voice, and Camdyn's arms tightened a fraction around her. She rested her head on his chest and closed her eyes as she thought over the vision.

"Declan is looking for someone. Or he will look for her. I don't know her name, or why he wants her," she said and opened her eyes. "But I felt his need to find her, and it was great."

Gwynn leaned back and rubbed her hands up and down her arms.

"Declan's magic is gone," Dani added. "I know because I pulled it from you."

"No one can touch you here," Camdyn said, his deep voice filling the kitchen.

Saffron nodded and tried to believe their words, but it was difficult when she knew in her gut that things with Declan were just beginning.

She looked up and her eyes met Camdyn's dark chocolate eyes. He looked only at her, his gaze penetrating, probing. Utterly captivating.

"You're safe." His voice was smooth and deep. The timbre of it made her blood heat.

And her heart race.

Dani cleared her throat and grabbed the basket of biscuits. "I think we need to take the rest of the food out to the others."

Camdyn took a step back and dropped his arms from around Saffron. "Are you all right?"

Saffron licked her lips and nodded. Camdyn frowned and turned on his heel and left.

"That's a strange one," Gwynn said.

Dani shrugged. "Not so strange. Just . . . quiet and withdrawn. I think there's more to him than anyone realizes."

Saffron merely watched his retreat without adding to the conversation, because she knew there was much more to Camdyn.

CHAPTER
FOUR

Camdyn resumed his seat at the table, inwardly chiding himself for racing to Saffron. Just because he felt the fear in her magic.

He wasn't her protector, nor did she need one in the castle. Especially now that she could see again.

So why had he found himself in the kitchen before he realized what he was doing? Camdyn dearly wished he knew the answer. Whatever it was about Saffron that pulled at him was a damned inconvenience. And he wanted it to stop.

Immediately.

He couldn't concentrate on the tasks at hand with his need so close to the surface and surging to life whenever she was near.

"What's this about a vision?" Larena asked when Saffron, Dani, and Gwynn emerged from the kitchen.

Saffron swallowed, nonplussed by the knowledge that Larena's advanced hearing, as well as that of the rest of the Warriors in the castle, had enabled her to hear about the vision.

"I saw Declan," Saffron said as she took her seat. "He was looking for a woman, and it was important. He was . . . anxious to find her."

"That doesna bode well," Galen said around a mouthful of food.

Saffron dished some eggs onto her plate before passing it on. "As I've told you all before, what I see in my visions is always incomplete. I don't know when it will occur or if it's something that has already happened."

"But you do know he's looking for someone," Ian said.

"It appears so," she answered. She sighed and licked her lips. "The female he was questioning feared him. Immensely. She's older, so the woman he searches for could be her daughter or niece."

Marcail leaned forward to look at Saffron. "You didn't happen to get a name, did you?"

"No. I just saw Declan, the woman, and someone holding her. Declan was furious and irritated." Saffron paused, her brow furrowed. "Almost as if he needed to find this other woman soon."

"Let us know if you learn any more, Saffron," Fallon said. "The more we know about Declan the better."

Camdyn watched her eyes harden and her lips flatten out of the corner of his eyes. He understood Saffron's anger. He had his own for Deirdre. If anyone was justified in killing Declan it was Saffron, for the spells and torture he put her through for those years. And God only knew what else the demented man had done to her.

Camdyn knew how vicious her nightmares were. The terror and dread that mingled with her magic when she was caught in a nightmare left Camdyn ill at ease. Agitated.

At least now he no longer felt that thread of *drough* magic mingled with Saffron's. He never thought anyone could rival Deirdre's black magic, but Declan, it seemed, came mighty close.

That Declan had been able to penetrate Saffron's mind and mix with her magic had definitely made Camdyn wary. But despite all that Declan had done to her, Saffron was steadfast in her views and her magic.

Declan might have taken her eyesight and her life for those years, but he hadn't dampened her spirit or destroyed her magic.

Although Camdyn would have liked to learn more

about what Declan had done to Saffron, everyone's attention was focused on getting to Laria and ending Deirdre. So his curiosity would have to wait. Which was probably for the best since he didn't trust himself to get too close to her.

Whenever he did, he wanted to hold her as he'd done in the kitchen. Granted, she'd been about to fall, but he'd held her much longer than he had needed to.

He fisted his hands as he thought about how she had trembled, her hands clutching at his shirt as she buried her head in his neck.

He recalled the feel of her curves against him, her breath against his skin. It was too much for a man that hadn't allowed himself pleasure in a very long time.

The need was tantalizing, the desire irresistible. The hunger . . . absolute.

How easy it would have been to tilt up her chin, to seal his lips over hers. Her hands had been eager to grasp him, and her body had molded to his.

"I think we should go back to the Ring of Brodgar right now," Arran said as he finished the last bite of his breakfast and pushed his plate away.

Reaghan set down her fork slowly before she looked at Arran. "My father told me there was a secret passage in order to get into the maze."

"The same father who told you Laria was buried in the mountains?" Broc asked. There was no anger in his voice as he repeated what Reaghan had told them after being released from her spell.

Reaghan shrugged. "I don't know how to answer that, Broc. Whenever he spoke of Laria it wasn't to say where she was buried, but what I would need to awaken her."

Galen put his hand atop his wife's and met Broc's gaze. "I've thought of that also, my friend. I suspect Reaghan's father knew she would go from artifact to artifact until she found the map hidden in the Tablet of Orn as Logan and Gwynn did."

"The stone rings have always been revered," Camdyn

said. "They are places of significant magic. It makes sense
to have put Laria inside one instead of a mountain."

Reaghan smiled at him before she said, "The spell I used
to erase my memories was meant to keep information from
Deirdre. It could be that if she discovered something, all
she might have gleaned was that Laria was buried in the
mountains."

"Thereby sending her on a wild-goose chase," Broc finished with a slight smile. "I doona fault your father, Reaghan.
I merely want to make sure we doona find ourselves on
something like that."

"We're all in agreement there," Fallon said. He looked at
each person at the table and sighed. "I'm more than ready to
end Deirdre. I have to agree with Arran on this. I think we
need to go there now and find our way in."

Lucan leaned back in his chair and put his arm around
Cara. "We know Deirdre hasna been there. Broc, where is
she?"

Camdyn and the others watched as Broc closed his eyes.
At one time, all Warriors had to call up their gods and trans-
form before they could use their magic. But the longer a
Warrior housed a god, the stronger that power became until
it was part of the Warrior just as breathing was.

Broc had had centuries to master his god and his power,
so all he needed to do was to call up that power.

"She's in her mountain," Broc said after several moments
of silence. He opened his eyes and smiled. "We should do it
now. She willna be expecting it."

Fallon nodded and stood, his chair sliding back on the
stones. The sound of the other chairs scraping back filled the
hall as everyone gained their feet.

"I'll bring everyone in groups. The castle will be safe and
hidden with Isla's magic."

"Nay, Aiden," Quinn said when his son also rose.

Aiden clenched his jaw. "I want to help."

Fallon raised his hand before Quinn and Aiden could
bicker more. "As leader here, Aiden, I need you, Braden,
Fiona, and Kirstin to remain behind."

"I think they should come," Saffron said into the silence that followed Fallon's decree.

Camdyn's gaze shifted to Fallon for his response.

Fallon's brows lifted. "And why is that? Did you have a vision of this?"

"It doesn't take a Seer to know that every Druid will be needed there, regardless of how much magic they hold. Even the tiniest drop of magic could make the difference in this battle."

Fallon blew out a breath. "Point taken. Aiden, Braden, Kirstin, and Fiona, prepare to leave with the others."

Saffron released the breath she had been holding and moved with the others as they put on their coats and grouped together as Fallon requested. Fallon was the leader, and though he liked to get others' opinions on matters, he had already made a decision.

She had countered that and, fortunately for her, it had gone well. Even if it hadn't, she knew she had to speak her mind.

While she tugged on a coat and scarf, Saffron found herself watching Fallon as Larena, Lucan, Cara, Quinn, and Marcail stood in a circle, each of them with a hand on the person's shoulder next to them.

She had heard the others talk about Fallon's power of teleportation. Or jumping as they called it. Now she would finally witness it for herself.

With a smile and a kiss on Larena's lips, Fallon put his hands on Larena's and Lucan's shoulder. And in the next instant they were gone.

Before Saffron could blink, Fallon had returned and the next group stepped forward.

Her mind was still reeling from how fast he moved from place to place when Fallon called her toward the group that consisted of Logan, Gwynn, Ian, Dani, and Camdyn.

Saffron walked to the open spot between Camdyn and Fallon, her heart in her throat. Fallon had jumped her from Declan's mansion to the castle when they rescued her, but she had been so happy to be free, not to mention blind, she hadn't realized what was going to happen.

"You willna feel a thing," Fallon said with a grin.

She nodded and met Gwynn's gaze across from her. Gwynn winked as Fallon placed his hand on Saffron's shoulder. In the next instant Saffron found herself standing on a snow-covered peninsula with water on either side.

Her head swiveled to Fallon only to see him disappear.

Saffron blinked as the bright sun hurt her eyes. She lifted a hand to shield her eyes as she desperately tried to see all that was around her.

A large shadow crossed in front of her, blocking the sun. She dropped her hand and looked up to find Camdyn.

"Better?" he asked.

"Better. Thank you."

He shrugged. "Your eyes are still adjusting. I think it will take a while for them to mend fully."

"I don't like appearing weak."

A dark brow rose in response. "Is that what you believe we will think? You survived Declan. Give yourself some credit."

She shifted her feet in the snow, causing their hands to brush. A current of something primal, needful, zoomed through her. Saffron sucked in a breath and glanced away from him.

"Do I frighten you?" he asked.

Her gaze jerked back to him. "Frighten me? Of course not. Why would you think that?"

"You try no' to look at me."

If he only knew the real reason.

Saffron cleared her throat while she shook her head. "I awoke just a few hours ago to find I had my sight back, Camdyn. I'm simply trying to take everything in. I meant no offense."

"Of course."

He lifted his gaze over her head, but Saffron couldn't stop staring at him. She knew he felt it, knew she should stop. But she couldn't.

Camdyn drew her gaze and her body. She forced herself to look away and took the time to look around her. The higher the sun climbed, the less Camdyn's tall, muscular form would be able to help her.

It had been so long since Saffron had seen the world. She would bet her sizable fortune that in the summer the grass was a brilliant shade of green. It was too bad she couldn't see it now since it was covered in snow, but the glorious blue sky together with the dark blue waters of the loch was a sight to behold.

"So many have gone," Reaghan said in distress.

Saffron whirled around to find herself staring at a huge ring of standing stones. She quickly counted twenty-seven standing, but there were spaces where many more should have stood.

"Look at where the stones are placed," Lucan said. "No snow, weeds, or anything, but the grass grows there."

Saffron sucked in a breath when she spied the bright green grass between and around the stones. It made a perfect circle, leaving the middle and the outside piled with snow.

"Magic," Camdyn whispered from behind her, his voice deep and seductive. "Can you feel it?"

Saffron wasn't sure who he spoke to, but she nodded. "It's so strong even I feel it. I've never felt anything like it."

"I have," Galen said.

Logan nodded. "At Loch Awe, and then again on the Isle of Eigg."

In a matter of seconds Fallon had everyone at the Ring of Brodgar. Saffron closed her eyes and lifted her face to the sun. The warmth of it seeped into her skin and made her smile.

Camdyn's presence behind her only made her more aware of her surroundings. And him. His cedar and power scent made her skin tingle, made her think of dark nights, tangled sheets, and cries of pleasure.

She couldn't keep her eyes closed for long though. She wanted to see everything. In all her travels over Scotland before Declan had found her, she had seen much, but she had never seen the Orkney Isles. And she had missed out on a treasure for sure.

"It's so beautiful here. So peaceful. Its almost as if you can feel the history and magic of this land standing beside you," she whispered.

Camdyn's dark eyes came to rest on her as he came to stand next to her. "Aye."

He stood so close she could lean against him, but somehow she held back. She might turn her face away from him, but her body knew where he was at all times.

They were clustered in a group watching as Reaghan paced back and forth. Galen was trying to talk to her, but she kept shaking her head.

Saffron grew uncomfortable as she realized how exposed they were out in the open. She had grown used to the safety of the castle. Now, there were just the stones. There wasn't a tree in sight to hide behind.

"We're safe," Camdyn said, reading her mind.

She snorted, not believing him. Saffron had learned her lesson with Declan. She wouldn't be caught unawares again.

By anyone.

"You think I lie?" Camdyn asked with such confusion it almost made her smile.

She shook her head instead. "I think you will say what you need to say in order to make me feel safe. You think because you're a Warrior you can battle anything."

"Because I can. I've battled Deirdre many times."

"Maybe. But you haven't battled Declan. He's a modern man, Camdyn. He fights differently. He'll come at you in ways you'd least expect."

"I'd like him to try."

"I'm sure he will."

Camdyn's lips lifted in a cruel smile. "Then I'll finish him."

CHAPTER
FIVE

Saffron didn't get a chance to say more as Reaghan's distress became more obvious.

"What is it?" Fallon asked when Galen finally took Reaghan in his arms.

Reaghan lifted her head and tucked a thick strand of auburn hair behind her ear as the wind picked up. "I can't find the entrance. Too many stones have toppled."

"What are you looking for exactly?" Cara asked.

Reaghan shrugged and stepped out of Galen's arms. "I don't know. I should recognize it, or at least that's what my father told me."

"Let's get closer to the stones," Galen suggested. "Maybe there you will be able to sense something."

Saffron followed the path in the snow made from everyone's footsteps. Behind her was Camdyn. Near her once more. As frightened as she was to be out in the open, he was right. She did feel safe with him close to her.

She glanced over her shoulder to find his gaze on her. Goose bumps raced over her skin that had nothing to do with the cold. She huddled deeper into her coat and faced forward once more.

But even that didn't stop her from feeling his gaze.

The closer they came to the massive stone ring the more the ancient magic washed over her. She inhaled deeply, feeling the magic fill her lungs and body. It was heady, un-like anything she had ever experienced.

Would she have felt it had she come here before Declan had taken her? It was rare for a Druid to feel magic, but with magic as strong as what was in the stones, Saffron suspected that anyone would feel it.

"It is said all of Britain once felt like this," Sonya said.

Saffron looked to the redheaded healer and saw Sonya's eyes closed and Broc staring at her with such love and devo-tion that Saffron had to look away. Embarrassed to have caught a glimpse of something so private.

And why was it that her first thought after witnessing the couple's love was of Camdyn? Was it because Saffron wanted the same kind of love herself? Or was she so messed up from her confinement and torture that she was clinging to the first person who had helped her?

Saffron inwardly shook her head. It was hard to know. What she did know was how good it felt to be held by him. It was a dangerous thing, the desire she felt.

Once they were at the edge of the snow that bordered the grass around the stones, everyone fanned out. Saffron wasn't surprised when Camdyn stayed by her. No one said anything as the wind picked up and clouds passed quickly above them.

Saffron kept her eyes on the ground, glancing up for only seconds at a time. She hated how her eyes hadn't adjusted yet. This was worse than being blind. Everything she longed to see was right in front of her, but the pain from the sun-light was too much for her eyes to take.

"It's just stones," Camdyn murmured. "The same stones you saw from afar. Stones and snow."

She shifted her gaze to look at the black combat boots he wore. He stood with his feet braced apart. She didn't need to look at him to know he was on alert, ready and waiting for whatever action came his way.

He was a warrior in every sense of the word. Coiled within him was a tangible violence that would have put her off years earlier. Now, she found it exhilarating, thrilling to be around someone so virile and dangerous.

But with Camdyn, there was more. She couldn't put her finger on it though. He wouldn't have a god inside him if he wasn't a formidable warrior, but there was something that set him apart from the rest.

A desolation she herself could relate to.

The lull of the stone's magic pulled at Saffron, turning her attention to magic ancient and powerful. It drew her. It lured her.

She was powerless to deny it as she stepped off the snow into the grass. Behind her, Camdyn said her name. But Saffron couldn't stop. She didn't want to stop. She kept walking until she came to the first stone.

Once she was beside it she closed her eyes as the magic began to shine brighter than the sun. With her eyes closed, Saffron stopped trying to see and used her other senses.

A smile pulled at her lips when she heard the magic whispering around her. She put one hand on the stone and gasped when the magic raced through her hand. The force of it, the sheer potency of it, made her sway on her feet.

A soft hand took hers, and Saffron glanced to her left to see Gwynn beside her. One by one the Druids lined up and linked hands between two of the standing stones.

Saffron knew the instant a Druid touched the other stone. The magic singed through her and into Gwynn before rushing through each of them then into the next stone.

She didn't know how long they stood there as the magic took them, but when someone broke away, Saffron felt as if her soul had been ripped from her.

"I know where to get in," Reaghan shouted happily.

Saffron dropped hands with Gwynn and turned to walk back to Camdyn. She lifted her hand to shield her eyes again, blinking rapidly to avoid the light.

Large, strong hands caught her shoulders and moved her to the right. She caught a glimpse of black combat boots, which all the Warriors wore, but she knew by the feel of the hands it was Camdyn who touched her.

Saffron was about to ask someone to escort her to where Reaghan had gone when Fallon appeared before her.

"Larena suggested I get these for you," he said, and held out something for her.

Saffron smiled when she grasped the sunglasses. She let out a sigh when she slipped them on and was able to fully open her eyes. "Thank you."

"No need."

Now that Saffron was able to see, she raised her face to Camdyn. "Are you my keeper?"

"Why would you ask that?"

She shrugged, unsure herself. She liked having him around, but she wanted to know if he was there because he wanted to be, or because . . . he had to be. "I'm no longer blind, but I'm not a hundred percent yet. I'm a hindrance. You Warriors are experienced in battle, so it makes sense that someone would be assigned to stay with me so I don't hamper things if we're attacked."

His gaze never wavered from her, but she saw a muscle in his jaw tick. What was he thinking? She was dying to know, but she suspected that whatever it was, he wasn't going to tell her.

"Most of the others have wives. I'm just making sure that you have what you need. Until you are a hundred percent."

It was a great explanation, and a plausible one. Why then did it hurt that he wasn't with her because he wanted to be? Saffron forced a smile and nodded.

"As I assumed. Shall we join the others?"

She began to walk away when his hand grasped her arm in a gentle, but ironclad, grip. Saffron looked at him, startled to find his brow furrowed.

"I've upset you," he said.

How could he have known that? Saffron was an expert in hiding her emotions. There was no way he could have known she was anything other than happy with his response.

But by the look he was giving her, he knew differently.

"I don't want to be a burden," she admitted. "I want my life back, the way it was before. My eyes will adjust, and until they do, I'll make sure I stay near the others so that I'm not a hindrance to anyone."

"You are no'," he murmured.

It was her turn to frown. "I'm not what?"

"A hindrance." He dropped his hand and took a deep breath, looking beyond her to where the others had gone. "I'm impressed with your courage."

This she hadn't expected. Her mouth dropped open, but before she could respond, he started after the others.

Saffron had no choice but to follow him. She lengthened her strides and hurriedly caught up with him as Reaghan walked southeast around a lone standing stone.

With Saffron half running, half walking, they reached the group. And just when she thought no one had noticed their absence, Ramsey turned and looked at them.

She gave him a smile, and then promptly ignored him and the grin that slowly turned up his lips. "Men," she whispered.

"What was that?" Camdyn asked.

"Nothing."

The huge stone Reaghan walked around stood on a low oval platform with two stumps of stones rising from the ground, signaling that the stone hadn't originally been alone.

"This is the Comet Stone," Reaghan said as she ran her hands over the monolith.

Saffron turned back to the Ring of Brodgar and the entrance caught her eye. She then looked back at the Comet Stone and around it to see the Standing Stones o'Stenness.

Reaghan smiled when she saw Saffron. "Aye," she said. "The Comet Stone and its two sisters that are no longer here were a midpoint between the two stone rings."

"Is this the entrance?" Isla asked.

Reaghan shook her head. "Nay, but I know how to find it."

"How?" Ramsey asked.

Reaghan pointed to the sky. "The entire peninsula we're on is aligned with the stars. Orion's Belt to be exact. Orion's Belt rises and sets in exactly the same place as the sun during the winter."

Camdyn, his arms crossed over his chest, chuckled as he nodded his head in understanding. "If you overlayed Orion's Belt where the stones are, it matches, does it no'?"

Saffron had studied and loved astronomy for as long as she could remember, and she didn't expect anyone to know about overlaying the alignment of Orion's Belt.

She was pleasantly surprised, and found herself looking at Camdyn in a new light. She'd figured him to be all brawn. And she'd assumed wrong.

"Exactly!" Reaghan said with a laugh to Camdyn. "The ancient Celts worshiped the sun and the moon and the stars. Every layout of stones is in direct relation to one of the three. Once you know which it is, you can sometimes divine its secrets."

"Such as?" Saffron asked.

Reaghan winked at Galen. "In this case, the entrance to the labyrinth where Laria awaits."

"What do we need to do?" Hayden asked.

For the first time Reaghan's smile slipped. She glanced at the sky and the clouds rolling in. "Once Orion's Belt rises we wait for the moon. The light of a full moon will shine the way. This was meant to be done during the winter. At no other time does Orion's Belt match up to these standing stones."

"It's two days until the full moon," Quinn said.

Fallon pinched the bridge of his nose with his thumb and forefinger. "Reaghan, are you sure you can no' find another way? I doona want to wait."

"I'm sorry. This was done with magic, Fallon. Magic and the reason why the stones were constructed. It's meant to be difficult so not just anyone could find Laria. If it were summer we'd have to wait until winter. And the landscape has changed in fifteen hundred years. Most of the stones are gone."

"And if one is gone that we need?" Camdyn asked.

Reaghan's apprehensive face said it all.

"We've got time right now," Dani said. "Let's look around."

Logan shook his head. "We're too exposed. I doona like it."

"We have to look sometime," Ian said. "I'd rather do it now than when Deirdre is attacking."

Fallon held up a hand for silence before he turned to Broc. "Is Deirdre still in Cairn Toul?"

Broc closed his eyes, and a moment later they snapped open. "Nay. She's headed north. Whether that means here or no', I doona know."

"It's no' a chance I'm willing to take with Reaghan," Galen said.

"Back to the castle," Fallon said.

A thread of anxiety raced through the Druids, and Saffron couldn't help but feel it as well. She found herself being moved toward Fallon by Camdyn.

"No arguments," Camdyn whispered.

Once she was in the group, Saffron turned and looked back at Camdyn. He gave her a small nod, which was all she saw before she found herself back at MacLeod Castle.

She waited to make sure everyone arrived safely home before she hurried to her room. She stripped out of her borrowed clothes and jacket and climbed into the shower.

Being out and seeing had been wonderful, and she'd enjoyed her banter with Camdyn. Though she had never encountered Deirdre herself, she recognized that she was a formidable enemy.

The fear that had spiked through her at the thought of Deirdre finding them reminded Saffron too much of Declan. It had left her cold all the way to her soul. A coldness she hadn't expected to feel again.

The fear that had taken hold of her had immobilized her. Thankfully Camdyn had been there to get her moving.

Saffron stood under the hot water for a while before she found herself reaching for the shampoo bottle with her eyes closed.

She snapped open her eyes and proceeded to wash her hair and body. It wasn't until she stood outside the shower drying off that she saw the mirror hanging over the sink.

Earlier she'd been too afraid to look in the mirror. But she would have to do so sooner or later. She'd forgotten what she looked like. Oh, she remembered that she had the same tawny eyes as her mother, but she had gotten her father's thick walnut-colored hair.

She wrapped the towel around herself and started for the mirror.

Camdyn knocked on Saffron's door and it creaked open slightly since it hadn't been latched. He grabbed the handle and opened it wider to call out to her when he saw her standing in the bathroom.

The dark blue towel wrapped around her still damp body made his balls tighten and his blood heat instantly. Especially when a droplet of water raced down her thigh, over her knee, and descended down her calf to drop into the rug she stood on.

He licked his lips, his cock growing harder by the moment as desire captured him, claimed him. Seized him.

Damn, he didn't want to be attracted to her, didn't want to feel the burn of need fierce and unyielding in his veins. He didn't want to yearn for her touch, to crave her kiss.

He didn't want to ache for a taste of her, to hunger to have her luscious body beneath him. Especially now that he saw so much of her creamy skin exposed.

Camdyn's hands fisted as he thought of going to her, of pulling her into his arms and turning her face up for his kiss. Would she accept him? Would she welcome the potent desire?

His thoughts skidded to a halt when he saw her reflection in the mirror. She took tiny steps toward the mirror, her eyes downcast as if she were afraid to look up.

When she bumped into the sink, she gripped the porcelain until her knuckles turned white. And then, slowly, she raised her face with her eyes still closed.

Her breathing was labored, the pulse at her throat erratic. Camdyn couldn't take his eyes off her as she gathered her nerve to face herself. His desire faded as worry and concern filled him.

He wanted to go to her, to help her, but this was something she had to do on her own. Camdyn found himself holding his breath as she kept her eyes closed, her body as still as a statue.

And then her eyes suddenly flew open. A heartbeat later they filled with tears before overflowing her eyes and falling down her cheeks.

Camdyn frowned, wondering what could be so upsetting. She was beautiful, and made more so by the determination and resolve to get her life back.

Realization dawned when she touched her cheek, nose, lips, and chin as if seeing herself for the first time.

And she was. It had been over three years since she had looked at herself in a mirror. Camdyn wondered what she was thinking. Did she see the same high cheekbones, the same full, kissable lips, and the same determined chin? Did she see eyes of a wild tawny hue that had always transfixed him?

Did she see the woman he knew her to be?

Her hands then smoothed over her clearly visible collar-bones. Her fingers stopped at an old half-moon scar on her left shoulder.

When her hands went to her hair and her face began to crumble, her shoulders shaking with the force of her tears, Camdyn knew Saffron didn't like what she saw. He could no longer stand back and watch. But just as he started toward her, he heard someone approach.

With the quickness and stealth of a Warrior, he disappeared before anyone could see him.

Saffron jumped when Dani called out her name as she walked into the room. No matter how quickly she swiped at the tears, Saffron knew Dani had seen them.

"Oh. Sorry," Dani said sheepishly. "Your door was open."

"It's all right," Saffron said as she moved away from the hated mirror.

Dani held out a blow-dryer. "I thought you might need this."

"It's been so long. Not sure if I know how to use it," Saffron said with a forced laugh.

"I've no doubt it'll come back to you. You're gorgeous, Saffron. I'm sure you were one of those girls in school I envied because they were able to do their hair in all the styles that were popular. Mine did this," she said as she lifted a lock of her straight, silvery-blond hair.

But her words reminded Saffron that she had something else to deal with. Her mother and stepfather. "It's amazing what money can do." She hadn't meant for the anger to come out, but her words were laced with it.

"I didn't mean—" Dani started.

Saffron held up a hand. "I'm sorry. I shouldn't have said anything. It's just that people were my friends because of my money. I didn't realize it still upset me."

"I'm your friend because you're a good person and a Druid. We have a destiny to help these Warriors end Deirdre. But you aren't just my friend. Every woman here is like a sister to me. Please remember you are one of us."

Now Saffron felt lower than a slug. Before she could apologize again, Dani was gone. Saffron squared her shoulders and spent the next ten minutes blow-drying her hair and devising a plan of action.

There was time before she would be needed to awaken Laria. Time for her to take care of family business.

CHAPTER
SIX

Saffron rolled up the waist of the borrowed burgundy sweats and hastily yanked on a sweatshirt. She walked soundlessly in her socks next door to Ian and Dani's room.

She heard Dani's laughter as she raced to the door, with Ian saying something in his low, deep voice that had Dani laughing again.

The door suddenly opened and Dani gave her a big smile. "We're about to start a movie, want to watch? I'm still getting Ian acclimated to this time. We watched *Die Hard* last night, which, of course, he loved. Something about men and blowing things up." Dani shook her head, but she was still smiling. "We're going to watch *Pride and Prejudice* tonight."

Dani leaned in close and whispered, "I have a feeling Ian won't enjoy this one as much."

Saffron couldn't help but smile. It had been so very long since she'd watched a movie. She used to love going to the movie theaters every week, seeing two shows back to back sometimes.

"Thank you, but no," Saffron said. "Actually, I came to ask if I could borrow your cell."

"Cell?" Dani said, her face scrunched up. Then she chuckled as she turned away from the door and walked to a bench where her purse sat. "Ah, you mean my mobile phone.

I know I was raised in Florida for several years, but I've gotten used to the British way of saying things."

Saffron gave a nod to Ian when she found him staring at her.

"Is everything all right, Saffron?" Ian asked.

She plastered on a fake smile and nodded. "Of course. I just have a few calls to make."

Dani walked back to the door and held out her iPhone to Saffron.

She took the phone and held it for a moment before she said, "I'm going to have to make some overseas calls. I'll pay you for the charges."

"No," Dani said. "We're sisters here. We may not be blood, but we're bonded by magic, which goes just as deep. Make your calls, Saffron, and don't worry about the charges."

Saffron smiled her thanks and returned to her room. She wasn't used to the kindness she had been shown at MacLeod Castle ever since she had arrived.

Why did she have to go halfway around the world and be abducted for three years by a deranged psychopath before she found the type of friends she had always longed for?

Saffron closed her door and walked to the bed as she stared at the cell phone. "Mobile," she said, mimicking Dani's Scottish brogue.

She smiled, but the smile soon faded as her stomach knotted with the realization she was going to have to make calls she'd rather not make.

But she'd start off easy. The first call went to her attorney, the same attorney her father had used in all his business and personal matters.

Saffron dialed the number she had known since she had been old enough to dial a phone. It took a moment for the call to connect. Three rings later, she heard the soothing, cultured voice of Arthur Myles, attorney extraordinaire.

"Arthur," Saffron said, and felt a huge weight lift off her shoulders just by saying his name.

"Saffron," he whispered, the surprise evident in the catch of his voice. "Is that really you, girl?"

He had always called her "girl" from the moment of her birth. Arthur and her father had been the best of friends growing up in Colorado, and that friendship had continued through the years.

"It's me," she said. "It's really me."

"But your mother has filed papers to have you declared legally dead. It's been three years since anyone has heard from you. Even I thought the worst when I saw nothing had been purchased with your credit cards, girl."

She blew out a breath and squared her shoulders. "I'm very much alive, Arthur. I need you to stop my mother's filing immediately."

"Of course. However, people are going to want to see you in person as proof. Especially Elise."

Saffron cringed at the mention of her mother's name. "I know. And I'm prepared to make myself available to you and a judge, if necessary."

Arthur paused, a soft sigh sounding through the phone. "You have no intention of seeing Elise?"

"Do you really need to ask that?"

"No," he said with a grunt. "I suppose not. Can you at least tell me where you are?"

"I'd rather not. Not yet. I'll be in touch soon."

"Take care, girl. It's good to hear your voice," he said, and the line went dead.

Saffron ended the call and rubbed the back of her neck, which had begun to ache. A stress headache was just what she needed, she thought with a roll of her eyes.

The next fifteen minutes were spent on the phone with her credit card companies getting new cards issued as well as obtaining a new cell phone. Since all the bills were paid automatically out of her bank account, no cards had lapsed, which was fortunate for her.

With all the calls made, there was only one thing left to do.

Saffron once more left her room. She gave Dani's iPhone back to her before she continued down the corridor and up a flight of stairs to the master chamber.

Fallon wasn't going to be happy with what she wanted, but he wouldn't have a choice in the matter.

She gave a quick knock on the thick wooden door. It was opened almost immediately by Fallon.

"Saffron."

"I'd like a word, please," she said.

He stepped aside and motioned for her to enter.

Saffron glanced around the spacious chamber, noting that even though the stone walls had been kept, everything else had been modernized.

The bed was a king-sized four-poster bed with simple yet elegant dark bronze and pale gold bedding. On the bedside table were two iPods charging. A medieval tapestry still hung on the wall, but there was also art from almost every era that Fallon and Larena had lived in.

There was a large flat-screen TV and a deep brown leather couch where Larena lounged, and a thick rug, in a soft cream color, in front of it. All in all the room was cozy and comfortable. The mix of the past and present was one that worked well.

"I'll leave you two," Larena said as she started to rise from the couch.

Saffron held out a hand to stop her. "There's no need. Everyone knows what happened to me and what my mother is trying to do."

"I still can no' believe it," Fallon said as he leaned against the footboard of his bed and crossed his arms over his chest.

Saffron snorted as anger flared inside her. "You don't know my mother or what money can do to people."

"That's what this is about?" Larena asked as she swept her golden-blond hair back away from her face. With a few twists of her hands it was set in a loose bun at the base of her neck.

"Yes." Saffron was embarrassed to admit it, but then again, her mother had only married her father for the money. Elise had never intended to get pregnant, but for a fluke of Fate. That fluke had been Elise taking cold medicine while also using the pill. They had canceled each other out, and the next thing Elise knew, she was pregnant.

Saffron was surprised Elise hadn't gotten an abortion. But she'd had no idea she was pregnant, she'd thought she was only sick. Saffron knew it was only by the grace of God that her father had taken Elise to the doctor and heard the news of her pregnancy himself or Saffron wouldn't be standing there now.

"Saffron?" Larena called.

She shook her head and pulled herself from her memories. "I wanted to let both of you know my plans."

"Of course," Fallon said.

Saffron licked her lips and said, "There are some . . . things . . . I have to take care of in London and Edinburgh, namely my bank and credit card companies and other odds and ends. Since we have some time before we can awaken Laria, I'd like to take this opportunity to do these things."

"Which will in turn prove to your mother and others that you aren't dead," Larena said with a smile.

"Precisely," Saffron said. "My mother will demand proof, so I'm going to give it to her. Now, I know the castle is shielded and can't be found, but I've arranged for a helicopter to pick me up in a few hours."

When Fallon didn't respond, she continued. "Nothing I have here is mine. For three years I was at the whim of a deranged lunatic. I need to find myself again, and not just to prove to everyone I'm alive so my mother can't get to my money. I want to—"

"Shop," Larena said with a bright smile. "I think that would be a wonderful idea. You have your eyesight back, but like you said, you need to find yourself."

Saffron couldn't believe Larena actually understood. She turned her gaze to Fallon. "I won't be long. I promise. The quicker I'm seen, and by the right people, the quicker this thing with my mother will end. I just need to know a location close by so that I can tell the helicopter pilot."

"Nay," Fallon said, and ran a hand through his thick brown

hair. "There's no need for you to hire a helicopter when you have me. Allow me to jump you where you need to go, and it'll be done much quicker."

Saffron blinked, surprised by his offer.

"My love," Larena said as she leaned up to whisper in Fallon's ear, "I think she's astonished by your proposal."

"That she is," Fallon said with a grin.

Saffron mentally shook herself. "I apologize. I'm just used to doing everything for myself."

"You'll find that while you're here we help each other," Larena said as she pulled on a pair of black high-heeled boots.

Fallon watched her with his lips flat. "And where are you going?"

"Shopping with Saffron, of course. She needs a Warrior with her, and who better than me?"

Fallon rolled his eyes, but there was a lopsided smile on his face. "Any excuse to shop, my love."

"Most certainly." Larena's smile was wide as she jumped up and kissed Fallon before turning to Saffron. "Are you ready?"

Excitement rose within Saffron as she nodded. "I am."

Fallon pushed off the bed and started toward the door. "We need to tell the other women. They might want to come as well."

"Tell them," Saffron said as she hurried to the door. "I'm going to change. I'll meet you in the great hall in five minutes."

Saffron didn't wait to hear what was said as she ran to her chamber and yanked off the sweats. She searched for a pair of jeans and boots. A quick brush of her hair and she was out the door again and on her way to the great hall.

To her surprise Gwynn, Dani, Isla, and Marcail were also coming with them.

"We're going to have to do this again once this is all over and I can come," Reaghan said as she glanced up from a map of the Ring of Brodgar. "I'm going to need it."

Cara stuck her head out of the kitchen and frowned. "If I wasn't in the middle of baking bread . . ."

Fallon shook his head while smiling and walked to the group. "Where do you want to go first, Saffron?"

She swallowed, her gaze searching for Camdyn in the great hall. She'd wanted to tell him where she was going, though she had no idea why. But he wasn't to be found. "London. High Street."

"It's a good thing I've been there over the last four centuries," Fallon said as he placed his hand on her shoulder.

The calm of the castle was replaced by thick traffic and so many voices it was hard to hear anything. Saffron looked around and smiled. London. She always loved to shop in London.

"Give us five hours," Larena said as she kissed Fallon. "We'll be waiting here for you."

With a wink, Fallon was gone.

"I can't tell you how convenient his power is," Gwynn said.

They all laughed as they walked from between two buildings out onto the sidewalk.

"Where to first?" Dani asked.

Saffron took a second to get her bearings, then went left. "First stop, my bank. This isn't just a pleasure trip for me. I have to be seen in person in order to halt my mother's claim that I'm dead. There will be some forms I have to fill out from my attorney, which shouldn't take too long. Second stop is a salon. I want a haircut."

"Oh," Larena said wistfully. "And I think I'll get a manicure."

"And a pedi," Gwynn said with a smile.

Saffron hadn't felt this free and sure of herself since she had first landed in Britain four years earlier. This time she had Druids with her, and a Warrior.

Even if the trip wasn't just for fun, she wanted to be there. Being seen at the bank should put a permanent hold on her mother's legal move to declare her deceased. It's too bad Saffron wouldn't be there to see her mother's face when she got the news.

As she walked down the street with her friends, Saffron's

happiness edged away as she faced reality. She had said she needed to find herself, but no amount of shopping or new haircuts would help her with that. Only time would.

And even then Saffron wasn't sure if she would ever find the peace and love she craved so desperately.

CHAPTER
SEVEN

Camdyn knew the moment Saffron left the castle. He was fishing on the beach with both Hayden and Quinn when the feel of her magic simply vanished.

He went on as if nothing had occurred, because if there had been an accident, someone would have come and gotten them. At least that's what he told himself, but he still found himself glancing up at the imposing structure of the castle as it rose from the cliffs.

"What's wrong?" Hayden asked.

Camdyn shrugged. "Nothing."

"You lie poorly," Quinn said with a chuckle before he tossed the net out into the water.

Hayden had already been swimming in the cold depths of the sea and returned with several fish, but Quinn liked to do it the way he and his father had done.

Camdyn adjusted the net in his hands and turned to the side before tossing it out into the water and slowly pulling it back in. "I doona like waiting around is all."

Hayden and Quinn looked at each other and laughed.

Camdyn rolled his eyes. "What now?"

"Have you always been such an awful liar?" Hayden asked with a wide smile and knowing gaze.

Camdyn knew he would have to give them the truth, or at least part of it. "I felt some magic leave."

"Aye," Hayden said with a nod. "Isla's is gone."

"So is Marcail's," Quinn said.

Camdyn looked at them with confusion. "And neither of you are worried?"

Hayden opened his mouth to answer when Fallon's voice reached them from behind. "They needn't be worried. Marcail and Isla went with Larena, Gwynn, Dani, and Saffron to London. To shop."

Quinn shook his head. "I figured it was something like that."

"Shouldn't she have told you?" Camdyn asked. He was baffled by how nonchalant both Quinn and Hayden were, knowing that Deirdre and Declan were still a threat.

He'd expected them to at least go after their women.

Quinn glanced at him with a half smile. "I know Marcail would never put herself in danger. She normally tells me when she leaves, and though I'd like to know before my wife departs the castle, I know through the feel of her magic."

"Saffron didna give them time to tell you or Hayden," Fallon said. "She was bound and determined to leave."

Camdyn's gut clenched at Fallon's words. The thought of never seeing Saffron again was like a sword slicing him in half.

"Why?" Hayden asked, his brow furrowed. "Surely she knows we need her magic."

"She's returning. Besides, there is the issue with her mother that has to be addressed, and Saffron knows this," Fallon said.

Camdyn didn't want to evaluate how much of his worry eased knowing Saffron wasn't alone and that she was returning. Saffron was a distraction he didn't need or want. Regardless of how the sight of her caused his body to flare with desire so great it left him gasping for breath.

"She'd already called a helicopter to pick her up," Fallon said with a chuckle. "I took them instead. Despite all she's been through, she's kept her backbone."

"Stubbornness is more like it," Camdyn grumbled.

Hayden raised a brow. "I think 'stubborn' can be applied to every Druid in the castle."

Camdyn glanced at Fallon. "She should have taken a Warrior with her."

"She did. Larena. Or were you no' listening?" Quinn asked.

Camdyn shook the net from the water and kept his gaze averted from the others. He shouldn't be so upset that Saffron was gone. Except that he knew how much Declan wanted her ability as a Seer. He could very well capture her again.

"With Larena and the other Druids accompanying Saffron she'll be kept safe, Camdyn," Fallon said.

"I know." He did know, and more than that he understood why she had to leave and prove she was alive and well.

"She's been through hell. Literally," Quinn said after a long moment of silence filled only by the crash of the waves. "Nothing here is hers."

"That's what Larena said," Fallon replied.

Hayden nodded. "Saffron pretends everything is fine, but it isna. Declan's magic may be out of her head, but what he did to her will live in her for a long time to come."

"Add on top of that her mother trying to claim she's dead, and us fighting Deirdre, and she's keeping it together better than I would," Quinn said.

"I agree. She's strong, but I'd like for us to keep an eye on her just in case. Camdyn, you seem to have developed a link with her. Keep close to her," Fallon said, and squatted down to pick up a rock. "You should've seen the excitement in her eyes when I left them in London. It lit up her entire face."

Camdyn growled, hating the way his emotions were rioting inside him. He had seen many of Saffron's false smiles. They were kind, but they didn't fully reach her eyes. It was a rare thing when anyone saw true happiness on her face.

But then again, who could blame her after all she had been through?

"She'll be back in a few hours," Fallon said.

Camdyn looked at him. "Why are you telling me?"

Fallon shrugged nonchalantly before he jumped back to the castle. Quinn turned his head, but not before Camdyn saw his smile. The only one who would meet his gaze was Hayden.

"She's pretty," Hayden said. "And wounded. A woman like that could find herself leaning on a man who was willing."

"Saffron doesna lean on anyone. She's a strong woman."

"Aye. So is Isla, but she does lean. And it's a fabulous thing, Camdyn."

Quinn nodded. "Oh, aye. A fabulous thing."

"I seem to remember you warning me about love," Hayden told Quinn with a lopsided grin.

Quinn threw back his head and laughed. "And look where that warning took you."

"To the love of my life," Hayden shouted to the sky with his arms wide.

Camdyn fiddled with the net, pretending there was a knot in it, when in fact there was a knot in his chest. The love of his life died hundreds of years ago. Not once in all that time had a woman ever snagged his attention.

Until Saffron.

He'd hoped it was simply because he'd been the one to free her from Declan. Camdyn had been the only one who had been able to reach her through the magic of the prison.

He'd been the one to carry her from that evil place and to MacLeod Castle.

Could it have been the way she clung to him, her body thin and fragile as he held her? Could it have been the way she ducked her head against his shoulder to hide her tears? Could it have been the nights he had been compelled to pass by her chamber as she cried out from the nightmares?

Whatever it was, he was powerless to keep his distance.

He'd loved once before and had had his heart torn out. Camdyn never wanted to experience that kind of pain again. Ever.

"You're awfully quiet," Hayden said as he grinned at Camdyn. "Each Warrior is finding his mate. Do you fear you'll be next?"

Camdyn looked up from the net as he went down on his haunches. "Nay," he answered.

"Nay?" Quinn asked, his brows raised in question. "What makes you so sure? Love is no' something you can run from, my friend."

"Love is no' for everyone. And I've already loved once."

Hayden frowned, his smile gone. "I didna know."

"It is in the past," Camdyn said with a shrug. "Long ago."

Quinn set aside his net and walked to stand between Hayden and Camdyn. "What happened to her?"

Camdyn briefly closed his eyes and let out a breath. "She died. In my arms. We had years together, but she aged while I stayed the same."

"So she knew what you were?" Hayden asked.

"Aye. I showed her."

Quinn shook his head. "How did you stay away from Deirdre and keep your female safe?"

"I got as far from Deirdre as I could. I was in the lowlands near the border with England," Camdyn said and tossed aside the net. He stood and looked out over the sea.

Hayden clamped him on the shoulder. "You loved her verra much."

"Aye."

Quinn crossed his arms over his chest and rocked back on his heels. "It doesna mean you can no' love again."

Camdyn looked at him. "If Marcail died, if you held her in your arms and watched the life drain from her, could you ever imagine loving again? I willna put myself through that kind of pain a second time."

"But Isla's magic prevents the Druids from aging," Hayden quickly pointed out.

Camdyn released his god. Claws extended from his fingers and fangs filled his mouth. A glance down at his skin showed the same dark brown color as the earth.

He didn't say another word to his friends as he bounded

up the cliff until he landed in the snow. With memories of Allison churning inside him as well as thoughts of Saffron, Camdyn ran into the forest. He ran and ran and ran, never slowing, never looking back.

When he finally stopped, he put his hands on his knees and bent over, his head hanging. He had no idea how long he'd been gone, but he was miles from the castle.

Yet, the run had felt good. It was just the thing to calm him.

Camdyn straightened and looked around. He gazed up at the imposing mountain and the vast land laid out before him. His mind was still in a riot with thoughts of Saffron, and he wasn't yet ready to return.

Instead, he walked. He kept the road at a distance and followed the mountain up and over. And then the next and the next, and the next. Until he realized most of the day had passed.

While he'd been walking, he had kept his mind blank and that had given him a measure of peace. Yet when he saw where the sun was, his first thought was to return to the castle and see Saffron.

Camdyn wished he knew what it was about her that drew him. With a resigned sigh he began to jog back to the castle. With his speed, it didn't take him long to reach the outskirts of MacLeod land. He looked to the sky and saw the moon visible in the blue sky. It was too bad the full moon wasn't that night because he was anxious to put an end to Deirdre.

Anxious and oh, so ready.

He slowed to a walk when he reached Isla's shield hiding the castle. As soon as he walked through it, Saffron's sweet, appealing magic slammed into him so hard Camdyn took a step back.

With a hand over his chest, he paused and let her magic surround him. Enfold him. Embrace him.

Her magic gripped him through his skin to his soul.

And how wonderful it felt. He hated that he yearned to feel her magic more and more each day. The more he felt it the more he wanted it. And the more he was becoming addicted to it.

A very dangerous thing, that.

It wasn't just her magic he longed for either. It was her touch, a look, a smile. Anything.

And the more he fought to stay away from her, the more he felt himself being drawn to her. As if Fate were tugging an invisible line between him and Saffron, pulling them together.

He shook away such thoughts and continued on to the castle. It was a few hours before sunset and supper. He wanted a shower and maybe some time playing the Wii with Broc.

When Camdyn entered the castle, his gaze instantly found Saffron. And he stopped dead in his tracks.

Her hair, which had been all one length and reached midway down her back, had been cut to just below her shoulders. And wisps of hair now graced her forehead. Her nails had a pale pink color on them, but more than that, she was in clothes that made him all too aware of her curves and the woman that wore them.

As if he needed reminding of the desire she caused.

Before, when she was borrowing clothes, everything fit just a little too loosely on her and hid her mesmerizing body. The dark blue jeans she had on fit her to perfection, accentuating her buttocks and long legs.

But it was the dark purple shirt molded to her breasts and abdomen that made his cock instantly, painfully hard. The cream-colored cardigan she wore over the shirt only brought more attention to the full shape of her breasts and her small waist.

Arran let out a low, soft whistle as he came to stand beside Camdyn. "Damn. I always thought Saffron was pretty, but whatever she did in London has made her stunning."

Camdyn moved closer to Saffron while she spoke with Cara and Reaghan and showed them the other things she had bought. He didn't care about her clothes, he just wanted to see all the changes she had had done.

It was something besides her hair and the color on her fingernails. Camdyn looked at her from head to toe, and it wasn't until his gaze moved back up her body that he realized what it was.

She had pink color on her eyelids and color on her cheeks. Even her eyelashes looked longer and thicker than before. And her lips! God help him, but the way her lips glistened made him want to taste her. A long, slow kiss or a hot, frenzied kiss. He didn't care as long as he could feel her mouth beneath his.

Hayden and Quinn were suddenly on either side of him. Both men had their arms crossed over their chests and were staring at Saffron.

"I like the bangs," Quinn said.

"Hm. The makeup is subtle but nice," Hayden added.

Camdyn could take no more. If he didn't leave he was going to do something crazy. Like kiss Saffron.

And kissing was definitely something he couldn't do with her.

He started for the stairs, but as he passed her, she looked up, their eyes clashing. The way her lips subtly turned up in a smile made his blood sing.

She turned toward him, their hands grazing as he passed. Camdyn clenched his jaw and took the stairs three at a time while every instinct, every fiber of his being, urged him to kiss her.

CHAPTER EIGHT

Saffron nodded as she listened to whatever Cara was saying, but her words had faded away the moment she saw Camdyn enter the castle.

She had hastily looked away. Even now she pretended that she didn't notice he was near. And watching her. She didn't understand how her body and senses came alive anytime he was close. As if she were attuned to him on a level far deeper than normal people.

As much as she hated it, she found herself wondering what he thought of her new haircut and the makeup and clothes. He came from medieval times, even though that was difficult to remember sometimes. Their women hadn't worn makeup or cut their hair.

Saffron drew in a deep breath and smiled when Cara stroked her hand over the coral-colored cashmere sweater Saffron had purchased.

"It's stunning," Cara murmured.

Saffron shifted her gaze to Lucan who stood behind and to the side of Cara. Then she mouthed, "Remember this."

Lucan nodded, a slow smile spreading over his handsome face before he stepped near Cara and wrapped his arms around her, nuzzling her neck.

Saffron's clothes were soon forgotten as Cara and Lucan walked away.

"They've always been like that," Marcail said.

Larena rolled her eyes and laughed. "The same can be said for you and Quinn."

"And you and Fallon," Saffron replied.

The two women looked at her, and Saffron shrugged. "I might have been blind, but the deep love between all of you can be felt through other senses."

Marcail laughed and began to gather up bags. "Come on. I'll help you carry up all these bags."

"Don't forget yours," Larena called.

Gwynn hurried and snatched up her own bags. "Or yours, Larena."

As the others walked away, Saffron could hold back no longer and looked at Camdyn. His emotions were closed off from her, but how she longed to know if he approved or not. She hadn't done any of it for him. Yet, it would be nice to know a man appreciated her efforts.

And then Camdyn was coming toward her after something both Hayden and Quinn had said to him. She turned toward him, and just when she thought he would stop, he continued on. But not before their hands touched.

It was the simplest of touches, innocent and accidental. But the contact left her light-headed and aching for . . . more.

Saffron gathered up her bags and walked up the stairs. She waited until she was in her room and everyone else had deposited her bags and left before she slumped against the door.

It had been exhausting going out, but it had felt magnificent. Her eyes hurt from everything, and her feet couldn't wait to get out of the heels. She had bought entirely too much in the way of clothes and shoes. And jewelry and makeup. And even soap and shampoo.

But they were her things, things she chose for herself. It was silly to want such mundane items, but it was the first time she had felt like herself. Like the woman she'd been before Declan kidnapped her.

Saffron had thought that woman gone, but maybe, just

maybe, she was still somewhere deep inside waiting to come out again.

She pushed off the door and began to pull things out of the numerous bags. It was the first time in a long time that she was glad she had the money her father left her. And it was a massive sum of several million dollars.

Money her mother desperately wanted.

Saffron refused to think about her mother as she sorted through the makeup she had bought. She was putting it away on the shelf in the bathroom when a knock sounded on her door.

"Come in," she called.

The door creaked open as she put the last bit of makeup down. Saffron walked out of the bathroom to find Fallon standing in her doorway.

"Thank you," she said. "I'm not sure I told you, but I do appreciate you jumping me to London and Edinburgh."

Fallon smiled and leaned against the door frame. "As Larena said, you needed it. I hope you doona think I'm trying to keep you here."

"Not at all," she said with a wave of her hand. "I know you worry about all the Druids. Right now isn't a good time to be out and about with us getting ready to awaken Laria."

"And what of Declan?"

She stiffened at the mention of the hated name. "I don't fear him, if that's what you're asking."

"It's no'. It's merely a question. He's out there and a danger."

"You don't need to remind me of that. Until he's dead, until I kill him myself, I'll always be reminded of him."

"You intend to kill him yourself?"

She smiled at hearing the surprise in his voice. "You don't think I can?"

"I didna say that," he replied, his hands held palm out in front of him. "We all saw what Declan did to Logan and Gwynn."

"You mean his mercenaries. Where Deirdre had Warriors, Declan has resorted to mercenaries to carry out his

unpleasant tasks. He wouldn't want to get his perfectly man-
icured hands dirty with such menial jobs."

"What did he do to you, Saffron?"

She turned away and pulled other items out of the bags to
layout on her bed. "Nothing I can't handle."

"Marcail has the ability to take away your pain if you
need her to."

Saffron jerked her head around to pin Fallon with a glare.
"I've carried this around with me for over three years, Fallon. I can handle it."

His eyes lowered to the ground for a moment as he nodded. When he next met her gaze he said, "If you change
your mind, just come to me."

Saffron went back to pulling out her new items as the
door clicked shut behind her.

All through Camdyn's shower he could feel the turmoil in
Saffron's magic a level below him. It made it difficult for
him to concentrate as her magic went from contentment to
anger to regret to anxiety.

He turned off the water and began to towel himself dry.
The shower with the nearly instant hot water was something
he had come to love immediately in this new time.

The clothes had been a different story. Giving up his kilt
was something he had done willingly to fit in with the new
time and culture. But still, he missed seeing the bold red,
black, and blue tartan of his clan.

It still felt odd to have something around his legs, but he
was getting used to the different pants. He pulled on a pair
of faded jeans and a tee.

He padded barefoot out of his chamber, only stopping
when he reached the corridor. There was nothing he could
do to help Saffron now. Going to her and asking her what
was wrong would only let her know that he felt her magic
differently.

Instead, he headed to Broc's chamber for some more video
games. Broc's chamber, however, was on the same level as
Saffron's.

Camdyn walked down the stairs and took a right to Broc's chamber instead of the left which would take him to Saffron's. As he neared Broc's room he passed Ian's where Dani was trying to explain some game that was on the telly. Rugby or was it soccer? He couldn't remember.

It wasn't until he knocked on Broc's door and there was no answer that Camdyn turned and stared down the long hallway toward Saffron's chamber.

Most of the couples in the castle were spending time together, alone. Which left as his options Ramsey, Arran, Fiona. Or Saffron. Even Braden and Aiden had taken an interest in Kirsten and rarely left her side.

Camdyn frowned as he thought of the newest Druid at the castle. There was something strange about Kirsten, but he couldn't put his finger on it.

Another glance at Saffron's door and the struggle to go to her or not remained. What would he accomplish if he went? He'd never been good with words, and he wouldn't do as his body urged and kiss her since he didn't want to complicate anything. So what was the point?

He shook his head and started retracing his steps back to his chamber. There were a few books he wanted to read, movies waiting for him to watch, and even his iPod Touch was filled with songs.

Camdyn smiled as he walked into his chamber and saw the flat-screen television and other modern accessories that seemed so foreign in the castle, yet at the same time looked as if they belonged.

He wasn't surprised technology had advanced so much, not after all the magic he had seen in his lifetime. With a click of the remote the telly was turned on.

Camdyn plopped in his chair and tried to concentrate on the movie and not think about the delectable images of Saffron as she stood in her towel, her body still wet from her shower.

Deirdre drummed her fingers on her beloved stones. Touching the rocks helped to keep her calm, and calm was exactly what she needed now.

She had used her magic to divine where Malcolm was. His task had been easy. Go to Edinburgh, find the Druid posing as a teacher, and kill all the children to flush her out. Then, Malcolm was to bring the Druid to her.

Yet, somehow, Malcolm had ended up in Glasgow. Without the Druid.

No one, not even Malcolm, could botch up a mission and not be punished for it. She had been waiting nearly three days for him to return, and her patience was growing perilously thin.

The screech of a wyrran behind her told Deirdre someone had come. She kept her back to them as she looked out over the vast cavern that had held hundreds of wyrran and dozens of Warriors before Declan had pulled her forward in time.

"The MacLeods got to the Druid," Malcolm said.

Deirdre gripped the stones with both hands as rage boiled within her. First they killed her spy, Charlie, and now they got to the Druid first. The MacLeods had been a thorn in her side since the day she unbound their god.

She had thought to keep them in her mountain, but she hadn't counted on their strength. Before she knew it, they had escaped.

Then they set about killing her pets, the wyrran, and recruiting other Warriors and Druids in their bid to kill her. She had gained a leg up when she had captured Quinn. Quinn had always been the one she wanted, the one she had wanted by her side to rule. The one she wanted to father the child of prophecy. A child of both her and him.

But Quinn's brothers, Lucan and Fallon, and the rest of the Warriors at the castle had stormed into her mountain. All because Broc had betrayed her.

They even managed to kill her body, but her magic had been too strong and her spirit remained until she was given another body by the Devil.

"Deirdre."

"I heard you," she said, and whirled around to face Malcolm. Her white hair, which hung to the floor, swirled around her, twitching with her anger. "It was a simple mission I sent you on. You said you had no problem killing children."

"I didna, nor do I. The MacLeods, along with Broc and Isla, were already in Edinburgh when I arrived. They had found the Druid before I did," Malcolm said.

"So they have her."

"Nay."

Deirdre perked up at hearing this. "Really? Where is she?"

Malcolm shrugged, his expression bored. "She's gone, and Fallon dumped me in Glasgow. Find another Druid."

"There are so few!" She clenched her jaw as she fought to keep her rage in check.

One side of Malcolm's lip lifted in a sneer. "You have powerful black magic, Deirdre. Use it."

She glared at him, wondering not for the first time if she had made a mistake unbinding his god. Malcolm had a strong tie with the MacLeods since his treasured cousin, Larena, was married to Fallon MacLeod.

Deirdre had used that connection between Malcolm and Larena to lure him to her side. She had used her magic to erase the ugly scars on his face and right side of his body. Even though it had been her order to her Warriors that had given him those scars. But that was before she realized he could house a god.

It was Malcolm's need to keep Larena safe that kept him from doing as she commanded. Since she no longer had the Warriors that used to fill her mountain, Malcolm was her strength.

"Where's Charlie?" Malcolm asked. "Should he no' be here by now?"

"My same thoughts. I found him by using my magic. He's dead."

Malcolm didn't even blink at her comment.

Charlie had been her only other Warrior, but he'd allowed himself to be caught spying at MacLeod Castle. All he'd had to do was return to her with the artifacts. Which he should have done easily.

She'd have punished him for taking his time returning to her if he wasn't already dead.

If she had those artifacts no one would ever be able to awaken Laria. And Deirdre could once more focus on ruling the world as she had longed to do.

As she had been promised would be hers by Satan.

But now everything had changed. Now the MacLeods had the artifacts. And they were set on waking Laria.

CHAPTER
NINE

It was past ten that evening when Saffron left her room to go for a walk. She had been sitting in her room with the lights off, which was easier on her eyes.

During her shopping trip, she purchased five pairs of sunglasses so she'd never be without one. But even they didn't always help her eyes adjust to the sun or some bright indoor lights. And flashing lights were another matter entirely.

The lights inside the castle and other places could hurt her more than the sun. To give her eyes a rest and to help the pounding that had begun in her temples, she'd sat and listened to her iPod for a couple of hours.

She had spotted the moon out her window and couldn't get outside quick enough. She had always loved the moon, thinking it used to follow her when she was a child.

The stars fascinated her. For her eighth birthday she had requested a telescope and astronomy books. From that first look through the telescope to see the moon she'd been hooked.

She gobbled up anything and everything to do with the stars, the solar system, and astrology. Her telescopes became larger so she could see farther.

As Saffron bundled up in her new wool coat and stepped out onto the battlements she wished she had a telescope with her at the castle. Maybe on her next trip she'd purchase one.

She lifted her face and smiled when she saw the blink of

stars through the clouds drifting lazily over her. How she had missed them. Back in Colorado, she would lie in the yard and spend her evenings staring at the sky.

The moon hung just shy of being full, its light making the snow look as if it were glowing. Saffron ran her hand over the stones of the battlements.

She had been on the battlements several times and learned the shape and size of them with her hands. But she had never seen them.

With a slow, measuring look, she took in the gatehouse, bailey, and even part of the castle. In the darkness of night the stones looked dark gray, but nothing could hide the magic inside them.

The towers, four that she could see, but she knew there were six, rose high above her. The bailey now held SUVs and cars when it had originally seen nothing but horses and people.

As her gaze raked over every stone, she saw the remnants of burns. Saffron squatted down on the battlements and ran her hands over burn marks.

She knew the story of how the entire MacLeod clan had been murdered by Deirdre while Fallon, Lucan, and Quinn had been away meeting Fallon's intended bride. By the time the brothers returned, everyone was dead and their home burning.

Saffron wondered how the MacLeods had been able to live after that, especially with their god unbound and giving them powers. But then again, the brothers had stayed holed up in their castle for several centuries before Cara came into the picture.

As she recalled Cara's story of slipping over the cliffs before Lucan caught her, Saffron stood and turned to the sound of the waves.

No matter how hard Saffron looked, she couldn't see the waves crashing into the beach from her vantage point. But she was able to see the vast sea stretch into the horizon and she saw sheer cliffs on either side of the castle that descended far below her.

"Is it what you thought it would be?"

She whirled around at the sound of Camdyn's voice but couldn't find him. She searched the shadows until he finally stepped out of them. The darkness clung to him, as if it didn't want to let him go.

She drank in the sight of him beneath the blue light of the moon. His eyes were hooded, his face set in hard lines, yet his voice had been soft, questioning. "It's more stunning than I could have ever imagined."

Camdyn nodded as he came to stand beside her. He wore no coat over his thin, short-sleeved tee. "There is a path to get down to the beach, but I wouldna suggest trying it out the first time at night. It's rather steep."

"Thanks for the warning."

He lifted one shoulder in a half shrug. "Were you no' happy with what you saw of yourself when your sight returned?"

Though he didn't look at her, she knew he was aware of her every action. Saffron stared at his profile hard before she answered. "No. I wasn't. The face I saw staring back at me wasn't the person I used to be."

"Nay. And the person looking back at you in the mirror three years from today willna be the same either. People change, Saffron."

"Not the way I have," she muttered before she thought better of it.

"Will the new clothes and hairstyle help?"

She turned to face him, resting her hip against the rock. "Everything I've been wearing since I was brought here has been handed down to me from the others, which I greatly appreciate. There was no reason I couldn't buy my own clothes so the others could have theirs returned."

"You know they doona care about clothes."

Finally he turned his head to her, and she was caught in his deep chocolate eyes, trapped in the interest she saw in them. Her stomach flip-flopped as she became all too aware of the very virile, very attractive male before her.

"Maybe not, but I did. I wanted, no," she said with a shake of her head, "I *needed* something that was mine."

"Clothes willna help you find yourself. You're no' lost, you just are no' looking in the right place."

She blinked. Twice. She had been so desperate to be the person she used to be, that she hadn't looked at the person she was.

"I like the hair, by the way," Camdyn said.

She was so taken aback by his compliment that she didn't see him move toward her or his hand rise to her face until his finger softly caressed near her eyebrow as he pushed aside a strand of hair that had been caught in her eyelash.

Her skin sizzled from where he touched it, and Saffron found herself leaning toward him. It had been so long since she'd been kissed, since she'd felt desire, that she was drowning in the emotions.

She yearned to close the distance between them, longed to lift her face and place her lips on his. To be desired, needed. To be loved.

The ache began in her chest and shifted lower, between her legs. Her breaths became shallow and she struggled to form a coherent thought. Which is when she realized he had complimented her.

"Thank you," she mumbled.

Her heart skidded when his eyes lowered to her lips. He was close enough that she could feel his heat, could practically taste the power within him.

It was a heady combination, especially mixed with the surging need rising within her. She licked her lips, and for a moment she thought she heard a growl.

"You shouldna be out here alone," Camdyn said. His voice had lowered, became more gravelly.

"I'm safe here."

His dark gaze lifted and caught hers. "You were caught unawares once. Doona let it happen a second time."

The mention of what had happened when Declan took her was like being doused with a bucket of ice water. Saffron took a step away as need was replaced with fury.

"How dare you," she ground out.

Camdyn's eyes narrowed. "How dare I? I'm trying to keep you from making the same mistake twice."

"You have no idea what happened. So don't be a jackass and pretend you do."

She whirled around and stormed back into the castle. She slammed the door shut with a hard shove, only there was no answering bang.

Saffron didn't need to look behind her to know that Camdyn had stopped the door. It had been childish of her, she knew, but she was mad, and she was so tired of having that anger inside her.

She made a beeline for her room, wanting only to be alone. But when she tried to slam that door as well, nothing happened. Somehow, she wasn't surprised to find Camdyn's large frame filling the doorway when she turned to look.

"What do you want?" she demanded as she jerked off her jacket.

"Had you no' stomped away, I would have told you." He paused and looked around the room as if suddenly aware they were in the dark. "Why are the lights no' on?"

"Then tell me what you want now so you can go." She crossed her arms over her chest and tapped the toe of her boot on the floor as she refused to answer him.

He raised a brow and glanced at her foot before he tossed another log onto the dying fire. The flames jumped higher, spreading an orange glow across the floor. "Tell me what happened with Declan."

Images of Declan's handsome face laughing with triumph as he tortured her, frightened her, and tormented her flashed through her mind.

Her stomach roiled with nausea as she thought of all the times he'd had her hit or kicked. Or both. Of the times he had starved her, froze her.

"No," she said when she could finally speak.

Camdyn lifted a brow. "It needs to be known, and if I have to, I'll go get Galen."

Saffron paled and dropped her hands. Galen's power was

the ability to see into a person's mind when he touched them. She didn't want him anywhere near her, not when her head was so full of atrocities.

"Why are you being so mean?" she asked. How could he have gone from making her feel so desired to this? Were her emotions so messed up she didn't know the difference?

"I'm trying to help."

"Bullshit. Do you like having me relive those memories? Do you get off on seeing how it upsets me?"

He frowned, his lips flattening the more she spoke.

"Whatever Declan did to me is better kept locked in my head," she said. She started to turn away when he took her arm and kept her facing him.

As much as she hated it at the moment, his touch sizzled through her sweater to her skin. And she wanted more.

His gaze was hard and calculating as he stared. "Do you always run away from problems?"

His mark hit too close to home. She elbowed him in the ribs, knowing it would do no damage other than surprise him. But she was able to wrench her arm out of his hold.

"Don't pretend to know me."

Camdyn laughed dryly. "No worries there, lass. You keep everyone at arm's length. No one can get to know you."

Saffron wanted to deny it, but she couldn't. She *had* kept everyone at arm's length. At first she used the evil from Declan's magic as an excuse, but the longer she stayed at the castle, the more she used her blindness as an excuse.

And it had been a poor one at that.

She never got a chance to respond because her cell phone rang at that moment. Glad an for excuse not to continue the conversation she'd been in, Saffron answered it without looking at the number.

"Hello," she all but shouted.

"Saffron? Honey, is that you?"

The sound of her mother's voice made all the blood rush from her head. Saffron swayed, and suddenly Camdyn was there. His strong arms held her as he sat her down on the bench in front of the bed.

"Saffron?"

She swallowed. "Hello, Mother." She didn't want to talk to her mother, not now, possibly not ever.

"Why haven't you called me? I've been worried sick."

"And that's why you tried to declare me dead?" she asked.

Elise tsked. "Honey, we hired private investigators to search for you. We found the car you rented in Edinburgh, but nothing else. All your luggage and your purse was gone. And you didn't answer your cell."

Saffron laughed. It was either that or cry. "So it took you only three years to give up and declare me dead so you could take the money."

There was a pause before Elise said, "You always make it about the money. Had your father left me more than a few hundred thousand, I wouldn't have need of more."

"So it is about the money. I gave you almost a million before I left three years ago."

"I have needs, honey."

Saffron closed her eyes. "Well, I'm not dead. I'm very much alive, and you won't get a penny of that money. I've already had Arthur draw up a new will. I'm leaving you as much as Dad left you."

"You ungrateful bitch!" Elise screamed. "Do you have any idea how much pain you put me through during the nearly two-day delivery? When you wouldn't come out they cut me open! Not only did you mess up my body, but I have a scar I've had to cover up ever since then."

"And we all know how important a good body is for a swimsuit, don't we? I'm so very sorry being pregnant messed up your perfect body, and that the C-section scar has been so difficult to bear."

"You have no idea," Elisa said, completely missing the sarcasm in Saffron's tone. "You do know you'll have to be seen in person to dismiss my claim."

Saffron laughed. "Oh, I took care of that today. Watch the papers tomorrow, Mother."

She disconnected the call, and sat there, desperately trying to get her breathing and raging emotions under control.

She had held out hope in the back of her mind that her mother might have actually missed her, that it was more than just the money.

But she had been wrong yet again.

It took her a few moments to realize she wasn't alone. Camdyn wasn't just in the room with her, he was sitting beside her. And she had a hold of his hand.

How long had she held it? Saffron looked down at their joined hands and the way her nails dug into his skin. Instantly she released him and rubbed her hands along her arms as she rose to her feet.

"I'm sorry you had to hear that."

When she turned around, he was standing right in front of her. His dark eyes had softened, and were almost kind. But it was the desire that wound through her, settling with a low heat between her legs, that made her all too aware of him. From his dark eyes to the closeness of his body to hers, she saw nothing but him.

CHAPTER
TEN

Camdyn knew he was standing too close to Saffron. Hell, he should never have followed her from the battlements to her chamber, but her anger had sparked his own. He wanted to know what drove her, what propelled the need for revenge that sat so heavily on her shoulders.

So he had followed her.

Of all the times he had watched Saffron he'd seen her always serene, always guarded, as if she couldn't show her true self.

When her anger began to show, he had pushed at her harder. He might have gotten the answers he sought if her mobile phone hadn't rung. And if it hadn't been her mother on the other end.

Camdyn's advanced hearing had allowed him to hear the entire conversation, and he was appalled that a mother could treat her child so.

When Saffron had taken hold of his hand, her nails digging into his flesh, he had kept still and given her whatever strength she needed from him.

But then he made his second mistake. He didn't leave.

Instead, he stood when she stood. And found himself mere inches from the most beautiful, alluring woman he had ever encountered.

Her tawny eyes looked up at him with a mixture of sadness and desire. And it was his undoing.

Camdyn had to taste her, had to feel her. Had to touch her. It might have been the worst decision he had ever made, but the need, the craving, gnawing at him was too great to ignore.

With only the desire clawing at him, he pushed aside all thought and gave in to his body. He wrapped a hand around Saffron's waist and pulled her the remaining few inches toward him.

Her hands came to rest on his chest, her lips parted and her breathing shallow. His head lowered to hers, their eyes locked.

Camdyn was giving her ample opportunity to escape him. When she remained in his arms, his god, Sculel, god of the underworld, roared with approval and appreciation.

Their faces were so close he could see the gold flakes in her eyes and the tiny scar near the corner of her left eye.

But it all became too much. He could wait no longer. He had to taste her. He slanted his mouth over hers in a hard, explosive kiss that left him reeling. Listing.

Completely unsettled.

Utterly adrift.

Her body was soft and curvy, fitting against him to precision. A small moan broke in the back of her throat as they continued the fiery, scorching kiss that fanned the flames of their desire higher and higher, consuming them. Her fingers dug into his chest before she wound her arms around his neck.

The feel of her molded against him had his balls tightening and his blood pounding in his ears. The need he had felt a moment before was nothing compared to what pumped through him now.

It was going too fast, and if he didn't stop now, he never would. It was the pleasure that thought gave him that somehow provided him the strength to end the kiss.

He reluctantly, slowly, pulled back and met her bewildered gaze. "Oh, shite," he muttered.

Camdyn had known she would taste of heaven, he just hadn't been expecting such a fierce and physical reaction to her, a reaction he'd never felt in his long life. One that had his cock aching he wanted her so desperately.

He made himself drop his arms from around her and step back. The loss of her body, her tempting curves against him, was nearly too much.

The words he wanted to say, to explain why he had kissed her, stuck in his throat. Because every one of them was a lie. He couldn't tell her the truth—that he had needed to kiss her, needed to know her taste.

Camdyn hadn't needed anyone in . . . a very long time, and he didn't want to find himself back in that situation. He wouldn't survive it.

He clenched his jaw shut and hurriedly walked from her chamber without another word. As he exited, he noticed Gwynn and Ian standing outside the chamber, but he didn't speak to them. He couldn't.

Camdyn was almost to the stairs when Broc walked out of his chamber. "I was just coming to find you. Want to play the hunter's game you were interested in?"

"Nay," Camdyn replied as he took the stairs three at a time.

He didn't stop until he was in his chamber. But he was too restless. His body was on fire, heated to the point that he was in physical pain. And the only one who could relieve him was the one person he couldn't touch again.

Camdyn rested his head on the cool glass of the window and struggled to calm his breathing. He fisted his hands before he spread them wide as he thought of touching, of holding Saffron, of how soft and good she had felt against him.

Of how wonderful she had tasted. The stroke of her tongue, the sound of her moan.

He swallowed and could still taste her on his tongue, could still smell the moonlight and snow scent that was hers alone.

Nothing he did could erase her from his mind, not even thoughts of Allison, which seemed to have faded to nothing suddenly. All he knew was that he had mucked things up tremendously.

Before he had only wondered how Saffron would taste or feel against him.

Now, he knew in excruciating detail just how perfect she felt, how seductive her kiss was.

Saffron gently touched her swollen lips and closed her eyes as she replayed the sizzling, consuming kiss again in her mind. The kiss had swept her away. Taken her. Seized her.

And she hated that it had ended so abruptly.

More confusing was Camdyn's reaction when he broke off the kiss. Had he been as affected as she?

Saffron shook her head and put a hand over her heart as it continued to race. No, Camdyn wasn't a man who let his emotions lead him. He had wanted the kiss, and initiated it, but he'd also been the one to end it.

Had he found her lacking?

Saffron frowned. It had been years since a man had kissed her or held her, and never with such raw, untamed desire that it made her shake with wanting.

She'd been unprepared for it at first, but her body soon caught up. And now . . . now need, hot and consuming, still throbbed within her.

After blowing out a breath, she started toward the bed when she saw her iPhone sitting on the bench. She had forgotten all about her conversation with her mother. Even now, she found she wasn't as angry as she had been before Camdyn kissed her.

Saffron put her hand to her forehead and groaned. How would she face him now? He had walked out of her room without a word. Tomorrow night was the full moon. The time to awaken Laria where they would all be together.

To take her mind off everything, she cleaned her room, then decided to move all her makeup onto the vanity before taking it back into the bathroom, then finally deciding it should be on the vanity.

Saffron was a ball of nerves, her body throbbing with

need. Every sound she heard she found herself looking to the door wondering if Camdyn was going to come back. Even when she knew he wasn't.

What was it about the Warrior that attracted her so? He was solemn, rarely smiling, and liked to keep to himself. He worked well with others because all the Warriors liked him, but even so, Camdyn was a loner.

Maybe that's what it was. Saffron was also sort of a loner. She hadn't started off that way, but as she grew older and discovered people only wanted to be her friend because of her money she began to distance herself from people.

It made it less likely that she would get hurt that way. But it also made life lonely.

She had thought she'd had a few true friends, but even they had dropped by the wayside when she rebelled against her family and gone on a European tour. Alone.

Saffron couldn't help but wonder if Declan would have convinced her as easily as he had if she'd had someone with her. Most likely, she never would have been in the small southwesterly town of Oban since it was so out of the way. She had been driving to the Isle of Skye, and going to Oban required a significant detour.

But she had heard so many great things about Oban from locals that she decided to see for herself.

Where would she be now if Declan hadn't imprisoned her? Would she be back home? Married maybe? With a career in her father's business as he had wanted?

Saffron knew it was pointless to think about what could have been, but it was easier than allowing her memories of the three years prior to pull her under. Which they always did.

She lowered herself in front of the fire and stared into the flames. There was something mesmerizing about a fire and the flicker of the flames.

It pulled her mind away from her tangle of thoughts and let her wander. She didn't know how long she sat there before she heard the sound of drums and the distant murmur of chanting.

Her magic instantly reached out to it, pulling her with it as the chanting and drums grew louder. It hypnotized her, until her eyes closed.

She could feel the magic swirling faster and faster inside her, growing stronger and stronger each moment. The louder the drums beat the more her magic surged. And the chanting seemed to suddenly come from all around her. Enveloping her. Encircling her.

Enfolding her.

The many visions she'd had over the years zoomed through her mind's eye. People she hadn't known and couldn't help, families she had diverted from disaster. All of them were wound together like a huge funnel in her mind before disappearing.

But some remained.

The visions she'd had of Deirdre, Declan, and anyone else involved in this war now were in the forefront of her mind. She saw them differently, examining every particle of the visions in the hope of finding some clue or missed message.

She felt the visions more than before. Declan's shouting was louder, and Deirdre's rages made her quake inside. Everything was amplified so she felt it twenty times more than before.

Her head began to pound, and she tried to pull away. However, the chanting only grew louder, taking away her pain and her fear.

"Who are you?" she asked the invisible force she could feel around her.

"The ancients," the thousands of voices answered between the chants.

For the first time in so very long Saffron found a place where she could let herself go, where her magic was stronger, and where she could be completely safe.

Somehow, instinctively, she knew neither Declan nor Deirdre would ever be able to reach her where she was. No one would be able to hurt her again.

CHAPTER
ELEVEN

Declan reclined on his leather couch in his office staring through the floor-to-ceiling windows at the snow that continued to fall. With one arm resting along the back of the couch he sipped on his single-malt whisky, relishing the heady taste while his thoughts centered on Tara and how to find her.

He had already located Tara's pitiful excuse for a mother. The same mother that had tried to kill her. But Declan had taken Tara away from all of that. He'd known there was something special about her. Too bad he hadn't realized just how special Tara was before she had run away.

It was bad enough that she had had the audacity to leave him, but to make matters worse, it was like Tara had never been. She had vanished, all but become a ghost. Even with all his considerable magic he couldn't find her. With all his money and connections, Declan couldn't find a trace of her.

Oh, there were instances where the person that had been there months before could have been Tara, but he didn't know for sure. Couldn't know for sure.

He should have known Marie would give him nothing no matter how much he'd made her suffer. She and Tara hadn't spoken in years, but Declan had held out a small thread of hope that Tara had given in to the need for her mother's love and contacted Marie.

But he'd had no such luck.

With Saffron gone, Declan needed another Druid. What made Tara so special was that she came from a long line of very powerful *droughs*. All he had to do was apply the right pressure and convince her she belonged with him, and he'd have another *drough* on his side.

Tara's magic was volatile, but he could help her control it. The thought of both Tara and Deirdre standing with him against the world brought a smile to his face.

If only he could convince Deirdre she needed him. She had survived for too long on her own to think she needed anyone, but Declan wasn't about to give up.

He was so lost in his thoughts he didn't see the black smoke until it was upon him. *"So you think you need Deirdre?"* the voice asked in his mind.

Declan wasn't afraid of the deep, booming voice. He smiled. "Welcome, Master. I wondered when you would visit. As to answer you, aye, I do require Deirdre. She's been around for over a thousand years. Her experience in controlling the world would be vital. No' to mention her ability to create wyrran."

"I could give you that ability."

"Aye, and I wouldna turn your gift away. You seem angry with Deirdre. What has happened?"

"She refuses to do as I command. I told her to forget the artifacts, but she will not."

"It was one of the reasons you allowed me to pull her to my time."

The black smoke swirled around Declan thick and heavy, Satan's fury evident in the way the smoke clung to Declan. *"That I did. I added much power to your magic, and I thought that with Deirdre, the two of you would have already conquered the world and allowed the darkness to take over."*

"And we will, Master," Declan hastily assured him. There was only one thing Declan feared, and that was the Devil. He'd do whatever needed to be done, say whatever needed to be said. Because the last thing he wanted was to find himself at the mercy of Satan. "I urge you no' to do anything rash when it comes to Deirdre."

"You would speak on her behalf?"

Declan swallowed. He knew he was treading on dangerous ground. Satan had been irritated with Deirdre for quite some time. "I do."

"I was about to take away all the magic I had given her, but even if I do, she would still be a powerful Druid."

Declan leaned up, causing the thick smoke to shift. "If I can persuade Deirdre that she is better off with me at her side, then your plan to have evil take over the world will happen. Give me a chance, Master, to prove my worth."

There was a long silence before the deep voice said, *"I will grant you this, Declan. But I warn you. Do not fail me."*

With that the smoke was gone. Declan ran a hand through his blond hair and sighed. He hoped he'd made the right decision, because his life now rested on gaining Deirdre's trust.

The double doors to his office flew open and Robbie filled the doorway clothed in all black fatigues, his favorite. He smiled when he spotted Declan and hurried over. "Your spy has done it again."

"Kirstin?" Declan asked. "What information did she ascertain?"

"I know where everyone at MacLeod Castle went yesterday morning."

Declan looked at the clock on his wall and realized it was nearing five in the morning. "Where?"

"Satellite imaging picks up twenty-four bodies on the Orkney Islands near the Ring of Brodgar."

A slow smile spread over Declan's face. "And you're sure it was the MacLeods?"

"I had the image enhanced. I saw three men wearing torcs. It's the MacLeods, Declan."

"Good work, cousin," Declan said as he gained his feet. "I wonder how much Deirdre would appreciate this information."

* * *

"Where is Saffron?" Gwynn asked when everyone gathered around the table to eat that next morning.

Camdyn didn't bother to look up as he attacked the pile of pancakes layered on his plate. He took a bite of crunchy bacon as the others all admitted to not seeing Saffron.

Finally he had to speak up. "I saw her on the battlements last night. Then she went to her chamber."

A chair scraped as Isla rose from the table. "I'm going to check on her."

Camdyn knew she was fine. He'd felt the strength of her magic all night as he tossed and turned in bed thinking about her full lips and creamy skin, of her curves molded along his body.

Even now he could feel the sheer power of her magic. It was stronger than before, but it was still Saffron's magic.

Hayden suddenly jumped up from the table and started running for the stairs. "Something is wrong with Isla."

A heartbeat later Isla's voice rang out from above, "I need help!"

Camdyn forgot about his food as he leaped to the top of the stairs, landing just in front of Hayden, and sprinted down the hallway to Saffron's door.

The door was open, and he skidded to a halt when he spotted Isla squatting beside Saffron, who sat rocking back and forth in front of the fire.

"The fire is magical," Hayden said from behind him.

Camdyn strode to Saffron, intent on discovering what was wrong, but when he went to touch her, magic shot from her body and hit him.

It didn't hurt. It didn't do anything but stun him. Yet he was unnerved. Unsettled.

Uneasy.

The others began piling into the chamber, each taken aback as they caught sight of Saffron. Camdyn walked slowly around Saffron until he stood directly in front of her. He lowered himself so that he looked her in the eye, but her tawny gaze that had haunted him all night wasn't the same one that stared back at him now.

"What's wrong with her?" he asked Isla.

"She's gone to the chanting," Isla answered.

"Get her back."

Isla's ice-blue eyes held a wealth of uncertainty that caused Camdyn's blood to turn to ice. "I don't know if we can."

"We also have no idea how long she's been with them," Marcail said.

"With who?" Camdyn demanded, his anxiety growing by the moment.

Reaghan laid a hand on his shoulder. "The ancients, Camdyn. Each of us Druids has heard the drums and the chants at one time or another. It is a haven for Druids, a place where we can discover answers or just find tranquility."

Camdyn recalled Dani nearly succumbing just a few days ago. How could he have forgotten such a thing?

"Every Druid has something that strengthens her magic," Sonya said. "For me it's the trees. I believe it's fire for Saffron."

"Douse the fire then," he ordered as he peered closer at Saffron, praying for some kind of response from her.

It was Hayden who stepped to the fireplace and put his hands in the fire. He grunted and shook his head. "Without magic, that will be impossible. Saffron is keeping this fire going, and no' even my power will douse it."

"Shite," Camdyn murmured and ran a hand down his face. "There has to be something we can do to bring her back."

Quinn caught Camdyn's eye. "You'd best hurry, my friend. I nearly lost Marcail when she was drawn to the chants."

Camdyn didn't want to be the one to try and pull Saffron back, nor did he think he was the right person. Already her magic was a beacon for him. And no amount of warning himself to stay away seemed to help.

"Do it," Ramsey said from beside him.

Camdyn gritted his teeth and reached out to touch Saffron's shoulder. This time her magic let him through and he took hold of her.

"Saffron, wake up." When she didn't respond, he called out to her louder, shaking her harder.

But nothing worked. For fifteen minutes he tried every suggestion thrown at him to wake her, until he had an idea of his own.

"Saffron, your mother is here. She demands to speak with you. She said she's come for the money."

Saffron heard Camdyn's voice from far, far away. It caught her attention, but the drums and chanting sounded so good she was loath to leave.

But Camdyn persisted.

Sometimes his voice sounded as if it were right next to her, while other times as if it were coming through a long tunnel. But always he was there, calling to her.

Saffron was determined to ignore him, even though his voice sparked the memory of their kiss and the way his wide lips had moved over hers with such passion and heat that it made her heart quicken and her body come alive.

She became curious as to what he wanted. Didn't he realize she was safe? Didn't he realize she didn't need anyone anymore?

The more she tried to listen to his words the more the chanting and drums faded. It wasn't long before she heard his words as clearly as if he were sitting in front of her.

Her mother. At the castle.

"No!" she screamed and tried to turn away.

Strong hands held her, hands and a touch she recognized all too well.

"Open your eyes," Camdyn demanded softly.

Saffron shook her head, reaching for him. He was steady, a rock she knew she could hold on to in the storm that was her mother. "Make her go away. Make my mother go away."

"She's gone," he murmured in her ear as he held her close. "She's gone."

Saffron took a deep breath and opened her eyes. She missed the chanting, but there was something altogether comforting and wonderful about being in Camdyn's arms.

She liked being there, wanted to stay there. Always in his embrace.

"Thank God," Gwynn said.

Saffron shifted her gaze to the right and saw Gwynn as well as most everyone else in the castle. She pulled away from Camdyn, her eyes locking with his.

Deep in his chocolate gaze she saw worry there. For her? Had he been concerned for her?

"You gave us all a scare," Isla said with a small forced laugh. "Please don't do that again."

Saffron nodded, but couldn't look away from Camdyn's dark, compelling gaze.

Dani threw her arms around Saffron from behind and hugged her. "Camdyn yelled for you for almost twenty minutes before he finally got through. We all knew he could do it."

Saffron patted Dani's arm, unsure of what to say.

One by one everyone left her room except Camdyn and Ramsey. Ramsey laid a hand on Camdyn's shoulder before placing his other hand on her shoulder.

"It's nice to have you returned to us, Saffron," Ramsey said before he walked out.

Camdyn cleared his throat and was the first to look away. "What happened?"

She shrugged. "I'm not sure. I was looking into the fire, then the next thing I knew I heard drums and the most beautiful chanting. I followed it, and . . ."

"And?" he prompted when her voice had faded away.

"Something strange happened with my magic. All the old visions I've had through the years evaporated, and the ones dealing with this war we're in grew stronger, clearer."

Camdyn stood and held out his hand to her. As he pulled her to her feet he asked, "Did you see anything different?"

"No. But . . . but I think my magic has grown stronger."

"It has."

She licked her lips and tugged at the hem of her shirt. "I didn't mean to frighten everyone. Thank you for pulling me out."

He turned to the side and glanced at the now dead fire. "Be careful, Saffron. You're needed here."

"Because I'm a Seer?"

"Because you're a Druid and your fate is intertwined with ours, and because you're a part of this family. It has nothing to do with you being a Seer."

CHAPTER TWELVE

Camdyn's words echoed in Saffron's head after he'd departed. Yet, when she walked, wincing at the stiffness in her legs and back, the morning sun that shone through the window caught her eye.

"Damn," she muttered as she hurried to pull on the snow boots she had bought.

It had seemed liked forever since she saw a sunrise, and she had planned to get up early that morning and watch her first one in years. The chanting, however, had changed all of that.

If she couldn't see the sun rise, she could at least go out and watch it climb into the sky. It was hours before they had to get ready to leave for the Ring of Brodgar, and she intended to make as much use of the free hours as she could.

Saffron snagged her thick coat from the peg near the door as she walked past. She had one arm in her jacket and the other about to go through as she started down the stairs into the great hall.

"Aren't you hungry?" Sonya called out.

"Later," Saffron said, an eager smile on her face.

She pulled on a lavender beanie and hurried outside. The cold slammed into her almost immediately, but she had been raised with snow. Colorado Springs might not be as damp as Scotland, but she knew snow.

A laugh escaped her as she hurried down the steps and jumped into the snow. Saffron then walked through the bailey, taking every bit of it in, from the stables to the blacksmith's shop to the church that had been used several times to marry the Warriors and their Druids.

She had been in that church, small though it was, and she was eager to see it. But not now. Now, she wanted to feel the wind on her cheeks, to squint up at the sun, and to play in the snow.

Before she walked through the small door in the huge gatehouse, Saffron pulled out a pair of the sunglasses she had stuffed in the inside pocket of her coat and put them on.

Already her eyes were adjusting better to the light. Soon, she wouldn't need the sunglasses all the time as she did now.

"Oh, my," she murmured as she spotted the cliffs and the dark, wild sea below.

Saffron drank in everything she saw as she walked closer to the edge of the cliffs, from the gulls that hung suspended along the strong currents to the water that rolled ashore along the rocks.

She took in the cliffs and caught sight of several cave entrances that would be too remote for anyone but a Warrior to get to.

When she reached the edge, she looked down to find the beach below filled with rocks of all dimensions, from some the size of baseballs to massive boulders that jutted from the ground. Much like the ones dotted around the castle.

"Cara fell not too far from where you're standing," a male voice said from behind her.

Saffron smiled as she recognized Arran's voice. "I've no intention of falling. I'm not sure you'd have as quick a reflex as Lucan did."

"Oh, ho," Arran said with a hearty laugh as he came to stand beside her. "Care to give it a test?"

"I'll pass, thanks," she replied with a bright smile.

"I'm glad to see you up and about after how we found you this morning."

She lifted a shoulder in a shrug. "I know there is cause to

worry about a Druid falling into the chanting and drums, and I even thought about it. There is safety there with the ancients. It's a place no one can hurt us. And it strengthens our magic in ways that I can't even begin to explain. Yet, if a Druid knows what they're doing, it's safe."

"Did you know what you were doing?"

"No," she answered with a chuckle as she glanced sideways at him. "I do now. Still, it's almost addictive, like a drug. It is such a beautiful, wonderful place to be, I understand why no one wants to leave, or has difficulty leaving."

"I'm just glad Camdyn was able to pull you out."

"Why did he do it?" she asked, and immediately regretted it. She didn't want to know the reason, not if it would hurt her.

Arran stuffed his hands in the front pockets of his jeans and hitched up his shoulders. He was wearing only a navy blue T-shirt and gray hoodie sweatshirt jacket. "Maybe because he reached you first? I really doona know, Saffron. All I know is that I wouldna have thought about telling you your mother was there for money."

She swiped at the bangs on her forehead and considered his words. "Unfortunately, Camdyn was privy to a rather nasty call between my mother and me yesterday."

"Regardless, it worked, and we're all glad of it."

They watched waves roll in and violently crash upon the cliffs for several quiet moments. Saffron found her thoughts turning again and again to Camdyn and that amazing, breathtaking kiss.

"So, did they send you out to watch me?" she asked when she couldn't stand thinking about Camdyn another moment or the way her body craved his touch and her mouth his lips.

Arran chuckled and turned toward her. "No' at all. I was with Lucan in the blacksmith's shop when I saw you leave the castle. I thought you might like some company."

"That would be nice. There's so much I want to see and do now that I have my eyesight back. There just aren't enough hours in the day."

He smiled and swept his arm around him. "You have a vast playground, milady."

Saffron threw back her head and laughed. "I do, don't I?"

"Just watch for the rocks hidden in the snow. They can ruin a day. So what do you want to do?"

Saffron had been balling up a handful of snow, and as soon as Arran asked his question, she lobbed it at him. It hit him square in the chest.

He omphed, looking from the snow falling down his chest to her. "You little minx," he said with a smile as he began gathering up his own snowball, which was three times the size of hers.

Saffron ran away from the cliffs, but she wasn't able to dodge Arran's snowball. It hit her in the shoulders, with snow then bouncing onto her face.

She slid to a halt and called, "My turn!"

Arran's laughter faded as he started running toward her. Saffron hurried, her hands cold and clumsy even with her gloves on. But she managed to get the snow packed together and tossed it at Arran before she took off running again.

She heard him coughing and looked over her shoulder to see she had thrown the snowball in his face. Her laughter took hold of her until she was doubled over from the effort.

"Oh, God, my cheeks hurt," she said between laughing as she tried to push her cheeks down.

Arran, meanwhile, was giving no quarter. He had a sizable snowball in each hand and threw them both at the same time.

All Saffron could do was fold her arms over her head seconds before they hit her. The force of them pushed her backward into the thick snow, which cushioned her fall.

She rolled to her side and began to gather up more snow as Arran's footsteps drew near.

"Saffron? Did I hurt you?" he asked, concern thickening his voice.

She waited until he turned her over and then she shoved the snow in his face and down his shirt. He bellowed with laughter and wiped the snow from his eyes.

Saffron pushed to her feet, more snow in her hands. She waited for just the right moment to throw again.

Camdyn was on his way to the village to do some more work on his cottage when he spotted Saffron and Arran laughing as they threw snowballs at each other.

An odd ache began in Camdyn's chest when Saffron's sweet laughter reached him. He had never heard her laugh with so much joy and happiness before, and he craved to hear more of it.

When she fell from the impact of Arran's throws, Camdyn had started toward her before he knew what he was doing. It was only when he was nearly upon them that he paused.

Arran caught sight of him, his smile wide and his eyes bright. "Did you come to join us?"

Camdyn held back the growl that had formed in his throat. It was obvious by Arran's attention that he was attracted to Saffron. Camdyn wanted to pound his fists into his face, plunge his claws into Arran's chest.

Anything to make Arran go away.

"I'd throw this at him if I thought it would make him smile," Saffron said as she nodded toward Camdyn.

Camdyn hated that her words bothered him so much. He might be morose, but he knew how to have fun. Didn't he?

It was Arran who ended up answering her. "A Warrior's idea of having fun, Saffron, is killing wyrran. And dreaming of killing Deirdre."

She nibbled at her lip and smiled. "I can see that. But this is a new time for both of you. There's a lot to do for entertainment. You both should give it a try."

Before Camdyn could think to form an answer, the snowball in her hand was suddenly flying toward him. He could have easily dodged it, but she had tried so hard to catch him unawares, that he allowed it to hit him in the side of the face.

The next thing Camdyn knew both she and Arran were tossing the snowballs at him.

Camdyn ducked, a smile forming on his mouth as he worked his way closer to Saffron even as she tried to back away. He managed to reach her and wrap a hand around hers that was about to throw the snowball at him. He turned her so that the snowball went toward Arran instead.

They were all laughing by that time. And then it became Camdyn and Saffron against Arran. Snow began to fly relentlessly as Camdyn drove Arran back with Saffron helping.

Then the heel of Saffron's boot hit a rock and she lost her balance. Camdyn reacted instantly and wound his arms around her as he turned them so he took the brunt of the fall in case there were stones below the snow.

He bit back a curse as he landed on several large rocks with his back. The same place Saffron would have landed had he not been there.

Camdyn rolled her over and smoothed back the hair from her face with his hands. Her tawny eyes blinked up at him, surprise still on her face.

Whatever he'd been about to say vanished from his mind as his body realized he was cradled atop her softness, one leg nestled between hers. He clenched his jaw to keep from moaning. His hardening cock was pressed against her hip, and there was no way she didn't feel him.

Camdyn's gaze lowered to her lips. Instantly he remembered how incredible her lips had felt beneath him, how marvelous it felt to have her respond so quickly to his touch. And how astoundingly fast his own body had reacted.

His head lowered toward hers. Nothing, he told himself, could stop the unimaginable hunger he had to taste her lips again, to breathe in the moonlight and snow smell of her.

To hear her moan in pleasure. For him.

He wanted her with a passion that surprised and frightened him. He yearned to make love to her again and again, if only to get her out of his blood.

Surely that's all it was. It had been a while since he'd had a woman. He just needed to find a willing wench. One who would make him forget the intoxicating feel of Saffron in his arms.

Arran's footfalls as he rushed up broke through the desire that had surged in Camdyn.

"Is she all right?"

Camdyn looked into Saffron's eyes and saw the passion there. His balls tightened, and he was thankful Arran was with him or he would have given in and kissed her. Again.

"She's fine," Camdyn said as he jumped to his feet.

He held out his hand to her, but she took Arran's instead. For some reason that rankled Camdyn so that he again wanted to punch Arran.

"You're reckless," he told Saffron. It was a ridiculous thing to say, but he had to do something to release the need and frustration inside him.

She raised a light brown brow. "Excuse me? What did you just say?"

"I said you're reckless," Camdyn repeated. "Your life is so short, so easily stamped out. You could get a cold from being out here, or hit your head on one of the stones beneath the snow. Your life would be over in an instant. You're reckless."

"Reckless?" she repeated, her voice low and her eyes staring at him with deadly intent. "Well, forgive me, Mr. High-and-Mighty. Maybe I should apologize for not being immortal or having powers to heal myself like other Druids, but I won't. I know better than anyone how short a life can be. Lest you forget, I was kept prisoner for three years. So, yes, I might be reckless, but it's my life to live. Mine!"

Camdyn opened his mouth to try and calm her, once he realized he might have overstepped, but she talked over him.

"People catch colds all the time. People break bones all the time. People die all the time. It's part of life. And if I want to be reckless with my life, I'll be the one to pay the consequences."

She started to walk off when Camdyn took hold of her arm and pulled her to a stop. Her body vibrated with anger, but he could see the hurt in her eyes. Hurt he had caused.

"I'm sorry. I've never been verra good with people." Camdyn released her arm and started toward the castle.

What was it about Saffron that sent his world spinning? He wasn't one who ever lost his cool, yet with Saffron, that's all he seemed to do.

CHAPTER THIRTEEN

Somehow Deirdre wasn't surprised to find Declan on her mountain. The stones let her know the moment he and his men set foot in her domain.

Deirdre commanded the stones to open the hidden door and waited. She smiled as Declan and his men reached the door and looked inside.

"Deirdre," Declan said with a lazy smile and his blue eyes crinkling in the corners. "It's good to see you. You're as beautiful as ever."

"As much as I love compliments, state your business, Declan."

He chuckled and pulled at the cuff of his shirt beneath the suit jacket and the long overcoat he wore. "It's cold out here. Why no' allow me to come inside."

It was just what she had wanted him to say. "All right."

Declan walked through easily enough, but when the other four men tried to follow him, her magic prevented it.

"What is this?" Declan demanded as his blue eyes swung to her. Gone was the teasing seducer who had begged for entry.

She shrugged. "A show of magic, maybe. You asked for entry, which I granted. If you would like to battle, I'm game. Your men could be killed with merely a thought from me to my stones," she said as she stroked the wall behind her.

Declan's eyes narrowed as he seemed to weigh her words. Finally he let out a breath and smiled as he began to unbutton his overcoat. "You win. I didna come here to argue or fight. I came to offer you information and hopefully a solution that could benefit us both."

As much as she hated to admit it, Deirdre was intrigued. She looked at the two wyrran who had been hiding in the shadows and had them guard the doorway as she commanded the stones to close the door.

"Follow me," she told Declan and turned on the heel of her leather boot.

"I see you favor leather now, just as I expected you would."

She chuckled. "Admit that you just liked seeing the way it conformed to my body."

"Exactly. Why else would I have given it to you to wear?"

He was certainly a charmer, but she had been alive long enough to know that beneath the charm was a man who was willing to do anything to get what he wanted. And right now, he wanted her.

But how far would he go? she wondered.

She walked into the small sitting room outside her chamber and took a seat on the plush sofa Malcolm had retrieved for her. Deirdre motioned for Declan to take the chair opposite her, but after he tossed his long coat on the back of the chair, he instead sat on the other end of the couch.

"What information do you have for me?" Deirdre asked.

Declan smiled and leaned back in the corner, one arm resting on the arm of the couch and the other on the back. "No pleasantries?"

"You pulled me from my time to this one, taking me away from all I had accrued, then kept me prisoner in your house for three months, and you want pleasantries? Maybe I should kill you now."

"You would do that to the person who saved you from our master?"

Deirdre's stomach clenched in terror, though she did not allow it to show on her face. "How did you do that?"

"He's pissed off, Deirdre. He wanted to take away all the

magic he had given you because you haven't given up on your need for the artifacts the MacLeods have."

She knew the Devil hadn't been to see her in some time, but that wasn't always so strange. However, she'd had no idea he was going to take away her magic.

"Do you know what those artifacts will do, Declan?"

He shrugged. "Enlighten me."

"They will awaken my twin sister, who has the ability to kill me regardless of how much magic I use to try and save my spirit once again."

One side of Declan's mouth lifted in a grin. "I confess, I knew that. I wanted to know if you did."

"So what is your information? That Satan is angry with me?"

"That's a portion of it, my sweet. The second part is that the MacLeods have found your dear sister's hideaway. And they are awakening her tonight."

Deirdre jerked to her feet and began to pace. Not tonight. It couldn't happen tonight. She wasn't ready to face Laria. All those years growing up she had thought Laria had no magic, but her twin had kept it from her.

If Deirdre was going to kill Laria she needed more Druids to take magic from, and she needed more Warriors. She paused and put her hands to her stomach.

"Get out," she told Declan.

"I thought you'd like to hear the rest of my proposal," he said as he leaned forward and braced his forearms on his knees.

Deirdre swung around as her magic raced through her. A strand of her floor-length white hair struck out and wrapped around Declan's throat. He didn't grab for it or even flinch as she began to squeeze.

"No' this time, my darling," he said, and cut the strand with a small dagger she hadn't seen him withdraw. He stood and brushed aside the hair around his throat.

He flipped the dagger end over end as he went to retrieve his coat. He looked at her. "Verra soon you will be coming to me for help. Verra soon you'll be begging me."

"Never."

"Ah, you should watch what you say."

As he took his coat and walked out of her sitting room, Deirdre wondered for the first time in thousands of centuries if she should have listened.

Saffron's happy morning turned dour after her argument with Camdyn. What was it about the man that set off her anger every time he opened his mouth?

Even though she had wanted to return to the castle, Arran had convinced her to let him show her around the grounds. They spent a few hours in the village looking at all the cottages that had been restored. He, Ramsey, and Camdyn all had cottages.

"But there's room enough in the castle," she'd said.

"It's getting tight. It was always the plan for the unwed Warriors to live here and all the Druids in the castle."

It had made sense to her, and though she hadn't wanted to know, she'd taken special interest in Camdyn's cottage when Arran pointed it out.

Next they had spent some time in the old ruins of the abbey. It saddened Saffron that so many innocent people had died upon MacLeod land. If she were one to believe in ghosts she'd expect everything to be haunted.

Saffron asked to be taken to the beach, and they were on their way to the side of the castle where Cara had her garden and the path that led down to the water.

They were standing at the path when Arran stopped her. "It's icy and no' safe for you."

"I can fly her down," Broc said as he strode out of the kitchen and released his god so that his wings sprouted from his back.

Saffron took in the indigo color of his skin and the dark blue of his claws as well as the huge leathery wings that rose high over his head as he folded them behind his back.

Gwynn had explained the transformation of the Warriors to her many times, but seeing the claws, fangs, and the way the color of the god took over their skin and eyes was another matter altogether.

"Nay, you can't," Sonya said as she poked her head outside. "Fallon is looking for you, sweetheart. I think he wants you to make sure Deirdre is still at Cairn Toul."

Broc shrugged, and just like that the indigo blue of his skin and eyes were gone as were the wings, claws, and fangs. "Sorry, Saffron. Another time."

She smiled and was ready to see if she could help in the castle when Broc paused and said, "Camdyn can take you, however."

Camdyn's dark head jerked up from where he was sitting near the kitchen door. Saffron hadn't realized he was there because Broc had stood in front of him, but now that she saw Camdyn, she couldn't look away.

He laid aside the dagger on the bench beside him and rose to his feet. With determined strides he moved toward her.

"I . . . ah, I'm going to go," Arran said, and hurried away.

Saffron took a deep breath and looked at her gloved hands. She cleared her throat and said to Camdyn, "You don't have to do anything. It's probably better if I wait until spring anyway."

When he didn't answer, she looked up to find him holding out his hand palm up. Saffron looked from it to his face and frowned.

"Do you trust me?" was all he asked.

Saffron nodded. "I do."

"Then take my hand."

She didn't hesitate a second time. As soon as she put her hand in his, his fingers closed around her hand and he pulled her against him so that his arms wrapped securely around her. It gave her the excuse she wanted to wind her arms around his neck.

"Hang on," he whispered in her ear.

A shiver of anticipation, of pleasure, raced down her spine. His arms tightened, and she had but an instant to get her breath. One moment they were standing on the cliffs by the castle, and the next they were falling through the air.

Saffron's stomach jumped into her throat, but she wasn't afraid. She'd heard that the Warriors leaped to the beach all the time. So, instead of burying her face in Camdyn's neck in fear, she threw back her head and laughed at the idea of just being alive.

All too soon they landed. More gently than Saffron had expected.

She was still smiling when she looked up into Camdyn's face. "That was amazing."

"You were no' frightened." It wasn't a question, and the confusion in his chocolate eyes startled her.

"No."

She felt his hands spread over her back through her jacket and clothes, felt him pull her tighter against him. It became difficult to breathe as she found herself drowning in his gaze.

Sinking.

Tumbling.

Into everything that was Camdyn MacKenna. She didn't want to feel this insatiable attraction to him, but it seemed there was no denying it.

She didn't stop him or turn away when his head began to lower to hers, even though she knew in her heart she should. She should run as far and as fast from Camdyn as she could.

Because he was the type of man who could hurt her far worse than anything Declan had ever done to her.

Saffron forgot about running, forgot everything but Camdyn and the wonderful feel of him as his lips took hers. He nibbled her mouth softly, seductively, teasing her before his tongue slid between her lips.

She gasped as his tongue stroked along hers, fanning the flames of desire that had been scorching her since their first kiss.

The feel of his hard arousal was pressed into her stomach. His moan, low and long, when she returned his kiss with fervor only pushed her further.

The longer they kissed, the hotter the kiss grew. It consumed them. Devoured them.

And she loved every hot, wonderful moment of it.

His hands slipped into her jacket and held her firmly, as if he couldn't let her go. His hands were everywhere, touching her, caressing her. Saffron was drunk with his kisses, her passion flying high as he grabbed her hips and ground his arousal into her.

She groaned and clung to him tighter.

Camdyn knew he was walking an edge as sharp as a blade, and any moment he was going to fall into all that was Saffron. Her scent was all over him, her body a temptation he couldn't ignore.

And her kisses . . . they spoke of her passion, of her longing. Of her yearning.

He turned her slightly and reached up to cup her breast. She gasped as he circled her nipple through her sweater before thumbing it into a hard peak.

Camdyn knew he had to stop soon or find himself past the point of no return. It was only the thought of going through another death that doused the flames of his desire.

He lowered his hand and slowly ended the kiss. Then cursed himself for ten kinds of fool when he saw Saffron's kiss-swollen lips and the question in her eyes.

"Camdyn?"

"I can no' do this." He didn't recognize his own voice it was so hoarse, but he had to get the words out. "Regardless of what my body wants, I can no'."

She nodded and let her arms fall from around him. Camdyn didn't want to release her, didn't want to sever what was between them, but he allowed her to do it as she stepped around him.

"I think it's better that you leave," she said and turned her back to him.

He watched her for several moments as she stared out to the sea, her back rigid and her arms crossed over her chest. The walnut-colored strands of her hair danced around her face in the sea air. In the end, he knew she was right. He did need to leave.

The only problem was, he could never get far enough away from her.

CHAPTER
FOURTEEN

Saffron found herself standing once more in the great hall waiting for Fallon to teleport her to the Ring of Brodgar on the Orkney Islands.

It wasn't that she wasn't ready and willing to help the others end Deirdre, because she was. It was the thought of having to go underground that had her quaking in her boots.

Literally.

Everyone was bundled warmly since the wind whipping off the two lochs along with the already frigid temperatures would make things very uncomfortable.

Several of the Warriors had backpacks filled with water and food, and everyone had PowerBars stuffed into the pockets of their coats just in case.

Saffron raised her scarf so that it covered her mouth to just under her nose so no one could see her teeth chattering. With her jacket no one could see how she was near to hyperventilating, either.

It was appalling that the mere mention of going underground could terrify her. Just another reason to hate Declan. For three petrifying long years she had been deep under his house in his dungeon. Tortured in ways that she could hardly wrap her mind around.

Tormented by her greatest fears.

Starved for days at a time.

Beaten until she finally begged them to stop.

But the worst . . .

Saffron mentally shook her head. She wouldn't venture down that road and open herself up to those memories. Not now.

Not ever again.

"Everyone ready?" Fallon asked as he glanced around him.

"I've been ready for over seven centuries," Quinn replied.

Lucan smiled at his brother and nodded. "Hell yes, little brother."

The other Warriors cheered, but as Saffron looked at the Druids, they weren't as joyous. They were more worried than their husbands.

Someone bumped into Saffron on her left and she glanced over to see Kirstin, Braden, and Aiden. Saffron rolled her eyes at the way the two guys were falling all over the young Druid, though Kirstin was certainly enjoying the attention. When it didn't appear as if her mind was taking a small vacation.

Isla stepped forward into the circle beside Fallon. The hall quieted almost immediately. "As before, the shield will stay in place protecting the castle. But just as before, whenever we leave here we won't be immortal."

"I'm hoping we awaken Laria before Deirdre gets there," Fallon said. "But if the worst should happen and one of the Druids becomes injured, get them to Sonya immediately so she can heal them."

As Fallon began to group people together, something slick and evil slid over Saffron. For a moment she couldn't breathe, couldn't move, as she recognized the feel of that malevolence.

She swallowed and tried to step to the side only to collide with Logan and Gwynn.

"Are you all right?" Gwynn asked, her brow puckering in worry.

She turned her head to them and gave a small shake of her head. "Need. Away."

Logan and Gwynn didn't ask any questions as they each

took an arm and led her into the kitchen. The farther Saffron got from the evil the better she began to feel.

"What happened?" Logan asked, his brows knit over his hazel eyes. "You were white as death."

Saffron shuddered. "I felt Declan's evil. It's here. In this castle. On someone."

"Are you sure?" Gwynn asked.

"I'd stake my life on it."

"That's good enough for me," Lucan said from the doorway of the kitchen.

Saffron hadn't realized he had followed them into the kitchen. But he wasn't the only one. Ramsey stood on one side of Lucan and Camdyn the other.

Camdyn didn't utter a word, simply watched her with his hooded eyes and blank expression. She couldn't tell what he was thinking, and that worried her. Especially after their kiss at the beach.

She began to sweat and jerked off her mittens, scarf, and jacket. Still it wasn't enough to calm her stomach. Saffron leaned over and braced her hands on her knees.

"What do you need?" Gwynn asked.

Saffron squeezed her eyes closed and tried to rid herself of the terror. "To kill Declan."

"He's next," Ramsey said.

She shook her head, her brown hair hitting the sides of her cheek. "He's here. Somehow he's here."

"Who was she standing near?" Camdyn demanded.

It was Logan who answered. "Aiden, Kirsten, and Braden."

The kitchen grew quiet, and it didn't take long for Saffron to realize what she had to do. Slowly she straightened and took a deep breath to calm her stomach.

Her gaze met the startling green ones of Lucan as she said, "There's only one way to be sure who it is. I need to get near all three again. Preferably one at a time."

Lucan gave her a nod and turned on his heel as he stalked from the kitchen. A glass of water was shoved into her hand. Saffron looked at the water and suddenly wished for something much stronger.

As if reading her mind, Camdyn took the water and gave her a glass with a dash of whisky in it. "Drink it. You'll feel better."

She tilted her head back and drained the contents. It burned down her throat before it settled in her stomach, its warmth spreading through her.

Saffron covered her mouth with the wrist of the hand that held the glass as she coughed. She blinked rapidly to stop her eyes from watering.

"Next time, try sipping it," Logan said with a grin.

She set the glass on the worktable as Fallon and Quinn walked into the kitchen with Lucan. Quinn's mouth was set in a hard line, his eyes trying to hold in his worry.

Fallon held out his hand to her. "Lucan filled me in. Are you ready?"

"No," she replied, but put her hand in his anyway.

"We willna allow Declan to harm you," Ramsey promised.

"I'm going to hold all of you to that."

Lucan gave her a wink of encouragement as they followed her and Fallon out of the kitchen. Saffron's steps faltered when she saw everyone seated around the table watching her.

Marcail sat beside Aiden stroking his hand as Aiden's gaze was locked on Saffron. Saffron prayed it wasn't Aiden for Marcail and Quinn's sake.

"In order for Saffron to determine who holds magic from Declan inside them, she'll need to stand alongside each of us individually until she finds it," Fallon told the great hall.

Saffron sighed. She was glad he was going about it this way instead of naming the three she knew had to hold it.

Fallon turned to her. "Do you feel Declan's magic on me?"

Saffron shook her head. Next was Lucan, then Quinn. After the MacLeods came Logan, Dani, Ramsey, and Camdyn. A small thrill went through Saffron when Camdyn's hand brushed hers as he came to stand beside her.

"No," she whispered, and dared to meet his chocolate

gaze. To her surprise, he squeezed her hand before he walked away.

One by one the rest of the castle came to stand beside her. When it was Aiden's turn, it was all Saffron could do not to look at Marcail or Quinn who stood off to the side holding each other.

Saffron held her breath waiting for the awful feel of Declan's magic. But there was nothing. She smiled and shook her head at Aiden, who returned to his parents with a bright smile on his face.

Next came Fiona, who Saffron knew wasn't part of it. But it was when Kirstin began to draw near that Saffron felt it. She stumbled backward until she hit the wall, holding up her hands to stop Kirstin from coming closer.

"It's me?" Kirstin asked with confusion.

Saffron nodded, and had to swallow twice before she said, "Yes."

Kirstin looked around her with wild blue eyes. "How? I've never met Declan Wallace."

Fallon stepped toward her. "Are you sure?"

"Yes!" she shouted.

"Where are you from?" Quinn asked as he drew closer.

"Kinlochleven."

Lucan walked to the other side of Fallon. "But you know who Declan is?"

"Everyone does," Kirstin answered.

Ramsey moved behind her, and that's when Saffron realized the men where boxing Kirstin in.

"You were walking along the side of the road when I found you," Ramsey said. "How did you get there?"

Kirsten shrugged. "That's the oddest thing. I have no idea. The last thing I remember before I woke up there was being at work."

Her words sealed her fate.

Reaghan's arm wrapped around Saffron and pulled her away from the wall where she had supported herself and walked her to the table. She, along with the rest, watched as the Warriors held Kirstin while Dani used her magic to delve into Kirstin's mind.

Almost immediately Dani jerked her hands away from Kirstin. "My, God," Dani whispered and shared a startled, shocked look with Saffron. "He's almost as deep into her mind as he was yours."

"Nay," Kirstin yelled and tried to break free.

Saffron couldn't watch anymore. She turned her face away and buried it in her hands. How had she not realized Declan's magic was in Kirstin before now? How had she missed it?

Had Saffron spent more time with the young Druid she would have recognized the feel of Declan's magic instantly. Because she hadn't, there was no telling how much information Declan knew about the goings-on at MacLeod Castle.

It was no coincidence that Declan had chosen Kirstin. She had very little magic, and obviously her mind was easily controlled. But what had he wanted?

Saffron's stomach roiled as she realized how much they had spoken about the artifacts and Laria in front of Kirstin. They had even taken her to the Ring of Brodgar because Saffron had said she would be needed.

Bile rose in her throat as she realized their mission had been compromised. She lifted her head at the same time Dani released her hold on Kirstin.

"We've been compromised," Saffron and Dani said in unison.

Camdyn's nostrils flared, his gaze on Saffron. "Explain."

"It's fairly easy to put together. Kirstin has little magic, and Declan must have manipulated her brain in order to spy on us," Saffron said as she rose from the table and walked to Kirstin.

Tears poured down Kirstin's face, but she no longer struggled against the Warriors holding her.

Dani blew out a breath and nodded. "That's exactly what Declan did. I felt his magic where it touched only certain parts of her mind."

"He knows where we're going," Saffron said. "He knows about the Ring of Brodgar."

Arran let out a string of curses and slammed his fist into the wall and stone crumbled around him as his fist went through it.

"Which means Deirdre knows," Broc said.

"Fuck," Galen growled.

Saffron couldn't have said it better herself.

CHAPTER FIFTEEN

Camdyn couldn't shake the fear that had clawed at his belly when he had felt the dread in Saffron's magic. It had slammed into his gut, wrapping around him like a vise. For a moment, he'd been so shocked by the assault of her magic that he'd been unable to move.

Then he had seen Gwynn and Logan helping her to the kitchen.

Every fiber of his being told him she wasn't his concern, but he found himself quickly hurrying after Lucan and Ramsey as they strode to the kitchen.

The last thing Camdyn had wanted was to see her put through feeling Declan's magic again, especially because of how pale and shaken up she was after the first brush. But he should have known Saffron would pull it together and face what was asked of her. Her resilience, her strength, made pride well inside him. Pride and . . . pleasure.

She'd stood with her shoulders back, her chin high, and her gaze determined. It was only when Aiden stepped forward that Camdyn spotted the slightest flinch from her. It was so faint he doubted anyone else saw it.

But he'd been looking for it.

Then when it was Kirstin's turn, she had taken just two steps toward Saffron before everyone could see she was the one being used by Declan's magic.

Yet none of them had really understood what Declan had done until Dani, with her ability to search a person's mind, and Saffron had put it together.

It had already been deduced that when Reaghan had tried earlier to use her magic to see if Kirstin had lied, Reaghan's magic had been stopped by Declan's magic somehow.

The fact that Declan had invaded the castle in several ways brought a worry, an alarm to Camdyn he didn't want to feel. He'd told Saffron she was safe from Declan, but it had been a lie.

Camdyn wanted to bellow his fury to the heavens. They had all worked so hard to have a place where they and the Druids were safe, but it appeared there was no such place.

Which put extra strain on every Warrior there. Camdyn could see it in their faces, the apprehension and nervousness about protecting what was theirs. The fact they were protecting not just Druids, but women who were mated to them was another matter entirely.

Camdyn was lucky that he wasn't bonded with anyone. But as soon as that thought went through his mind his gaze locked on Saffron.

Warriors were powerful. They were immortal and could heal wounds quickly. They were given special powers from their gods, but no matter how potent the god was, a *drough*'s magic—and even that of a *mie*—could stop a Warrior in his tracks, if their magic was strong enough.

Deirdre's *drough* magic had hampered all of them at one point or other.

"We need to get to the stones," Marcail said, a small tremble in her voice.

Hayden nodded. "The sooner the better."

"It won't matter what time we get there if we miss the alignment. We have to time it perfectly. Now that we know Deirdre is going to be there, arriving early might not be a good idea," Reaghan said.

Arran jerked his chin to Kirstin, who he still held. "What do we do with her? She can no' come with us, and I doona want her hearing any more of our plans."

Braden rose to his feet, a muscle in his jaw working. "I'll escort her to her chamber. She willna harm anyone from there."

But Camdyn wasn't so sure. Still, it wasn't his castle. Fallon gave his consent and Kirstin was released to follow Braden up the stairs.

They all waited until the pair was out of sight before Fallon said, "Broc, I need you to locate Declan and Deirdre. I want to know where they are before we arrive at the stones."

Broc gave a nod and sat, his hands braced on the table as he closed his eyes. Camdyn still had trouble getting used to some of them being able to use their power without calling forth their god.

Because he, Ian, Logan, Ramsey, and Arran had been brought forward in time, the others had had centuries to hone their skills as Warriors. He was looking forward to the time he could do the same.

And though he hated to admit it, he was worried about how Saffron would react when she saw all the Warriors with their gods unbound. She had been around them when they had done so, but that was when she was still blind.

The last time he had cared what a woman thought of him was when he had been with Allison. Now, he found himself worrying about what Saffron would think when he released his god. And he hated the anxiety of it.

"Mother!" Braden's panicked voice filtered down from the upper floors.

Fiona rose and started toward the stairs, but Galen was quick to stop her.

"Let us go first," he told her.

Camdyn glanced at Saffron to see her hands gripping the table so hard her knuckles were white. He started after Galen when Fallon's voice halted him.

"Galen, Lucan, Ramsey, Hayden, Larena, and Logan, come with me," Fallon barked. "Camdyn, Ian, Quinn, and Arran, stay with Broc and the Druids."

Camdyn gritted his teeth, but did as commanded as the others raced up the stairs.

"We shouldn't have left her alone," Saffron said.

Isla frowned. "Why?"

"If Declan knows we have discovered what he's done to her, there is no telling what he'll make her do."

"Make her do?" Camdyn repeated, the knot of worry in his stomach growing larger. "I doona understand."

It was Dani who sighed heavily. "He was controlling her," she explained. "Not all the time, mind you, but he was controlling her. I don't know what he was after, but he sent her here to spy is my guess."

"Just like Deirdre sent Charlie," Arran said.

Ian crossed his arms over his chest as he stared up the stairs. "Did Deirdre and Declan make a pact, you think?"

"Hard to tell," Gwynn answered.

Saffron rubbed her hands up and down her arms. Camdyn shifted so that he was in her line of sight. "What else do you think?" he asked her.

She lifted a slender shoulder. "Declan is devious. He will do anything, and I mean anything, to achieve what he wants. He doesn't mind using a young woman who is expendable for his cause."

As soon as she finished speaking they heard Braden bellow a "nay," and then silence.

A few moments later, Larena, her eyes red, appeared at the top of the stairs. "Kirstin jumped from the tower into the sea. She apologized and said she had known something was wrong with her, but she hadn't known what. Braden tried to catch her and nearly fell himself. Hayden and Galen barely caught him in time."

Fiona's soft crying filled the hall. But Camdyn's gaze was still on Saffron. He could see how the touch of Declan's magic, even on someone else, had affected her. It made him want to know all she had gone through at Declan's hands even more.

And he feared what that knowledge would do to him at the same time.

Fallon and the others walked back into the great hall subdued, but determined. "As soon as Broc tells me where

Deirdre and Declan are, I'll start jumping everyone to the stones."

Time stretched as they waited for Broc to open his eyes. The only other time it had taken him this long was when Declan had pulled Deirdre into the future, and Ian with her.

Camdyn's nerves were stretched taut, his god growling inside him, eager for a battle and bloodletting.

After what seemed like an eternity, Broc opened his eyes and his shoulders slumped. "Deirdre is still on Cairn Toul, but Declan . . . I couldna find him."

"Damn," Lucan muttered.

Fallon's jaw muscle jumped. "Everyone stay alert. I want a mix of Druids and Warriors each time. I'll jump us as near to a stone as I can to give us some shelter. The sun is going down, so that will help. Are all the artifacts ready?"

"Aye," Larena and Reaghan said in unison.

"Then let's go," Fallon said.

Camdyn managed to maneuver himself into the second group with Saffron. He didn't wonder why or question the urgent and overpowering need that filled him to protect her. He just did it.

He inhaled, and before he could release the breath they were at the Ring of Brodgar. True to his word Fallon had jumped them to a stone near the ring.

Camdyn and the other Warriors circled the Druids as they awaited Fallon to return with the last group. When he did, they turned as one to stare at the sky where the sun was sinking.

"Orion will rise there," Saffron said, and pointed to the sky.

Reaghan smiled and nodded. "Exactly. How did you know?"

Saffron shrugged. "I used to study the stars."

More and more about Saffron intrigued Camdyn, which was a very dangerous thing. He and the others kept a wary eye on the surrounding landscape with their enhanced sight and hearing while the Druids waited for the stars and moon to light the way.

The longer they stood out in the open, the antsier the Warriors grew. Camdyn knew they needed to get underground soon. He could practically feel that danger was on its way.

"We need to hurry," Broc muttered. His obvious wariness showed by the way his gaze darted around. "Deirdre must have left Cairn Toul after I checked on her last time because she's nearly here."

Camdyn growled and released his god just when the others did. He saw the surprise in Saffron's eyes as she caught a glimpse of him.

He knew what he looked like. He'd seen himself in the mirror. The fangs could be a lot to take in, but the claws were more than off-putting. Then there was the color each god favored.

For Sculel, the god inside Camdyn, it was a deep, rich brown. The same brown as well-tilled earth. As Saffron's gaze caught his, her eyes widened a fraction. He wanted to ask her if he frightened her the way the brown filled his entire eye, from corner to corner, even coloring the whites. It was the same for all Warriors and the color their god chose.

The tension inside him loosened a tad when Saffron offered a shaky smile. If she was frightened, she hid it well, but she would have to get used to their appearance since it was better for all if their gods were unbound.

"I see movement to the west," Logan whispered.

After a moment, Quinn's voice was full of contempt as he answered, "It's wyrran."

Camdyn smiled. It had been too long since he'd killed wyrran. His claws were eager to rip their heads off their skinny bodies, ready to remove that bit of evil from the world.

"Here it comes," Reaghan said.

Camdyn turned to see the sky darken enough so that the three stars in a line, Orion's Belt, could be seen by all. It appeared directly over the second standing stone on the peninsula.

"We wait for the moon now," Saffron said.

Clouds obscured the light of the moon, and with each second, the wyrran were gaining on them. Their shrieks filled the air, causing the Druids to flinch and the Warriors to flex their claws in anticipation.

"We're no' going to make it in time," Camdyn said as he crouched down in front of Saffron, ready to take out the wyrran heading his way.

Beside him Hayden grunted. "Doona let the little buggers touch any of our Druids."

Saffron's head whipped around as she heard a dangerous growl near her and realized it was Camdyn. She'd wondered what he looked like with his god unbound, and all her imaginings hadn't prepared her for the amazing and fearsome and impressive sight of him.

She wasn't afraid for herself. She knew none of the Warriors there would harm her, yet even getting a glimpse of Broc before hadn't prepared her for what the sight of Camdyn in Warrior form would do to her.

Her heart raced, her blood pumped loudly in her ears. There was power within him, power and domination. Authority no one would dare take from him.

Supremacy no one could deny.

And it thrilled her that she was a part of it all, a part of something to do with Camdyn.

She gasped when he leaped away from her and landed atop a diminutive yellow creature that let out a shriek, which had her covering her ears. Soon all the Warriors were fighting the wyrran in a battle full of roars, growls, and pure dominance by the Warriors.

Saffron didn't think the clouds would ever move from over the moon, and when they did, it gave them the briefest of moments to see where their path lay.

She and Reaghan gripped hands as they watched the moon's bright light touch first the Comet Stone before it shed a path from the Comet Stone to the Ring of Brodgar.

Upon the Comet Stone, lit only by the light of the moon, was a double spiral which looked like an *S* lying on its side. Saffron watched the double spiral grow brighter and brighter.

"That's where we need to be," Reaghan said. "The Comet Stone. The doorway is there."

Saffron started to follow the others as they ran to the Comet Stone, but she looked back to see Camdyn fighting five wyrran. His shirt was cut in five long rows across his chest, and she was sure there was blood as well.

"Aren't you going to help him?" she asked Ian.

Ian laughed, his hand holding on to Dani tightly. "Camdyn doesna need my help."

Sure enough, by the time she looked back at him, Camdyn had killed all five.

"What are you waiting for, woman?" Camdyn demanded as he ran toward her and took her arm to pull her after him.

They flew over the ground so quickly her feet barely touched earth. Exhilaration filled Saffron as they raced toward the Comet Stone. Until she skidded to a halt and saw where Reaghan had placed her hand over the double spiral and the earth suddenly gave way, opening a large section in front of the stone.

The others soon disappeared into the earth. Into the dark. The very thing she feared more than anything.

CHAPTER
SIXTEEN

Camdyn cleaved the head off the last wyrran he'd been fighting while his friends filed into the opening, and smiled as the body hit the ground. He glanced up when he heard shrieks. More were coming.

He turned to find Lucan, Hayden, and Arran trying desperately to get Saffron to go into the tunnel that had opened before the Comet Stone.

"We doona have time for this," Hayden said as a ball of fire erupted in his hand and he threw it at a wyrran racing toward them.

The wyrran erupted in flames, its screams echoing around the peninsula.

"I can't," Saffron said, and jerked out of Arran's hold.

Camdyn let out a roar when he saw the way Arran roughly gripped Saffron's arm. He pushed his friend away from Saffron and glared at Arran.

Arran threw up his hands. The white skin of his god glowed in the moonlight. "Then you handle her," he ground out.

Before Camdyn could turn back to Saffron, Arran cursed and shot a ball of ice at an approaching wyrran, knocking its head clean off.

Camdyn faced Saffron and took note of her wild eyes and rapid breathing. "You willna be alone down there."

"I wasn't alone before," she muttered.

Not for the first time Camdyn wondered what Declan had done to her, but it would have to wait. For now, he needed to get her below before the wyrran got her.

Camdyn gripped her shoulders and gave her a slight shake. "Saffron, we need to get in there to awaken Laria."

"It's beneath the earth." Her tawny eyes met his, and she didn't try to hide her fear.

"Bloody hell," Lucan called as he drew upon his power to control shadows and darkness. The shadows covered him, concealing him from the wyrran. "The door is closing!"

Camdyn glanced to see that indeed the doorway into the labyrinth was closing. "Everyone needs you, Saffron. Please. I give you my oath as a Highlander and a Warrior, that I willna let anything harm you down there."

She brushed away a lone tear that seeped from the corner of her eye and gave a single nod. Camdyn didn't wait for more. He lifted her in his arms and used his incredible speed to get inside the tunnel.

A second later, Lucan, Hayden, and Arran were right behind him. The sound of the stone door closing was a loud boom belowground. The Druids winced at the screeches of anger from the wyrran above them.

"Deirdre is here," Broc suddenly said. "She saw where we entered, but it willna take her long to realize she can no' get to us."

Fallon asked, "And Declan? Do you know where he is?"

"Nay," Broc answered. "He's using his magic to obscure himself. That's the only explanation."

"Ah, not to be a girl or anything, but I'd really like to be able to see," Gwynn said into the silence.

To his relief, Camdyn heard Saffron chuckle along with the others at Gwynn's comment.

"Never let it be said I doona bow to the wishes of my woman," Logan said as he nudged Hayden. "Give us some light."

Camdyn knew the Warriors could have guided the Druids

effortlessly through the labyrinth with their ability to see in the dark, but it was probably better for all if everyone could see.

Hayden lifted his hand above his head and a flame suddenly appeared. The yellow-orange glow danced upon the red skin of Hayden's Warrior and the small, red horns that appeared at the top of his head through his blond hair.

Broc had tamped down his god because the ceiling of the labyrinth was too low and his wings kept scraping against them, and one by one the others did the same.

"What now?" Ian asked.

Fallon walked through their group until he stood in front of Ramsey. "You said there would be a male Druid from the Torrichilty Forest."

"So I did," Ramsey replied with a small lift of his chin. "I didna lie, Fallon."

"I doona see anyone else."

"You're looking at your male Druid."

Camdyn could only blink, he was so taken aback. It had never dawned on him that a Warrior could also be part Druid. Why hadn't Ramsey said anything before?

"As I thought," Larena said with a smile.

Fallon grinned and held out his arm to Ramsey. They clasped each other's forearms. "I wish you would have trusted us enough to tell us sooner."

"I didna want Deirdre to know," Ramsey said by way of explanation.

"Holy hell," Quinn muttered. "How did you keep that from Deirdre all these centuries, Ramsey?"

Ramsey, always a man of few words, shrugged. "It wasna easy."

"We can discuss this later," Reaghan said. "Right now we need to determine which way to go."

Camdyn peered through the others to see that they were indeed at a crossroads. There was a huge wall that rose up above them into the earth. On either side was a corridor for them to choose.

"I doona suppose you could have a vision to steer us in the right direction, could you?" Camdyn whispered to Saffron.

She stiffly shook her head. "Not once have I ever had a vision that involved my fate. I doubt that would cease now."

"Aye," he muttered dejectedly.

Nothing was ever easy, and Camdyn had a sneaking suspicion that it was going to cost all of them a lot more than they expected just to get to Laria.

Charon sat in a corner of his pub, his hand around an untouched pint of ale. He'd returned to his village to discover the wyrran hadn't come back.

And neither had Deirdre.

He had almost driven back to the MacLeods. Almost. But in the end, he knew his place was here, with his people. They were powerless to protect themselves from wyrran or even Druid magic. Charon had sworn to defend them four hundred years ago. He wouldn't abandon them now.

A sputter of something magical, something urgent, raced along his skin. His god, Ranmond, answered with a roar that nearly tore from Charon's throat.

He lifted his head and rose from the table to walk outside. Without knowing how or why, Charon found himself facing north. And he knew without a doubt he needed to go there. Immediately.

Phelan was leaving the theater from seeing his third movie that day. He paused as he glanced up at the sky and the full moon. He'd been in Aberdeen for nearly two weeks and found he quite liked the city.

He turned and started back toward the small, abandoned house he was using when the force of the magic stopped him in his tracks.

The urge to go northwest was overwhelming. Crushing. Overpowering.

Phelan had been on his own so long, had felt so little

magic over the past four centuries, that the feel of such strong magic made his skin itch.

It didn't hurt. It felt like it did when he was a lad and a wound was beginning to heal and it would itch.

The more Phelan tried to ignore the pull of the magic, the more it engulfed him. Before he knew it, his feet were taking him to where the magic dictated.

Malcolm stood beside Deirdre overlooking the peninsula where the two stone circles stood. The entire peninsula hummed with magic. *Mie* magic.

It raced over his skin, leaving a trail of goose bumps he didn't try to hide. The appeal of the magic was persuasive. Compelling.

He wanted to go with the men he had called friends. He yearned to stand by Larena's side as they awoke Laria. He craved to watch as Deirdre was killed.

But he could do none of those things.

Malcolm had promised himself to Deirdre in return for Larena's safety. He wouldn't jeopardize that to save his own soul.

Besides, his soul had been lost long ago.

"Find where they went," Deirdre commanded him.

He turned and raised a blond brow at her, the maroon skin of his god appearing darker in the moonlight. "The wyrran couldna find it and they were right upon the MacLeods, and you want me to find it?"

"I do not repeat my commands, Malcolm. Do as you're told."

Malcolm clenched his teeth and started walking along the long, thin peninsula. He could barely breathe because of the force of the beautiful, pure, magnificent magic that filled the air.

He'd been around such magic at MacLeod Castle, but then he'd been mortal and hadn't felt the magic. The heavy, cloying feel of *drough* magic made him want to shred his skin from his bones with his own claws.

But the feel of *mie* magic . . . It wouldn't last long, only until he returned to Deirdre. But he would savor this small piece of heaven, this tiny relief from the hell that was his life.

The wyrran saw him approach and gathered around him. Malcolm didn't spare them a glance as he walked past the first ring of standing stones.

Littered throughout the peninsula were remnants of more stones that had either fallen over or had been knocked down through the centuries. It was a shame. Malcolm would have liked to have seen it when all the stones stood tall and brilliant against the sky.

By the time he reached the large center stone where the MacLeods and his cousin Larena had disappeared, Malcolm could feel the pulse of magic grow.

He knelt at the base of the stone and ran his hand over the grass. Nowhere did he see evidence that the ground had been disturbed. Then again, Camdyn's power was the ability to move the earth. Yet Malcolm had the suspicion this was done by Druid magic, not Warrior power.

Malcolm lifted his head and looked at the imposing stone before him. The moon had shifted but some of its light still fell upon the stone. And that's when he saw part of what looked like a spiral.

"A Celtic symbol," he muttered as he stood and ran his fingers along the spiral.

It wasn't etched in the stone. It was like it appeared only by the light of the moon.

Malcolm smiled. "Druid magic, of course."

He glanced down at his feet again. Somehow the moon upon the stone had allowed the earth to open and the others to enter. But it couldn't be that simple or anyone could have stumbled upon this earlier.

Then he remembered how Reaghan had told them she was the key to finding Laria. So it was Reaghan who had opened the doorway.

"Good luck, my friends," he whispered to those below him. He couldn't call out to the MacLeods or any of the other Warriors by name. The wyrran would hear him and report back to Deirdre.

So he kept his hopes to himself and turned on his heel to run back to Deirdre. As usual he kept all expression from his face.

It wasn't that hard to do. He had no feelings inside him. Deirdre had killed all of them when she'd unbound his god.

CHAPTER
SEVENTEEN

Saffron dearly wished she was able to tell the others which way to go, but no matter how hard she tried, no vision came to her.

It was so frustrating, especially when she knew how desperately they could use the information.

"Go right," Reaghan suggested.

It was Hayden and Isla who were the closest and began to go down the right-hand hallway. The light from Hayden's fireball showed what looked like holes in the rectangular stones that made up the walls, ceiling, and floor.

Saffron rose up on her tiptoes and looked over shoulders so she could see what was going on. Fallon and Larena were the next to follow them. Hayden was in front of Isla and walking with slow, measured steps when his foot landed on a stone that cracked beneath his weight.

The sound was like a shot in the silence.

"Son of a bitch," he yelled and grabbed Isla in his arms as he raced back to the crossroads.

"Hayden," Isla cried out as she reached over his shoulder and pulled out a small arrow.

Saffron's mouth fell open as Hayden turned and she could see a dozen or more poking from his back. Isla began to yank them out, and thankfully Hayden healed almost instantly.

"No *drough* blood," Fallon said as he inspected one of the arrows. "The tip is made of stone, no' metal."

"Which means they booby-trapped this place when they built it," Gwynn said.

Arran snorted, his lips twisted in resignation. "Just what we need."

"Shall we go left then?" Camdyn asked.

Saffron had intended to stay near Camdyn because he'd promised to keep her safe, but if he was going to lead the way down a dark, dank, small tunnel, she'd prefer to stay behind.

She'd never been claustrophobic before, but three years in Declan's prison had changed all of that. Now, she couldn't stand to be closed in.

Already her scalp tingled and her nerves were stretched tight from every little sound she heard in the labyrinth. And they hadn't even really gotten started yet.

No one had any idea how big this maze was or how long it would take them to reach Laria.

"Left it is," Fallon said. He held out his hand and Larena took it with a small smile.

It was better to have the Warriors go down a corridor first since they were immortal. But eventually the Druids would have to walk that same path.

Saffron had seen plenty of movies in her life. She knew how things could happen with one small misstep. The last thing she wanted was for anyone to get hurt.

But what they were doing was extremely dangerous. Not just belowground, but above as Deirdre awaited them. It would be a miracle if everyone returned to the castle hale and whole.

She looked at Camdyn. She couldn't imagine him injured. He had always been so resilient and tough.

"We're through," Fallon called, breaking into Saffron's thoughts.

The next to follow were Hayden and Isla, and when they made it through unscathed, the rest of them followed. When it was time for Saffron to walk the long corridor, she wanted to keep her eyes ahead of her to where the others waited to help ease her anxiety, but she was so worried about stepping on a wrong stone that her eyes were glued to the floor.

It seemed an eternity before she, Camdyn, and Braden reached the others. Saffron inhaled a deep breath and slowly let it out.

Camdyn knew Saffron wasn't handling being underground well, but so far she was keeping it together. At the rate they were going, however, he didn't know how long that would last.

He noticed how she sidled closer to him when she thought there was a threat. Unfortunately, he quite liked having her so close.

Unlike the other Druids, Saffron hadn't removed her jacket, though her gloves had been stuffed into her coat pockets and her scarf now draped loosely about her shoulders.

Her walnut-colored hair hung down her back, its thickness and silkiness causing him to lean close and inhale her moonlight and snow scent.

No matter what he did, no matter how he tried to walk away from her, he couldn't seem to do it. And after holding her, tasting her, caressing her, he didn't want to walk away.

Ever.

"Sonya," Lucan called.

Sonya and Broc worked their way through the group until they stood at the next crossroads.

Broc scowled at Lucan. "Why did you call Sonya?"

Cara lifted her finger, and said, "Reaghan was the first artifact, and Sonya found the second in the amulet. We assume it's the second to be used."

"She has a point," Sonya said. She pulled out the amulet she wore around her neck and lifted it over her head. "But what do I do with it?"

"Good question," Quinn mumbled.

Dani stepped forward and moved Hayden's arm to see

more of the wall in front of them. "There has to be a place to put it, is my guess. What else would you do with it?"

"Maybe just wearing it will aid her," Marcail offered.

Sonya returned the amulet to her neck. "We have to choose a way again. Left or right?"

It was decided to try left again. Camdyn kept Saffron beside him, though he made sure to move a bit in front of her to safeguard her.

They went through four more crossroads before they came to a dead end and had to turn back. Since they had gone left each time, it was easy to return to where they had been.

"It would be so much easier if we could split up," Ramsey said.

Logan nodded. "And faster."

"But we need the artifacts in certain places before we go forward," Reaghan said.

Camdyn felt Saffron's fingers tighten around his hand, and he answered with a slight squeeze of his own. "It's with an understanding this could take a very long time, but we need to move forward."

"Aye, we do," Sonya admitted. She and Broc once more stepped forward and they turned right this time.

As before, nothing happened. It put Camdyn on edge. He'd been fully prepared for something to shoot out of the walls at Sonya and Broc since they'd gone through fine when they turned left. But the same had happened going right?

Never knowing if there was a booby trap or not was only going to make this expedition of theirs even more nerve-racking.

Sonya and Broc took a left at the next crossroads and had them walking down a hallway that Camdyn didn't think would ever end.

When it did, they all thought they had reached another dead end until the fire from Hayden's hand showed a massive double spiral that took up the width of the entire door.

"It's the same as the amulet," Sonya said. She lifted it over her neck to hold it up to the etching when a pulse of magic flew from the door over them, causing everyone to take a step back from the force of it.

At the same time, a slot in the door appeared that was the exact shape of the amulet. Without hesitation Sonya stepped forward and put the amulet in the hole.

There was a loud click, then a bang as the door began to lift upward. Dust and earth rained down upon them while the door slowly moved upward, allowing them entrance farther into the labyrinth.

They all hurried quickly through the door since they didn't know how long it would stay open. When the last of them were through, the door began to lower.

"Wait," Sonya said as the door shut with a boom. "The amulet."

"The maze took it," Reaghan said. "At least now Deirdre won't ever get it."

Camdyn had bent over to get the dirt out of his hair when he heard Fallon's low hiss just before the sound of metal hitting stone filled the silence.

He lifted his head to find the sword they had stolen from Deirdre lying on the floor. "What happened?"

"It burned me," Fallon answered.

Quinn wrapped his hand about it, and promptly released it. "Mine as well."

Without pause Lucan tried, but just as with his brothers, he was burned.

"We all try then," Ramsey said.

One by one the Warriors tried to touch the sword, and each time it rejected them. Camdyn was the last to step forward.

"Maybe a Warrior is no' supposed to carry it," Camdyn said as he studied the sword.

Hayden shook his head. "A Warrior is supposed to carry it."

Camdyn released a breath and gripped the hilt of the sword. He expected to feel pain, but all he felt was the cool touch of metal against his palm.

"Bloody hell," Galen muttered.

Fallon smiled. "Looks like the sword found who it wanted. You're up next, Camdyn."

Camdyn dreaded this part. He could either leave Saffron with Ramsey and Arran to watch, or take her with him. And he suspected she wouldn't like either option.

"Aye," he called. Camdyn felt a tremble run through Saffron. He turned to her and said, "Ramsey will keep you safe."

He wasn't finished speaking before her head was moving back and forth. "You promised," she said.

Just as he figured. He let out a sigh. "All right."

He walked forward, Saffron on his heels. Now, it was up to him to make the decisions. He looked to the left of the crossroads, then to the right.

Nothing could help him make a decision on which way to go. And there was no way he was going to put Saffron's life in danger, not if he could help it.

Camdyn went down on his haunches and put his hand on the floor. He commanded the earth to answer him, to help detect patterns where there was something other than rock and stone to help keep them safe.

But the Druids had been too smart for him. Their magic coated every inch of the labyrinth. He rose with a curse and pointed to the right.

"I'm going to try this way."

He took two steps and looked back at the others. On his third step, he felt the earth move in a way that had nothing to do with booby traps.

"Get clear," he shouted as he reached out and grabbed hold of Saffron's arms.

He yanked her out of the way before the rocks collapsed on her. For several more minutes dirt and rocks continued to rain around them, but Camdyn used his power to keep it away from him and Saffron.

When he lifted his head he found himself being attacked, but not by wyrran or Deirdre.

By Saffron.

It was all Camdyn could do to keep her from breaking out of his hold. Whether she knew it or not, she was using her magic mixed with her terror and it was a powerful combination.

Almost instantly Camdyn sensed the unmistakable feel of *drough* magic from above him. There was no doubt it was Deirdre. With Deirdre above him trying to break through his power, and Saffron in front of him doing her damnedest to get away, Camdyn was holding on by a thin thread.

He had to get Saffron under control somehow, someway.

"Saffron," he called.

By the way she kept clawing at his face it was obvious she couldn't hear him. If he couldn't get through to her that way, he would have to use another.

Camdyn didn't want to touch her with his claws and risk cutting her, and he needed his god unbound in order to keep the earth from crushing them.

With no other choice, he urged his claws to disappear before he grabbed first one wrist, then the other and held them above Saffron's head. Her head thrashed from side to side as she screamed at him to let her go.

Somehow he managed to tamp his god down enough that his fangs vanished, but he was still able to use his power. That was all he needed to do to claim her mouth. She bucked against him and tried to turn her head, but he wasn't about to give up. He had to calm her so they could fight Deirdre together.

He licked at her lips, pressing his mouth against hers hard and with all the passion he'd held in check until that moment. She took a breath, and when she did he swept his tongue inside her mouth and ran it along hers.

Her soft moan was his undoing. His cock hardened as her leg wound around his waist. Camdyn kissed her with all the abandon, all the need, he'd held back from her—and himself.

He kissed her as if there were no tomorrow. Because for them, there might not be.

He kissed her as if he'd waited his entire life to taste her. Because he had.

He kissed her as if he never wanted to kiss another woman.

Because he didn't.

CHAPTER
EIGHTEEN

Saffron knew the moment Camdyn's lips touched hers that she was powerless to resist his temptation. His kissed coaxed, teased. Enticed.

His hard body pressed against hers, urging her passion higher, driving her need deeper. Even through her thick jacket she could feel the passion radiating from his body. She was drowning in it. And it felt blissful.

When his tongue slid between her lips, Saffron melted against him. She wanted to touch him, hold him, but Camdyn wouldn't release her wrists.

With one hand he held her arms above her while he continued to ravish her mouth with need so strong it never entered her mind to turn him away. All she wanted was more of him and his kisses that made her weak all over.

She moaned when he tilted his head and deepened the kiss. He took, he demanded. He claimed.

He released her hands and slid his beneath her jacket and under her sweater to touch bare skin. Saffron lifted her leg to wrap around his waist and bring him closer, to have him against her.

The hard length of his arousal only heightened her own desires, which were quickly blazing out of control. It had been so long since her body had found release, so terribly long since she'd been in a man's arms.

She wanted Camdyn. Yearned for him, craved him. His kisses were like a drug, an intoxication she couldn't get enough of.

"By the saints, you taste so damned good," he muttered and kissed her again.

Deeply. Intensely.

And Saffron was captivated.

She arched against him as his hand slid over her buttocks and rocked her against his rigid length. Her body pulsed with unquenched need as she felt herself grow damp. Need, forceful and urgent, slid over her like silk.

Her body wasn't her own as she waited to feel more of Camdyn, hungered to touch him as he was touching her.

He held her still against the stone wall with his hard body while he kissed her to reckless abandon, wild need. His kiss took, it seized. And she was more than happy to give him everything he wanted.

She could only stand there, her body on fire, as his hands rubbed down her arms before dragging her against him.

Saffron plunged her hands into the cool strands of his coal-black hair and kissed him with all the desire, all the longing, within her.

His kiss turned insistent, almost desperate as the fires raged amid them. Saffron could feel the need tightening between her legs as he continued to rock against her.

And then he ended the kiss as suddenly as he began it.

Saffron blinked open her eyes as she fought to get her breathing back under control. For several moments they simply stared at each other, their ragged breaths the only sound to be heard.

She could only make out his silhouette in the darkness, and she longed to look into his eyes, to see if the passion she felt had been real.

"I need your help," he finally said, his breathing harsh, his lips wet from their kisses.

Saffron lowered her leg and nodded though she couldn't

dispel the desire within her as easily as Camdyn could. She drew in a ragged breath, trying to calm her racing heart. "What do you need?"

"Deirdre is the one who collapsed the tunnel. I doona know how, but she did. She's also using her magic against me so I can no' put the earth back the way it was."

Saffron adjusted her sweater and tried to step out of his arms, but he wouldn't allow it. "And I made it worse by fighting you."

"I doona blame you. But now that you are under control, your magic mixed with my power could overwhelm Deirdre's black magic."

"I doubt it," Saffron muttered, but she was willing to try anything to get some space back, even if it was the narrow tunnels of the labyrinth. "What do I do?"

"Concentrate and focus your magic into me."

She saw his head lower to hers, felt his warm breath on her skin. Her eyes drifted closed and her body moved toward him. Just before their lips touched again, he turned away. Saffron's mouth parted as she licked her lips and took a deep breath.

Surprisingly, her magic was stronger than she had ever felt it as she called for it. It rushed through her body like a tidal wave, the force of it taking her breath.

Saffron channeled the magic toward Camdyn. She pictured it invading his skin and filling his body much like it did hers.

He grunted, his body stiff. The groan that rumbled from deep within him had nothing to do with pain. "Shite."

She smiled at his reaction, but that soon faded as she felt something push against her magic.

"It's Deirdre," Camdyn said, his voice low and clipped.

Saffron knew how powerful black magic was. She had experienced it firsthand for three years. She had been pulled from that hell, and there was no way she was going to die buried beneath tons of earth and rock.

She put her hands in the middle of Camdyn's back as she

closed her eyes. The drums and chanting filled her ears as if they had been waiting for her.

All Saffron wanted to do was go to them, but she held herself in check. She could feel her magic strengthening, but it was nothing compared to when she had been staring at the fire. When she found herself forgetting Camdyn and listening only to the chanting, she stopped it immediately.

It wasn't just her and Camdyn who were trapped. The others could be as well. And regardless of her fears, she needed to step up and do what she could to fight Deirdre.

"Saffron," Camdyn murmured, his voice rough with desire.

Her stomach flipped at the sound of his voice, the way her name was like a caress upon his lips. No one had ever said her name like that before, and she knew no one would again.

Saffron heard something moving around them, but she didn't open her eyes. Not yet.

"I'm getting it," he said.

She smiled and took a step closer to him. The feel of his heat, his hard muscles beneath her palm, sent her heart pounding. There was no fear in her now. She knew Camdyn would keep her safe. He'd already proven it by preventing them from being crushed.

Even when she had flipped out, he had gotten her under control while still keeping them safe. She couldn't imagine how much power it took to keep all that weight from falling on top of them.

Just thinking about it made a chill rush down her spine. Declan would enjoy it if he knew that he had made her afraid of being underground. And she hated that.

"Almost," Camdyn gritted out. "Doona let go of your magic."

"Never," she whispered, and tightened her grip on him.

His body quivered beneath her hands, but whether it was from the task of fighting against Deirdre or her magic, Saffron didn't know.

She heard their names being shouted frantically. "Camdyn."

"I hear them," he said.

Saffron turned her head to the side, but all she saw was darkness. She could hear the others as if they were getting closer. And then suddenly, she saw a ray of light break through the rock.

"I told them you both were still alive," Hayden said as he looked between two rocks.

Saffron had never felt so happy to see light again. Being in the dark had reminded her of when she was blind, and though it was something she had gotten used to, now that she had once again taken in the amazing array of colors in the world, she couldn't imagine not seeing them again.

Camdyn gave a massive heave and Saffron looked up to see the top of the tunnel shift back into place. Hayden jumped back as the earth blocking them also returned to where it had been.

Saffron dropped her hands as Camdyn turned to face her. She could see he wanted to say something, but before he could they were swarmed by the others.

"It was Deirdre," Camdyn said.

Broc's lips flattened. "Aye. We know. She didna break through the ground and see us, however."

"We've wasted enough time here," Fallon called out. "Sonya has already healed those who were injured. Are either of you hurt?"

"No," Saffron said and glanced at Camdyn.

Fallon gave her a quick smile. "Let's move on then."

Saffron thought that a brilliant idea until she looked at the spot where Camdyn had kissed her as if there were no tomorrow, as if his very being had gone into that kiss.

She allowed Dani and Gwynn to pull her with them as they began to walk. Camdyn had retrieved the sword he had dropped and was soon back up at the front leading them. And she found she wanted to be with him.

Regardless of the dangers.

Camdyn had gotten her out of Declan's prison when no one else could have. He had brought her out of her trance when no one else could have.

And he had calmed her when she knew no one else could have after the cave-in.

Her gaze was on the back of his head as he shook it from side to side, clearing his black locks of debris. She bit back a smile as he pulled his long hair back from his face and tied a strip of leather around it at the base of his neck.

A queue she'd heard him call it.

Yet, strands of his hair fell around his face to curl lightly. Again and again he raked them back from his face, but those locks of hair were determined to fall as they would.

"Are you all right?" Dani asked her.

Saffron smiled, her gaze still on Camdyn. "I am."

"We thought you'd be freaking the hell out," Gwynn said, her voice thick from her worry.

"Oh, I did." Saffron was embarrassed to think of just what she looked like.

Gwynn's head swiveled to her. "But . . . you're calm now."

Saffron shrugged. "Camdyn calmed me."

"Ah," Dani said, a smile in her voice.

But Saffron didn't care. She battled through her terror, been kissed like never before, and helped to achieve a small victory over Deirdre.

All with Camdyn.

He turned a corner, and just before he walked out of sight, he looked at her. Their eyes caught, held. Saffron missed a step as her body hummed with the answering desire she had seen in Camdyn's dark gaze.

Without a word, she walked away from her friends, meandering through the others until she stood beside Camdyn.

"You shouldna be here," he muttered angrily.

She raised a brow to look at him. "And who else will protect me from the very thing I fear most?"

He let out a loud sigh. "You are better away from me."

"Maybe, but I'd rather not stake my life on it tonight."

Camdyn came to a halt and stared hard at her. "Which way then?"

Saffron ran a hand through her hair and grimaced when she felt the dirt there. She leaned her head to the side and ruffled her hair to get out as much as she could while she looked to the left. Then she switched sides and repeated it as she looked to the right.

"The left smells funny. I say we go right."

A hint of a smile appeared on his lips before he turned away from her to start down the right-hand corridor. It was short, and he had just reached the corner where it only allowed him to go left when Saffron started after him.

She heard a loud crack ahead of her. Without thought to her own safety, she began running toward Camdyn even as the others tried to hold her back.

Camdyn let out a loud curse before she heard what sounded like claws sliding down rocks.

The Warriors tried to get around her, but the tunnel was too narrow. Saffron twisted away from Quinn and rushed to the corner where she slid to a halt when she saw the floor missing.

"Camdyn!" she bellowed as she fell to her knees and looked over the edge of the broken floor.

She found him dangling from one hand, his claws caught in the rock. Her heart plummeted to her feet as she realized how easily he could have dropped. She peered below him, but all she saw was darkness. There was no way to know when the hole ended. Or even if it did.

Saffron leaned over the edge to help.

"Have you lost your mind?" Camdyn demanded calmly. "Get back so I can jump up."

She rolled her eyes, but stood to find the other Warriors behind her. Some were openly smiling at her exchange with Camdyn.

Before she could explain why she had rushed to him,

Camdyn landed beside her and gripped her shoulders to turn her to face him.

His mouth opened, but he clamped his shut as a muscle in his jaw ticked repeatedly.

Saffron cleared her throat. "So, the left corridor then?"

CHAPTER
NINETEEN

Deirdre's rage knew no bounds. She lashed out with her hair at anyone standing close to her, including her precious wyrran.

When a lock wrapped around Malcolm's neck and squeezed, the maroon Warrior simply raised a blond brow at her. "Killing me wouldna be in your best interest. Especially since I'm your last Warrior."

As much as she hated to admit it, he was right. She released her hold on him and threw back her head to shout her anger at the heavens.

She had heard and felt the ground move beneath her. She knew there had been a cave-in, but why couldn't she get below the surface?

It was bad enough she couldn't get close to the stone circles because of *mie* magic, but now she couldn't even get below the ground where the MacLeods were to reach Laria before they did.

"*Mie* magic shouldn't be able to stop me," she said when she'd gotten control of her rage. She looked at Malcolm. "Do you know what I've done to have the black magic inside me? Do you know what I've had to sacrifice?"

"And how many innocents you've killed?" Malcolm retorted.

There was something in his tone that caused her eyes to narrow on him. "Do you feel sorry for those innocents?"

"Nay. Nor do I feel sorry for you. You chose this path, Deirdre. Doona try to make it seem like this was forced on you. You were the one who pushed it on Isla."

Deirdre spat at the mention of Isla. "That bitch will pay for betraying me. Everyone who has betrayed me will get their comeuppance."

"You mean if they doona awake Laria first."

Her chest expanded as she took a deep breath. There was no mistaking the smirk on Malcolm's face. "You find this humorous? They will kill you as well for aiding me."

"I know my fate. I doona try to outrun it as you have," Malcolm stated. He crossed his arms over his chest. "You willna get under the ground. Why no' prepare for when Laria is awakened?"

"You have a point," she conceded. She looked over the peninsula.

She would set up a blockade. The MacLeods and their group trying to kill her would have to get through her, her wyrran, and Malcolm.

Camdyn didn't care that he'd almost dropped into the hole that appeared to go on forever. What scared the hell out of him was that Saffron had tried to save him.

Him!

He was immortal. Why did she keep forgetting that, especially when he couldn't forget that outside the castle she was mortal? Her life could be wiped out with the simplest of occurrences.

Camdyn backtracked his steps until he came to the left corridor. Like Saffron, he didn't like this hallway. It wasn't just the smell either. Something just seemed . . . off.

"We doona have a choice," Ian said from beside him. "This is our only way to go."

Camdyn shook his head. "We could get over that broken floor. Broc could fly the Druids or Fallon could jump them. As for us, it would be nothing to leap over it."

"True," Ramsey conceded. "Except I have to believe that

it was meant to keep us from going forward. This has to be the only way."

Fallon gave Camdyn a nod, and Camdyn took a step forward when he felt Saffron's magic move beside him. He'd thought he'd tortured himself by kissing her with such recklessness and no restraint, but the feel of her magic as she pushed it into him to fight Deirdre would be with him for eternity.

Her magic had felt wonderful before. But now . . . now it was as if it were living inside him, melding to his bones and muscles and flesh. As if it had taken residence in his soul.

Where he would sense Saffron. Always.

Forever.

He glanced at her to find her tawny gaze watching him with trepidation. She thought he was angry, and he was. He didn't want her risking her life for him. He wasn't worth it.

"Ready?" he asked her as they moved along the hallway, which was much longer than the last one.

"Not at all."

He took her hand as he led the way down the hall that switchbacked several times. They walked endlessly, and appeared to be going down a slight slant.

"This doesn't feel right," Saffron murmured.

He squeezed her hand. "It'll be fine," he lied.

Behind them Camdyn could hear the other Warriors telling the same lie to their women. All of them were on edge, and none of them knew why.

Camdyn used his enhanced senses to look and hear ahead of them for anything that might be lying in wait. The labyrinth hadn't been opened in centuries, so the idea that something or someone was alive down there was ludicrous.

Yet, none of the Warriors should be alive and they were. So who knew what awaited them?

The farther they walked, the more his apprehension grew. But nothing happened. The air didn't even stir. It was eerie, even to Camdyn. Eerie, and just not right.

After one more switchback, Camdyn found himself facing

a huge door with a knocker on it. The knocker itself was a massive dragon's head that appeared to have been hung there by its long neck. It held the knocker in its mouth and had sapphires for eyes.

"It feels as if it's watching me," Saffron said.

Cara nodded. "I agree. I swear his eyes are moving."

"You can no' see in this half light," Lucan told his wife. "Those eyes are just stones."

Camdyn was about to agree with Lucan when white smoke poured from the dragon's nostrils. "I doona know if it's alive, but it's certainly something."

"Do we use the knocker?" Saffron asked.

Camdyn took a deep breath. Only one way to find out. He released Saffron's hand and stepped forward. As he lifted his arm to grasp the knocker, he too felt as if the sapphire eyes of the dragon had just focused on him.

"Wait," Saffron said before his hand took the knocker. She gave him a slight shove so that she stood directly before the dragon.

"Saffron, what are you doing?" Camdyn demanded.

She shrugged. "I don't know. It just feels right that a Druid should do this and not a Warrior."

"You could get injured."

She smiled and looked over her shoulder at him. "Maybe. Maybe not."

Camdyn fisted his hands so he wouldn't reach over and yank Saffron away from the dragon's head. He held his breath as she reached up and gently stroked down from the dragon's forehead to his nostrils.

She repeated the caress again, this time lingering on the dragon's head. When she drew closer and wrapped her arms around the dragon, Camdyn managed to keep his feet rooted to the spot by sheer will alone.

"Camdyn, bring the sword," Saffron whispered.

He didn't question her. He cautiously held out the sword.

"Lift the sword above the dragon's head. There is a slot there where I believe the sword belongs."

Camdyn met her gaze and saw that she was now asking

him to trust her. How could he not? She, as well as everyone there, knew the stakes and what could happen if they failed.

He lifted the sword so that the tip was over the dragon's head. Again, he felt as if the dragon watched him, waiting for him to make a wrong move.

Saffron took the tip of the sword, and when she did the blade sliced her fingers. She didn't utter a sound. Gently, she guided the tip of the sword into the back of the dragon's head near its neck.

Camdyn slid the sword downward until the hilt of the sword rested across the dragon's neck and the blade stuck out through the bottom of the dragon. At once the dragon's eyes began to glow a bright blue as if lit from within. Camdyn grabbed Saffron's hand and tried to drag her backward.

They had taken two steps when more smoke poured from the dragon's nostrils. So much that they were able to follow it as it disappeared beneath the wall to the right of them.

"That's where we need to go," Saffron said as she walked to the wall and put her hand where the smoke had gone. "I feel air."

Camdyn and the other Warriors stepped to the wall and tried to shove it, lift it, slide it. Anything. But it wouldn't budge.

Saffron watched them for several moments before she put a hand on Camdyn's shoulders and said, "This place was made with magic. Doesn't it seem logical that in order to get inside you'd need magic?"

"Ah, yes," Reaghan said with a short laugh as she rubbed her hands together and joined Saffron before the door.

Once all the Druids were there they looked at one another. It was Marcail, whose magic was strengthened by being underground, who put her hand on the wall first.

Saffron and the others followed suit and poured their magic into the stones. Excitement rang through Saffron when she felt the door move. It was just a smidgen, but it was enough to know they were doing the right thing.

"It's not enough," Isla said. "For *mie* magic to be as powerful as black magic, we need to combine our magic."

With their hand still on the wall, the Druids placed their other hand on the person next to them. The force of the magic that raced through Saffron was incredible. She let it seep into her, through her, and into the wall and the Druids on either side of her.

The wall began to slide open. Step by step the Druids opened the door until they stood inside a small cavern. Saffron looked at the eight different doorways and inwardly groaned.

"What now?" Dani asked.

"We keep moving," Camdyn said.

Logan walked to one of the doorways and peered inside. "Taking the wrong tunnel could be disastrous."

Saffron wished she could have a vision to know which tunnel to take. She felt the others looking at her and she folded her hands in front of her so they wouldn't see how nervous she was.

"We're Druids," Sonya said. "We have magic. There has to be a way we can determine which way to go."

Gwynn nodded. "Or at least narrow it down."

"But how?" Cara asked.

Saffron met their gazes. "You know I can't have a vision about my future."

"Nay, I have a better idea," Reaghan said. "Broc, do you think you can find Laria?"

Broc smiled. "Unless she's blocked as Declan is."

They waited as Broc closed his eyes and used his power to find Laria. Saffron once more called up her magic. The more she used it the more it seemed to come easily to her. For so long she'd been afraid of her visions, and so she'd tried to pretend she didn't have any magic.

It had been her father who told her of her great-great-grandmother who had been a Druid. Saffron had done research on the Druids, which had proved annoying since no one knew for certain what they could and couldn't do.

With nothing else to do, Saffron had begun to use her magic after she went away to college. It had begun small at first, but grew quickly. By the time she took her trip to Europe her magic was as strong as it had ever been.

Until she had been brought to MacLeod Castle. And met Camdyn MacKenna.

Her mind was on Camdyn and how they continued to circle around their attraction to each other, and how they could either move on or see where the passion led them.

The idea of being in Camdyn's arms, of being loved by him and waking in his arms, was something she both feared and desired.

"There," Broc's voice rang out.

Saffron's eyes flew open to find Camdyn watching her. The others hurried to the entrance Broc had pointed out, but Saffron and Camdyn stood their ground.

Only when the others had passed did Camdyn take the four steps separating them. She looked up into his dark, fathomless eyes and asked, "What are you thinking?"

"It's better for both of us if I doona answer."

CHAPTER TWENTY

Camdyn was playing with fire, and he was about to get burned. The way Saffron watched him with longing and need sparkling in her tawny eyes made him yearn to pull her into one of the darkened caves and pin her against the wall as he had earlier.

To kiss her sweet lips and along her sexy neck. To have his hand on her bare skin again and to cup her breast.

His heart rate increased as he remembered how she rubbed against his cock, her soft moans music to his ears.

Camdyn had to turn away before he went to her the need, the hunger for her was so strong. He found the others gathered around the third entrance from the right, which Broc had pointed out.

"What is it?" he asked, anything to get his mind off Saffron so he could get himself back under control.

"I doona know," Fallon said. "None of us can pass through the door."

Camdyn watched as Hayden and Ian tried to walk through the doorway, only to be held back by an invisible barrier.

"The magic is so thick," Ian said as he took a step back, his brows furrowed deeply in his forehead.

"None of the Druids can go through?" Camdyn asked.

Reaghan shook her head. "Nay. It's very odd."

"The only ones who haven't tried to go through are you and Saffron," Cara said.

Camdyn looked to Saffron, who stood next to Dani. Saffron's gaze swung to him, and she lifted her shoulders in a shrug before stepping toward the doorway.

He held his breath, both wanting her to be able to get through, but also wanting her to be held back like the rest of them.

Her head was high as she paused before the arched doorway. She touched the outside stones, a small smile playing over her lips. "There are Celtic symbols marked around the doorway."

"They're the same symbols as those on the cylinder that held the map within the Tablet of Orn," Ian said.

Camdyn held his breath when Saffron dropped her hand to her side and took a step through the doorway. There was an audible gasp as she was allowed to pass.

He clenched his hands into fists, the urge to be with her crushing. Somehow Camdyn held himself in check as she stopped and turned to look at him.

"Why me?" she asked, her gaze moving from him to look at the others. "Why did it let me through?"

Gwynn hurried to the door and tried to go through again, but just like before she wasn't able. "Maybe because you touched the dragon?"

Isla walked to the dragon's head and stroked it just as Saffron had before she returned and tried to follow Saffron through the door. But it didn't allow her through either.

"I don't understand," Saffron said. "I cannot be the only one it allows through."

Camdyn heard the tremor of fear in her voice as every eye turned to him. He wanted to see if he could go through the doorway, but if he couldn't . . .

With no other choice, Camdyn moved forward. He tried to look away from Saffron, but he couldn't. His gaze, along with every fiber of his being, was trained on her.

He stopped before the doorway and glanced at the markings etched into the stone. Saffron stood still as stone, but he could feel the thread of fear in her magic that was growing as each moment passed.

Camdyn took a deep breath and lifted his foot. To his surprise, the doorway allowed him through. The relief that filled Saffron's eyes made him want to take her in his arms and hold her, to tell her everything was going to be all right.

When he doubted very much it would.

She leaned a hand against the wall next to her and smiled. "Thank you, God. I didn't want to be alone for this."

He understood exactly how she felt, because he hadn't wanted her to be alone either. Camdyn turned back to the others and scratched his neck.

"Now what?" he asked.

Galen leaned a shoulder against the doorway and smiled. "It looks like you and Saffron are meant to do this alone, my friend."

"If that's the case, you're going to need this," Logan said as he tossed something across the threshold.

Camdyn caught the gold cylinder that was the Tablet of Orn.

"And this," Dani said.

Camdyn reached out and snagged the ancient iron key from the air, and handed it to Saffron.

Ian stepped to the doorway, a cylinder in his hands. He moved the wooden dials around the cylinder. "This is the exact order the symbols need to be," he said.

Camdyn took the cylinder Ian held out and looked at the small squares with the same symbols that were on the doorway.

It took no time for him to memorize the order of the symbols from the cylinder, but still he handed it to Saffron so she could also have a look.

"Be careful," Lucan said.

Camdyn nodded. "You doona have to remind me."

"We'll try to find a way to you," Fallon said.

No sooner had the words left Fallon's mouth than the wall the Druids had used their magic to open shut with a resounding thud.

"Shite," Ramsey said, and tried to walk through one of the other doorways.

But whatever had held them back from entering with Camdyn and Saffron prevented them from entering any of the other doorways now.

Lucan caught Camdyn's gaze. "It looks as though we'll be waiting here until you can find Laria."

"Make it fast," Arran said as he rammed a shoulder into one of the invisible barriers at a doorway.

"Wait," Sonya called out. She unzipped the backpack she was carrying and tossed several bottles of water across to them.

Saffron smiled and shoved them into the pockets of her coat. "Thank you."

"Be careful," Quinn told them.

Camdyn gave a nod and turned on his heel. He shifted sideways to squeeze past Saffron and sucked in a breath when his hand brushed her hip. One small touch was all it took to make him burn. And how he burned for her.

She fell into step behind him as they walked away from the doorway and their group of friends.

"I hate to admit this, but I'm scared."

He glanced over his shoulder at her. "I know. We'll make it though."

"Why did it only let us through? Because of the dragon?"

"Maybe. It's hard to tell. This place is so full of magic and traps that I doona know its intention."

She snorted. "Its intention is to keep Laria from being found."

"Even if we have the artifacts?"

"What if it was Deirdre that had found all the artifacts? What if her spy, Charlie, had been able to get Dani to tell him where the artifacts were kept in the castle?"

Camdyn growled. "I doona want to even think about what could have happened, but I see your point. If it was Deirdre or some other evil down here, the labyrinth would want to keep them out."

"Do you think the magic here senses the god inside you?"

Camdyn stopped and turned to look at her. "You mean, does it know that I have evil inside me?"

She shifted her feet and shrugged. "Yes."

"Most likely." He looked over her shoulder, but the tunnel had curved and he could no longer see the others. "Regardless, it allowed us to come this far."

"Does nothing frighten you?" she asked, her head cocked to the side so that a lock of her hair brushed the top of her breasts.

There was one thing in particular that scared the hell out of him, but Saffron didn't need to know she was it. Camdyn arched a brow and said, "I'm an immortal Highland Warrior. What do I have to fear?"

They resumed walking, and Camdyn tried to keep his senses sharp for anything ahead as they made their way through the tunnel. The sound of her breathing, every step she took, every time their bodies brushed accidentally, sent his blood heating until his body sizzled with longing, a yearning that consumed him.

He was aware of everything regarding Saffron, and it was driving him to distraction. A wonderful, painful distraction. He longed to hold her against him, to feel her soft body and sweet curves.

Camdyn found himself staring at three steps that led down into a small room. He raised a hand so Saffron would know to wait and walked into the room himself.

He moved about every inch of it to make sure it was safe before he waved Saffron to him. Camdyn crossed his arms over his chest and stared at the walls and the evidence that they weren't able to move onward.

"Did we miss an exit somewhere in the tunnel?" Saffron asked as she looked around her.

"Nay."

"Damn. Now what?"

"We rest for a time."

Saffron leaned against a wall and let herself slide down to the floor. "Good. I'm starving."

Camdyn turned away so she wouldn't see his scowl. He'd

been so intent on keeping her away from danger he'd forgotten that she needed to eat. As a Warrior, he could go indefinitely without eating, though it weakened his body.

"I've got enough PowerBars in my pocket if you'd like one."

He shook his head while he examined the walls in the round room. "Nay. You'll need them."

"You need to eat as well. I know you can go without, but despite being immortal, your body will grow weak. And . . . well, I need you, Camdyn."

He slowly turned to face her. The last person that had needed him was Allison. He'd forgotten what it was like to be needed, that warm feeling that spread through him that he wasn't alone in the world.

Camdyn took the proffered bar and tore open the wrapper. The bar was tasteless, but he ate it because she'd asked.

Saffron ate her bar, drank as much water as she dared, and then sat. And sat and sat. She walked around the room, looking for any clues to how they could move forward. But there was nothing.

Finally, she resumed her seat and raised her knees to her chest. "I can't stand this silence. Talk to me, Camdyn."

He sat on the steps in the doorway, his elbows resting on his knees. His inky black hair had all but come out of his queue. "What do you want to talk about?"

"Tell me about you? Where do you come from? What time?"

He sat up and removed the leather holding his hair. His black hair fell around his face and neck, making him look even more rakish than his normal brooding face did.

Saffron waited as he fiddled with the leather strip, almost as if he were trying to decide what to tell her. He was much more interesting to look at than the spiderwebs that seemed to grow bigger and more numerous the deeper into the maze they went. Was it some kind of cosmic law that said spiders had to be everywhere? Especially underground?

But her thoughts of spiders were halted as Camdyn's voice filled the small room.

"I was born in 1333. My parents were like any family back then. They fought alongside our laird, raised sheep, and tried to make the best of life. My father was . . . a hard man. My mother a woman with a kind heart."

She knew the Warriors were immortal, but to put an age on him, to know he was almost seven hundred years old, boggled her mind. "Did you have any siblings?"

Camdyn gave a short nod. "Two older brothers and three younger sisters."

"A big family then."

"The more children, the more help with chores."

The way he spoke so matter-of-factly had Saffron trying to read more into his words. "You weren't happy then?"

"It was the only life I knew. Until Deirdre found me. What about you? What was your life like?"

Saffron didn't like how he had turned the tables on her. She wanted to ask him more questions, especially about how Deirdre captured him and how he got away from her. But fair was fair. He shared a portion of his life, so she would share hers.

"I adored my father. My mother was another story, one which you heard part of."

He looked down at his hands. "My hearing is much better than yours, so, aye, I heard the conversation you had on the mobile with your mother."

Saffron grimaced. "You heard everything she said?"

Another nod.

"The first thing I remember growing up was how I was always with my father. We did everything together. I'd see my mother at dinner or when she had bought me an outfit. She didn't like having a daughter, but if she was going to have one, she wanted me to be perfect. I can't tell you how many times she told me that throughout the years."

Saffron laughed and leaned her head against the stone to look at the darkened ceiling above her. Her eyes had adjusted to the darkness well enough that she could see better than before.

"Mother treated me like a doll. Always dressing me up

and presenting me to her friends, then forgetting about me when she was ready to move on. My father was always there when it happened. He'd scoop me up in his arms, and we'd go do something fun.

"The older I got, however, the harder it was for Mother to control me as she wanted. I began to rebel. The fights were horrendous. And then, she stopped everything. Stopped talking to me, stopped acknowledging me, stopped looking at me."

"I'm sorry."

Camdyn's deep, rich voice jerked her out of her memories. She smiled at him, and shrugged. "Things got better then. For me at least. For a while I was happy. Until my father began to push for me to attend the University of Denver so I'd be near them."

"What did you want?"

"To get away. Far, far away from my mother."

"What did you do?"

Saffron tucked a strand of hair behind her ear. "The best thing in my life was my father. He begged me to stay in Colorado, so I did. Until I graduated college. All those years I was trying to begin my own life while he tried to keep me near him. I did everything I could to stay away from Mother, which meant I didn't see my father. And then it was too late."

She wiped at her eyes as she looked away from Camdyn's piercing gaze. "My father had wanted me close because he was dying. He had a bad heart and never told me. I didn't realize his intent until he lay dying and he told me. All those years I spent away."

"But he understood."

Saffron sniffed. "He did. I thought it would all end with his death, but then came the reading of the will. Mother thought she would get the money, but Dad had one last card to play. He gave her only a very small portion, and the rest was given to me. You can imagine how that went. I just *thought* I had problems with my mother up until that point."

CHAPTER
TWENTY-ONE

Camdyn hated the sadness in her voice, but the more she talked, the more he wanted to know. "When did you come to Scotland?"

"After my father's funeral, I had to get away from my mother. For a woman who never wanted me, she suddenly wanted to be my best friend. It was all for the money."

"I discovered in my learning of this time that money is important to people."

Saffron fiddled with her fingers as she lifted a slim shoulder. "To some. So many wanted to be my friends because of my father's wealth. Even the guys I dated were only after the money. It got to a point that I didn't think anyone was my friend just for myself."

"What did you do?"

She chuckled, the sound dry and humorless. "I did the cowardly thing and ran away. I flew into Rome and spent a week there before I began a yearlong tour of Europe. I'd always wanted to come to Britain, so I made it my last stop, intending to spend the most time here."

"You did all this by yourself?"

"Yes," she said, and glanced at him. She seemed particularly interested in her fingers. "I had been in Scotland for just over a month when I met Declan Wallace."

Camdyn's breath locked in his lungs as he waited for Saffron to continue. He knew for certain he wasn't going to like what he heard, but he had to know what Declan had done to her so he would know how much to make Declan suffer.

Saffron let out a bark of laughter. "Declan swept me off my feet. No man had ever done that to me before. He said it was because we both came from such wealthy families that we could understand each other. Like a naïve schoolgirl, I believed every lie that fell from his lips."

Camdyn watched the way her body stiffened slightly when she spoke of Declan. Hatred for Declan was in every syllable, every word.

He recognized such hatred because it was what he felt for Deirdre. That loathing had festered in his soul for two hundred and fifty years before he time-traveled to the future.

"You know, I cannot believe I was so gullible," Saffron said. "It felt so good to have someone like me for myself. Or so I thought. It took less than a week for him to make his intentions clear."

"What did he do?" Camdyn hated that his voice came out mostly as a growl, but the rage inside him was building quickly.

Saffron suddenly rose to her feet and began to pace slowly, running her fingers along the stone wall. "First, it was all about me. He wanted to know every detail of my past, but then he began to toss around words like 'magic' and 'Druids.' It startled me at first, but when I didn't jump in and tell him I was a Druid he decided to show me he was one."

She paused and frowned. "At the time I didn't realize there were two sects of Druids. I thought we were all just Druids, that we'd be like the rest of the world with there being mostly good people and a few bad people. I didn't know . . ."

"How could you have?" Camdyn said. "You weren't raised as a Druid."

"No, and no research I did led me to anything about *mies* and *droughs*. Had I known, I'd have been more cautious. Had I known, I could have tried to defend myself against Declan."

Camdyn caught her gaze. "As potent as Isla is with her mix of *drough* and *mie* magic inside her, someone like Declan or Deirdre could overpower her with their black magic. You didna stand a chance."

"I suppose not," she murmured and looked down as she leaned a hand upon the wall. "He wanted me to join him, Camdyn. Declan painted this picture of power and domination that made me sick to my stomach. He said all I had to do was perform a ceremony and my magic would increase tenfold."

"The ceremony to become *drough*."

She nodded. "I didn't know it at the time, but that's exactly what it was. I made him explain what was needed of me, and I figured out what would happen, that my soul would belong to Satan. I refused. He begged me, pleaded with me, but I wouldn't change my mind."

Camdyn flexed his shoulders. He continued to track Saffron with his eyes. "Good for you."

"Maybe not," she said with a snort and lightly kicked the wall as she faced it. "His patience ran out when I tried to leave the mansion. The next thing I knew he was torturing some guy with his magic. Declan said he was demonstrating what would happen to me if I didn't join him. I'd never been so scared in my life."

His claws extended from his fingers as he felt the icy dread run through her magic. She kept her back to him, but he didn't need to see her face to know the memories were difficult for her to return to.

"You survived it. Just like a true Highlander," he told her.

She put her forehead on the stones and made a choked sound. "He wanted me because I was a Seer. He thought I could control my visions."

"What did he do to you?"

"Which time?" she asked.

Camdyn closed his eyes as he felt his god rising up through the fury that ran rampant through him. How could anyone dare to hurt someone as beautiful and pure of spirit as Saffron?

All he knew was that Declan was going to suffer a slow, agonizing death.

"He stripped me bare in front of his men." Her voice intruded on his thoughts. "Every last stitch of clothing was taken from me. He strung my hands above my head. I thought he was going to beat me, but he stepped back. His men . . . his men began to fight over who would get to have me first.

"Declan then whispered in my ear that I could be his alone if I would join him. I almost agreed, but I couldn't. Even the fear of being raped by his men wouldn't allow me to give my soul to Satan."

Camdyn cleared his throat twice before he was able to ask, "Did they touch you?"

Finally Saffron turned to face him. "When I still refused Declan, he had his cousin beat me. When the other men grew enraged at not getting to have me, Declan killed two of them. With just a few words I couldn't even understand. Up until that moment I thought I could get away from Declan, but I saw the force of his magic. And I knew the truth then—that I was never getting out."

Camdyn released the breath he'd been holding. It was small consolation that Saffron hadn't been raped. But beaten? A woman was to be cherished and loved. Protected.

Not beaten.

"I survived the beating," Saffron said with a half smile and eyes that swam with tears. "He locked me in the prison, and I lost all track of time. I had no idea how many days had passed. He would come to me and ask me to join him. Every time I refused he would punish me.

"If I had a vision, he would demand to know every detail of it. If I attempted to hold anything back, Robbie would get to hit me again."

"I'm going to kill that son of a bitch," Camdyn growled.

Saffron wrapped her arms around her middle and leaned a shoulder against the wall. "I tried to escape. Three different times. One time I got all the way out onto the road and was flagging down a car when they reached me. After the third attempt, Declan used the spell to blind me."

Camdyn knew that wasn't the end of her story. There was more, but she wasn't ready to share it yet. Already she had told him more than she had told anyone else, and for now, that was enough.

"You're free of him now."

Saffron's head swiveled until her tawny gaze pinned his. "I won't be free of Declan until he's dead."

"That will be taken care of."

She laughed and pushed off the wall to walk in the center of the room. "Don't underestimate him. He has powerful black magic."

"And so does Deirdre," Camdyn said. "There is always a way to kill evil. You just have to know how to do it."

"Will you help me?"

He was taken aback by her soft question. Camdyn stood and walked to meet her. "I'd like nothing better."

Her smile was slow but radiant as it filled her face. He gripped his legs to keep from reaching for her. She had opened herself up to him, shown him her vulnerability, and all he wanted to do was comfort her.

Hold her. Caress her.

Love her.

Camdyn could barely draw breath into his lungs as he imagined Saffron with her wealth of thick brown hair spread around her, her head thrown back, and her legs open as he positioned himself over her.

Sweat popped on his forehead as he struggled to keep from touching her. Because one touch would be all it took to break the thin thread of control he had over himself.

Her gaze drifted over his shoulder, and her smile slowly faded. "Camdyn, look."

He pulled in a breath and briefly closed his eyes as she walked past him. Only when he knew she was far enough away from him did he turn to see what she was looking at.

Camdyn saw the faint outline of something carved in the stone. He strode to her and they looked at it together.

"Has it faded?" she asked.

"Nay. I think this was done like this on purpose."

"Why?"

"So it wouldn't be seen easily." Camdyn slowly walked along the wall.

Saffron went in the other direction, and they both searched for more. "I found another one," she called out.

"As have I."

"These markings are the same as the one on the doorway we went through earlier."

"The same as from the cylinder," Camdyn muttered.

Saffron pulled out the cylinder from her pocket and they both lined up the small squares in the correct order.

"We can't move the stones," Saffron said.

Camdyn leaned close to one of the carvings and smiled. "We push the stones."

"Push?" she repeated.

Camdyn searched the room until he found the carving that was the first one on the cylinder. He took a deep breath and gave the stone a push.

CHAPTER TWENTY-TWO

The sound of stone sliding on stone filled the room as it sank into the wall. Saffron bit her lip as elation swept through her.

One by one, she and Camdyn took turns finding the next symbol and pushing in the stone. The etchings were scattered throughout the room, some high, some low. It would have been easier to find them with a light, but they made do without.

"Here," she said as she knelt by the last etching. Just as she placed her hand on the stone, Camdyn's joined hers.

They shared a look before he gave a nod, and together they gave the stone a shove. For a moment nothing happened, and Saffron was just about to say they must have done it wrong when the floor dipped.

She screamed, and strong arms wrapped around her as they began to fall. Saffron held on to Camdyn with all her might as they hit something that reverberated through her body. Her teeth knocked together even though Camdyn took the brunt of the impact. With her mind still reeling they began to slide.

Saffron felt a nail break off as she clutched at Camdyn's shirt while they continued to slide. If it hadn't been so scary, she'd think she was on one of those huge slides at the fairs.

But this wasn't a theme park. This was a labyrinth with booby traps and God only knew what else in store for them.

The steady beat of Camdyn's heart beneath her ear helped to keep her somewhat calm.

Until they were dumped unceremoniously into a room.

Saffron hardly felt a thing as Camdyn shifted and she landed on top of him before he rolled her onto her back. She blinked up at him, noticing too late how her hands were fisted in his shirt.

Cautiously he smoothed away the hair from her face. "Are you hurt? Is anything broken? Bleeding?"

"No, though I think my heart leaped out of my chest."

She thought she saw a hint of a smile before he stood and helped her to her feet, then he turned away.

Saffron dusted off her jeans and looked around them. She didn't know how far they had fallen, but it was obviously quite some ways judging by the dampness and dripping of water she heard.

The air didn't smell old, just . . . still. As if it were rarely disturbed where they were. The way Camdyn walked sound-lessly and didn't speak had Saffron doing the same.

She let out a soft breath. Where would this adventure take them next? And would she survive it?

"I've found something," Camdyn whispered in her ear.

She jerked, startled to find him right behind her. She hadn't even heard him approach. Saffron turned and followed Cam-dyn to the other wall.

When he pointed to something, she had to squint and lean forward to make out the etching of the silhouette of a dragon's head. The water that dribbled over the etching had begun to erase it so that it was barely visible.

Saffron looked over her shoulder at Camdyn. He gave a nod, and together they started down another corridor. This one was wider than the others, but here the air smelled al-most rotten.

She was so busy looking around her that she wasn't pay-ing attention to where she was stepping. Saffron felt the rock crumble beneath her foot, and the next thing she knew she was falling again.

Before she could gather a scream she was jerked to a halt

by her arm, then hauled against the wall with Camdyn standing in front of her.

Once more she found herself clinging to him. "I'm a menace," she muttered.

There was a slight rumble in his chest that might have been laughter, but when she looked into his face, he wasn't smiling. In fact, his glower had her rethinking holding on to him.

As the fear melted away, Saffron was all too aware of the rock-hard muscles against her. All too aware of Camdyn's heat, of his hands wrapped around her arms.

All too aware of how his bottom lip was fuller than his top. And how delightful his kisses were.

She swallowed as his hands tightened around her arms a moment before he released her and took a step back.

"It's the dragon's head stones we have to keep to. Step where I step," he said, and turned his back to her.

Saffron drew in a shuddering breath and glared at his back. But her gaze caught on the way his T-shirt was cut and she was able to get glimpses of his back and the way the muscles shifted and bunched with each of his movements. She hated how her body reacted so quickly to him, when apparently she didn't affect him at all.

Damn her body. It was just like her to find herself falling for a guy who would only hurt her. She hadn't asked for her life to be turned upside or to live in the hell she'd been in.

Even now Saffron wasn't sure how she'd survived. There had been times she'd prayed for death. On several occasions she thought she might get her wish during the beatings.

Saffron hurried to follow Camdyn as he moved from one spot to another. She thought the stones beneath her might have something etched on them, but in the dark, she couldn't see that well.

She had to keep her arms stretched out on either side of her to help keep her balance, and more than once her fingers snagged in a spider's web. It took all her control not to screech each time. Somehow, she managed to bite her lip, but there was no stopping the shaking that took her as she peeled the sticky web off.

When she looked up to see the next stone wasn't just a step away, but a jump, she got worried.

Then she took too long wondering how to get to the next stone, because when she glanced up at Camdyn he'd moved so far ahead she had no idea where to go.

"Camdyn, wait," she said as he picked out the next stone and stepped.

He paused and turned his torso to look at her. "What is it?"

"It's too big of a jump. I can't make it. Are you sure there isn't another between these two?"

His lips flattened as he slowly shook his head.

"Damn," she whispered. There was nothing else for it. She had to do it or stay there forever.

Saffron took a deep breath and jumped. The toe of her boot caught the correct stone, but she quickly lost her balance and flailed about with her arms.

She desperately tried not to put her other foot down, but she was so off balance that she was liable to place it anywhere but on the dragon stone.

Without really knowing how, Saffron managed to grab a hold of the wall next to her to help right herself. She put her other foot down and scooted her first fully onto the stone.

"You're going to be the death of me," Camdyn said into the silence.

Saffron was too weak from the adrenaline rush to do anything other than stand there and shake. How had she ever liked going on roller coasters? How had she ever enjoyed the feeling of her stomach lifting as the coaster plummeted down the tracks?

After this, she'd never even look at a theme park or fair again.

"Saffron?"

Camdyn's dark tone, edged with worry, brought her head up. "I need a moment."

"And I need you off those stones."

She tried to push her bangs out of her eyes, but her hand shook too badly. And she wouldn't release the wall with the other one.

"You have to keep moving," Camdyn said.

"I know." And she did. She just needed to convince her body to get moving.

The last thing she wanted was for Camdyn to leave her to complete the quest. Saffron pulled herself together and looked at the stones in search of the next dragon one.

"I can't see it," she said as her fear began to rise again.

"Three stones to your right and then two up. Do you see it?"

"Not really. It's too dark."

Camdyn paced back and forth. He'd hurried to reach the other side of the trap so he could help Saffron, but now he wasn't sure how he could do that if she couldn't see.

"I can see the three over, but it's the ones going up," she said. "I can't quite make out where one ends and the other begins."

He damned the Druids who had added these traps throughout the labyrinth. "I'm coming back to help you," he called.

"What if it doesn't let you? What if you cause everything to cave in?"

Camdyn paused with his foot over the first stone and frowned. He hadn't thought of that, but then again, she could be right. "You watch too many movies."

"Probably. Regardless, I could be correct, and you know it or you'd already be over here."

He wanted to go to her to prove her wrong, but the idea that he could be the cause of her death kept him still. But if he didn't do anything it could also cause her death.

Camdyn was in a position he never thought to find himself in. Either way, he could damn her to die. He didn't know what to do.

But then it was out of his hands as Saffron moved from her place to the other stone.

He bent forward with his hands on his knees as she managed to land on the correct stone. It was a good thing he was immortal, because she had already taken off decades from his life.

She met his gaze and blew out a breath so that it made her bangs lift off her forehead. "I overstepped. This isn't the stone I was aiming for."

Camdyn straightened and rubbed his hand over his jaw as he tried to get control of his heart pounding in his chest. "There's just three more stones to find."

"Three?"

He heard the horror in her voice and gave a hard nod. "Aye, and I'll get you through them. The next one is two to the left and two up."

"You know they didn't exactly place these so they're in order."

"I know. Count the ones in the row first."

She threw up her hands, but did as he asked. She leaned as far to the left as she could. "One . . . two."

"Nay. Doona count that small one after the first one. It's part of a larger stone behind you."

Saffron's nostrils flared as she gave him a hard look. "Fine. Then that means the second one is there," she said and pointed.

"Aye. Now, two up," he coaxed.

She squatted down to try to see. "Are there any stones I shouldn't be counting?"

Most of them, but he didn't want to frighten her more than she already was.

"Screw it. Here goes nothing," she said as she stood and took the step.

Camdyn knew the instant before she chose the stone that it was the wrong one. "The next one up!" he shouted.

With her nimble feet she was able to quickly move to the right stone with her other foot. Yet, the entire area of the trap began to tremble and rock.

"Give me your hand," Camdyn called.

She stretched out her hand, but she was still too far away. The stones began to crack and fall away around her, and

Camdyn knew he had to do something quickly. He took a few steps back, his eyes trained on her.

Then he ran and leaped into the air. He planted a foot on the right-hand wall and shifted his momentum to the opposite wall. When he did, he grabbed Saffron up in his arms as he pushed off from the wall.

They landed where he had been waiting for her as the stones fell away to leave a huge gap in the floor.

But Camdyn's attention was on Saffron. He held her, his arms wrapped tightly around her while her head was buried in his neck, and she trembled in his arms.

"I'm not going to live through this, am I?" she whispered.

Camdyn cupped the back of her head. "Aye, you are. I willna let anything happen to you."

"Some things are out of your control."

"Some things are no'." He pulled back to look at her and saw her exhaustion.

He lifted her in his arms and started down the hallway. Camdyn wanted to find a place where she could rest. He didn't want to think about how right it felt to have her head on his shoulder or her arms around his neck.

He didn't want to think about how right it felt that he was the one protecting her.

Camdyn turned the corner and paused. The air seemed clearer. There was a spot in the corner where water didn't seep through the stones.

He set Saffron down and sighed. She needed a fire, but there wasn't any wood, nor a place for the smoke to vent to either.

"Sit," she said, and patted the spot beside her.

Camdyn did as she asked, thinking he'd only help keep her warm.

And knew it for the lie that it was.

CHAPTER
TWENTY-THREE

Fallon paced from one doorway to another, his gaze going again and again to the entry where Saffron and Camdyn had ventured through.

"They'll be all right," Hayden said.

Fallon raked a hand through his hair. "I hope you're right. I just wish we were there to help them."

"So do I," Larena said as she pulled him down to sit beside her. "Wearing a hole in these stones as you pace isn't going to help them though."

"There has to be another way to get to Laria," Arran said as he punched a stone.

The rain of the rock falling onto the stone floor echoed around the cavern.

"We'll awaken Laria," Logan said.

Broc grinned. "And watch her defeat Deirdre."

Fallon met his brothers' gazes. If for some reason Camdyn and Saffron failed, their one and only way to kill Deirdre was gone.

After all the heartache and death Deirdre had given them, Fallon wanted her to suffer as they had suffered. He wanted her to feel the pain as they had felt pain.

Fallon kissed the back of Larena's hand. They had waited over four centuries to have their gods bound so they could have children and have the family both so desperately wanted.

Larena smiled sadly, her gaze telling him she knew exactly what he was thinking. They had spoken many times about the family and the future they wanted.

Now everything rested in Camdyn and Saffron's hands.

Fallon was a doer. He didn't like waiting for someone to do a job for him, yet in this instance, he had no other choice. The magic wouldn't let any of them pass to follow Camdyn and Saffron.

Dani had used her magic to look into each doorway. She had been insistent that none of them force their way into any of the other doorways. What awaited them if they did Fallon didn't know. And he'd rather not find out.

Camdyn wasn't surprised when Saffron fell asleep almost immediately. Her head had lolled to the side to rest on his shoulder.

He would have been content to stay just like that if he hadn't felt a shudder run through her. The water might not have been leaking through the stones there, but the air was damp and cool.

Camdyn shifted so that he wrapped an arm around her and pulled her tighter against his body. She slept like the dead after that.

All the while, his thoughts went over everything they had endured since stepping into the labyrinth. If it was any indication, there was more in store for them. How much more was the question.

There were three more artifacts to use. Which meant three more perils at least. Could his heart take it? He knew it couldn't. Every time Saffron's life was threatened, he felt it like a blade in his gut.

He was responsible for her safety. He alone. Before, he might have been looking out for her, but then again so had the others. If she died, it would be his fault.

Camdyn didn't know how long he sat there with that

mind-numbing thought rolling through his mind. But the next time he glanced down, Saffron was staring at him.

"What's wrong?" she asked.

Her voice, rough and seductively low from sleep, sent heat pooling into his aching cock. "No' a thing."

She sat up and yawned before raising her arms over her head and stretching, her back arched so that her jacket parted and her breasts pushed forward.

Camdyn tried to look away, but desire had him in its grip. And it wasn't letting go.

"You're a very bad liar," Saffron said with another yawn. "How long did I sleep?"

He shrugged and hurriedly rose to his feet. The fact he missed having her pressed against him, her scent filling his senses, he did his damnedest to ignore. "I doona know."

"We need to get moving, I suppose."

"Nay," he said, and held out his palm to stop her from rising. "Eat something. You need to keep your strength up."

The fact she didn't argue with him told him she must be starving. While she pulled yet another bar from her jacket and peeled back the wrapper, Camdyn looked down the hallway to where they had to go.

"The labyrinth is taking back the artifacts," Saffron said around a bite of food.

Camdyn turned his head to her. "What do you mean?"

"I mean that every artifact we've brought down here that's been used has been taken back by the labyrinth. The next three will have to be used in that same fashion, is my guess."

Camdyn nodded. "Of course. We have the Tablet of Orn—"

"That's not really a tablet," Saffron interjected.

"True. It's a cylinder case. Then there is the cylinder that was inside the Tablet of Orn."

She wiped her mouth with the back of her hand. "And the key."

"Aye. The key. That could be used in any number of ways. It's the other two artifacts that have me thinking."

The crinkle of the wrapper as she wadded it in her hand and stuffed it in her pocket drew his attention. "Let's find out, shall we?"

Camdyn's appreciation for her courage and fortitude rose. He should have known she would rise to the occasion. She was a strong, independent, and amazing woman.

He waited until she caught up with him before he started down the corridor. The tunnel narrowed, forcing Camdyn to have to turn his shoulders to be able to fit through.

"I have a feeling this won't lead to anything good," Saffron said.

"Has anything else?"

She gave a snort of laughter. "No. I thought getting us into the maze would have been the greatest feat. But, come on. It should be easier to find and wake Laria than this."

"The Druids never did anything halfway. They wanted to be sure Deirdre wouldna be able to get to her sister."

"They certainly succeeded. We're lucky to have gotten this far. What if there hadn't been any more Druids in the world? Did they think of that when they built this? Nope. Then were would we be? In this shit, that's where."

Camdyn coughed to cover his laugh. She was agitated, which anyone would be, but he knew women well enough not to let them know he found their annoyance humorous.

He kept in front of her to knock away the spiderwebs he found blocking their way. If she was afraid of being belowground, then spiders could very well send her over the brink.

"Ick," he heard behind him. Then it turned into a gasp before he felt her rubbing her hand back and forth on his back.

"What?" he asked as he turned around.

"I . . . I . . ." she stuttered as she tried to get something off her hand.

It was obvious by the way her eyes had grown large that she was indeed afraid of spiders. Camdyn saw the web and hurried to help her in order to keep her calm.

"There," he said when it was off her hand and arm. He looked up to tell her not to be worried when he saw the spider on her shoulder.

He inwardly groaned as his mind raced to come up with a way to get it off Saffron without her knowing it. The fact they were in a cramped tunnel didn't help.

"I need to get out of here," she said as she pushed against him. "Keep going. If there's a web, there's a spider, and I don't want it anywhere near me."

"Why be afraid of a little insect?" Although he had to admit, the one crawling on her was anything but little.

She shuddered, her face scrunching in horror. "All those hairy legs crawling. And the eyes." Saffron scratched her head. "Just thinking about them makes me feel as if they're crawling all over me. Are they crawling on me? I know they're crawling on me. I have to get them off. Get them off!"

Her hysteria grew with every word, and Camdyn had no idea what to do. He didn't want to tell her about the spider and make things worse, but neither could he ignore the fact that it sat on her shoulder.

Since the spider was getting closer to her neck, Camdyn knew he needed to do something immediately. He flicked it with his hands and pulled at her hair.

"What?" she screamed and tried to get away, only succeeding in bumping into the wall. "Do I have one on me? Oh, God, please tell me it's not on me."

"It's no'," Camdyn answered with all honestly. "Just a bit of webbing in your hair."

She gave him another hard push. "Thank you, but I really need to move away from this place. Now. Move!"

Camdyn faced forward again and continued along the tunnel, his shoulders constantly hitting the wall, even though his torso was turned sideways. He grinned at her demand to get moving. She really was afraid of spiders.

He was thankful that he had got the spider off Saffron before she noticed it. As scared as she was, she'd probably have climbed over him to get away from it.

"Declan used them against me," she said softly into the silence.

"When we found you, you thought they were crawling on you."

"Before he took my sight, that was one of the ways he tortured me. He knew it was the one thing I was truly petri-fied of. I always have been, even as a little girl. He had them all over me, and the spell used was one where I couldn't move. It was horrific. I cannot even look at spiders now."

Camdyn was rapidly beginning to hate Declan as much as he did Deirdre. "Larena said when she first discovered Declan was keeping you that you thought the spiders were on you. But they weren't. He knew it would scare you."

"Is it wrong that I want to find his greatest fear and make him suffer again and again?"

Camdyn glanced at her. "Nay."

"I want to kill him."

"As I want to kill Deirdre."

There was a pregnant pause before Saffron asked, "Did Deirdre hurt you the way Declan hurt me?"

Camdyn sighed. "Deirdre is evil like Declan, but Deirdre came from a different time. She did things differently. De-clan tortured you, but Deirdre had nothing stopping her from killing our families if we didna do as she wanted."

"Did she . . . ?"

Camdyn rubbed the back of his neck. "It's a long story."

"I suspect we have enough time."

He opened his mouth to begin the tale when the tunnel suddenly widened and torches flared to life.

"This place gets freakier and freakier," Saffron said as she peered around his arm.

The light danced upon the wall, flickering over the stones in a wild dance. Camdyn let his gaze slowly move around the widened part of the tunnel. "It gets narrower ahead."

"Ah, but is that where we're supposed to go? Look," she said and nudged his left side.

He followed her finger as she pointed to the wall.

"It looks like the stone has been hollowed out in the shape of a cross."

Camdyn made his way to the cross and peered at the stone. "It's a Celtic cross," he told her. "See the carvings?"

"Stunning," she said as she ran her finger along the markings.

"But why hollow out the cross? Why no' just carve the cross as they did the knotwork?"

She fumbled in her pocket and produced the Tablet of Orn with its gold cylinder. "Maybe because this goes in there?"

Camdyn looked from the Tablet of Orn to the cross. Both the horizontal and vertical areas of the cross were the same exact shape. "Aye. But which way?"

"Just once I'd like them to make this easy," she muttered.

Camdyn had to agree with her. He spotted something in the hollowed stone. "Look. There's something here."

"A spiral and a trinity symbol on the horizontal portion. On the vertical there's a triskelion and a spiral. Do you know what it means?"

"Nay."

"Then we have a fifty-fifty chance of picking the right one."

Camdyn looked at Saffron. "What do you think?"

"Vertical."

"Vertical it is," he said as he took the Tablet of Orn from her and slid it into the slot.

CHAPTER TWENTY-FOUR

Saffron's heart raced, her blood pounded in her ears. All those times she had sat watching the adventure movies she loved so much saying she wished she could have a life like that seemed eons ago.

And now she knew she didn't want a life like Indiana Jones because her heart simply couldn't take the constant surprises and life-threatening episodes.

There was a soft click as the Tablet of Orn fit perfectly into the slot. Saffron looked down at the floor and hastily jumped to the wall.

"What is it?" Camdyn asked.

She shrugged as she stared at the floor, waiting for something to happen. "I'm tired of falling. I'm tired of the floor shifting beneath my feet. These Druids seem to have a thing about plunging people to their deaths."

Camdyn licked his lips and hastily turned his head away to try and hide his smile. "I doona believe the floor will cave in this time."

"You doona believe," she repeated, mimicking his brogue. She gave a very unladylike snort that would have appalled her mother. "Well, I feel all better now."

Saffron didn't mean to allow her anxiety to show, but she was tired, cold, and wanted more than another PowerBar to eat. She was at her wit's end with this entire ordeal, and she knew more was coming. That's what scared her the most.

"I have been wondering why they supplied fire."

She lifted her gaze to the four torches and cringed. "Now that you mention it, why would they? Nowhere else in this hell of a labyrinth has there been any light. Why now?"

"Why indeed?" Camdyn murmured as he peered closer at one of the torches.

"At least I can take one with me now and be able to see." Saffron grasped the iron at the bottom of the torch and lifted.

Yet the torch didn't budge. She thought it might be stuck, so she gave it a harder yank, but still nothing.

Finally, Camdyn tried to pull out the torch he was standing near. Not even his considerable strength could move it. He looked at Saffron and shrugged.

"Great. So the Druids won't allow us to take the torches with us, and didn't supply light earlier. This can't be good."

Camdyn shook his head. "Nay, I doona suppose it will be. And putting the Tablet of Orn into place didna do anything."

"There aren't any doors I can see, so it looks like we're stuck again until we put the Tablet of Orn the right way."

Saffron pulled out the cylinder and turned it horizontal. It made the same soft click as it had the first time as she pushed it into place.

When nothing happened, Saffron gave it a push to see if it was meant to go farther back. The cylinder didn't move. Saffron slapped her hands on her legs in frustration and stalked away.

She stood against the far wall and watched as Camdyn walked to where the Tablet of Orn was held in the cross. He ran his fingers over the knotwork slowly.

"Do you see something?" Saffron asked.

"Maybe."

When he tapped at something on the stone, Saffron straightened. "You did find something."

Camdyn looked over his shoulder at her. "Come see."

She hurried to him and looked to where he pointed. With the fire flickering on the walls, she had a hard time seeing anything clearly. And then she saw the thin, barely visible line.

Her finger traced it to a perfect circle around the cross. She stepped back, the lump of fear growing.

"We have to turn it," Camdyn said. "I think the entire cross turns based on the line around it."

"But which way? And which way do we put the cylinder?"

Camdyn's nostrils flared as his eyes narrowed on the cross and the Tablet of Orn. "Only one way to find out."

Saffron took another step back as Camdyn pulled out the cylinder and turned it so that it was once more vertical before he put it back in the cross.

With his hand still on the artifact, he glanced at Saffron before he turned it to the right.

Her eyes were drawn to the torches as they flared high overhead. She saw them shift toward her, and even though her mind screamed for her to move, it happened too fast for her to do anything.

Suddenly, she was hauled roughly to the side and shoved against the wall. Camdyn's hard body blocked her from the flames as he bent over her, but the heat soon had sweat running down her face and between her breasts.

Camdyn grunted, his body stiff and his hands braced on either side of her head. But none of the flames touched her. After a moment, the torches went back to normal as if nothing had happened.

Saffron lifted her head from Camdyn's chest to see him staring at her. Smoke filled the small area and wafted around them, and she smelled something burning. It dawned on her then exactly what Camdyn had done.

"You're hurt."

He shrugged, and she saw the pain that caused him. "I will heal."

"Immortal or not, I don't like the idea of you getting hurt." She couldn't stand the heat anymore and shrugged out of her jacket.

He pushed away from the wall, and what was left of his T-shirt fell to the floor. Saffron saw the scorch marks around the edges of the shirt and knew he had suffered terribly.

Because even though a Warrior always healed, they felt the wounds.

She gently touched his face, her heart aching. "Thank you."

"You're a Druid, someone to be protected. There are so few of you left."

"So you did it out of obligation?" She really hated how much the idea of that hurt.

He let out a breath. "I gave you my vow that I would keep you safe."

She nodded and he turned away. Saffron covered her mouth with her hand when she glimpsed the extent of the burns that covered his back. His back was a mass of burned flesh twisted and misshapen. His back was already healing, but she knew he had to be in considerable pain.

Camdyn walked back to the cross. "Ready for another try?"

"No."

He smiled then, a lopsided half smile, but a smile. And it melted her heart.

Saffron's lungs seized, her world tilted. Because that small smile made the already handsome Camdyn into a devilishly good-looking rake. And if her heart had been in danger before, there was no question of it now.

"Stay there," he cautioned as he moved the cylinder back to its original position.

Saffron gripped the stones behind her and found herself praying it was the correct way. She met Camdyn's gaze as he turned the cross to the left.

Once more the flames leaped upward, but this time they didn't shift toward her. The flames continued as the Tablet of Orn sank farther into the stone.

"Give me the other cylinder," Camdyn said as he held out his hand.

Saffron hurried to her jacket and yanked it out of the pocket and placed it in his hands. "What is it?"

"I think both are supposed to go here. See how the first sank farther back in the wall? It leaves room for the other one."

She shrugged. "Try it."

His gaze met hers before he fit the second, smaller cylinder into the open slot on the cross. As soon as he did, the cross turned on its own, making a complete circle.

When it was upright again, both artifacts were gone. Of a sudden, the flames flickered out and the entire chamber began to move in a circle.

Saffron squatted down, her nails chipping as she clung to the stones. In two strides Camdyn was beside her. His arms wrapped around her.

As abruptly as the room had begun to move, it stopped. They both found themselves looking at the same doorway they had entered earlier.

"That looks to be our way out."

Saffron shook her head. "There is nothing for us if we retrace our steps."

"I have a feeling we willna be retracing our steps," Camdyn said as he pulled her to her feet.

Sure enough, as soon as they stepped into the hallway, they could tell they were in a different location. No more water ran down the walls, but they were covered in even more spiderwebs.

Saffron walked with her shoulders hunched forward in the middle of the tunnel so she wouldn't have to touch the walls. She didn't look down, not even when she felt something crunch beneath her foot.

"Duck," Camdyn warned her.

Saffron didn't look up, just did as he told her. She bent as low to the ground as she could without actually touching the stones beneath her feet.

"You can stand now."

She could feel the terror fill her, the absolute spine-tingling chills that raced along her skin. Because there were spiders.

Camdyn took her hand and they began to run down the tunnel. She should have cautioned him about booby traps, but all she wanted to do was get as far from the spiders as she could.

A glance upward showed there were spiders hanging on the walls and from the ceiling. Huge spiders, small spiders. It didn't matter the size, they were spiders.

The tunnel led them to the left, right, left, right, and left again until Camdyn skidded to a halt. Saffron was out of breath, but she would have run for days if it got her away from her fear.

"I think we're past it now," Camdyn said as he looked at her.

She could feel his gaze searching her face. Saffron nodded. "Yes. Thank you."

He turned and looked around them.

"Where are we?" she asked as she ran her hands up and down her arms, wishing for her jacket once more. She should have known better than to forget it, but the maze with its magic was sending her emotions on a never-ending roller coaster ride.

"Looks like we need to decide whether to go left or right."

"We have one more artifact," she said.

He gave a single nod and touched his pocket where the key rested. "One more, then we awaken Laria."

Saffron smoothed the hair away from her eyes with her hand and tried to keep a tight rein on her anger and frustration that were slowly mounting. If she didn't get out of the maze soon she was going to erupt like Mount Vesuvius.

"You decide," she told him, and put her hand against the wall.

Instead of her hand propping her up, she felt herself falling.

"Camdyn!" she screamed as the wall turned and she tumbled into a darkened room.

She turned and pounded on the wall, hoping she could get back to Camdyn.

"Camdyn! Camdyn, can you hear me!"

She shouted until her throat was raw, but not once did he answer her. But even worse, she heard the unmistakable sound of spiders.

CHAPTER
TWENTY-FIVE

Camdyn tried to reach Saffron before the wall turned, but he missed her. He shoved his shoulder into the wall twice to try and move it as it had for her.

"Saffron! Saffron, are you all right?"

Her scream echoed in his head, reminding him he had failed to protect her. His god raged inside him, and Camdyn didn't bother to try and tamp him down. He released his god, and threw back his head with a roar.

"Saffron!"

When she didn't answer, he punched the wall, kicked the wall, and even scoured the stones with his claws. But nothing would make it budge.

Camdyn splayed his hands on the wall, and that's when he felt the thrum of magic. "Damned Druids," he muttered.

He had no idea where Saffron was or if she was injured. But he wouldn't give up finding her. He told himself it was because of obligation and his promise to her, but he suspected it went much deeper than that.

Camdyn moved along the wall until the steady feel of magic began to fade. Then he balled his fist and rammed it into the wall. The stones crumbled around him.

He peeled back his lips over his fangs and growled as he began to tear down the wall stone by stone. If it took him dismantling the maze in order to find Saffron he'd do it.

"I'm coming, Saffron!" he bellowed. "Doona give up!"

He shoved aside another weighty stone. "Doona give up," he muttered. "I'll find you."

The fear held Saffron in its steely grip. She couldn't move, even though she knew spiders were all around her. All she had to do was run, to step on them, but her body was frozen.

She couldn't see the spiders, but she knew they were there. Thousands of them, and they were all coming toward her. Her breathing was ragged, her heart pounding like a drum in her ear, and her blood had turned to ice.

Saffron hated the terror inside her, the anxiety and fright, but the years of Declan torturing her with spiders had only expanded her arachnophobia into something more than just a fear.

It paralyzed her.

"Is this your fear?" a voice like dozens of people speaking at once whispered.

Saffron felt the tears run down her cheeks as a spider dangled in front of her face. All she had to do was swipe it away and step on it.

If she could only move.

"You are a Druid. With magic."

Saffron screamed when a spider landed on her arm from above and bit her. That scream released her from her paralysis and she screamed and screamed and screamed.

All those years of holding everything in so Declan wouldn't know she was terrified, all those years of hiding how hurt she was by her mother's indifference. All those years of pretending she was fine by herself exploded.

She threw out her arms and magic erupted from her hands. Saffron moved her hands everywhere she thought there were spiders. She might be too afraid to get near them, but her magic could do it for her.

The more she used her magic to kill the spiders, the more her fear began to fade. Everything she had held in all those years dissipated until the spiders were no longer giants in her subconscious ruling her life.

The magic was healing her, and it felt glorious. Saffron closed her eyes and let the magic pour from her, surround her.

Take her.

Camdyn's stomach plummeted to his feet when he heard Saffron's screams. He bellowed her name and clawed through the stones faster and faster.

He called to his god to help him. It was a risky thing. The gods inside them wanted control, and if a Warrior was weak minded or gave too much to the god, the god would rule them.

It was a gamble Camdyn was willing to take. For Saffron. She had suffered as no Druid ever should have, and she was suffering again.

He'd kept in contact with other Warriors like Galen who he'd seen through the centuries. But Camdyn had retreated into himself after Allison's death.

It wasn't until he'd met Saffron that he'd felt such a riot of emotions. She made him angry, made him want to throttle her. But she made him want to smile and laugh. And she made him yearn for her with a hunger that consumed him.

Although he knew he needed to put distance between them before he got too close to her, he did the unthinkable and shifted part of his control to his god, Sculel.

Camdyn felt the increase in his strength immediately. He roared when he heard Saffron scream again. He tore through the wall that was several feet thick and found himself in another tunnel that ran alongside the chamber Saffron was in.

The magic surrounding the chamber was enough to stop even a Warrior from entering.

"Nay," he bellowed and slammed a fist into the stones.

The fact that the stones didn't even shake against his onslaught told him how powerful the magic was. He was cursing his luck when he spotted a door.

Camdyn ran to the door and put his hand on it. He could feel the magic in it, could feel the potent power. He laid his hands upon the door and dropped his forehead against the thick wood when he heard Saffron scream again.

If anything happened to her . . .

Nay. He wouldn't let himself think it. He couldn't. He had to stay focused and find a way to reach her. He was all she had to save her from whatever was inside, and by the sounds of her screams, she was terrified.

"Saffron!"

Her screams fell silent, and Camdyn lost what little hold he had on his rage. He pounded on the door, slashing it with his claws as he bellowed her name over and over again.

He didn't know how long he stayed like that before the door suddenly opened. Camdyn was instantly wary. His claws were ready and eager for blood, his god hungry for death. If anything was in there besides Saffron, it was dead.

Camdyn spotted a faint light through the crack in the door. He nudged the heavy door with his toe and peeked around it. What he saw stopped him in his tracks.

Saffron hung suspended in the middle of the chamber with her arms held out to the side. A faint, pale light emanated from her hands and feet. Her eyes were closed, her face serene.

And then the force of her magic slammed into him.

Camdyn doubled over, not from pain, but from the intense pleasure of her magic. He went instantly hard, his need so strong, his yearning so powerful, he wanted to take Saffron right then.

To lay her down on the stone altar he saw behind her and cut away her clothes with his claws. He wanted her body bared to him so he could look his fill at her breasts.

He wanted to spread her legs wide and slowly enter her. To hear her moans of pleasure, her cries of passion as he thrust in and out of her sex.

Camdyn cupped his aching cock and shifted it to help ease his need, but nothing was going to help him until he was inside Saffron. Claiming her.

He straightened with a grimace and looked around the

chamber for whatever had harmed her. But all he saw was the altar behind her, and a door beyond that.

"Camdyn."

His gaze jerked to Saffron, whose eyes were open and looking at him. He took a slow, measured step toward her. Camdyn wasn't sure if she had done this to herself, or if someone else had. The last thing he wanted to do was hurt her.

"You came for me," she whispered.

"I told you I would. I doona make promises I doona intend to keep."

A single tear fell down her cheek, and it was his undoing. He tamped down his god, briefly noticing the ease with which he did it, and strode to her until he had to look up at her to see into her face.

The light emitted from her hands and feet began to fade as she lowered to the floor. And with it, her magic diminished as well.

Camdyn ached at the loss of it, but at the same time, he was able to gain a measure of control over the yearning he felt for her. It was a small amount, but more than he had had a moment before.

Her feet touched the floor and she walked over to him. Camdyn stood silently as she wrapped her arms around him and laid her head upon his chest. Hesitantly, he folded her in his arms and simply held her.

"What happened?" he asked.

"The spiders. They were everywhere. All over me, the walls, the floor, the ceiling. I couldn't get away. Couldn't move because of my fear."

Camdyn ran a hand up and down her back as she began to shake.

"I heard a voice, but I was too scared to listen. And then a spider bit me." Her head lifted so that he looked down into her face. "I don't know what happened, Camdyn. It's like something flipped inside me. My magic took over."

He cupped one of her cheeks and smoothed away the

remnant of the tear. "Whatever happened, it's over now. There are no spiders."

She frowned and glanced at the floor. "The voice. It asked me about my fear. The spiders. I killed them. Thousands of them. Where are the bodies?"

"I see none."

"Exactly. The voice then told me I was a Druid, that I had magic. After that is when I snapped."

"So you think this was a test?"

She sniffed and gave a half shrug. "If it was, who ever came up with this idea needs to suffer their own fear a hundred times over."

He had to agree, because the terror that had taken him at not being able to reach Saffron had been the worst thing he had ever experienced in his very long life. And he didn't care to ever repeat it.

A test for her? Or had it been a test for him? Maybe for both. He had managed to give a measure of control to his god, and somehow he'd gotten it back. He'd never attempted that before, but he hadn't hesitated. Because it had been Saffron who needed him.

"A test or no', you defeated whatever was in this room so that I could get to you. There was magic blocking me from getting in."

"Me? I defeated what was in the room?"

"Aye. You."

She shook her head and tried to step out of his arms, but he held her tight. "I don't have that kind of power in my magic."

"I think you do."

They stood locked in each other's gazes for several moments before Camdyn looked away. He had to or take her lips again. Need rode him, and he wanted nothing more than to taste her, but now was not the time to give in to his desires.

"There is a door behind the altar," he said.

Saffron turned to look at it. She walked toward it, and as she passed the altar she let her hand run over the stone.

Camdyn followed her, never more than a step behind. He

wasn't going to let them be separated again. Next time he might not be able to reach her.

She turned to look at him, excitement making her tawny eyes dance. "There's a lock on the door."

"Perfect, since we have only the key left."

She nodded. "You do it."

"We do it together," he said.

Camdyn pulled out the key. When she had taken it he wrapped his fingers around hers, and together they inserted the ancient key and turned. The click as it unlocked seemed overly loud in the quiet of the room.

They paused as the walls began to shake around them. Camdyn strained his ears to listen. "It sounds like doors opening. Or closing. I can no' tell which."

"Let's finish," Saffron said.

"We have."

"Nay, we haven't."

Camdyn turned the key once more with her, and to his surprise there was another click before the key was yanked out of their grasp and disappeared into the lock.

He moved so that he was in front of Saffron as the door creaked open.

Fallon and the others jumped up as a gust of wind poured into the cavern from one of the doorways, as if inviting them in.

"Saffron and Camdyn must have done it," Logan said.

Dani paused beside the door and smiled. "This is the way we need to go."

"Then let's hurry," Fallon said as he took Larena's hand in his own.

Finally, Deirdre was about to be ended.

Finally, they could have their family and the future they'd craved.

Saffron didn't mind that Camdyn was walking ahead of her into the room, but when she heard his sharp intake of breath she hurried to stand beside him.

Then gasped herself.

In the middle of the large chamber was another altar, and upon it lay a woman with long golden-blond hair wearing a medieval dress of dark green.

"We did it," Saffron whispered.

Camdyn turned his dark eyes to her. "You did it."

Saffron briefly forgot all about the woman as Camdyn's fingers wrapped around hers. Never in her life had she thought she could have survived all those spiders, but she had. It wasn't on her own though. Camdyn had given her that strength, he had given her the courage.

Because she hadn't wanted to give up as she had so many times in Declan's prison. No, she had wanted a life, and she was willing to do whatever it took to have it.

To have Camdyn, even if just for a little while.

CHAPTER
TWENTY-SIX

Camdyn lost himself in Saffron's tawny gaze. He was adrift, floating. Swept away. And he never wanted it to end.

The mix of excitement and passion in her gaze was too much for him. As one, they faced each other. He rested his hand on the small of her back and pulled her closer as her hands lay atop his arms.

She had dirt smudged on her cheek, her hair was disheveled, and her clothes dirty. But in his eyes she was the most beautiful thing he had ever seen.

"Camdyn," she whispered as she leaned toward him.

He desperately wanted to kiss her, to drink in the exquisite taste of her. How he ached to drown in her scent of midnight and snow.

His fingers curled, pulling her toward him. Her lips parted and it sent a jolt of longing through him straight to his cock. A longing so profound that Camdyn knew if he kissed her, if he gave in to the desire pulsing for her, he would be lost in her.

Her lids slowly closed as his face drew near hers. A soft exhale reached his ears. Her face tilted up to his, as eager for his kiss as he was for hers.

But just before his lips touched hers, his enhanced hearing heard the unmistakable sound of feet running toward them.

Camdyn's eyes memorized Saffron's face for the long years ahead of him before he released her and took a step back. It was the last thing he wanted to do, but he knew he had saved himself by doing so.

Saffron's eyes fluttered open. The passion melted from her face to be replaced by confusion and a thread of anger. She had every right to be cross. Camdyn couldn't keep his hands off her. Couldn't stop looking at her.

Couldn't stop hungering for the one thing he couldn't have.

But he also couldn't give her what she wanted.

She took a deep breath, her eyes brimming with fury. But before she could let loose with the scolding he knew he had coming, Arran and Logan came to a halt at the doorway.

Camdyn turned to them as the others filed in behind the Warriors. He wasn't sure what to say or do. He felt like the worst kind of arse for continually kissing Saffron yet pushing her away at the same time.

There were words he needed to say to her, but they caught in his throat. He wasn't a charmer, wasn't one who always knew what to say. And in this instance, it was better to keep his words to himself, to keep Saffron from knowing how much he wanted her.

Because if he told her, if she knew, things would only get worse for him.

He had to get control of himself. For a hundred years he had lived as a recluse in the forests after Allison's death. He'd been content with his life. While other men wanted to find a woman to share their life with, Camdyn had been happy being alone.

Well, not exactly happy, but at peace with his lot.

What was it about Saffron that drew him like a dying man to water? What was it about her magic that sent his desires to a state that he'd never felt before?

What was it about her that made him want to be with her always?

"I knew y'all would do it," Gwynn said as she walked to them with a huge smile.

Fallon pounded Camdyn on the back. "Good job. Both of you."

Camdyn and Saffron accepted the gratitude of the others. He didn't need to look at her to know her every move or reaction.

She was hurting, and it was his fault. He drew in a deep breath and turned to the others, who all stared at Laria as she lay sleeping peacefully.

Camdyn fisted his hands as Dani wrapped an arm around Saffron's shoulders and drew her into the large circle they had formed around Laria.

"She looks like she just lay down," Cara said.

Camdyn found his gaze traveling to Saffron. He could tell by the way her lips were pinched and her shoulders tight that she was holding in her anger.

Just moments before he'd pulled away from her he'd seen her eyes alight with happiness. He'd seen her withdrawn, angry, frightened, furious, and even filled with passion. But he'd never seen her so joyful.

And he'd ruined it.

Now that he knew what Declan had done to her, he of all people knew she deserved to be happy. It just proved to him that he wasn't the person to give her that.

"Camdyn?"

He started and jerked his head to Quinn who stood beside him. "Aye?"

"I asked if you or Saffron touched anything when you came in?"

Camdyn shook his head. He'd just touched Saffron. A touch that was likely to be his last. "Nay. We unlocked the door and then stepped inside. A few moments later the rest of you arrived."

"As much as I'd love to find out what you and Saffron had to go through to get here, I want to awaken Laria and get this battle over with," Galen said.

Fallon nodded. "Agreed. Ramsey, it's your turn."

Camdyn licked his lips as he too was eager for Laria to awaken. He'd waited for the moment of Deirdre's death for too long. It was made even worse when they'd thought they had killed her when they had freed Quinn.

But Deirdre's black magic had been stronger than any of them had realized. Her body might have been killed that day, but her magic had allowed her soul to remain. It hadn't taken Deirdre long to generate another body.

Ramsey paused beside the huge slab of rock and looked down at Laria.

"Maybe you kiss her like all the princesses in the Disney movies," Dani said with a smile.

There were a few chuckles in response.

Ramsey glanced at Dani and grinned. "If only it were that easy."

"What do you have to do?" Hayden asked the question before Camdyn could.

Ramsey shrugged as he slowly walked around the slab. "That's what I'm trying to determine."

They grew quiet as they watched him. When Ramsey knelt and touched something on the slab, Hayden produced a ball of fire in his hands and leaned close so everyone could see the intricate carvings that looked part Celtic and part something much older.

"Those are no' like any Gaelic writing I've seen," Logan said.

Broc grunted. "Or Celtic artistry."

"These are writings of my people," Ramsey told them.

Camdyn was still in awe of the fact that Ramsey was part Druid as well as a Warrior. He wondered if his magic strengthened Ramsey's power from his god or hindered it.

"What happened to your people?" Camdyn asked.

Ramsey lifted his gaze to Camdyn. "I wish I knew."

Camdyn looked at the carvings in the stone and wondered what they meant. It was obvious by Ramsey's furrowed brow that he didn't know either.

"The magic around Laria is stifling," Ramsey said as he wiped his forehead with the back of his arm.

"We can feel it," Lucan replied.

Camdyn became impatient. He knew it was just a matter

of time before Deirdre tried to trap them again, although he suspected they were so far beneath the ground her magic couldn't penetrate.

But once they were back on land Deirdre would be waiting. Camdyn just hoped they had Laria awake by then. And then there was Declan.

So many had put him in the back of their minds, but Camdyn hadn't. His gut told him Declan could very well join in the upcoming fray.

Just thinking of that had Camdyn's gaze moving once more to Saffron. He watched her hand push her hair out of her face and behind her ear in an elegant motion. The exposed expanse of her neck made him wish he had kissed that portion of her skin. It had him wanting to skim his fingers down her neck to touch flesh he knew to be as soft as silk.

A swell of magic, ancient and strong, suddenly filled the chamber. Camdyn swung his gaze to the altar and Laria. Ramsey knelt at the base of the altar and held one hand over a carving, his head cocked to the side and his eyes closed.

Like Camdyn, Arran, and Logan, Ramsey still wore his hair long, as it had been in the fourteenth century before they'd time-traveled to the future. Ramsey's hair hid part of his face, but there was no denying the smile that pulled at his lips.

There was no warning as Ramsey reached out with his other hand and placed it on another etching. The blast of magic that rushed by Camdyn had him taking a step back, it was so fierce. And he wasn't the only one.

Everyone, including the Druids, had been affected by the magic.

"Oh, my gosh," Saffron whispered breathlessly, her hand on her throat.

The chamber began to buzz with magic. Several small white lights zoomed from beneath the altar like small flying bugs. They darted this way and that, over and around Laria so rapidly the trails of their lights could be seen long after they had moved on.

Ramsey's head was tilted back, words Camdyn had never heard before falling from his lips. The more Ramsey spoke the faster the lights moved until they were nothing but a blur.

There was a loud pop and the lights disappeared. The ancient magic, though still present in the chamber, felt different. Almost as if it had been awoken. Roused.

Revived.

Camdyn drew in a ragged breath, his god affected by such potent ancient magic it hadn't felt since it was pulled from its prison in hell.

He put his hand over his chest as his god raged inside him, urged him to run away. This was the first time Camdyn had felt his god fearful of anything, and it unsettled Camdyn.

One look at Quinn on one side of him and Arran on the other told Camdyn he wasn't the only one whose god wasn't happy.

"What is going on?" Arran bit out.

Fallon gritted his teeth and said, "Stay steady."

But the longer the magic pushed against them, the more their gods railed inside them.

Marcail moved in front of Quinn and placed her hands on his chest with her eyes closed. At once Quinn's body eased. Camdyn looked around to note that each Warrior with a Druid as a wife was having the same process done to them.

Fallon and Larena, both Warriors, weren't able to help each other, but Fiona was quick to step in and aid them before she went to Arran.

Camdyn felt Saffron's gaze on him and he looked at her. He wanted it to be her that eased him, but he knew he had no right to ask. Not after all he'd done to her.

To his amazement, she walked to him and softly, gently touched him. At once Sculel quieted, calmed. Camdyn took a steadying breath and opened his mouth to thank her.

But she turned her back to him and returned to her spot before he could.

"What did you do to her?" Arran leaned over and whispered.

Camdyn glanced at the floor. "I was myself."

Arran's lips twisted in a frown, but he didn't say more. There wasn't anything more to say.

Camdyn turned his attention to Ramsey and Laria. Sculel might be calm once more, but the magic had yet to diminish. And that worried him. They needed to be able to fight against Deirdre, but the way their gods had reacted to Laria's magic might make that impossible.

Of a sudden, Laria's chest rose as she took a deep breath and slowly released it. They stood silently as Ramsey got to his feet and looked down at Laria while more of his strange language tumbled from his lips.

A surge of anticipation filled Camdyn when he saw Laria's fingers twitch.

Ramsey's words grew louder, his magic stronger. Yet the feel of his magic was odd, because mixed with it was his god. It wasn't as pleasurable as other Druid magic, like Saffron's, but neither was it distasteful.

Just . . . different.

And then Laria's eyes opened.

CHAPTER
TWENTY-SEVEN

Saffron was busy staring at Camdyn so she didn't see when Laria's eyes opened. It wasn't until Laria sat up that Saffron focused on the Druid.

Though Saffron had seen visions of Deirdre, she was unprepared for Laria's stunning beauty. Her skin was unblemished and as smooth as cream. Her golden locks hung straight down her back to pool around her hips. Her eyes were so bright a blue that Saffron was mesmerized by them.

Laria's oval face had the bone structure of nobility, and the beauty of a supermodel. She looked slowly around the chamber until her gaze came to rest on Saffron.

Saffron grew uncomfortable under her direct gaze. Then Laria spoke in a language that Saffron recognized but didn't understand.

"Gaelic," Ramsey said. "She's speaking Gaelic."

Gwynn sighed. "Then communicating with her won't be easy."

"*Fáilte*, welcome," Ramsey said in Gaelic.

Laria turned her head to him. "*Fáilte*."

"I'm Ramsey."

Laria held up a hand and turned her gaze back to Saffron. She motioned Saffron to her with a finger.

Saffron swallowed uneasily. She didn't know why Laria was so interested in her, but she was about to find out. Saffron walked to the altar so that she stood across the slab from Ramsey.

"Doona be afraid of her," Ramsey said.

Saffron looked into his gray eyes. "What does she want with me?"

In answer, Laria put her hand on the side of Saffron's face. A jolt of powerful magic shot through Saffron, making her cry out from the shock of it as well as the small amount of pain.

Saffron's gaze was locked with Laria's, but out of the corner of her eye she saw Camdyn start toward her only to be held back by Quinn, Arran, and Hayden.

As quickly as the minor discomfort had begun, it ended. Warmth flooded Saffron. And peace. The same peace she had experienced with the chanting and the drums.

"Don't be afraid of me," said a female voice in her head. *"I need to learn your language and your time."*

Saffron didn't know how long she stood there as Laria touched her, but when Laria dropped her hand, Saffron knew she would never be the same again.

She had been touched by magic unlike anything she could have imagined. It was so pure, so potent, that it brought tears to her eyes. And the fact that two of the most formidable Druids she knew—Isla and Reaghan—were standing in the same room with them said something.

"Thank you," Laria said, and smiled at Saffron.

Saffron looked down at her hand upon the stone, which was covered by Laria's. "Why me?"

"The labyrinth chose you to find me." Laria turned away to look at Ramsey. "You are Druid and Warrior?"

Ramsey gave a slight bow of his head. "No' by my choosing."

"Ah," Laria said with a small measure of distaste in her voice. "My sister."

Saffron couldn't believe no one was freaking out to hear that Laria had learned their language so quickly. But then again, with magic like Laria's, Saffron imagined she could do almost anything.

"Aye," Fallon said as he stepped forward. "Deirdre must be stopped."

"Then let's not waste any more time." Laria was helped off the stone slab by Ramsey.

She took Saffron's hand and led her through the group. As Saffron passed Camdyn she glanced at him to find his dark eyes creased with worry.

There wasn't any time to tell him not to worry as Laria walked toward the stone wall and held out her hand, palm out, as she murmured a spell Saffron had never heard before.

The stones shifted, and a door slid open.

"You can talk to stones, too?" Quinn asked her.

Laria looked at him. "No. That was Deirdre's gift. The only way out of the labyrinth is through spells only I know."

"Wait," Lucan said, stopping her before she could go through the door. "You should know Deirdre is waiting for us."

"I'd expect nothing less from my sister," Laria said with a smile before continuing on.

Saffron didn't know why Laria wanted her beside her. Behind her, Saffron could feel Camdyn's eyes on her. Each time Saffron slowed Laria would smile and motion for her to hurry.

"Your man thinks I mean to do you harm," Laria whispered.

Saffron frowned. "My man? Oh, you mean Camdyn. He isn't mine."

"Really?" Laria asked with an arch of a blond brow. "He certainly acts as if he is."

"He's only doing that because I made him promise to keep me safe."

Behind them Isla snorted. "Saffron, he's protecting you because he wants to, not because you made him promise. I give you my word on that."

Laria shared a look with Isla before she nodded at Saffron. "She's right. A Warrior, but most especially a Highlander, doesn't do anything he doesn't want to do."

Saffron didn't know how to respond to that. They hadn't been alone with Camdyn. They hadn't tasted his kisses and felt his passion.

Or experienced his rejection.

Then she didn't have to answer because Laria slowed as they reached a set of steps that were cracked and weathered by time. "I can feel Deirdre," Laria said softly.

She turned to look at those around her, meeting each of them in the eye. At Fallon, she paused. "Deirdre will be focused on me. Give us room for our battle, but above all else, keep your Druids safe."

"It will be done," he answered.

Camdyn glared at Laria. He didn't know why she wanted Saffron with her, but he didn't like it. If Laria was going to battle Deirdre then Saffron needed to be with the other Druids, not in the line of fire.

Laria's eyes shifted to him then. He narrowed his gaze. It was difficult to look at her and not see Deirdre. Though Laria's hair was blond and not white, and her eyes blue and not white, they were still the same.

Same build. Same mannerisms. Same voice.

"Don't worry, Warrior. Saffron won't be in any danger."

"She better no'."

In response to his threat, Laria simply smiled. Laria then gave a small sweep of her hand and the ground above the stairs began to move.

Camdyn and Arran hurriedly moved ahead of Laria. Camdyn looked at her and said, "We'll draw Deirdre out for you."

He blinked against the glare of the setting sun as they reached the top of the steps. A second later and a wave of *drough* magic slammed into him and tossed him backward into one of the standing stones while being held immobile above the ground.

Camdyn saw Arran had also been held. There was a smile on Deirdre's face as she stood about fifty paces from the steps leading out of the maze.

"I knew you would fail in awakening my sister," Deirdre said with a laugh.

"Oh, but they didn't."

Camdyn began to laugh as Deirdre's smile faded at the sound of Laria's voice. Laria's head appeared, and with it, a blast of magic aimed at Deirdre.

Almost instantly Camdyn and Arran were dropped. Camdyn didn't waste another moment as he rushed to where he saw Saffron beside Dani and Ian as they exited the labyrinth.

Camdyn spotted a wyrran running toward Saffron. He let out a roar and called for the earth to answer his power. The ground rolled beneath the wyrran before swallowing the petite yellow creature.

Camdyn reached Saffron and Dani in time to help Ian battle six wyrran. Dani and Saffron were using their magic against the wyrran, but it wasn't enough for Camdyn.

His god bellowed for blood and death, and Camdyn was in complete agreement. His body ached from his need for Saffron. This battle was a perfect release for him.

Saffron winced as a wyrran shrieked near her ear, but it was nothing compared to Camdyn's roar of rage. It was a Warrior's call to battle, a signal to the others that it was time for death, time to exact vengeance with blood.

Three years ago she'd have been horrified by what she was witnessing, but now she stood in awe of the way Camdyn moved. He was fleet of foot, quick of body. His claws had deadly aim. And once his gaze had pinned an enemy, there was no escape.

Saffron forgot about using her magic against the approaching wyrran. She was too riveted by the sight of Camdyn in his Warrior form with his deep brown skin. Around them were the other Warriors from MacLeod Castle each with their gods unbound and using their vast array of power.

"Saffron!"

She heard Camdyn's yell the same moment she felt the wyrran's claws in her leg. Saffron reacted instantly and shoved against the creature while her magic shot from her.

The wyrran went tumbling backward. Before it could

gain its feet Camdyn stood upon its chest with one foot and severed its head with his claws.

Camdyn's head swiveled to her. He had spatters of blood on him, and his hands were covered in it. Gone was the sun-bronzed skin she knew, replaced with the deep brown of his god. His claws flexed, reminding her they were his weapons. And his fangs gleamed in the sunset.

His eyes were filled from corner to corner with the same deep, dark brown, watching her, his bare chest heaving.

"I'm fine," she said.

He gave a nod, and they were both back in the battle. It didn't take long for Saffron to realize not all of them had made it out of the labyrinth.

She sent a wyrran barreling into Camdyn, who quickly killed it, and chanced a glance at Laria and Deirdre. The twins were locked in battle.

Deirdre with her white hair that hung to the ground and black leather bodysuit that was molded to her like a second skin. Her hair swirled around her in an eerie display of magic.

Laria's blond hair lifted behind her as if caught in the wind while her green skirts tangled about her legs. Both sisters sent the full force of their magic against the other.

It looked to be a deadlock until, somehow, Deirdre got the upper hand and began to push Laria back.

"We need to help," Saffron said as she grabbed Dani's arm and pointed.

There were eleven Druids from MacLeod Castle, but only five of them were aboveground and fighting. Saffron, Dani, Isla, Cara, and Marcail soon sent their magic to mix with Laria's.

It took everything Saffron had not to recoil at the power of the *drough* magic from Deirdre. It reminded Saffron too much of Declan and the memories she wanted desperately to bury.

It wasn't just the memories she had to deal with, however. There was strength in Deirdre's black magic that Saffron hadn't been prepared for.

Finally she understood why it had taken the others centuries to find a way to kill Deirdre. The knowledge scared her far more than she wanted to admit, because she couldn't imagine Declan escaping as many times as Deirdre had.

Yet he had the same potent black magic. That same cloying *drough* magic.

But Saffron wasn't about to give up. She gave a shout and channeled more of her magic against Deirdre.

Deirdre screamed her frustration. She couldn't believe her sister's magic was so powerful that Deirdre hadn't ended her instantly.

She had thought it was be so easy to kill Laria. But Deirdre hadn't been able to trap all the Druids in the maze. A few had managed to get out, and they soon added their magic to Laria's.

A *drough*'s magic was amazingly powerful.

But a group of *mies* could overpower a *drough*.

In all her centuries of living Deirdre had never been bested. And she wasn't going to be now. Because if Laria won, Deirdre wouldn't just lose. She'd die.

She wasn't ready to die, but by the way things were going, that's exactly where she was headed. Deirdre decided it was time she pulled back and found another way to win. Because she would win.

"Until next time, sister!" she shouted before disappearing.

CHAPTER
TWENTY-EIGHT

Declan watched the battle from a vantage point far enough away that Deirdre didn't see him, but close enough that he was able to see what was going on. He could have stepped in and aided Deirdre. He could have helped her win.

But if he had, he wouldn't have her where he wanted her.

Now that she had left without defeating Laria, Declan knew it was just a matter of time before Deirdre came to *him*.

He'd grown up hearing the amazing tales of Deirdre. She was the reason he'd embraced being a *drough* instead of turning his back on magic as others in his family had.

For so many nights Declan had dreamed of having Deirdre for his own. He'd brought her to his time. And now, she would be his.

Declan smiled and looked at Robbie. "It willna be long now."

"You should have helped her. We could've ended the Mac-Leods once and for all. Then taken their Druids."

"I have no need for Druids," Declan said. "As for ending the MacLeods, doona worry, cousin. That will be happening verra shortly."

Declan turned on his heel and made his way down the hill to where Robbie had parked the sleek black Jaguar.

"By the by, I think we might have a lead on Tara," Robbie said as Declan opened the car door.

Declan paused and shifted his gaze to Robbie. "And what might that be?"

"We know she spent some time in Aberdeen three years ago. After that, her trail disappears. For a wee bit." Robbie leaned his forearms on the hood of the car and smiled across to Declan. "Tara has gotten sloppy, Declan. We found her trail again in Edinburgh."

"Good. Verra good. Now you need to find her and bring her to me."

"All in good time," Robbie said with a smile.

Declan knew that smile. Robbie wasn't about to allow Tara to disappear on them. Not again. Tara had bested Robbie and made him look like a fool, and for that Robbie would hunt Tara until the end of her days.

As Declan reclined in the backseat of his car, he couldn't help but grin. Everything was coming together just as he wanted. The only mishap was losing Saffron, but even that would be corrected. Soon.

Very soon.

Camdyn stared at the spot Deirdre had been just a moment before. He couldn't believe she had gone, couldn't believe she had left without them killing her.

"What happened?" he demanded of anyone who might answer.

Isla leaned against Hayden wearily and said, "We needed the other Druids."

"I thought Laria was supposed to be able to kill her on her own."

Laria turned to Camdyn then and sighed. "It isn't as easy as that, Camdyn MacKenna. While my magic is strong, Deirdre has taken the magic of other Druids as well as having hers strengthened by being *drough*. I can hold my own against her, but to defeat her, to end her, I will need the Druids of MacLeod Castle."

"Damn," Hayden muttered. "That would've been nice to know before we started to battle her."

Camdyn agreed silently. He looked to where Deirdre had

caved in the exit to the labyrinth and easily called the earth to do his bidding. The ground opened, separated, and the others hurried out, their faces a mixture of fury, surprise, and confusion.

"What happened?" Fallon ordered.

Camdyn returned the earth to its rightful place and put his hands on his hips. "Deirdre left. Laria needs all the Druids from the castle to help her."

"Bloody hell," Lucan said as he ran a hand through his hair.

Camdyn caught movement out of the corner of his eye and turned to see Saffron with her eyes closed and a hand on Dani's arm.

"We need to get back to the castle," Camdyn said.

He kept an eye on Saffron as Fallon began jumping everyone back to the castle. Camdyn purposely made sure he was in the last group with Saffron.

Camdyn knew better than to touch her, or even get near Saffron, but he couldn't help noticing the dark circles under her eyes or her pallor, which was ashen.

"I'm just tired," he heard Saffron tell Dani.

She had only gotten a few hours of sleep while they had been in the labyrinth, and the maze itself had taken a hard toll on her.

When it was their turn for Fallon to jump them to the castle, Camdyn found himself standing next to Saffron since the others had put them together. He didn't question it. The way Saffron's magic clung around her, as if giving her extra support, told him how exhausted she was.

Just as Fallon put his hand on Camdyn's shoulder, Camdyn heard Saffron suck in a breath. He looked over to find her eyes go milky white as a vision took hold of her.

There was no time to tell Fallon, and when they arrived in the great hall, Camdyn was the one who caught her against him when she started to fall.

He watched, helpless, as her eyes swirled from the vision. The magic that had clung to her now swelled and wrapped around him. It drew him, lured him with unmistakable ease.

Camdyn closed his eyes at the heady feel of it. Of how it seduced. Enthralled.

Captivated.

It was only the sound of Saffron dragging in a ragged breath that opened his eyes. She blinked up at him before she rested her head on his shoulder.

"Ramsey," she whispered.

Camdyn's gaze searched the great hall until he found Ramsey toward the back and called to his friend, "Ramsey."

Ramsey hurried to them, his brow knitted in concern. "What is it?"

"I doona know," Camdyn said.

Saffron lifted her head, feeling weaker than she had a moment ago. She needed food, a bath, and sleep. And not necessarily in that order.

Somehow she wasn't surprised to find herself in Camdyn's arms. The fact that she enjoyed being there so much was the only thing that ruined it.

It took her two tries but she straightened, and was only able to step out of Camdyn's hold with his help. Then she turned to face Ramsey. Ramsey's gray eyes were trained on her. She rubbed her arms with her hands as chills ran through her while she thought of her vision.

It had been so clear, so vivid. That had never happened to her before, and it scared the hell out of her.

"Saffron. What did you see?" Ramsey urged.

She swallowed and took a deep breath. "I saw a woman. She was being chased and her very life was in danger."

"By who?" Camdyn asked.

"I don't know," she said as she glanced at him. "He was . . . dangerous, evil. And she was petrified. I still feel her terror."

Ramsey's brow lifted in question. "You felt her fear?"

Saffron began to shake her head no, when she paused. "I didn't feel it exactly, but I knew it. I saw you," she told Ramsey. "You are part of the vision, and if Tara is to be saved, you have to find her before whatever is after her."

"Tara?" Ramsey repeated the name.

"Yes. That's her name." Saffron hadn't heard the name,

hadn't heard any voices, but she somehow knew it was Tara she had seen being chased. It was Tara who Ramsey stood beside, protecting her from evil.

Ramsey looked over her head to Camdyn, then turned his head to Fallon. "I can no' leave now."

Saffron wanted to argue that he did, but she had no idea of the timeline of her vision. It could happen that day or the next month. And as much as she wanted to help Tara, Saffron knew Deirdre had to be taken care of first.

She put a hand on Ramsey's arm. "I'll help you find Tara after we kill Deirdre."

Ramsey covered her hand with his and smiled. Saffron blinked, her eyes feeling as if sand coated them. She extracted her hand and started for the stairs. She wanted out of her dirty clothes and into a hot shower that lasted for at least three days.

After that, maybe sleep.

Saffron couldn't remember getting up the steps or walking to her room. As soon as she kicked her door closed she pulled her sweater over her head and tossed it to the floor. Her T-shirt and bra soon followed.

She had to hop on one foot to untie her hiking boot before she kicked it off and repeated the process with the other foot.

Her jeans, damp and dirty, and panties she yanked down over her hips and wiggled her way out of them as she walked to the bathroom. She used her feet to hold down the jeans as she pulled her legs out of them.

A giggle escaped her as she looked back and saw the trail of clothes leading from her door into the bathroom, but she didn't care. She'd pick them up later.

Saffron turned on the water and then stood beneath the spray, letting the steam and spray soothe her tired, aching muscles. She put her hands on the shower wall and simply stood there, her eyes closed.

It wasn't until she drifted off to sleep that she knew she had to get washed and get out of the shower before she collapsed.

* * *

Charon stayed in his squatting position, one finger idly rubbing his chin, as he stared at the spot where the battle had played out. Dead wyrran still littered the ground. Deirdre wouldn't be pleased about her pets being killed.

Though Charon chafed at not having helped in the vile creatures' slaughter.

He shouldn't be surprised that the Warriors and Druids from MacLeod Castle had awoken Deirdre's twin, Laria. What disappointed him, however, was that they had failed to kill Deirdre.

Charon had almost joined the Warriors as they killed wyrran, but he'd seen—and felt—the magic shift in Deirdre's favor. Charon had spent too many years beneath her control, and he would rather die than be at her mercy again.

He wanted her dead. Desperately. But he wouldn't put himself in a position where he was on the losing side. He'd made a home for himself, and his village depended on him.

Charon sighed as he thought about Ian's urging him to join the Warriors in battling Deirdre. Maybe he should. Another Warrior against her would favor the MacLeods, and it would feel good to fight her.

But then Charon recalled Deirdre's prison. He remembered what she had done to his family. And more importantly, what she had made him to do his father.

There was a hole in his chest, in his heart, for what he'd done. Nothing would ever fill that hole.

Charon rose to his feet and ran a hand down his face. For now, he could continue to watch from the sidelines.

As he turned to walk back to his Mercedes, which he'd parked a few miles away, he caught sight of something. Charon paused and stood silently as his gaze narrowed.

It was a person, a man. And he was staring at the same battle scene Charon had been watching. Who was this man? And was he on Deirdre's side?

Charon's jaw clenched when the man's gaze lifted to him. Almost instantly Charon realized he was a Warrior. Only a

Warrior would be able to see across such a vast distance so clearly.

The Warrior hadn't joined Deirdre, nor had he helped the MacLeods. Whose side was he on?

Charon laughed at his own question. "What right do I have to that knowledge since I have no' taken a side either?"

Without a backward glance at the Warrior, Charon started for his car. Once he reached the black CLS Mercedes, he slid behind the wheel and simply sat there.

Every instinct he had told him to go to the MacLeods. But he'd done the right thing once before and it had delivered him into Deirdre's hands. He'd had his god unbound and had turned into a monster.

Then Deirdre had shoved his father in the cell with him. Charon would never forget straining to gain control over his god only to realize he had killed his father.

That haunted Charon even now.

He might want to help the MacLeods, knew he should. It was the right thing to do to fight against such evil as Deirdre.

But he'd learned his lesson the hard way the first time. He didn't need to learn it again.

CHAPTER
TWENTY-NINE

Camdyn paced his cottage over and over. He sat at the table, sat on the bed, and paced some more. No matter what he did, he couldn't stop thinking of Saffron.

Of her soft skin.

Of the sweet taste of her kisses.

Of her body that was made for sin.

Camdyn wanted to go to her. He wanted to find her and give in to the unquenchable desire that scorched his blood since kissing her so thoroughly in the labyrinth.

But if he did, if he gave in, he would set himself up for pain again.

He halted, amazed that he hadn't thought about Allison in days. She had faded from his mind over the years to the point he couldn't remember the color of her hair or the exact shade of her eyes.

It wasn't until he'd been tempted by Saffron that Allison filled his mind once more. But even now his long dead wife had been overtaken by Saffron. It was as if everything around him was somehow connected to Saffron.

The only way to save himself would be to get as far away from the castle as he could. Even as he thought it, he knew he wouldn't.

He'd waited too long to see Deirdre dead to leave now when his brethren needed him the most.

But he couldn't stand the ache for Saffron another moment. He either needed to find release with another woman, or find Saffron and take her as he'd thought about taking her from the first time he had held her in his arms.

Camdyn leaned his hands on the table and dropped his chin to his chest. He couldn't remember wanting another woman as much as he wanted her. He couldn't remember hungering for a taste of another woman as he hungered for her.

He straightened and stalked from his cottage. He jogged to the castle and leaped to the battlements, landing with his knees bent and a hand on the stones. He rose and looked around him.

Ramsey and Arran were in the bailey, and Logan was on the battlements coming toward him. There would be no going through the front door and greeting anyone still in the great hall. He was in no condition for small talk. With anyone.

Camdyn turned his back to Logan and started for the door that led into the castle. He had scarcely a moment's notice that he wasn't alone when Ian stepped out of the shadows and blocked his way to the door.

"Camdyn," Ian said in greeting.

Camdyn clenched his jaw and nodded. "Ian."

His friend sighed and glanced down at his feet before meeting Camdyn's gaze once more. "Are you sure you should be doing this?"

"What am I doing?" Camdyn didn't like the fact that Ian knew who he was going to see, because if Ian knew, then that meant the others probably did as well.

"Going to see Saffron."

"So?"

"She's been through a lot. Dani is worried you might hurt her."

Camdyn fisted his hands. There was no doubt he would most likely hurt Saffron, but even that couldn't make him stay away from her.

"You doona deny it?" Ian asked, surprise in his deep voice.

"I'm no' fit for anyone, much less Saffron."

Ian's gaze sharpened, as if he'd just realized something. "Then why go to her?"

"Get out of my way." There was nothing that would make Camdyn admit to any of them why he had to see Saffron. It was better if none of them, most especially Saffron, knew how much she affected him.

Cara and the other women were matchmakers. If there was a hint of something between him and Saffron, they would set about throwing them together any way they could.

And that could never be. A night, yes. One night of pleasure and passion was all he could allow there to be.

For several seconds Ian simply stared at him. Then, finally, he shifted to allow Camdyn to pass. Only when Camdyn drew near did Ian reach out and grasp his upper arm to stop him.

"You're a good man, Camdyn. Doona hurt her."

Camdyn pulled his arm out of Ian's grip, went through the door, and strode down the corridor to Saffron's chamber door. He braced his hands on the stones on either side of the door and tried to calm himself.

He banged on the oak door twice and resumed his stance. The door opened and his gaze feasted on Saffron with her damp hair and a gold robe wrapped around her lithe body.

Camdyn knew he should say something, but his need was too great. He grasped her as he hauled her against him for a hard, ravishing kiss as he stepped into her chamber.

He kicked the door closed with his foot and tossed her back onto the bed. Camdyn quickly laid his body atop hers and kissed her again. He kissed her with all the desire, all the yearning, he had.

If he couldn't put into words what he wanted to say, he would show her with his mouth, hands, and body.

As soon as he had touched her, his already heated body had gone up in flames. They licked at him, urging him for more of her, to have more of her.

Her hands skated up his arms and around his neck as she

opened her mouth to him. Her moan, soft and seductive, filled his ears as their tongues slid against each other.

Camdyn was soon sinking in all that was Saffron. Falling. Tumbling.

And he didn't want to stop it.

He groaned when she lifted her hips to rub against his cock. A wave of passion burned through his veins so great he had his knee between her legs before he knew what he was doing.

Camdyn drew upon his legendary control and stopped himself from taking her right then. He wanted her, there was no doubt, but he wanted to savor Saffron. To put every inch of her into his memory.

He rose up on his hands and looked down at her. Her lips were wet and swollen from his kisses, and her tawny eyes were heavy lidded and filled with passion.

"Don't you dare stop," she whispered before she pulled his head back down for a kiss.

Camdyn slipped a hand inside her thick robe. With just a twist of his wrist, her loosely tied belt came undone and he spread her robe wide.

He sucked in a breath when he found her naked beneath. Camdyn broke the kiss to gaze at the body he'd been craving to see. His hand caressed between her full breasts, past her small waist, and over her flat belly, and then to her gently flared hips.

Camdyn paused for a heartbeat to let his fingers skim over the light brown curls that hid her sex from him. His hand continued down her thigh until he reached her knee where he tugged her leg up so he could touch down her leg to her foot.

She was more beautiful than he ever imagined. Her skin was still pale from being kept out of the sun, but it was luminous now as it glowed with health.

Camdyn met her gaze and knew in that instant he'd been a fool to fight against what was between them. He'd lost long ago and just hadn't realized it.

But if he was going to have her, he was going to take his time and relish every moment.

He cupped her breast and gently massaged it. Saffron's eyes closed and her lips parted. But when he thumbed her nipples he heard the moan he'd been listening for.

Camdyn was merciless as he began to tease her nipples. He closed his lips around one and let his tongue glide over the tip while his hand rolled her other nipple between his fingers.

Her fingernails bit into his back as she arched off the bed. Camdyn didn't relent as he shifted to her other breast and suckled the turgid peak deep into his mouth.

He couldn't stop a groan of his own as her hips rocked against his. He burned hotter with each moan, each rub of her hips.

Camdyn rolled them until he was on his back and she rested on his chest. She sat up, and with a simple shift of her shoulders, the robe puddled around her hips.

He'd never seen anything so bewitching in all his long years. If he'd hungered for her before, he was ravenous now. There was nothing, not even Deirdre, who would stop him from claiming Saffron's body that night.

She reached for the hem of his tee, but Camdyn was quicker. He flung the robe to the floor and cupped her breasts. She sucked in a breath as he pinched her already sensitive nipples, mixing pleasure with pain.

Her hips rocked forward as her head dropped back. Camdyn couldn't take his eyes off her. Her passion was a thing of beauty, as if she had been waiting to come alive for someone.

Before he could think too much on that, he moved a hand down to her curls and pressed.

She moaned his name as her breath became ragged.

Camdyn licked his fingers before he pushed them through her curls and found her clitoris. And began to softly circle it. Tantalizing them both.

She stilled, her thighs squeezing his sides as a cry locked in her throat.

Camdyn shifted his hand between them and felt her arousal on his fingers. Whatever control he'd had snapped in that moment.

He flipped Saffron onto her back and wedged himself so he lay between her legs. He had a finger inside her before she had landed on her back.

The feel of her slick walls nearly made him spill right then. Her wet heat and soft moans drove him to want to hear her scream her release. He wouldn't be satisfied until then.

Camdyn began to stroke his finger in and out of her. Over and over he plunged his finger into her heat before adding a second finger.

She clutched at his arms, her hips rising to meet his thrusts. He knew she was close. He could see her body tightening and ready to break loose.

And just as her breathing changed, he withdrew his hand.

Saffron's eyes flew open. She'd been so close to climaxing, so very close. She opened her lips to ask Camdyn why he'd stopped when he rose and knelt on the floor.

He grabbed her ankles and pulled her to the edge of the mattress. Her gaze met his just before his mouth touched her sex and his tongue licked her.

Her thoughts scattered as his tongue laved at her swollen clit. His arms were wedged so they held her thighs open while his large hands spread her labia.

Saffron had never been so exposed. And she'd never felt anything so good before.

Her hands fisted the coverlet as her eyes rolled back in her head. No one had ever kissed her like Camdyn did. No one had ever looked at her the way Camdyn did.

And certainly no one touched her the way he did.

Her body was ablaze with need that tightened in her belly with each lick of his tongue. Bringing her closer and closer to release.

A cry tore from her throat when he slid a finger inside her as his tongue continued to lick her. She rocked against him. His fingers filling her, his tongue teasing her.

The climax, when it hit, came suddenly. It took her away

on a tide of blissful glory that had her falling into an abyss of pleasure.

Camdyn continued his assault, prolonging her orgasm until a second wave took her.

With her body still shuddering from so much pleasure at once, Saffron realized Camdyn had risen. She opened her eyes to see him staring at her.

His black hair hung loosely to his shoulders, the ends curling slightly around his face. His chocolate eyes were filled with a need that made her breath catch.

He ripped off his T-shirt, giving her another glimpse of his chiseled abs and thick shoulders. But she really paid attention when he pulled off his jeans.

Saffron had seen Michelangelo's *David* while in Florence, and others might think *David* was a perfect specimen, but none of them had seen Camdyn.

His muscular chest made a vee to his waist and narrow hips. Legs, long and muscular, stood braced apart, letting her look her fill.

But it was his heavy, thick arousal jutting upward that caught her attention.

Saffron sat up and wrapped her hand around his length, marveling at the smoothness and hotness of his rod. She glanced up to see his eyes closed and his jaw clenched as she ran her hand up and down his length.

Knowing that he was feeling the same kind of desire still rushing through her veins was a heady experience. She wanted more of that control.

She leaned her head down and wrapped her lips around his cock. His hands instantly framed her head as he said her name with a mixture of desire and agony.

Before she could do more, she found herself on her back and Camdyn leaning over her. He held one of her legs in his big hand as he positioned his arousal at her sex.

Slowly, leisurely, he rubbed the head of his shaft along her sex.

Her sensitized flesh cried out for more as she moaned in

pleasure. And then he pushed inside her with slow, measured thrusts.

He held her hips as she tried to buck against him. She could feel herself stretching to take all of him in. But it had been so long since she'd had sex, and her body hadn't adjusted.

And then suddenly it did.

She groaned as he slid fully into her, stretching her, filling her until she didn't know where she ended and he began.

He leaned over her and kissed her fiercely, passionately. She wrapped her arms around his neck as he deepened the kiss. And then he began to thrust.

CHAPTER
THIRTY

Saffron's breath locked in her lungs as he moved with short, soft strokes and long, hard thrusts. He pounded into her, setting up a relentless tempo.

She held on to him, her body no longer her own. It was his to do with as he pleased. And she responded to his every touch, every breath as if she'd been waiting her entire life for him.

Her eyes opened to find Camdyn looking down at her, his dark chocolate eyes capturing hers and refusing to let go. Saffron had never looked into a man's eyes before while making love.

It had seemed too intimate, too personal.

But with Camdyn everything was different. She wasn't able to guard herself as she normally did, and somehow she didn't want to. She wanted to be herself, the person she kept from everyone.

She wound her arms around his neck when he bent and kissed her. The kiss held as much longing and craving as she had seen in his eyes.

He plunged deep within her and held still as he deepened the kiss. It swept away her breath. The walls around her heart began to crack with each sweep of his tongue against hers, with each stroke of his arousal within her.

"Saffron," he whispered, and kissed down her neck as he began to pump his hips once more.

She lifted her legs and wrapped them around his waist. It moved the angle of her hips and he sank even deeper into her. A gasp tore from her as his rhythm grew faster.

With her arms locked tight, she held on as he claimed her body stroke after stroke. He plunged faster, harder. Deeper.

Her body tightened. The passion rose higher, winding quicker, tighter. Saffron felt the rapid, smooth movements of his hips as his body slid against hers. Into hers.

She closed her eyes, giving her body up to the climax building within her. Her breath locked as she was engulfed by the flames of desire.

A scream tore from her throat when the orgasm hit.

Camdyn leaned up and watched Saffron peak for the third time. Her eyes were closed, her lips parted on her scream, and her back arched.

But it was the feel of her walls tightening around his aching cock that had him fighting back his own release. It had been too long, and he'd wanted her too desperately to hold back the climax.

With the shudders of her last orgasm still racking her body, Camdyn desperately pumped his hips. The combination of her slick heat and need were too much.

He threw back his head and gripped her hips tightly as he gave in to his release. Its power staggered him, amazed him. Astounded him.

Never, not once in his centuries of living, had he ever experienced anything so . . . poignant.

It was enough for warning bells to go off in his mind, but instead of leaving, he fell next to Saffron. She turned her face to him, locks of hair sticking to her cheek.

He saw the question in her eyes and waited for her to ask why he had come to her. But he prayed she wouldn't voice it because he couldn't answer. At least not in the way she wanted to hear.

"I don't think I can move," she said with a tired smile.

Camdyn noticed the goose bumps on her skin and rose to pull back the covers before he moved her so that her head was on the pillow. He covered her, but just as he was about to turn away, he found he didn't want to. He slid into the bed next to her, and the smile she gave him had him grinning as well.

"You should do that more," Saffron said as she ran a finger lightly over his lips.

He grabbed her hand and turned it so that he kissed the backs of her fingers. "Do what more? Make love to you until you can no' move?"

"Oh, that definitely," she said with a breathless laugh. "But I was really talking about your smile. It looks quite charming, you know."

"I've no' had much to smile about."

"You will once Deirdre is gone."

Camdyn sighed and rolled onto his back to look at the ceiling. "I've waited centuries for her death. I willna believe it's real until I see it with my own eyes."

"Will you tell me what she did to you?"

He looked down at their hands still joined between them. "My story is no' so different from the other Warriors here."

"Maybe not, but I'd like to hear it. What is it that you don't want me to know?"

"Everything. You're better off no' knowing me at all."

"It's a little late for that." She turned so that she was on her side facing him.

Camdyn sighed and ran his thumb over the back of her hand. He really should release her, but even that small gesture he couldn't seem to make himself do.

"Unlike the others, Deirdre didna have family to use against me. I was an orphan. My mother died giving birth to one of my brothers who didn't last the night, and my father a year later in battle. I was only a small lad at the time with nowhere to go. I was raised by the clan."

"I don't understand."

He shrugged. "I was passed around from family to family."

"What of your brothers and sisters?"

"My sisters were put to work in the castle, and my brothers were taken by different families."

"That's so sad. Were you happy?"

"I didna know any other way. As soon as I was old enough, I had to earn my keep in the clan since I had no family. I hunted for food as well as watched over the sheep. The next step for me was defending my clan and learning to use a sword."

"I gather you were good."

He turned his head to her when he heard the smile in her voice. He raised a brow, one side of his lips rising in a smile. "I was verra competitive."

"Was? You aren't anymore?"

"Maybe a wee bit. Immortality tends to change a man's views."

"Did you go to Deirdre as Logan did, then?"

Camdyn shook his head. "Nay. I was in the middle of a battle between my clan and another. I'd been injured. A sword to the stomach."

He paused when her finger traced the faint scar on the left side of his stomach slowly, her touch light.

"I knew it was a mortal wound, but I continued to fight. I killed the man who had wounded me. I doona know how long I fought before I'd lost too much blood to continue. By that time we were winning. I tried to make it back to my horse. But it was too late."

"You didn't die, did you?"

"It was close. I was out of my mind with the pain as well as delirious. I thought the beautiful woman with white hair and eyes was just something I made up in my mind. And the wyrran that dragged me into the woods and away from my kinsmen I thought were just children."

"So you didn't know what was going on?"

"Nay. I could hear her speaking, but I couldna understand what she was saying. And then the real pain began as she unbound my god."

Camdyn paused, because even nearly seven hundred

years later, he still could feel the way his bones had popped out of joint and broken as his god stretched. He could still feel the way his muscles had shredded before they'd knitted back together.

"It healed your wound, didn't it?"

He nodded. "Aye, but it left the scar because I was still mortal when I received the wound."

"I see. What happened next?"

"I think I lost my mind for a time." He couldn't believe he'd said that. It was a secret he'd kept from everyone.

Her soft hand lay over his heart. "And only a Highlander as strong as you could have found your way back."

"Only because I was left alone. She had others who she was trying to turn to her side, and since I was on that road already, she focused on them. But that solitude gave me the time I needed."

"Today was the first time I've actually seen Deirdre," Saffron admitted. "I've only seen her in my visions, but it's so much worse seeing her in person. Her evil. I can still feel it on me."

Camdyn found himself pulling Saffron into his arms. He didn't think about his reason for doing so, only allowed himself to feel the rightness of it as her head rested on his chest and her body molded against his side.

"The evil of Cairn Toul is just as bad," Camdyn said. "It seeps from the rocks and surrounds you until you are suffocating with it. Combine that with your god, who is raging inside you for control, and it's no wonder so many Warriors succumbed to her."

"It must have been a lot for you to deal with in addition to seeing your wound healed."

"I never saw the wound heal, but looking down and seeing the flesh mended, as well as hearing and feeling the god inside me when I knew it was wrong, was too much for me. I tried to go back to my clan, but Deirdre stopped me and brought me to Cairn Toul. She threw me in her dungeons where other Warriors battled themselves for control. So few won."

"Who is your god?"

Camdyn released a long breath. "Sculel, god of the underworld."

"How did you gain control?"

"I doona know exactly. I've always been stubborn, so maybe it was that I never gave up, no matter how easy it would have been. I fought against him day after day, decade after decade."

Saffron's fingers leisurely traced designs upon Camdyn's chest. "How long were you in Deirdre's mountain?"

"A score and ten years."

"Thirty years?" she echoed and looked up at him. "And how did you escape?"

Camdyn smiled then. "Deirdre liked to see us fight. We were immortal after all, and as long as we didna take each other's heads, we could survive to fight another day. The Warrior I was supposed to fight had given in to his god fully. It took nothing to get him agitated enough that he began to slash his claws at those around him.

"I waited until everyone was trying to pull him off one of the Druids Deirdre used as slaves and then I ran. I had met Galen years before and he'd told me of a second exit that he knew of. I chanced everything on Galen's word and ran for that exit."

"And you found it."

"I found it." Camdyn looked at the ceiling, memories of that day assaulting him. "And I ran."

CHAPTER
THIRTY-ONE

Saffron ached for all that Camdyn had been through. His reservations about being close to anyone made perfect sense now that she knew he'd been an orphan.

At least she'd had the love of her father. It also put her life into perspective. Even with a mother that was a first-rate bitch, her life had been good. She'd been safe, clothed, fed, and loved. She'd been able to live a life she'd wanted for the most part.

"Once you left Cairn Toul, what did you do?"

As soon as the question left her mouth and she felt Camdyn tense, she knew it had been the wrong thing to ask. But she wanted to know all about his life.

"I wandered," he answered blithely.

"If you don't want to tell me, then just say so. But don't lie," she said, and sat up to turn away.

She found herself on her back with Camdyn leaning over her in the next heartbeat. His face was inches from hers and she felt his cock harden against her leg.

"Why do you want to know?"

"Why did you want to know what Declan did to me?" she answered with a question of her own.

Camdyn gave a slight shake of his head. "You doona want to know about my life."

"I wouldn't have asked if I didn't wa—"

Her words were cut off as Camdyn kissed her. Fervently. Ravenously. Frantically.

In an instant her body came alive. His hands were everywhere, touching every part of her as he kissed her senseless, kissed her so that she forgot who she was. Forgot everything except the man touching her.

Saffron found herself flipped onto her stomach with Camdyn's hands on her hips as he raised her so that she was on her knees. She had her hands beside her, ready to push up when he put a palm between her shoulder blades.

"Nay," he whispered between kisses he rained upon her back.

She stayed as she was, her body ready and open for him. His hands glided down her back, over her bottom to the crease between her buttocks. He stopped short of touching her sex.

Saffron groaned at the need coursing through her. Once more his hand ran down her back and between her bottom, and this time, his fingers skimmed her curls.

She sucked in a gasp when there was a feather-light touch on her already swollen clitoris.

"Camdyn. Please," she begged when he teased her twice more.

He leaned over her, his mouth next to her ear. "What do you want?"

"You. I want you."

His teeth lightly scored her skin where her neck met her shoulder before he kissed it. "I want you screaming."

At the rate he was going Saffron knew he'd get his wish. She'd never known her body could react like this, never knew a man could bring out her passion so diligently.

The engorged head of his arousal brushed against her sensitive sex. Saffron leaned her hips back for it, but Camdyn held her still.

He reached around and cupped a breast to gently massage it before pinching her nipple. Saffron gasped as her breasts swelled at his touch.

"Yes," he whispered in her ear.

She could feel herself growing damp the more he teased and touched. Her sex throbbed, ached. She'd never been so close to release with so little touching.

Her breath hitched as he thumbed her turgid nipple and his cock slid along her sex. She rocked her hips back and was rewarded with a groan from him.

"Minx," he muttered.

Saffron stilled, her fingers digging into the rumpled covers as the head of Camdyn's cock filled her opening. His hands held her hips tightly so she couldn't move no matter how hard she tried.

"By the saints, you're wet," Camdyn said.

Then slowly, inch by agonizing inch, he filled her.

She whimpered into the blankets as her passion rose the more he entered her. She wanted him hard and fast, and he was making her wait, prolonging her desire until she was in a fever pitch to have him.

When he was fully seated, he rotated his hips. Saffron moaned, wanting, needing more. She was exposed to him, her body at his mercy. And he was giving her more pleasure than she'd experienced in her life.

Slowly he pulled out of her until only the tip of him remained. And then he thrust deep.

Saffron cried out from the feel of him sliding inside her, deeper, harder than before. His fingers bit into her flesh as he pulled out again, this time holding still longer.

She wiggled her bottom trying to get him to thrust again. Instead, it was his fingers on her clit. Fondling, stroking, thumbing the little nub until Saffron's entire body trembled from the need gripping her.

All the while Camdyn kept just the head of his rod inside her. But now he jerked his hips forward and plunged inside her.

Saffron screamed his name. He pumped furiously inside her, his thick cock stroking her higher and higher. The feel of his flesh slapping against the back of her legs only heightened her passion.

The climax swept over her rapidly in a blinding flash of

pleasure that sent her spiraling down a chasm of bliss. And just as he'd asked, Saffron screamed for him.

Her body still racked by the aftershocks of such an intense orgasm, Saffron heard the harsh sound of Camdyn's breathing matching her rapid heartbeat.

He never slowed, just continued to thrust in and out of her channel, prolonging her pleasure. Until he gave a shout and she felt his seed pour into her.

Camdyn slumped over her, cheek to cheek. He was still inside her, still hard as her sheath clenched around him.

How had he been foolish enough to think that one taste of Saffron would release her hold on him? In fact, it had only tightened that hold.

Even now, he wanted her again.

He pulled out of her and rolled to his back. When he turned his head, their gazes clashed and she moved her hand to join his.

It was such an intimate and simple offering, but it made him realize she had shared her secrets with him. He needed to do the same, even if it killed him to do so.

He owed it to Saffron, to Allison, and even himself.

"I was married," he said into the silence.

Her brow furrowed slightly, but she didn't utter a word.

"It was after Deirdre unbound my god. I'd been wandering for almost twenty years when I came upon Allison. She was alone and the wheel of her cart had broken. So I helped her."

Camdyn smiled at the memory. "There was an easy grace about Allison that drew me. After I fixed the wheel I offered to help with anything else. I stayed one night, then one night became a week, and then a month. Soon, we were lovers. I'd never been so happy."

He looked at Saffron to find her watching him quietly, intently.

Camdyn shrugged. "I wanted her. I didna think of anything but that. Before I asked her to marry me, I told her—and showed her—what I was. She was frightened, but she didna run away."

Saffron's smile was small and sad.

"We married the next day. The next few years were some of my happiest. Until Allison began to age."

"And you didn't."

Camdyn nodded. "I didna care that her hair turned white. But she did. She tried to get me to leave, but I wouldna. It was five years later that we had a terrible winter storm. I had gone out to hunt. Allison had left the cottage to get some firewood I'd stacked outside the house. I was gone longer than I had anticipated, and she'd run out of logs inside.

"I returned to find her lying in the snow. She didna know how long she'd been there. She'd slipped on some ice and hit her head. Her body was too weak to fight off the fever when it struck. I stayed by her day and night for a week as she fought to live. I was there, holding her, when she took her last breath."

Saffron's fingers tightened on his.

"She gave up in the end," Camdyn said. "I saw it. I knew it. But I didna say a word to her. She hadna been happy in so long. How could I ask her to stay with me when she wanted to leave?"

Saffron pulled his hand to her lips and kissed it.

Camdyn couldn't look away from her tawny eyes. Her skin glowed and her hair was disheveled. Her lips were swollen, and her skin still flushed from their lovemaking.

She was stunning. Mesmerizing. Beguiling.

And he wanted her again.

Without any words she rose up and straddled his hips before she leaned down and put her lips on his in a soft kiss. He slid a hand around her neck to cup the back of her head as he slanted his lips over hers and slipped his tongue between her lips. A moan rumbled from his chest when she reached between them and wrapped her slim fingers around his hard cock.

She lifted her hips and guided him inside her. Camdyn ended the kiss and opened his eyes to look at her.

Before she'd just been a female who tempted him. Then she'd become a woman who had suffered needlessly.

Now she was a Druid who had managed to find the last shreds of his soul and touch him.

His hands caressed down her sides to squeeze her buttocks as she gently rocked against him. They'd had passionate sex, and hard, fast sex. This was something new, something Camdyn wasn't sure he could handle.

It was slow, seductive. And felt entirely too good.

It was also too dangerous.

He smiled when Saffron sat up, her hands resting on his chest and her hair wild about her shoulders. Back and forth she rocked her hips, pulling him deeper and deeper into all that was her.

Camdyn cupped her breasts and watched as her nipples hardened as he teased them. Her head fell back, a soft cry falling from her lips as he surged upward.

He closed his eyes at the sound of his name whispered with such pleasure.

It was impossible for him not to touch her. The more he ran his hands over her body the more she moaned. Her soft cries filled the chamber as their passion mounted once more.

"Camdyn," she screamed as she peaked.

This time he didn't hold back. As soon as her body clamped around his cock, he gave in to the release and followed her into paradise.

It washed over them, gripped them. Held them.

Bound them.

And when Saffron collapsed onto his chest and fell asleep, it never entered his mind to leave.

CHAPTER
THIRTY-TWO

Declan didn't bother to look up from signing papers at his desk when the knock sounded on his office door. "Enter!" he called out.

He set aside the papers and reached for another to look over all the legal speak his lawyers had added for the next property he was buying.

"What is it?" he asked Robbie as he glanced up and spotted his cousin standing in the doorway, Robbie's hand still on the knob.

"You're going to want to come to the front door."

Declan sighed and tossed aside his pen as he leaned back in his chair. "The only thing that's going to get me out of this chair is if Deirdre is here."

Robbie's smile was slow but broad. "You're going to want to come to the front door, cousin."

Without another word Declan rose and followed Robbie to the front door. Declan's heart was pounding with excitement at finally having Deirdre come to him. He knew it had only been a matter of time and now . . .

His train of thought ground to a halt as he found a man on his front steps, not Deirdre.

Declan looked at Robbie. "What is this?"

"Wait," Robbie cautioned and held up a hand. "Trust me."

Declan swiveled his head back to the man. "Who are you?"

"I'm Toby, and I'm here on behalf of my mistress, Deirdre," the man answered, though his eyes had the vacant look of someone whose mind was under the control of another.

Declan crossed his arms over his chest. He'd rather have had Deirdre come to him, but the fact she had sent one of her slaves got his attention. "And what does Deirdre want?"

"A meeting," Toby replied.

"She knows where I live."

Toby smiled. "She wants to meet on neutral ground. Somewhere private. And only you."

"Is she going to come alone as well?"

Toby gave a slow nod. "Yes."

Declan might not have wyrran as Deirdre did, or even a Warrior. But what he did have was mercenaries with X90s and bullets filled with *drough* blood that would fell a Warrior instantly.

He had wanted Deirdre to come to him begging for his help, but he should have known she'd be too prideful for that. The fact she wanted to meet him could very well get him everything he wanted.

"Where? And when?" he demanded of Toby.

"Noon tomorrow at the Ring of Brodgar."

Declan dropped his arms and slammed the door in Toby's face before he turned on his heel. He smiled at Robbie. "I told you she would come to me."

"Careful, cousin. She hasna asked for your help yet."

"Ah, but she will."

"Are you going alone?" Robbie asked.

Declan shrugged and clapped Robbie on the shoulder. "For the most part."

Saffron woke, but she didn't open her eyes. She inwardly smiled as she listened to Camdyn's heartbeat in her ear. His breathing was even, steady.

She opened her eyes and glanced at the window. It was still dark, but with the gray of approaching dawn. Since she'd been eager to see her first dawn in over three years, Saffron slowly moved out of Camdyn's arms. She walked barefoot to the window, thankful for the rugs she had bought that helped to keep the cold away from her feet.

With her fingertips on the cool glass, Saffron watched the sun peek over the horizon. The reddish-gold hue reflecting on the water was an amazing sight. But it was nothing compared to the color explosion in the sky.

Saffron blinked away the tears that filled her eyes as she stared at the clouds drenched in color from deep red to purple to the brightest pink.

It wasn't until she had her eyesight taken from her that she'd realized she'd taken so many things for granted. Like watching a sunrise. There had been many times she'd stayed up all night looking at the stars and had seen the sun crest the horizon.

She'd always thought it beautiful, but now it was even more so.

The smile on her face would last for weeks, she was sure. After an amazing night with Camdyn, and then finally getting to see her sunrise, nothing could dampen her day.

She looked over her shoulder to see Camdyn still asleep. Her body was sore from their lovemaking, but it was a wonderful feeling. No one had held her as Camdyn had. No one could come close now or ever. Of that she was sure.

Her gaze returned to the magnificent sunrise. She watched the way the sea moved, displacing the rainbow of colors. Suddenly, familiar arms wrapped around her from behind.

"It's beautiful," Camdyn murmured near her ear.

Saffron smiled as he nuzzled her neck. "I didn't mean to wake you."

"You didna."

She licked her lips as the worry that had filled her mind right before she went to sleep came again. "Camdyn, we didn't use protection last night."

"Protection?"

"To prevent pregnancy. I know from listening to the others that none of the Warriors carry diseases, but—"

His whiskers gently scraped along her cheek as he smiled. "Cara and Sonya have been making brews to keep everyone from getting with child since Sonya came here. It is given to every Druid every month unless they specifically ask no' to have it."

Saffron frowned. "I didn't know they did that."

He shrugged. "There's naught for you to worry over. I'm going to get us something to eat."

"Sounds great," she said, and turned in his arms to smile up at him. "I'm going to get in the shower."

Camdyn watched the way her hips moved sensuously from side to side as she sauntered naked away from him. He'd known the moment she left the bed.

To his surprise, he'd actually slept. He hadn't expected that since he rarely did more than doze for a few hours at a time.

Maybe it had been because he'd finally given his body the release it needed. He refused to think it could have anything to do with holding Saffron.

She paused at the door to the bathroom and looked over her shoulder to give him a smile. As soon as she disappeared into the bathroom and he heard the shower turn on, Camdyn jerked on his pants and shirt and headed for the door.

He yanked open the door and stepped into the hallway, softly closing the door behind him. There, he paused and leaned back against Saffron's door.

His eyes squeezed tight, he knew he was in trouble. The night had been everything he could have imagined and more. Holding Saffron, caressing her, kissing her. She was etched into his mind, branded into his soul.

He ran a hand down his face and let out a soft sigh as he opened his eyes. He'd wanted to avoid this very thing, but it seemed when it came to Saffron he was at her mercy.

What he needed to do was return to his cottage and forget the way her body had felt sliding against his, forget the way it felt to be buried deep inside her.

But Camdyn knew he would never forget.

He pushed off the door and took several steps toward the

stairs when he found Ian leaning against the opposite wall. Camdyn halted as Ian's words from the previous evening filled his head.

"I know that look," Ian said. "That's the look of a man who has found himself in a spot he doesna want to be in."

Camdyn didn't respond.

Ian shrugged and straightened from the wall. "Fallon has asked that everyone be in the great hall by ten."

Camdyn stayed where he was for several long minutes after Ian walked away. Ian knew what he had done last night. Camdyn could see it in his eyes. There had also been disappointment there.

Though maybe Camdyn only saw that because he was disappointed himself that he had failed to keep away from Saffron. Because despite his words, Camdyn knew he was going to hurt her. And she didn't deserve it.

It wasn't her fault though. He was the one who couldn't suffer losing someone else that he loved.

Camdyn took a deep breath and continued on to the stairs. When he reached the great hall he was surprised to only find Braden and Aiden at the table.

He gave them a nod in greeting, but didn't stop to talk. The sooner he gathered food and returned with it to Saffron, the sooner he could get back to his own cottage.

But when Camdyn returned to Saffron's chamber, the thought of going back to his cottage alone didn't appeal to him. He could still smell her on his skin, taste her on his tongue.

And he wanted more. So very much more of her.

He was standing by the hearth holding the food and drinks in his hand when Saffron walked out of the bathroom in her gold robe. He knew the treasures beneath that robe. Camdyn held the plates tighter in an effort not to reach out and drag her against him.

"Hmm. That smells good," she said as she grabbed a biscuit and pulled it apart.

Camdyn set the plates and orange juice down on the small table.

"What is it?" Saffron asked.

He looked at her to see her brow furrowed and her gaze searching his. How could he tell her that he'd done the unthinkable by coming to her last night? How could he tell her that no matter what, they could only have the one night together?

It was what he needed to tell her, but the very idea of never holding her again made his god roar with fury. Camdyn wasn't sure he could stay away from her. Which was the crux of his problem.

"Camdyn?"

He shook his head and turned to the bathroom. "Nothing. I'm going to take a shower."

Saffron took a bite of the biscuit as Camdyn turned on the shower. For a moment she had thought he was going to leave. She'd seen it in his eyes.

She drank deeply from the orange juice as she tried to tell herself to guard her heart. But it was too late. Her heart already belonged to Camdyn.

The thought gave her a moment's alarm, but then she recalled how he had held her, how he had touched her. She remembered the taste of his kiss and the way he had looked at her.

And that alarm turned to joy.

She hadn't expected to find love in Scotland.

Even though she knew it would probably end in disaster, she couldn't push him away. Being with him, near him, steadied her. He gave her the courage to face the memories of her years with Declan and look ahead.

Camdyn was the one who had given her courage in the labyrinth. It was the knowledge that Camdyn was there with her that had helped her face the spiders.

She finished off her biscuit and was in the middle of blow-drying her hair when there was a knock on her door. Saffron opened it to find Laria.

Saffron was so shocked that for a moment she couldn't speak. "Please, come in," she said, and motioned Laria inside.

Laria smiled and entered the room. Saffron noted that her medieval gown was gone, replaced by a pale pink velour track suit that belonged to Larena.

No sooner had Saffron closed the door than Camdyn came out of the bathroom with a pair of unbuttoned jeans on, his hair still wet and dripping on his bare chest.

Laria raised a brow at him, a grin pulling at her lips. "Good morn, Camdyn."

"Laria," he said with a nod of his head.

Saffron cleared her throat and motioned to the food. "Are you hungry?"

"Nay," Laria answered. "I came here to speak with both of you. Privately."

Saffron met Camdyn's gaze. While he pulled on his shirt, Saffron nervously waited for whatever it was Laria wanted of them.

Only after Laria sat in the chair at the table did Camdyn motion for her to take the seat opposite Laria. With no other recourse, Saffron did as he asked and watched as he seated his large frame on the long bench before the bed.

"What is it you want from us?" Camdyn asked.

Laria shrugged and looked from him to Saffron. "The labyrinth chose the two of you to find and wake me. Do you know why that is?"

"Because I touched the dragon head?" Saffron offered.

Laria shook her head. "Nay. The labyrinth chose the two of you because each of you has a connection to Deirdre that can help me defeat her."

"We all have a connection to Deirdre," Camdyn said. "She is the one who unbound our gods. Besides, other Warriors have been closer to her than I ever was."

Laria's smile was soft. "You take my words with literal meaning, Warrior. Open your minds and you will find what it is I speak of."

Saffron frowned. "But I don't even know Deirdre. I've never even met her. She doesn't know of me either."

"Not yet, but she will. Very soon," Laria said. "And once she does, she'll do everything to have you. Saffron, you're a

Seer. There were always so few Seers among Druids to begin with, but now that Druids have turned away from their magic, you've become even more special."

"She was already imprisoned because she's a Seer," Camdyn ground out.

Saffron was surprised to hear the anger in his voice. She looked at him, but his gaze was focused on Laria. Saffron turned and found Laria staring at her.

"And now you've found your connection to Deirdre," Laria said.

CHAPTER
THIRTY-THREE

Camdyn wanted to roar his fury. He wanted to deny everything Laria was telling them.

But he knew in the very depths of his soul it was the truth.

"How do you know this?" he demanded.

Laria's fingers played with the ends of her long blond hair and looked into Saffron's eyes. "When I touched Saffron to learn of your time and language, I felt a glimpse of something . . ."

"Cloying," Saffron offered.

Laria nodded. "Aye. In that brief look I detected an evil that nearly matched my own sister's."

"Declan Wallace," Camdyn said through clenched teeth. He couldn't look at Saffron. If he did he would remember how she looked when he pulled her out of that prison.

And he would recall all the nights he helped her through her nightmares without her knowing of it. Declan had done all of that to her.

"Aye," Laria whispered. "I learned from Danielle that Saffron was taken by Declan because she's a Seer. Add that to the fact that Declan brought Deirdre forward in time. With as great of black magic as Declan has, it's simply a matter of time before they unite."

Camdyn shook his head. "Deirdre doesna share power."

"She'll kill him."

Camdyn's gaze jerked to Saffron at the husky sound of her voice and the surge of her magic to see her eyes had gone milky. He was at her side in an instant, his hands gripping her arms.

Laria rose and took Saffron's hands. "What do you see?"

"Deirdre," Saffron said. "I see Deirdre standing over Declan's body. She's killed him. And . . ."

Camdyn's grip tightened when Saffron began to shake. "What is it?"

"Deirdre is heavy with child." Saffron blinked, and when her lids rose, tawny eyes swung to him. "I saw Declan killed."

Laria began to pace before Camdyn could respond. He could see the excitement in Saffron's gaze at the thought of Declan's death, but there was more to it than that.

"This isn't good," Laria said as she stopped in the middle of the room. "If Deirdre is heavy with child, then I must have failed."

"Or you didn't fight her again," Saffron said.

Camdyn let his hands drop as Saffron rose to walk to Laria. He straightened, his gaze caught by Laria's intense one.

"What?" Saffron asked, and tightened the belt on her robe. "What is wrong with both of you? Declan needs to die. What better way than by Deirdre's hand?"

Laria smiled sadly. "There was one other time in my life that I was in the presence of a Seer. She saved my life as well as gave me information with which to help me when the day came that I had to battle my own sister. Some things a Seer sees will help you. Others will hinder you."

"There was nothing in my vision that I saw that would suggest you had been defeated," Saffron argued.

Camdyn laid a hand on her shoulder and stood behind her. "What Laria is trying to say is that although it is good news for you that Declan dies by Deirdre's hand, it is no' necessarily good news for us."

Saffron turned so she could see him. "Declan has to die.

I cannot go through the rest of my life hiding from him. I won't do it."

"Nor will you have to," Laria said. "Rest. I'll see you both at the meeting Fallon has called. Saffron, please share your vision with the others then."

Camdyn gave a nod to Laria before she left the chamber. No sooner had the door shut than Saffron whirled to face him.

"What are you keeping from me? I have to know," she demanded.

He ran a hand down his face and lowered himself into a chair, staring at the food he'd gotten to eat. "I doona know anything for sure. What I'm about to say is just speculation."

"Maybe," she said as she took the other chair. "But I want to know."

Camdyn tugged a strand of her light brown hair behind her ear. "I doona believe Deirdre will allow Laria to wait long. It is a matter of hours, most likely, before Deirdre attacks."

Saffron's stomach fell to her feet with the weight of lead. But she wasn't going to give up that easily. "Possibly. But it could be that they haven't fought yet. My vision didn't show me that. We cannot know for sure."

"Nay, we can no'."

She was about to say more when her cell phone rang. Saffron rose and walked to retrieve it from her purse. She sighed heavily when she saw her mother's name pop on the screen. "It's my mother."

"I'll go so you can talk privately. I must see to my duties anyway."

She didn't want him to leave, but with a castle this large, there was always something for everyone to do. With a sigh, she answered the phone as Camdyn shut the door behind him.

"Hello, Mother."

"I wanted to give you another chance to apologize for the way you treated me," Elise said.

Saffron rolled her eyes and fell back on the bed. "If this

is about the money, I think we should end the conversation now."

"It's partly about the money. I'm actually calling to tell you I landed in London last night. Albert and I are going to fly up and see you if you'll tell us where you are in Scotland."

Saffron sat up. She wasn't surprised her mother had tracked her to Scotland. Though she wasn't exactly happy with her, Elise was still her mother and she didn't want her endangered. "Now isn't a good time, Mom."

"I flew all the way from Colorado Springs," Elise said, her voice getting higher the more agitated she became. "Why are you so selfish?"

"Maybe because you could be walking into a dangerous situation and I want to keep you safe?" Saffron said, trying the truth.

"Oh, please." Elisa gave a delicate snort. "I'm your mother, and the only parent you have left. I thought you were dead, Saffron. I want to see my daughter."

Saffron dropped her forehead into her hand and closed her eyes. Her mother always managed to make her feel guilty. "Fine. I'll see you, but not until next month. Now is not a good time."

There was a loud, drawn-out sigh. "At least reimburse me the first-class plane tickets for Albert and me for the inconvenience you've given us."

"Mom, I'm just not going to do this now."

Before she'd even finished speaking her mother had hung up on her.

Saffron looked at the phone before she tossed it on the bed. As if she didn't already have enough to deal with, the threat of her mother being in Scotland was enough to send her into hiding.

She blew out a breath and rose from the bed to finish dressing. There were a lot of people in the castle, and she needed to help the others cook.

After a quick brush of her hair and a light dab of makeup, she chose a pair of khaki cargoes and a burgundy sweater.

She opened the door to find Gwynn standing there with her fist raised, ready to knock.

"There you are," Gwynn said with a laugh. "I wanted to see how you were feeling."

"Better," Saffron said as she exited her room and they started down the corridor to the stairs.

"I could hardly sleep last night after all that has happened," Gwynn said.

Saffron smiled at her friend. "I didn't get as much sleep as I wanted."

Gwynn turned her head, but not before Saffron saw the smile.

She stopped and turned Gwynn to face her. "What?"

Gwynn shrugged with a knowing look. "Nothing."

"Gwynn."

"Oh, all right," Gwynn said with a laugh. "I saw Camdyn bringing food to your room this morning."

Saffron hit the toe of her boot against the floor. "He did."

"Did he stay the night?" Gwynn asked in a low, conspiratorial voice.

Saffron couldn't stop the smile. "Yes."

Gwynn yelped and covered her mouth with her hands as they both laughed. "I knew something was going on by the way he stayed next to you in the maze."

"Well, it may not go anywhere," Saffron said, a warning to Gwynn as well as herself.

"Oh, yeah. Right," she said, her voice heavy with sarcasm.

They started down the stairs to the great hall to find almost everyone there. Food was already on the table and people were eating.

Saffron took the seat next to Gwynn, and Dani soon sat on her other side. She turned to Dani to answer a question when her gaze fell on Camdyn, who stood against the wall, his arms crossed over his chest and his dark gaze on her.

Everything she'd been about to say just floated away. He'd left his hair loose so that it curled lightly around his face. A tight-fitting black shirt hugged his body, showing every defined muscle, muscles she had stroked just hours before. Sitting low on his hips were a pair of faded denim jeans.

He could have been the poster child for exactly what a bad boy should look like. Except Camdyn surpassed the bad boys she'd known and dated.

His immortality, the power that radiated from him as strong as the sun's rays, and his confidence that said he had no trouble taking anyone out made her heart beat double.

Her attention was pulled from Camdyn and all the fantasies he evoked by the sound of Fallon's voice.

"Our goal to wake Laria was achieved thanks to Camdyn and Saffron," Fallon said. "But the real battle is only beginning. Before we get into that, I've been told Saffron had another vision this morning."

Saffron licked her lips and stood when Dani urged her. "As some of you know, the visions I receive are sometimes very detailed. Other times, I get very little. The one I saw this morning only showed me three things."

"What were those?" Lucan asked.

She looked around the table, swallowing hard. She recalled Camdyn's words and knew that no matter how much she wanted her vision to work to their benefit, the chances were slim. "I saw Deirdre standing over Declan's body. She had killed him."

Logan nodded, a smile on his face. "That would certainly solve our problem with how to kill Declan. What else did you see?"

This was the part she didn't want to tell them. "Deirdre heavy with child."

"No," Marcail said, as she shook her head again and again. "No."

Quinn wrapped his arms around his wife and looked to Saffron. "Are you sure? It was Deirdre?"

"I'm most positive. Why?"

Arran was the one who answered. "Deirdre captured Quinn because she wanted him to father a child, a child foretold through a prophecy that would hold evil in its purest form."

Saffron's knees grew weak, and she slowly lowered herself to the bench.

"That child can no' be conceived," Ian said. "If it's born, our chance to win against such a force of evil is nearly impossible."

A muscle jumped in Quinn's jaw. "I'll cut that baby from her stomach and kill it myself if I have to. Deirdre almost killed Marcail in her effort to have me in her bed. I willna allow her to become with child."

"The baby is most likely Declan's," Camdyn said. "Why else would she kill him?"

"Because she doesna share power," Galen said.

Saffron lifted her gaze to meet first Laria's and then Camdyn's. "Deirdre needs to be ended before she can conceive this child."

"Exactly!" Hayden shouted, and pounded a fist on the table.

Saffron knew it was the right thing to do, but it meant that Declan would be around even longer. She had thought to let Deirdre kill Declan, and then Laria could kill Deirdre. Everything would have been tied up so nicely.

But life was never so polite and tidy.

"We will kill Declan," Camdyn whispered in her ear from behind her.

She turned her head to look at him over her shoulder. She hadn't even seen him move from his spot. "Promise?"

"I promise."

CHAPTER
THIRTY-FOUR

Deirdre lifted her face to the harsh winter wind as it raced off the water and hugged her long coat against her. How she missed her fur-lined cloak.

Her gaze was riveted on the spot where Laria had emerged from beneath the ground between two standing stones.

Her sister. Her twin.

How could Laria have hidden her magic from Deirdre all those years ago? If Deirdre had sensed just a smidgen of magic, she would have killed Laria as she had the rest of their family.

But there had been no trace of magic.

Now, Laria threatened to ruin it all. The mere thought of all the hard work Deirdre had done to secure her position as ruler made her sick to her stomach.

What was worse was that she had only one Warrior to call upon now. Finding Druids in order to steal their magic was as difficult as finding more men who housed a god inside them.

There were too many people, and none of them feared her.

All because Declan had pulled her forward in time. The imbecile had thought to rule her, but no one ruled Deirdre.

Yet she couldn't forget that she was now alone. All those years of devoted service to Satan, and he had abandoned her as well. With no other recourse, Deirdre had turned to Declan. Just as that arse wanted her to do.

How she hated him. But he could serve a purpose. Once she had defeated Laria, Deirdre would make sure Declan didn't survive the day.

"Are you remembering your defeat?" shouted a male voice over the wind.

Deirdre turned to face Declan. His blond locks were windblown, and his long wool coat billowed about his legs, but there was no mistaking the costly suit beneath. It would be so easy to use her hair to strangle the life out of him. Or rip his ballocks off.

The thought brought a smile to her lips.

"Now you're smiling?" Declan asked. "Is it because you're happy to see me?"

"You came alone," she stated. Of course she knew he had. She had wyrran posted around the area, and they communicated with her through the mind link she had with them.

Declan raised a blond brow. "It is what you asked. What can I do for you, Deirdre?"

"You know what I want."

"Aye, I do." Declan smiled then and walked closer to her so they were only inches apart. "But, my dear, I want to hear you say it."

How Deirdre despised him. She'd begged of no man in the millennia that she had lived. But if she wanted to continue with her plan to dominate the world, this once she would act the meek, needy woman.

And hopefully Declan would believe it.

"I need your help."

"Please," Declan added, his blue gaze holding hers.

Deirdre put her hand on his chest and smiled seductively. "Please, Declan."

"I've waited a long time to hear those words." He roughly hauled her against him. He stared into her face a moment before he claimed her lips in a kiss.

Deirdre was pleasantly surprised at how good the kiss

was. Declan was a handsome man with his square jaw, bright blue eyes, and rakish charm. Had he approached her differently, instead of locking her in his mansion for three months, she might not hate him.

She wound her arms around his neck and returned his kiss with fervor. His answering moan made her smile.

Deirdre let the kiss continue and deepen, she allowed it to grow frantic as their passion mounted. Only then did she end the kiss and lean back to look at him.

"Will you help me?"

Declan's blue eyes blazed with desire. "Aye, but I need something from you in return."

This she had expected. "You want me."

"Of course," he replied, and ran his hand down from the base of her throat and pushed her coat open so that his finger plunged into her cleavage. "That goes without saying."

"You want me and something else?" she asked, suddenly seeing him with new eyes. Maybe he wasn't such an idiot after all.

"There is a Druid with the MacLeods. She was mine, and they took her."

Deirdre laughed. "If she was yours, why hasn't she returned?"

"She was mine, she just needed a bit more time to come to terms with it."

"Ah," Deirdre said as she pulled out of his arms. "Who is this Druid?"

"Her name is Saffron Fletcher."

"And why is she so important to you?"

Declan shrugged and put his hands in his coat pockets. "She's a Seer. My Seer."

"A Seer?" Deirdre repeated, her interest piqued. Now this was something she certainly hadn't expected. She'd had a Seer of her own for many centuries, a Druid who just happened to have been Isla's sister. It was one of the only things that had made Isla comply with what Deirdre wanted from her.

Declan's eyes narrowed. "You will leave her for me."

It wasn't a question and Deirdre knew it. "I will leave her for *us*."

"Us. I like that."

"Good. Then let us begin."

Declan wasn't at all fooled by how easily Deirdre had agreed to his terms, or how she had fallen into his arms. But he was a patient man. She had come to him for help. He'd work his way into her trust after he proved himself to her.

In the end, he knew he would have her for himself. And in his bed.

Camdyn stood with his arms crossed over his chest behind Saffron as he watched Fallon pace in front of them as they sat in a circle before the fireplace. On either side of Saffron was Isla, with Hayden behind her, and Gwynn, with Logan behind her.

"I doona understand," Fallon said as he stopped near the chair where Larena sat. He put his hand over hers and stared at Laria.

Camdyn and Saffron had already heard this part when Laria had visited them in Saffron's chamber. And Camdyn didn't understand any of it better now.

"There isn't much to comprehend," Laria said. "I called Gwynn and Logan, Isla and Hayden, and Saffron and Camdyn to this meeting because they have the deepest connection to Deirdre."

Fallon shook his head. "We all have that connection to Deirdre. All of the Druids need to be protected, and all of them can help you."

"All of them will need to help me," Laria said softly, patiently. "You are leader here, Fallon, and you have done a wonderful job bringing together the Warriors and welcoming the Druids. But I know my sister better than anyone. I saw with my own eyes what she was capable of. I was hidden for centuries until the day I could defeat her. Will you trust me to do that?"

Fallon nodded. "Aye. I didna mean for you to think I doona trust you."

"These people are your family. I understand. I don't want to put them in harm's way, but unfortunately I must."

Isla leaned forward and put her hand on Laria's. "And we gladly do it if it means Deirdre's death."

Camdyn glanced down to find Saffron's head bowed. He had seen the disappointment in her tawny eyes when she had realized they had to kill Deirdre before she could end Declan.

"I'm curious," Gwynn said. "Why me? I only saw Deirdre for a brief moment. It would seem that Cara or even Marcail have a deeper connection to Deirdre than I do."

Laria smiled. "It isn't just you. Deirdre was deep into Logan's mind. You saw that for yourself while you both were beneath the Isle of Eigg searching for the Tablet of Orn."

Camdyn grew uncomfortable as the conversation continued. He'd thought he was there to protect Saffron, but could he be involved as well?

"You and Logan are two halves of a whole. You need each other," Laria continued. "Deirdre will try to split you, but you must remain together."

Camdyn's heart began to pound in his ears.

Laria's gaze swung to Isla and Hayden. "Isla, Deirdre will want revenge for you turning your back on her. She will come for you."

"Let her," Hayden said with his teeth clenched.

Laria smiled. "It is the love that binds you and Isla that Deirdre will attack."

Isla turned and smiled at her husband. "After all we've been through, it would take more than Deirdre to sever our love."

Camdyn shifted from foot to foot. All this talk of love made him more conscious than ever of Saffron. She had been silent, her body still. But her magic didn't lie. It swirled around him in agitation and panic.

He wanted to pull her into his arms, to tell her everything

was going to be all right. But he'd fought Deirdre for too
many centuries to lie. There was no telling how soon they
would be able to kill Declan.

Deirdre had survived before when they had killed her.
How did they know Declan wouldn't do the same thing?
And Declan didn't have a twin hidden away somewhere that
could end him.

Damn, how he hated this.

"Saffron," Laria called.

Camdyn watched as Saffron gave a small jerk and lifted
her head.

"If Deirdre doesn't know you're a Seer, it's simply a matter of time. For someone with her amount of black magic, a
Seer is a powerful tool. And I don't believe Declan is going
to give up on having you himself."

Camdyn clenched his jaw when Laria's gaze lifted to his.
He waited to learn how his link to Deirdre was greater than
that of Quinn or Broc. He waited to learn why he was so
important.

And he prayed Laria wasn't going to tell him that Saffron was his. He couldn't handle that now, not when he was
too conflicted about his need to be with her. Fate wouldn't
be that cruel, to give him another woman that he had to
watch die.

"Be vigilant," Laria told him.

Camdyn let out a breath. "You have my word."

"Wait," Larena said. "After what you told Logan and
Hayden, all you tell Camdyn is to be vigilant? What is his
connection to Deirdre?"

Laria smiled softly. "Someone needs to be there to protect Saffron. Who better than Camdyn?"

Relief unlike he'd known in decades coursed through
Camdyn. If he and Saffron were meant to be together, then
Laria would have stated it.

Since she didn't, it might mean that Camdyn could consider continuing his dalliance with Saffron.

"What of the others?" Saffron asked. "Deirdre tried to get
to every Druid here."

Laria rose to her feet and clasped her hands at her waist. "Deirdre's main focus will be me. When she sees the other Druids with me, she'll choose certain ones to attack simultaneously."

"And you know for certain it will be us three?" Gwynn asked.

Laria slowly shook her head. "Nothing is certain. Saffron may see a vision of the future, but one small event could change everything. I learned all I needed to about everyone here. I also know how my sister thinks. You three are my best guess."

"Maybe the others should be informed just in case," Logan suggested.

"Of course," Laria said as she started toward the stairs.

"I have one more question," Fallon said.

Laria stopped and turned to face him. "Ask it."

Fallon glanced at Larena before he said, "Do you know the spell to bind our gods?"

For several moments Laria didn't move. Finally, she said, "I'm sorry, Fallon. I do not."

"The Druids did once," Larena said, desperation in her voice. "Someone has to know the spell."

Camdyn hadn't realized until that moment how much some of the Warriors must want their gods bound. At one time, he'd have gladly cut off his own arm to know that spell. Now, it didn't matter.

Laria licked her lips, her blue eyes holding a wealth of sadness. "Deirdre killed any Druid she found to have the spell. She also destroyed every scroll where it was written. Every scroll but one."

Logan jerked. "Where is it?"

"At one time it was hidden in the library at Edinburgh Castle. I have no idea where it is now. I'd heard a spell was used to mask what it was in an effort to hide it from Deirdre. For all I know she's already found and destroyed it."

"We need to search," Hayden said.

Laria looked at each of them. "I wish you luck."

Before Camdyn could talk to Saffron, she, Isla, and

Gwynn rose and went into the kitchen as Laria walked to the stairs.

"What do you think about what Laria said regarding Deirdre?" Hayden asked him.

Camdyn looked at him, Logan, Fallon, and Larena, who all watched him. "I think no matter what, Deirdre is going to come after all of us."

"But Laria must think you six are important," Fallon said.

Logan scratched his chin thoughtfully. "Aye. But how?"

"Does it matter?" Hayden asked.

Camdyn snorted. "Nay. All that matters is that Deirdre dies. Once and for all."

CHAPTER
THIRTY-FIVE

Saffron wasn't sure how she got through the rest of the morning. She had thought to get outside and take a walk, but another snowstorm had arrived, keeping her inside.

She even missed lunch because of a phone call with her attorney. Arthur had some good news regarding her mother's bid to try and have her declared dead. He had obtained a statement from a few people who recently saw her in Edinburgh and London and could confirm it was indeed her.

One more thing she could cross off her list to do.

When she left her room and ventured into the great hall she had hoped to find Camdyn. She didn't like how she found herself needing him, but she didn't want to take the time to look deeper into her emotions. With her mother, the vision about Declan, and the threat of Deirdre attacking at any moment, she couldn't handle any more.

The mood throughout the castle was strained. Saffron noticed it when she entered the hall and found Cara, Marcail, Reaghan, and Fiona playing cards.

In the kitchen Isla and Larena were baking. Usually the kitchen was a place where there was lots of conversation and laughter. But today there was nothing.

Saffron retraced her steps and made for the back tower

that was closest to her room. She sank into the oversized chair and propped her feet on the ottoman. After a moment she picked up a book on the table next to her.

"Jane Eyre," she read the title aloud.

She'd always liked the book, but no matter how many times she read the first page, her mind kept wandering to the problems surrounding her.

Saffron gave up and put the book back. She stared out the window to the sea that seemed to stretch into eternity. She'd never felt the urge to go to sea, but now with all the walls closing in around her it sounded like a good option.

She had told everyone, including herself, that she was better, that she had gotten past what Declan had done to her. But the truth was, she was far from getting over it.

It would always be there in the back of her mind, reminding her of what he could do. Of how powerless she was against him.

She hated the thought of ever seeing him again. Saffron found it ironic that she had told Camdyn she wanted to be the one to kill Declan when she knew she wouldn't be able to do it.

One look at Declan and she'd freeze. She'd remember the torture, the threats. But most important, she would recall how easily he had taken her sight with just a few words.

Someone with that kind of magic scared the hell out of her. And if Declan could do all of that, what would Deirdre do to her?

Saffron leaned her head back against the chair and wondered again what she was doing as a Druid. At one time she might have been able to help her friends, but now . . . now she would just get in the way.

Camdyn blinked against the snow that landed on his eyelashes. He stared across MacLeod land from his vantage point on the battlements. The ground was covered with unmarred snow.

The soft whistle of the wind from the sea was the only

sound that broke the silence. With the sky heavy with thick clouds, it was difficult to determine where the sun was.

His ears picked up at the crunch of snow beneath a foot. Camdyn glanced to his left to see Hayden approach.

"I hope the bitch doesna make us wait long," Hayden said as he stopped near Camdyn.

Camdyn rested his hands on the stones before him and looked at the trees swaying, knowing Hayden was referring to Deirdre. "I doona think she will."

"Have Sonya and Broc returned?"

"No' yet. They've been gone a while."

Hayden grunted. "Aye, but hopefully whatever the trees tell Sonya will help us."

"Broc still has no' been able to locate either Deirdre or Declan?"

"Nay," Hayden replied with a quick shake of his blond head, sending snow falling to his shoulders. "Laria thinks they are blocking themselves to us."

"Which means they could arrive at any moment." Damn but Camdyn was tired of this game. He wanted the battle to start so he could either get on with his life or be killed as the warrior that he was.

Hayden turned his head to Camdyn. "Gwynn could get nothing from the wind. All it would tell her was that trouble was coming."

"It's been telling her that."

"And we didna need the wind to tell us what we already knew."

"If Sonya comes back empty-handed, what is the plan?"

Hayden blew out a breath. "That I doona know. Maybe Saffron will have a vision."

"She doesna have visions that include her future."

"Damn. Then we pin all our hopes on Sonya."

They lapsed into silence, and Camdyn found himself thinking of the other battles they'd had on MacLeod land. So many innocents, including the MacLeod clan Deirdre had murdered, had been taken on this land.

"I used to hate going into battle," Camdyn said. "I did it because my laird demanded it of me, and because I was good with a sword. But I often wondered why they couldna sit down and talk it out."

"That's the first time I've heard you speak of your past," Hayden said.

Camdyn shrugged and looked at the iced-over gray stones of the castle. "What is there to tell? We all have our pasts."

"Verra true words, my friend."

"You know we willna all survive this battle."

Hayden briefly closed his eyes. "It is unlikely that we would all come away unscathed."

"Deirdre is going to come at us with all she has."

"Do you think Declan will join her?"

Camdyn smoothed away a lock of his hair that fallen into his eyes. "Aye. Why else would Laria choose Saffron?"

"Or you to watch her?"

He looked into Hayden's black eyes and nodded. "Or me."

Hayden's eyes widened a fraction as he turned to face Camdyn. "You expect to die during the battle," he said with surprise and fury lacing his voice.

"I doona have a wife. The only ones who are no' mated are me, Ramsey, and Arran. I would rather it be my life than yours or that of one of the other Warriors with a wife."

Hayden shook his head, disbelief hardening his features. "If you fall, who is going to keep Saffron from Declan?"

It was if Hayden knew exactly what to say to rile Camdyn. He took two deep breaths before he said, "Ramsey or Arran would gladly watch over her."

"Hm. Of the three of you, why did Laria choose you to watch over Saffron?"

Camdyn gave a nonchalant shrug. "I doona know."

"You do know. You know and you willna admit it." Hayden took a step closer and looked deep into Camdyn's eyes. "I know you lost a wife. I know you doona want to feel that kind of pain again, but I've also seen the way you look at Saffron. It's no secret where you slept last night, Camdyn.

So if you want to lie to yourself, go ahead. But do your brethren the courtesy of no' lying to us."

Hayden stalked past Camdyn, knocking his shoulder into Camdyn's.

Camdyn blew out a breath and turned around. "Hayden. Wait."

Hayden halted and spun around.

"Aye, I was with Saffron last eve, even when I knew I shouldna be."

Hayden's face relaxed and he walked back to Camdyn. "I know you, Logan, Ian, Ramsey, and Arran are all still adjusting to this time. Relationships between men and women are no' taken as seriously as they were four centuries ago. Saffron is . . ."

"No' like others," Camdyn said. "Aye. I know."

"We doona even know what Declan did to her."

"I do." Camdyn saw Hayden's surprise and nodded. "I know why she doesna want to tell anyone. I doona know why she told me, but if I get the chance, I'm going to rip his head from his body."

Hayden took a deep breath and glanced at the sky. "Saffron trusted you. It was that trust that got both of you through the labyrinth and to Laria. It could very well be that trust that Deirdre will attack."

"I should never have gone to her last night. I can no' give myself to someone as I did Allison. Watching Allison die broke me, Hayden. If I was a different man, a whole man, I might see where this leads with Saffron. But I can no'."

"I think I understand. I know how lost I felt, how my soul shattered when I thought Isla was dead. She is my life. There will no' be another woman for me."

Camdyn nodded, but he had no words because he could see another woman for him.

Saffron.

"What are you going to do?" Hayden asked.

"I've no idea."

"Do you know how Saffron feels? Has she said anything?"

Camdyn shook his head. "It's no' as if we've talked about

this. The attraction is nigh crushing. I see her and I have to have her."

"She's one of the only single females in the castle. Maybe that's all this is. Verra casual."

"Casual?" Camdyn mulled that over for a moment and recalled how the passion had taken them, swept them. Seized them.

Casual it was not.

"Aye," Hayden said. "Two people coming together who need each other during a short time. It can be an explosive relationship, from what I've read."

Explosive. That could certainly apply to the hunger for Saffron that had consumed him last night. And even now.

"These relationships never last long," Hayden continued.

"Do they end badly?"

Hayden shrugged. "Sometimes."

"How do you know this?"

"Books, the telly, and of course the Internet."

"How do you know the difference between a casual relationship and one that's much more serious?"

Hayden scratched his cheek as he looked around him and leaned close. "Isla has a thing about reading romance novels. I picked one up to see what it was about. It's amazing what you can learn about women from those books. Those books tell about serious relationships. You should borrow one sometime."

"Aye." Camdyn cleared his throat, still not totally convinced Hayden was speaking the truth. It was difficult not to believe him though.

Hayden had lived through four centuries while Camdyn had leapfrogged over them. So much had changed during that time, much more than just how women dressed.

"Maybe you're right."

"Of course I am," Hayden said, and slapped him on the shoulder as he turned on his heel and walked away.

Camdyn watched Hayden walk away, thinking over all he had said.

Suddenly Hayden paused just before jumping down to

the bailey and said, "At least you have no' felt her magic different than other Druids. Because then you'd really be in trouble, my friend."

Camdyn could only stare at the spot Hayden had been in, his mouth hanging open. He took two strides and leaped to the bailey, landing near Hayden.

"Stop," he said. "Tell me what you mean."

Hayden's smile slowly disappeared. "As a Warrior you feel a Druid's magic, aye?"

"Aye."

"They all feel the same, aye?"

Again Camdyn said, "Aye."

"I knew Isla was different the moment I felt her magic. It was unlike anything I had experienced before. I know where she is at all times because her magic has a different feel than that of other Druids."

Camdyn's chest constricted, his gaze going to the ground as the world tilted precariously around him.

"Lucan, Quinn, Galen, Broc, Logan, and Ian all say the same thing about their wife's magic. So you have nothing to worry about."

Camdyn slowly lifted his gaze to Hayden.

"Oh, fuck," Hayden muttered.

CHAPTER
THIRTY-SIX

Camdyn's ears began to ring as his mind refused to believe what Hayden had told him. After all he had suffered, Fate couldn't have done this to him again.

". . . you'll see."

Camdyn blinked and realized Hayden had been talking to him. He had no idea what Hayden had said, and at the moment it didn't matter. He was still reeling from what he had learned.

"Just because I feel her magic differently doesna mean she's meant to be mine, right?"

Hayden rubbed his hand over his jaw. "I can no' answer that for sure. I doona know if anyone can."

Camdyn turned away when he saw Quinn emerge from the castle and start toward them.

"What's going on?" Quinn asked.

Hayden glanced at Camdyn before he said, "A wee bit of trouble."

"It's no' anything to concern yourself over," Camdyn said before Quinn could question him. "I'll deal with it."

"You shouldna have to deal with anything alone," Quinn said.

But Camdyn was used to being alone, used to doing things on his own. Even at the castle, he kept to himself. It was a fact no one had questioned before.

Camdyn had learned at a very early age after being moved

from family to family that if he wanted anything he had to rely only on himself. That became even clearer when Deirdre unbound his god.

"Quinn's right, you know," Hayden said.

Quinn's green gaze was steadfast. "We'll help you through whatever this is."

Camdyn let out a bark of laughter. "The only thing that can help me now is distance, and I willna be getting that anytime soon."

"This has to do with Saffron, does it no'?" Quinn asked.

"He feels her magic," Hayden said to Quinn.

Quinn let out a long, low whistle.

Camdyn ran a hand through his hair and sighed loudly. "I was content by myself. Happy even. I didna ask for this."

"Running away willna help. You can no' run away from this," Hayden said.

Quinn inhaled a deep breath. "You doona have to be alone in this world. Why no' take what is before you?"

"I did take it," Camdyn said with a curse. "I took Saffron even knowing I could never be anything more to her."

Quinn's brow furrowed. "Why is that?"

"I will never give my heart to another woman. I did that once already. And I certainly willna give it to a mortal woman so I can watch her grow old and die again." Camdyn peeled back his lips and let loose the growl that had risen within him. "Never again."

Hayden's gaze followed Camdyn as he stormed away and leaped back to the top of the battlements. Hayden turned to Quinn and said, "This isna going to turn out well."

"For Saffron's sake, I hope it does."

"It willna," Ian said as he came out of the shadows of the stables.

Quinn jerked his chin to Ian. "You heard?"

"Aye. And I tried to warn Camdyn away from her last eve," Ian said. "Dani says Saffron is vulnerable right now."

Hayden grunted and crossed his arms over his chest. "She certainly is, but there's no denying there is something that is pulling those two together."

"They would make a fine pair," Quinn said.

Ian brushed the snow from his shoulder. "If Camdyn will allow her. He's closed himself off, and no' just to Saffron."

"He's always been a loner," Hayden said. "I only knew of him because of Galen. But I had never met Camdyn before he arrived here."

Quinn said, "I also lost a wife before Marcail came into my life. Maybe I can help him."

"Camdyn is a stubborn one. The only one that will be able to change his mind and open his heart is Saffron," Ian said.

Hayden nodded as he considered Ian's words. "She's certainly strong enough. We'll need to keep a close eye on those two."

"Especially since Laria has said Deirdre will target Saffron," Quinn stated.

The three looked at each other, their faces grim.

Saffron ended her phone call with her bank and stretched her arms over her head before she fell back on her bed. The hours were crawling by as everyone waited anxiously for Deirdre to attack.

She had cleaned, she'd watched a movie, she'd listened to music, and she'd stared out the tower windows. And still it was only early evening.

The men were guarding the castle and keeping watch around the area. With night falling Broc was supposed to take to the skies and look for anyone approaching.

The mood in the castle had turned from strained to troubled when the only thing Sonya learned from the trees was that Deirdre and Declan had met at the Ring of Brodgar. Then they reiterated what the wind had already told Gwynn, that trouble was coming.

Saffron rolled her eyes. As if they needed to be warned of that. It was a given.

Yet, from the moment Sonya had told them about Declan and Deirdre meeting, Saffron's stomach had been in knots.

Declan had used considerable magic to pull Deirdre to their time. He'd never told her why, but she had heard the exhilaration in his voice when he had succeeded.

Declan didn't give up on the things he wanted. He just pursued them harder. If Declan wanted Deirdre for something, then she suspected that he had made some kind of alliance with her.

She'd told the others that, and for several hours they had discussed what Declan and Deirdre could do together. Saffron's mind had gone numb with all the things she had come up with. Added to that were the stories the Warriors had told of things Deirdre had done.

And it just made Saffron nauseous.

She'd been saved when the call she had placed earlier to Arthur had been returned. She wasn't much help to everyone at the castle since her visions came on their own, but there was one thing she had that they could use. Money.

Saffron had transferred a million dollars into an account at the Bank of Scotland that was set up so that the MacLeods could access it at any time.

She'd bought an entire houseful of furniture that Lucan had designed and built. What house she planned to put it in she hadn't decided yet.

The idea of staying in Scotland appealed to her in many ways. If she survived the battle, that is. Even if she didn't find a house, the furniture would be placed in storage, with the key given to the MacLeods at the reading of her will.

Saffron swiped at her bangs and sat up. Her will had been something else she'd taken care of that day. It was revised and heading overnight through UPS to arrive at her bank in Edinburgh where she hoped she could convince Fallon to jump her tomorrow.

The quicker she got the papers signed, the quicker the will would go into effect.

She rose from the bed and glanced at the clock. It was time for her to help with dinner. She'd never enjoyed cooking, but being with the others and actually being able to help was something she found she did like.

But once she opened her door the delicious aroma that was unmistakably pizza reached her.

Saffron hurried to the stairs and descended into the great hall to find boxes and boxes of pizza. New York pizza, at that. There was a huge bucket filled with snow and packed with just about every brand of beer available.

"There you are," Cara said. "We were just about to go looking for you."

"What's this?" she asked.

Gwynn shrugged sheepishly. "I wanted pizza."

"And I didn't want to cook anything," Isla said.

Sonya laughed. "So I suggested Fallon use his power and get us some authentic New York pizza."

"He wasn't exactly happy with how many pizzas we ordered," Reaghan said.

Larena picked a pepperoni from a slice and dropped it into her mouth. "It was all bluster. Trust me, he wanted this."

"Aye, he did," Marcail said with a laugh.

Dani opened another lid and inhaled the aroma. "I'm starving."

"Eat," Fallon said as he strode into the castle from the bailey. "The men will eat in shifts since we're keeping guard so doona wait on us."

The women promptly ignored Fallon. Only when Galen, Quinn, and Ian walked in did Reaghan, Marcail, and Dani get their food. Saffron watched the couples as they interacted. The ease with which they touched, the secret smiles they shared, the soft words whispered only between them.

It made her realize just how much she wanted a relationship like theirs. For the longest time she hadn't believed there could be such a thing except in books and movies.

Yet the couples at MacLeod Castle had changed her views long before she got her sight back. She might not have been able to see the shared intimacy before now, but she had heard it in their voices when they spoke to each other.

Maybe it was that longing that drew her to Camdyn. He hadn't wanted her, or she hadn't thought he wanted her.

Until the previous night. What had changed? And did she really want to know why he had come to her?

She hadn't gotten to speak to Camdyn because he'd been on guard, but even if she had, she wouldn't have known what to say. Her past relationships had all been complete failures. Either because of the men, or because she hadn't been willing to give herself completely to them. Because she hadn't trusted them.

But she did trust Camdyn. Of that she was sure. Would that be enough to allow herself to open up to him, to see if there was more between them than incredible sex?

Saffron bit her lip and reached for a beer and a slice of pepperoni and sausage pizza. She didn't have anyone to wait for. Oh, she could wait for Camdyn, but they hadn't talked about the future. And she had gotten the feeling he wasn't interested in a future with her.

The here and now was what mattered to him.

And maybe it should for her as well. Who knew what tomorrow would bring, or when Deirdre would attack. The only thing Saffron was sure of was that when the battle between Laria and Deirdre did occur, all hell would break loose.

With Declan now aligned with Deirdre, there was no doubt in Saffron's mind that Declan would come for her.

There was no way she would go back to his prison, no way she would allow him to get close enough to put another of his spells upon her.

But Declan wouldn't give up. He would come for her again and again. Saffron would fight again and again. Only one of them would win, and she knew it wouldn't be her.

She sank onto one of the benches around the table and bit into the pizza. It had been four years since she'd tasted New York pizza. She'd had a layover in New York before her flight out to London and she'd made sure to eat a slice.

It brought back memories of the girl she had been then. A girl full of naïve dreams, uncaring if she traveled alone or not. A girl who thought the worst that could happen to her was being robbed.

A girl who couldn't outrun her fate.

She'd always thought of herself as a strong person, but she hadn't really had to reach for that strength until she'd been in Declan's prison.

How she survived that, she'd never know. But she had, and it made her look at life differently.

Made her look at *her* life differently.

She didn't want to be alone anymore. She wanted someone beside her, someone who made her knees weak when he looked at her. Someone who could make her forget her own name when he kissed her.

Someone who made love to her as if she were the only woman for him.

Someone like Camdyn.

CHAPTER
THIRTY-SEVEN

Camdyn managed to stay out of the castle and away from Saffron until midnight. That's when his shift guarding was over. He wanted to stay, but Fallon was adamant about each of them having a rest.

Camdyn walked into the great hall and looked at the few pizza boxes still on the table. He'd never eaten pizza, and though he wanted to try it, his thoughts were on something else.

Some*one* else, actually.

Saffron.

All he had to do was close his eyes and he could pinpoint exactly where she was in the castle just by the feel of her magic. Her magic that affected him alone. Magic that made him want to bury himself deep inside her.

He'd always had control over himself and his god, but that control was rapidly unraveling as he recalled the feel of Saffron's silky skin beneath his palms and her hot, wet sheath pulsing around his cock as she peaked.

No matter how many times he told himself he had to stay away, he couldn't.

Camdyn turned to the stairs, taking them three at a time as he climbed to the top and paused. She was walking the corridors. Alone. Her magic calling to him, whispering to him.

Beckoning to him.

He groaned, his body reacting instantly. Camdyn leaned back against the wall and let his claws lengthen from his fingers to dig into the stones.

The desire, the longing. The yearning.

It was too much.

Sculel demanded he make Saffron his, insisted that Saffron succumb to the passion. And for once Camdyn was in complete agreement with his god.

Camdyn straightened when he felt her move closer to him. His gaze moved to the next set of stairs leading to the level above him. As silent as the shadows, Camdyn walked to the steps and waited.

Saffron hated when she couldn't sleep and had decided a walk around the castle might help. She was returning to her room when she was suddenly yanked off the stairs and against a chest she knew all too well.

"Camdyn," she whispered just before he pressed her against the wall and kissed her.

He swept his tongue into her mouth and claimed her with a kiss full of fire. And hunger. Just one touch from him and her body ignited, ready and waiting for him.

She clung to him, returning his kiss with all the need inside her. He tilted his head and deepened the kiss, a low moan rumbling from his chest.

Saffron's slipper fell off her foot when his hand slipped behind her knee and pulled her leg up to his waist. She eagerly followed his direction. Wanting, needing him with an intensity that shook her to her very core.

She'd never felt anything remotely close to this with anyone else, and it scared her. But not even that hint of foreboding could make her leave his arms.

"I need you," he whispered between kisses.

"Take me. I'm yours."

As if he'd been waiting for her approval, he swung her up in his arms and strode toward her room.

"My slippers," she hissed as the second dropped to the floor.

"Leave them. I'll get them later."

He nudged open her door, and with his shoulder, closed it behind them. Saffron next found herself standing. Camdyn's dark eyes were filled with a potency that held her spellbound. He lifted a hand and his claws lengthened from his fingertips.

Saffron pulled in a shuddering breath as her arousal grew. She licked her lips when he placed one of his razor-sharp claws on her bare breast above the neckline to her jammie top.

"Do you fear me?"

His voice, all dark and husky, sent a thrill rushing over her, through her. "No," she answered without hesitation.

With the barest of movements he split her top down the middle. Saffron glanced down at her torso, and just as she expected he hadn't touched her skin.

She barely noticed his claws were gone when his hands gently, seductively pushed her top over her shoulders so it fell from her arms and fluttered to the floor.

"Lovely," he muttered, and fell to his knees before her.

Saffron closed her eyes and dropped her head back when he cupped her breasts and kissed the inside of each one. Her fingers slid into his glossy black locks.

Her breasts swelled, eager for his touch. His hot, wet tongue flicked over a nipple before he suckled it deep within his mouth.

She cried out and gripped his head tighter. His hands roamed over her back and buttocks, touching and caressing. He gave a light nip on her turgid nipple and her knees buckled from the spike of pleasure.

His arms tightened around her, supporting her as he moved his mouth to her other breast. Where he repeated his teasing until her legs could no longer support her.

In an instant he stood, lifting her so that her legs wrapped around his waist. He turned them so that her back was to the wall. She whispered his name as he ground his thick rod against her aching flesh.

He kissed down her neck, leaving a trail of heat in his

wake. He paused when he reached her ear where he sucked the lobe into his mouth and gave it a quick nip.

Saffron heard a rip and then felt cool air on her lower body. She smiled when she saw him toss aside the bottoms to her jammies.

The smile faded when she realized she was naked, but Camdyn was not. She clawed at his T-shirt, inching it up as they kissed. Somehow she managed to get it tangled about his arms when he tried to pull it off without letting her go.

She giggled, and a moment later his deep laughter joined hers before he ripped off the shirt and discarded it. Their eyes met, clashed, and the laughter died as the passion flared once more.

With his hands cupping her bottom, she worked desperately to unbutton his jeans and get them over his hips while he kicked them off his legs.

And then they were flesh to flesh.

Camdyn's world had narrowed to include just him and Saffron. Nothing else existed. Nothing else mattered.

The way her body responded so quickly and heatedly to his touch left him aching for more. No matter how much he touched her, no matter how many times he kissed her, it was never enough.

And God help him, but he feared an eternity would never be enough.

He raised her by the hips so that she hovered above his cock. Her lids lifted and her tawny gaze found his. Slowly he lowered her until the blunt head of his cock touched her entrance.

She sucked in a breath, her pulse beating rapidly at the base of her throat. Her nipples stood hard against his chest and her wetness coated his rod.

He held her gaze as he lowered her upon his arousal until he was sheathed. Her lips were parted and her eyes dilated with passion.

And then he tilted her hips so that he went even deeper.

She cried out as her nails sank into his shoulders. But he

wasn't nearly done with her yet. He pulled out of her only to thrust hard. Once. Twice.

When she tried to rock against him, he held her still and smiled.

"Please," she whispered, and kissed across his jaw.

Camdyn turned and started for the chair.

Saffron gasped, her entire body going taut, as she felt his cock shift within her every time he took a step. The way he rubbed against her clitoris and stroked her sex had her ready to peak before he reached the chair.

"No' yet," he said with a chuckle.

She shifted her hips, seeking more of the wonderful feel of him. But once more his large, callused hands held her steady.

He lowered them into the chair and her legs draped over the sides with her toes skimming the cold stones. His hands shifted from her hips to her breasts.

"So beautiful," he whispered as he thumbed her nipples.

Saffron arched her back toward him as pleasure spiked through her and tightened into a pulsing mass at her sex. She rocked her hips forward.

His answering groan was all she needed to hear. She sensuously rotated her hips forward and back, taking him deeper. The feel of him so hot and hard inside her only heightened her arousal.

She gasped then moaned when he began to lift his hips. Each slide and answering plunge of his cock inside her wound her desire tighter and tighter.

"No' yet," he whispered.

Saffron tried to hold the tide of pleasure back, but it was so strong. She rocked faster as her desire built.

Camdyn was lost. Adrift.

He couldn't look away from Saffron's gaze. She held him captive, enslaved. Charmed.

Every instinct he had told him to run far away from her. But his body wouldn't obey. His body wanted her, had to have her.

He held her hips, urging her faster as she rode him. Sweat glistened on their skin, their breaths harsh and ragged.

His gaze dropped to her breasts that bounced enticingly. He bent and captured a nipple in his mouth and suckled. She moaned and rode him harder.

Camdyn reached between them and found the small, swollen nub. His fingers circled her clitoris in time with her hips.

Her body jerked as her climax hit her. Camdyn gripped her hips and thrust deep inside her with urgent, jerky movements. The feel of her body clutching around his cock sent him over the edge to his own orgasm.

She fell onto his chest, and he wrapped his arms around her, holding her tight as he spilled his seed inside her, his climax continuing each time her sheath tightened around him.

The power of their joining mixed with Saffron's magic to surround them, envelop them. Hold them.

He didn't try to hold back the peace and serenity that surrounded them, didn't try to deny the exquisite pleasure he'd found in Saffron's arms.

Camdyn didn't want to look deeper into what had just happened. He couldn't. Not yet. Mayhap not ever.

He stood, still holding Saffron, and walked to the bed. After he lowered her onto the mattress, he briefly thought about leaving, but then she opened her eyes and smiled contentedly.

Camdyn lifted the covers and climbed in next to her. He sighed as she snuggled against him, her head on his chest. It felt right to hold her, which was why he knew it was so wrong.

"Those were my favorite pair of jammies," she murmured.

He chuckled and kissed the top of her head. "I'll buy you some more."

"I've got more. You can destroy those, too. That was amazing."

He stared at the ceiling and frowned. "Saffron—"

"Sh," she interrupted him. "No words. Not tonight. Not

after what we just experienced. They can wait until morning."

He squeezed her and relented to her request. It was probably better that way since he really had no idea what he was going to tell her.

He wanted to tell her how wonderful and strong and beautiful she was. And he needed to tell her whatever was between them had to end.

But how could he when he didn't want it to end?

Camdyn slung his other arm over his eyes. He'd known he had to stay away from Saffron. He'd known the attraction between them could only bring him trouble.

Yet he hadn't turned away from her as he had countless other women through the years.

Whatever made her different from those faceless others also made her impossible to leave. And it wasn't just for himself that he wanted to end this. He recalled all too well how Allison had suffered as his wife. That wasn't the kind of life someone as vibrant as Saffron should lead.

Camdyn held her tighter because he knew it was going to be the last time. No matter what he might dream about when he slept, he had to walk away.

CHAPTER
THIRTY-EIGHT

Phelan looked at the naked woman beside him as she slept. He hadn't even gotten her name, but then again he didn't care to know it. He only wanted to relieve his body. That's all women were good for anyway.

It had been Isla and Deirdre that showed him women—most especially Druids—couldn't be trusted.

Still, he couldn't seem to get the battle at the Ring of Brodgar out of his mind. It had only taken one look at the blond beauty who was with the MacLeods to know she was Deirdre's twin.

He had watched the battle begin and how those from MacLeod Castle had helped the beautiful Druid against Deirdre. And just when Phelan thought Deirdre might be vanquished, she disappeared.

It was too bad. He'd hoped all the Druids would kill each other. However, the thought that there were Druids rising up against Deirdre intrigued him.

He'd seen Isla, of course, and the giant Warrior who guarded her constantly.

Phelan didn't understand the Warriors from MacLeod Castle who readily and willingly protected Druids. Didn't they realize it would be better for all if the Druids were wiped from the earth?

He blew out a breath and pulled his arm from beneath the

wench at his side. She rolled onto her stomach, her shoulder-length ginger hair stark against the white sheets.

Phelan sat up and scrubbed a hand down his face. The battle had certainly been on his mind, but it was the other Warrior he'd spotted that really nudged his curiosity.

Who was he? He hadn't helped either the MacLeods or Deirdre and the maroon Warrior at her side.

Phelan had thought he was the only Warrior left who hadn't chosen a side. But then again, there had been four hundred years where Deirdre hadn't been seen or heard from.

He hadn't cared to discover what she was about. The simple fact that she'd left him alone was enough. Now, though, Phelan was beginning to wonder if he should find some answers.

The bed creaked as he rose and pulled on his jeans and black biker boots. It took him a moment to find his red T-shirt and black leather jacket.

Phelan ran his hands through his dark hair that now reached just past his shoulders. He should probably get it cut again, but he liked it long.

He grabbed his helmet and quietly walked from the room. Once in the hallway of the small inn, Phelan let his gaze wander first to the left then to the right before he made for the stairs.

Dawn was a couple of hours away when he put on his helmet and fastened it. He straddled his Ducati motorcycle and started it.

He revved the motorbike before he put his foot on the concrete and gunned it so that he did a quick one-eighty, his tires screeching in the wet pavement. He'd watched the direction the other Warrior had taken as he drove away, and Phelan had even followed him for a time.

Though Phelan didn't know exactly where this other Warrior lived, he had a feeling it wouldn't take long to find out.

Saffron came awake slowly, a smile upon her lips. She rolled to where Camdyn had been lying only to find the sheets cool to her touch.

Her eyes opened and the smile faded when she realized he was gone. She sat up and looked around the room, hoping he had just risen from the bed, but the silence surrounding her told her all she needed to know.

"Maybe it was his turn to guard again," she mumbled to herself even though she knew it for the lie it was.

There was only one reason for a man to leave a woman's bed before she woke. It was because he wanted to avoid any kind of conversation about what they had done.

Saffron squeezed her eyes closed as the hurt flowed through her, choking her so that she could barely breathe.

"Damn you, Camdyn. Damn you."

She would have been fine had he not come to her last night. She hadn't expected more from him, hadn't thought there would be more.

But he had given her hope in the dark hours of the night as he made love to her then held her against him.

It didn't take long for anger to replace her hurt. She threw off the covers and rose from the bed. She yanked open a drawer and pulled out clothes before she stomped into the bathroom and turned on the water.

Saffron stepped beneath the steaming water and began to wash away Camdyn's scent from her body, though she would never be able to rid him so easily from her heart.

A tear dropped onto her cheek, but she refused to acknowledge it. She had been but a girl of eighteen the last time she had cried over a guy. And she wouldn't do it now.

She washed herself three more times before she reached for the shampoo. Her fingers scrubbed against her scalp. She leaned her head back into the spray of the water to begin rinsing her hair when her magic welled inside her.

Saffron had little time to grab hold of the shower wall before the vision took her. Blackness swirled around her before she found herself staring into a bright blue sky.

She heard laughter—a man's and a child's. In the next instant Camdyn's face filled her vision. His hair was shorter, and there was a light growth of a beard on his face. He laughed again, the corners of his dark eyes crinkling.

And then she saw the boy.

He had Camdyn's same black hair with a slight wave to it, the same chocolate-colored eyes. Saffron's heart stilled as she recognized that she was looking at Camdyn with his son.

The vision ended abruptly. Saffron leaned over in the shower and wrapped her arms around her stomach. She blinked the soap from her eyes, not trying to stop her tears from flowing.

Not once in her twenty-seven years had she had a vision that involved herself. Not once. No matter how she felt about Camdyn, her vision had proven to her that they didn't have a future together.

Camdyn would be happy though. He would find peace and the freedom to open his heart. His child could very well be the reason for it.

Saffron straightened, her body still weak from the vision. She wiped at the tears and finished rinsing her hair. It took all of her strength to shut off the water and wring out her hair before she reached for the towel.

She opened the shower door and stepped out onto the small rug. When she lifted her gaze it was to find herself looking at her reflection in the mirror.

Her eyes were red rimmed and her face blotchy. She always looked horrid when she cried. At least makeup would fix that.

She vigorously toweled off. It took extra time, but she used the flatiron to straighten her hair. She even put on additional makeup. She had an impression to make at the bank after all.

Saffron ignored the jeans and sweater she had pulled out earlier and reached for the black pencil skirt, the snug-fitting thin cream shirt that came to a low point over her breasts, and the matching cashmere cardigan. It showed enough to draw attention to her chest without being over the top.

She then slipped her feet into the four-inch black heels, added a Cartier watch, the platinum ring her father had given her at her college graduation that had been kept in the safe at the bank, and a Tiffany necklace with matching earrings.

Saffron gave herself one last look before pulling on her form-fitting long black coat and grabbing her purse. She took a deep breath and left her room. Her heels clicked loudly on the stones as she walked up the stairs to the master chamber where Fallon and Larena resided.

With her head held high she gave two quick knocks on Fallon's door.

"Just a moment," came Fallon's muffled voice from inside the room. A few seconds later the door opened to show Fallon bare chested and in jeans. He glanced over her attire, and frowned. "Saffron. Is everything all right?"

Before she could answer Larena peeked her head over Fallon's shoulder and raised her eyebrows. "Wow. You look stunning."

"I need a favor," Saffron said. "I wouldn't ask if it wasn't important. Especially knowing that Deirdre could attack any moment."

Fallon's brow furrowed as he nodded. "What is it?"

"I need you to jump me to Edinburgh again. To the Bank of Scotland. I need to sign some papers."

"Papers?" he repeated.

Larena gave him a light punch on the arm. "She said it was important, love."

"I wouldn't ask if it wasn't vital," Saffron added. When he didn't respond she knew she had to tell him. "I wanted this kept a secret until later, but if I must, I'll tell you now. Fallon, I wasn't jesting when I said I had a lot of money, money my father taught me to use wisely. I've set up an account at the Bank of Scotland in Edinburgh with money for everyone residing at the castle."

Larena covered her mouth with her hand.

"I've also made a significant purchase of Lucan's furniture that I need to have moved into storage once it's complete."

Fallon rubbed his eyes with his thumb and forefinger. "We doona expect any of this from you."

"I know. What you all have done for the world these centuries cannot be repaid. But I can help. I don't know if I'll survive the upcoming battle, but in the event that I don't, my new will, which I also need to sign, states that half of my fortune will go to the account I set up for you. The other half will go to charities I support."

"Saffron," Larena whispered.

Saffron cleared her throat. "Please. I've set it up so that the bank will see me early, before it opens for business. We'll be back in less than an hour. We won't even be missed, we'll be gone for such a short time."

"It could be dangerous," Fallon said.

She shook her head and said, "I set all of this up yesterday. Only my attorney who drew up the papers and the CEO of the bank knows what is going on. It's safe."

"Take her," Larena urged her husband.

Fallon sighed. "It'll be quick?"

"All the papers are in order," she said. "I just need to sign them and then have you sign so you can access the money."

"I doona like this," Fallon said as he leaned against the door.

Larena kissed his cheek. "It'll be safe, my love. If it'll make you feel better, take another Warrior."

"There's no need," Saffron interjected before Fallon could respond. "Less than an hour. Please."

After a moment Fallon gave a quick nod. "Give me a moment to put on some clothes."

He walked away but Larena remained. Her gaze searched Saffron's face before she asked, "Is everything all right?"

"I'm just anxious about the upcoming battle." Saffron spoke the practiced lie.

She didn't enjoy lying to her friends, but she didn't want them to know what had happened between her and Camdyn. It was bad enough that everyone already knew they had slept together.

"Of course," Larena replied.

But Saffron heard the doubt in her voice.

"I'm ready," Fallon said as he appeared next to his wife.

He gave Larena a kiss on the lips before he walked out of his chamber and came to stand by Saffron. "I should probably tell Lucan and Quinn."

"I'll do that," Larena offered. "Just go."

Fallon looked at Saffron. "Ready?"

"Yes."

He placed his hand on her shoulder and in the next instant she was standing outside the bank. Few people were milling about on the snow-covered streets at the early hour, and no one noticed their sudden appearance.

Fallon had brought them to the side of the bank, and with his hand on her elbow, they walked to the front doors. An armed guard caught sight of them and immediately unlocked the doors.

"Good morn, Miss Fletcher. Daniel said you'd be paying us a visit," the guard said with a friendly smile.

She returned his smile and glanced at the name tag on his shirt. "Thank you, Angus. Is Daniel waiting for me in his office?"

"Nay, ma'am," he said as he locked the door behind them. "He knew you'd be in a hurry so he brought everything down here. It'll be the third door on your right."

Saffron started to walk to where Angus had pointed when she glanced at Fallon and saw his frown. "What is it?"

"I doona know. I thought I'd feel better about us being here alone, but something feels . . . off."

"It's a huge building, and when there aren't many people it can feel that way."

He grunted in response.

Saffron adjusted the clutch in her hand as they reached the third door. Inside was Daniel but also another man that looked vaguely familiar.

She didn't think anything about it since she had been to the bank several times before she'd been taken. "Thank you for seeing me so early, Daniel. Shall we get started?"

Something popped and Fallon clutched his stomach and bent over. Saffron glanced down to see blood seep through his fingers.

Fallon lifted his stunned gaze to her. "Run!"

Saffron looked up to see the man she'd thought looked familiar holding a gun, a sadistic smile on his face. It was then she realized he was one of Declan's men.

She dropped her clutch and turned to run when a figure stepped in her way. The woman had white hair that fell to the floor and eerie white eyes.

"It's been a long time since I've been in the presence of a Seer," Deirdre said.

CHAPTER
THIRTY-NINE

Camdyn jerked up in his bed as soon as the feel of Saffron's magic vanished. He jumped off his bed and was out of his cottage a heartbeat later.

He released his god and ran like the wind to the castle. He leaped over the castle wall in one jump. As soon as he landed in the bailey, he was running for the door of the castle.

The door flew open beneath his hands and he rushed into the great hall to see Larena sitting with Lucan and Quinn at the table.

"Where is she?" Camdyn demanded.

Larena looked from her brothers-in-law to Camdyn. "Who?"

"He's speaking of Saffron," Quinn said as he stood. "You might want to come hear what Larena is telling us."

"Tell me she's all right," Camdyn urged.

Larena nodded. "Aye. She's fine."

He let out a breath he hadn't known he was holding and lengthened his strides to walk to the table. He didn't sit though. Instead, he stood beside Lucan.

Larena tugged on the braid that hung over her shoulder. "As I was just telling Lucan and Quinn, Saffron came to our door this morning and asked Fallon to take her to Edinburgh."

Camdyn crossed his arms over his chest so that no one could see how his hands shook. She had left. Saffron had left the castle without a word to him.

But what had he expected? He'd exited her bed in the middle of the night.

"Why?" Lucan asked. "Why was it so important for Saffron to go to Edinburgh now?"

Larena clasped her hands together on the table. "She has set up an account for us as well as changed her will. Those papers had to be signed."

"Does she no' think she'll survive the battle?" Quinn asked.

"That's my guess," Larena replied. "Saffron looked . . . distressed. As if something had happened. She did set up the signing early in the morning so no one would be there. It's safe."

"Nowhere is safe for her as long as Declan is alive," Camdyn said.

"Get Broc," Quinn told Lucan after a glance at Camdyn's face. "We'll make sure she's all right. It'll calm Camdyn, and reassure us."

Camdyn could no longer stand still. He began to pace, each stride making his worry grow until his stomach was in knots. He didn't know why, but he couldn't dispel the thought that Saffron was in trouble.

"She's with Fallon," Larena said. "If something was wrong, Fallon would jump them back here immediately."

"I know." And Camdyn did know it but that didn't stop the unease.

He looked up when he heard footsteps to see Broc and Sonya rushing down the stairs following Lucan. Camdyn drew in a shaky breath and clenched his jaw shut.

Broc's gaze landed on him. "Give me a moment. I'll find Saffron."

Before Broc could begin Fallon appeared in the great hall. But he wasn't standing. He was lying on the stones with blood covering him.

"Fallon!" Larena screamed, and rushed to his side.

Camdyn stood behind Larena looking down at Fallon as his brothers surrounded him.

"What happened?" Quinn demanded as they all gawked at the blood.

Lucan suddenly pulled back. "I smell *drough* blood."

"Shite," Broc ground out as he moved so Sonya could get to Fallon.

Camdyn could do nothing but watch. Fallon was fading fast. Sonya's magic washed through the hall as she used her gift of healing.

"They . . . have . . ." Fallon tried.

Camdyn's gut clenched painfully. "Declan has Saffron, doesn't he?"

Fallon nodded. "Sorry."

"Let Sonya heal you," Camdyn said before he turned and started for the door.

He reached for the knob and started to pull it open when a large hand slammed it shut. Camdyn turned his head to find Hayden on one side of him and Ian on the other.

"You go to her now and they'll kill you," Hayden said.

Camdyn growled and spun away from the door. "If I doona go to her there is no telling what they will do to her!"

"I can no' find her," Broc said, his voice harsh and sweat covering his face. "Saffron is as hidden as Deirdre and Declan."

Camdyn didn't try to suppress Sculel when he broke free. Camdyn embraced his god and smashed his hand into the stone wall. His fist plunged through the rock, breaking bone and cutting his skin.

But he didn't feel the pain.

Everything inside him was roaring its refusal that Saffron was gone. That Declan had her.

"We have to find her," he stated as he pulled his hand from the stones.

Ian shook his head. "No' until Fallon is healed."

"You doona know what he did to her! I do. She told me, Ian, and I willna sit here while he tortures her again!"

Camdyn realized then how quiet the hall had gotten. He shook his head and looked around to find everyone had gathered in the hall and was watching him. All except Sonya, Fallon, and Larena.

He watched the way Larena hovered over Fallon, holding his hand and kissing his cheek as Sonya healed him.

"I have to find Saffron," Camdyn said again, more quietly than before.

A hand clamped on his shoulder as Ian nodded. "We will."

"But you willna do it alone," Hayden said.

Arran nodded. "Precisely. I want my own shot at Declan for hurting a Druid, especially one as special as Saffron."

"You better include me in on that," Ramsey said.

Logan snorted. "Besides, you should know that if something affects one of us, it affects all of us."

"We will do this for Saffron. And for you," Galen told him.

Camdyn drew in a ragged breath. They had all conveyed to him that he was part of their family, but Camdyn hadn't understood what that entailed until that moment.

He hadn't allowed himself to be a part of them because of his past. What had he missed out on because he'd been so stubborn?

Camdyn looked over at Fallon to find the other Druids had gathered with Sonya to add to her magic. Even Laria had joined in. Larena gave her blood to pour into Fallon's wound, much like he had done when she'd been dying from *drough* blood. It was several tense moments later before Fallon took a deep breath.

"The *drough* blood is fading," Sonya said as she stood.

It was Larena's smile as she gazed down at Fallon that told them he was going to be all right. After a kiss that made them all look away, Fallon got to his feet.

He immediately headed to Camdyn. "I knew something was wrong the moment we got there. I should have brought her back then."

"What happened?" Camdyn asked.

Fallon tore off his blood-soaked shirt and gave it to Lucan to toss into the fire. "Nothing at first. We were allowed into the bank by the security guard who recognized Saffron. It wasna until we were inside the bank that something felt wrong."

"Did you no' sense any magic?" Quinn asked.

Fallon slowly shook his head, his eyes full of remorse as he gazed at Camdyn. "I should've known they would mask themselves and their magic. We walked into the conference room and one of Declan's men shot me with the X90 bullet. I told Saffron to run, but before she could, Deirdre was there."

Camdyn tried to swallow past the lump in his throat. "How did they know?"

"It doesn't matter how they knew. Deirdre has made the first move," Laria said.

Arran's face grew dark with rage. "I thought the battle would be here."

"I never said where the battle would be," Laria replied.

Camdyn slashed his arm through the air. "It doesna matter where we battle Deirdre. We all knew it was coming."

"I warned you to keep Saffron safe," Laria said as she swung her blue eyes to him.

Fallon held up his hands. "It wasna Camdyn's fault. I take the blame for Saffron being taken."

"Nay," Camdyn said. "It is my fault. Had I no' left Saffron while she slept she would've taken me with her. I vowed to her that I would protect her, and I have no' done that."

Laria walked in a small circle as she looked at the Warriors surrounding her. Camdyn narrowed his gaze on her, wondering what she was up to.

"All is not lost," Laria said.

Beside him, one of Ian's brows rose. "And how is that?"

"Deirdre knows we will come for the Seer."

Camdyn let the growl rumble from deep within him. "They willna let her go easily."

"Nay," Laria said softly. "If they release her at all."

He refused to acknowledge those words.

"But if Deirdre is dead surely Declan willna try to hold Saffron," Ramsey said.

Camdyn squeezed his eyes closed as Laria's gaze dropped to the floor. The fact that she didn't reply was answer enough.

But Camdyn had no intention of giving up so easily. He would do whatever it took to free Saffron, even if it meant his own life.

He'd feared allowing himself to feel for Saffron because she would grow old and die as Allison had. He'd never thought she'd be taken by Declan again.

Camdyn could still hear the terror and distress in her voice as she had told him what Declan had done to her. Saffron had survived, but barely. Would she again?

He refused to think along those lines.

His heart was already heavy with the knowledge that she was gone, possibly from him forever. It was enough to make him wish he could turn back time and stay with her instead of sneaking out of her chamber while she slept.

It was enough that he admitted, if just to himself, that Saffron meant more than he had ever thought a woman could mean to him.

He rubbed his chest as the ache, which had begun when he knew she was gone from the castle, increased. It pushed against him, clawing at his insides so that he felt as if he were bleeding from the inside out.

Nothing in his very long life had ever felt so dreadful, so horrific.

Everything he was, everything he had become since meeting Saffron, began to fade. It was as if with her absence the light that had begun to fill his life was leaving.

He'd thought he was a broken man before. Now, he knew he would shatter into a million pieces if he couldn't have Saffron back in his arms again.

CHAPTER
FORTY

Saffron groaned and tried to put her hand to her head, but was halted, the sound of chains making her eyes fly open.

"No," she whispered as she found herself in Declan's prison once more. "No, no, no, no, no."

The deep chuckle came from the shadows outside her cell door. And with the sound came the terror. Her lungs seized, her heart pounded.

And her soul withered.

"Did you actually think you could escape me?" Declan asked as he shifted into the light.

Saffron tried to swallow, but all the moisture had left her mouth. There was no use in even bothering to answer him. If she fought him, it would only provoke him. If she tried to reason with him, he would only retaliate another way.

Silence was her best option.

"Robbie, I do think the cat has her tongue," Declan said.

Saffron began to shake as Robbie appeared next to Declan. Robbie balled one fist up and punched it into his other hand. How many times had Robbie's fists hit her? How many times had his laughter rung in her ears until she had passed out?

There was more movement and Deirdre came into view. She walked to the bars and wound her fingers around the metal. "I had a Seer once."

Saffron watched a lock of Deirdre's long, white hair lift

and reach for her. It extended, lengthening before her eyes. Saffron turned her face away and pressed herself as close to the wall as she could. But she was trapped.

She'd heard what Deirdre could do with her hair, but when it touched her, the strand merely caressed her cheek.

"Seers are very important," Deirdre said. "Especially to us. Join us, Saffron, and I'll free you from those shackles."

"Never," Saffron said with as much force as she could despite the tremor in her voice.

Declan chuckled again. "Oh, but Saffron, you should know better than to try and fight me. Remember what happened to you last time? Though I see your eyesight has returned."

"No thanks to you," Saffron said through clenched teeth.

The door to her cell swung open with a wave of Declan's hand and he walked inside. His smile held a sadistic lilt as he squatted in front of her. "I can make this easy, or I can make this hard. The choice is yours, Saffron."

She had never been more frightened in her life, but she'd never hated anyone more. The two emotions warred and mixed inside her. "What did you do to Fallon?"

"Doona worry about him. He's no' feeling anything anymore."

Tears welled in Saffron's eyes even though she knew better than to show any kind of emotion in front of Declan. He would use it against her.

"*Drough* blood kills Warriors," Deirdre said with a smile. "I never understood why. The gods are evil, and black magic is its own kind of evil."

"You're going to die," Saffron said as she glared at Deirdre. "No amount of black magic is going to stop Laria from ending you once and for all."

Saffron was prepared for Declan's slap, but it was his fist instead. Her lip split instantly and her head jerked back, slamming against the bricks at her back.

The metallic taste of blood filled her mouth until she nearly gagged on it. She slowly turned her head and looked at Declan.

"You've found some backbone, I see," he murmured.

Deirdre snorted as her hair wrapped around Saffron's throat. "That can be dealt with easily enough."

"I thought you both said you needed a Seer," came a deep voice from the shadows.

Saffron jerked against the chains holding her as Deirdre's hair tightened. The choking paused and Saffron strained to see who had spoken, but the shadows were too deep for her to even make out the outline of his body.

"Unfortunately, he's right," Declan said, and tapped a finger on Deirdre's hair.

Instantly, the white strands unwound from Saffron's throat and returned to Deirdre's side.

"A warning then," Deirdre said.

Declan twirled a cuff link with his fingers as he stood and smiled. "Aye, a warning. As I said, Saffron, we can do this the easy way or the hard way. You have thirty minutes to decide."

He left, the iron door clanging shut behind him. She watched him, Deirdre, and Robbie walk away, but Saffron knew she wasn't alone.

Whoever was in the shadows was still there. Watching. Waiting.

She closed her eyes, her mind instantly going to Camdyn. She wished he was with her, but more than that, she wished she had listened to Fallon's warning and left the bank.

"It'll take more than one X90 bullet to kill Fallon."

Saffron's eyes jerked open. "How do you know?"

"I know," was his response.

Saffron licked her lips as she realized who the voice belonged to. "You're Malcolm, aren't you? Larena's cousin."

Silence greeted her question.

"She worries about you," Saffron continued. "They all do."

"I've told them to forget."

She let out a slow breath. Malcolm might be on Deirdre's side, but he hadn't always been. Maybe she could get him to help her.

"Larena won't forget, and neither will the others. You're family to them."

Suddenly Malcolm stepped forward into the small light outside her cell. His blond hair was long and hung loose about his thick shoulders. His face was handsome with his square jaw and aquiline nose.

But his blue eyes, as beautiful as they were, were filled with emptiness. "It's too late for me."

"It's never too late. Help me get out of here."

He shook his head, a thick lock of blond hair falling over his forehead and into his eyes. "Deirdre's and Declan's magic is too strong. No one will find you nor will you be able to escape again."

A tear she couldn't hold back rolled down her cheek. "I will fight them. I won't submit."

"Then they will take your body and mind by force. Are you strong enough to resist them?"

She drew in a shuddering breath as the comprehension that she was well and truly fucked sank into her mind. "You can get away though. You can save yourself."

Malcolm's eyes narrowed as his head cocked to the side. "Why?"

"Because I've heard the stories from Larena and Fallon and the others. I know what kind of man you were before . . ." She faltered as his nostrils flared. "Before the Warrior attack that left your arm unable to function."

"You didna see me, Druid. You didna see the scars upon my face and body." He lifted his right arm. "I'm able to use this limb now only because of Deirdre."

"Are you so vain that you think you have to be perfect in order to do the right things? Larena hasn't given up on you, but you gave up on yourself long ago."

"I do this to protect her," Malcolm said in a low, dangerous voice.

Saffron paused, reminded yet again how deadly Warriors could be. "Deirdre has yet to defeat the MacLeods. You do those fighting against her a disservice by not believing they could win again."

"This time they can no'," he said softly. "I will do anything to keep Larena safe."

"How do you think she'll feel if Fallon dies? Grateful that you made sure she was spared? And what of the others? Do none of them matter?"

All emotion fled from his face as he turned sideways. "You have little time left to make your decision."

"Wait," Saffron said when he started to leave. "I beg a favor of you. It is a small one."

A muscle jerked in his jaw but he said, "You can ask for this favor, but I doona agree to carry through with it."

"Will you tell Camdyn that I . . . I love him?"

Malcolm's head slowly turned and regarded her silently for several moments. "I make no promises."

Instead of leaving as she expected him to do, Malcolm remained. The longer Saffron waited for Deirdre and Declan to return the more her fear grew until she shook with it.

She closed her eyes and tried to think of her father and how he would handle the situation, but she couldn't focus long enough.

Finally she took a deep breath and let her magic envelop her. That's when she heard the drums as if from a great distance.

The more she pulled her magic around her the louder the drums became. And then she heard the chanting. It was strong and vibrant and welcoming.

Saffron knew the risk of giving herself up to the chanting, but at least there maybe Deirdre and Declan wouldn't be able to harm her or make her do something she didn't want to do.

It was a hefty price she would have to pay, but she would gladly do it if it meant Declan would no longer be able to use her, especially against the people she now considered her family.

And Camdyn.

Another tear joined the first as she thought of him. It gave her a measure of joy to know that he would one day be happy. She'd wanted it to be with her, but she loved him enough to let him go.

The chanting was all around her, the beat of the drums so strong it reverberated through her body. They wanted her to give in. To give herself to them.

The ancients were waiting.

And with a smile, Saffron went to them.

Malcolm watched the Druid carefully. He could have called to Deirdre that the Druid's magic was growing, swelling, so that it filled the entire prison below Declan's house.

But he didn't.

He couldn't.

Her simple request to tell Camdyn that she loved him had chipped away at the wall he thought surrounded the place where his heart used to be.

So instead of alerting Deirdre, Malcolm allowed Saffron to delve into her magic. What would happen he had no idea, but he assumed whatever the Druid was doing would only help her against the evil coming her way.

"It's time!" Declan declared as he banged open the door atop the steps and descended the stairs.

Beside him, as always, was Robbie with a gun and the *drough*-blood-filled X90 bullets trained on Malcolm. Deirdre walked next to Declan, her smile triumphant.

"Yes, Saffron. Let's hear your decision," Deirdre said as they drew closer to Malcolm.

When they reached the cell Declan looked at Saffron before his head jerked to Malcolm. "What did you do to her?"

"Nothing," Malcolm answered.

Deirdre put a hand on Declan's chest. "Malcolm knows better than to go against me. Right, Malcolm?"

Malcolm allowed his god to surface. His fangs filled his mouth, and he clinked his claws together. Declan's eyes widened but a fraction, but it was enough. And just what Malcolm had been looking for.

"I'm yours to command, mistress," he told Deirdre.

"Good. Now tell me what happened here? Why isn't she answering?"

Malcolm turned his gaze to Deirdre. "She tried to get me to release her; when I didna she closed her eyes. I assumed she was resting."

"And her magic?" Declan asked. "Did you feel her magic?"

Malcolm slowly shook his head. "Nay."

CHAPTER
FORTY-ONE

"I'm tired of waiting," Camdyn said as he slammed his hand down on the table.

They'd been sitting in the great hall trying to figure out how to find Declan and Deirdre. And Saffron.

Camdyn couldn't take any more. He had to act. He had to do something to find her.

"Whatever Declan is doing, it's powerful black magic," Broc said. "He's the only one that has ever blocked my god's power."

Sonya tucked a short, red curl behind her ear. "The trees will only repeat that danger is coming. Nothing else. They're frightened."

Fallon leaned forward on the table and caught Camdyn's gaze. "As soon as Deirdre or Declan lets us know where they want the battle to take place, we'll go. Until then, I doona think it wise for anyone to leave the area."

"It won't be long now," Laria said. "My sister was never known for her patience. I'm sure she would already have contacted the castle if it wasn't for Declan."

Camdyn couldn't stand to hear another round of what might happen. He rose and strode from the castle. The blast of cold air filled his lungs, but he welcomed it.

It made him feel something besides the crushing helplessness that filled him. He'd never wanted to care for someone again, never wanted to be put in a position to lose someone again.

But somehow Saffron had found her way into his soul without him knowing it. She was well and truly in his heart whether he wanted her there or not.

"We'll find her," Arran said from behind him.

Camdyn hadn't even heard the door open. "But will it be in time?"

"We'll find her, and we'll bring her back to you."

Camdyn looked at Arran and his light brown eyes. "Thank you."

He didn't wait for Arran to say more. Camdyn walked aimlessly around the bailey recalling Saffron's laughter and the way her tawny eyes darkened when she was aroused. He remembered the feel of her thick, silky hair as it glided through his fingers, and the softness of her skin.

He recalled how special and wonderful it felt when they made love.

Camdyn stopped next to the castle wall and leaned his forehead against it. He let loose the roar he'd held within him and punched the wall once, twice, three times.

"Saffron," he whispered.

He couldn't breathe, couldn't think beyond the despair that had taken hold of him. Camdyn closed his eyes and rolled so that his back was against the stones.

With his face lifted to the sky, he felt the first snowflake against his cheek. He touched his cheek, his throat clogged with emotion, as he recalled seeing her playing in the snow.

He put the heels of his hands against his eyes and slid down the wall until he was sitting in the snow.

Hayden stared at Camdyn's bent head from the battlements and crossed his arms over his chest. "He might no' have wanted to fall for Saffron, but he did."

"Aye," Quinn replied. "We're going to have to watch him. He may do something reckless in order to get to her."

Hayden's lips thinned as he sighed. "Wouldna we all if it was our women Declan and Deirdre held?"

"Aye," Lucan said softly.

Ramsey leaned his hands against the gray stone. "We've never faced two *droughs* before. Whatever they took Saffron for, you can guarantee that it's to be used against us somehow."

"Just as Deirdre used Isla's sister," Logan said.

Arran shifted from foot to foot. "Deirdre is doing this because Laria has the magic to destroy her. We need to trust in Laria."

"Tell that to Camdyn," Ian said.

Fallon shook his head, anger hardening his features. "We've no' let anyone down in this family before. I willna begin now. Laria has requested verra little of us. We just need to keep the Druids safe."

"While finding Saffron," Hayden added.

Fallon looked at Camdyn. "And keep him alive. I refuse to loose another Warrior."

Phelan knew the moment he entered the small village near Ferness that he'd found where the other Warrior lived. It was the way the men were stationed around the road leading into the village and perched atop buildings that alerted him.

He'd kept what he was a secret from everyone. There hadn't been a single person in four centuries that he'd trusted enough to even show them what he was.

But somehow this other Warrior had not only done it, but also had an entire town behind him.

"Interesting," Phelan murmured as he pulled his Ducati to a stop beside a sleek black CLS Mercedes in front of a pub that looked as if it had been around for at least seven centuries.

Phelan put the kickstand down on his bike and turned it off. He removed his helmet and let his gaze roam over the buildings around him.

The door to the pub opened and a burly man with a huge barrel chest stepped outside, his gaze on Phelan.

Phelan swung his leg over the bike to dismount and raised a brow at the man.

"Enough, Tom," said a voice behind Phelan.

Phelan turned and saw the Warrior. He stood still as the Warrior approached him after Tom returned to the pub. "Who are you?" Phelan asked.

The Warrior lifted a dark brow. "I might ask the same question. Warrior."

"The name is Phelan Stewart," he said as he hung his helmet on one of the handlebars of his motorcycle.

"Well, Phelan, doona be getting comfortable here. I doona know what you want, but you willna be staying."

"You didna help the MacLeods. Or Deirdre. Why no'?"

The Warrior sighed. "You're persistent."

"Tell me your name. You know mine."

"Charon Bruce."

"It seems, Charon, that you and I have something in common. Neither of us is on Deirdre's side, and neither of us feels inclined to help the MacLeods."

"How long have you been a Warrior?"

Phelan shrugged and said, "Five hundred and sixty years about. You?"

"Six hundred and twenty-two. How long did Deirdre have you?"

Phelan's nostrils flared and his lips flattened. "Isla tricked me when I was but a lad of four. I was kept in that damned mountain until I reached a score of years. Then Deirdre unbound my god."

"That means . . ." Charon's voice trailed off as his gaze lowered to the ground. When he looked back at Phelan he said, "Come with me."

Phelan followed Charon into the pub and up a flight of stairs to what was apparently Charon's private office. Fine works of art by Michelangelo and da Vinci graced the walls while expensive Persian rugs covered the floor.

Charon's desk was about as old as he was, but had been well preserved.

"Sit," Charon said as he poured whisky out of a crystal decanter into two glasses. He handed a glass to Phelan and said, "I do believe we were both held by Deirdre at the same time. I was there for several decades. It wasn't until the Mac-Leods attacked the mountain that I was set free."

Phelan lifted the glass to his lips and took a sip. "Ah. Fine, single-malt whisky. Deirdre kept me far below the ground in a chamber where I was only visited by her and Isla."

"Who set you free?"

"Isla." Though Phelan hated to admit it. He detested the Druid, but she had come to him and released him.

He'd thought she had died from her wound, but imagine his surprise when he'd seen her not so long ago.

"Isla is with the MacLeods now. Whether you know it or no', Deirdre used Isla's sister and niece against her. It was the only way Deirdre could control Isla."

"I really doona give a shite about Isla. I want to know why you doona help the MacLeods."

Charon swirled the amber liquid in his glass. "I know their cause is just. I know the world would be a much better place without Deirdre, but she forced me to spy on Quinn while she held him in the mountain. Deirdre has a way of manipulating people to her advantage. The MacLeods might welcome me, but it's no' a chance I'm willing to take. What's your excuse?"

"I refuse to fight alongside Druids. Actually, I came to see if you would help me kill them."

"Kill who?"

"The Druids. All of them."

Charon set down his glass and looked at Phelan with new eyes. "How much do you know of the history of the War-riors?"

"What is there to know?"

Just as Charon thought. "No' all Druids are evil, Phelan. This land, our Scotland, was built upon magic. Without the Druids, that magic will fade and cease to exist."

"So?"

"A verra long time ago the Romans invaded Britain. The Celts, our ancestors, fought them for years. They were able to stop the Romans from venturing into the Highlands, but the Romans refused to leave.

"The Druids in those days had split into two factions. The *mies* kept to their original Druid ways and continued to heal, teach, and guide the clan leaders. The *droughs*, however, turned to black magic by giving their souls to the Devil.

"The clan leaders turned to the Druids for help, but the *mies* had no answer for how to defeat the Romans. The *droughs* did. They called up primeval gods long imprisoned in Hell. These gods took the host of the strongest warriors of each family."

Phelan lowered his eyes to the glass in his hand.

"These men became the first Warriors. They defeated the Romans and had them retreating from Britain. But the gods were no' satisfied. They wanted to keep killing. It took the combined magic of the *mies* and the *droughs* to bind the gods inside the men. They were unable to force the gods back into Hell, and the gods traveled through the bloodlines, going to the strongest warrior each time.

"The spells were no' supposed to have been written down, but they were. And Deirdre found the spell to unbind our gods. That scroll listed one clan—the MacLeods. So, Deirdre began there. When she found Fallon, Lucan, and Quinn, she murdered their entire clan in order to have them for herself."

"Stop," Phelan said. "I doona want to hear more."

"But you must. You need to know your history. You need to know who you can trust and who you can no'."

"Can you trust the MacLeods?"

Charon nodded. "The MacLeods were able to escape Deirdre. They retreated to their castle where they stayed for three hundred years. Then Lucan fell in love with a woman who had no idea she was a Druid. Other Warriors who sought out the MacLeods found them. And the MacLeods opened their castle to any Warrior willing to fight Deirdre. As well as any Druid—*mie* or *drough*—looking for sanctuary."

Phelan took another drink of the whisky and contemplated the liquid for a moment before he asked, "Are there really good Druids?"

"Aye. You saw them at the Ring of Brodgar. Even Isla, who was forced to become *drough* by Deirdre, is no' truly a *drough*. She has the power of the black magic, but the evil doesna rule her."

"Is that why she released me?"

"I think she released you because she never wanted to bring you there to begin with. Isla had many opportunities to harm me while I was in Cairn Toul. Yet, she never did."

Phelan leaned forward and set the glass on Charon's desk down carefully. "If all you say is true, and you believe it so much that you're trying to convince me, I ask you again. Why no' help the MacLeods?"

CHAPTER
FORTY-TWO

A war raged inside Malcolm. His claws were sunk into his palms as he fought to keep himself still and not kill those around him.

Not that he could kill them. Deirdre had survived death once, and Declan, well, Malcolm was relatively sure the bastard would somehow survive death as well.

Yet, Malcolm couldn't take his eyes off Saffron. Deirdre and Declan had taken turns trying to wake her from her magic-induced sleep. When that hadn't worked, they had begun using magic on her.

It hadn't taken long for the smell of blood to fill the dungeon. That hadn't satisfied them though. And somehow Saffron had slept through it all.

"Robbie, string her up," Declan called.

Malcolm growled as Robbie slung his machine gun around so that it rested against his back. Robbie smiled at him and walked into the cell where Saffron was still sitting. Blood trickled from the corner of her mouth and her nose, but she hadn't moved a muscle.

"Help him," Deirdre ordered Malcolm.

He wanted to refuse, wanted to tell Deirdre to go to hell where she belonged. But then Malcolm thought of Larena. He bit back his words and strode into the cell where Robbie had grabbed Saffron's upper body.

Malcolm bared his teeth, showing Robbie his fangs. A low, menacing growl followed that had Robbie taking a step back so quickly Saffron listed over, banging her head on the cement floor.

Without another look at Robbie, Malcolm lifted Saffron in his arms. All he could think about as he walked her to where Declan and Deirdre awaited was her asking him to tell Camdyn she loved him.

Love.

Malcolm certainly believed in it. He'd seen it with his own eyes between Larena and Fallon as well as the other couples at the castle.

Though he never expected to find it for himself.

Somehow, against all odds, the quiet, withdrawn Camdyn had found it. Malcolm couldn't help wondering if Camdyn knew where Saffron was. As soon as Malcolm thought it, he knew Camdyn didn't. Because every Warrior from Mac-Leod Castle would have descended upon Declan's mansion to rescue Saffron.

Declan raised a brow. "What are you waiting for, Warrior? I said to string her up."

Rage began to burn inside Malcolm, making it difficult for him to keep his face impassive. He held Saffron with one arm around her upper body while he released her legs. Malcolm reached for the rope hanging from the ceiling and wound the loop around Saffron's hands.

As soon as he did, Saffron was yanked from his arms as Robbie pulled on the rope.

Robbie's smile was pure evil. "Is something wrong, Warrior?"

He and Declan called Malcolm that as if Malcolm were embarrassed to have a god inside him with powers none could comprehend. When in fact, the opposite was true.

Malcolm walked to Robbie and jabbed a claw against his shoulder until blood bloomed and soaked the black shirt. "One day verra soon you and I are going to have a serious disagreement."

"I'm no' afraid of you."

Malcolm's smile was slow as it pulled at his lips. "We shall see how brave you are without your precious gun."

"Enough," Declan bellowed. "Malcolm, resume your place."

Malcolm didn't move. He took orders from only one person, and then only when he wanted to.

Deirdre's laugh filled the dungeon. "Ah, Declan, you should know better. No one orders Malcolm or my wyrran but me."

"Then control your Warrior," Declan ground out.

There was a pregnant pause before Deirdre said, "Malcolm, you've made your point. Let us continue."

With great effort Malcolm returned to his post in the shadows. Saffron's body hung by her wrists, slowly swinging back and forth.

Malcolm was wondering what they were going to do to Saffron when Deirdre's hair lashed out like a whip and connected with Saffron's back.

Camdyn walked into Saffron's chamber and softly closed the door. He looked around the room, picturing her as she sat in front of her vanity and brushed out her hair, or how she twirled a lock of light brown hair around her finger as she talked on her mobile phone.

He walked to the bed and sank onto the mattress. Images of the times they had made love flashed in his mind. Camdyn leaned forward to brace his elbows on his knees and dropped his head into his hands.

He'd left Saffron that last night because he hadn't been able to face what he'd known from the very beginning. That she was special. Not just because she was a Druid, but special to him.

She was meant for him. He knew that now. Now that it was too late.

He hadn't wanted to love a woman again, hadn't wanted to put himself in a position to be hurt as he had been in the past. Even though he hadn't gone looking for love it had found him. And there was no escaping it.

No matter how much he tried to deny it, Saffron was a part of him. She was in his soul, his psyche. And he wanted her there.

"If only I'd realized this sooner," Camdyn muttered.

His idiocy could very well have cost him the second woman he had ever loved.

"Nay!" Camdyn bellowed and got to his feet. "I willna give up that easily."

He stalked to the door and threw it open with such force that it crashed into the wall behind it. Camdyn paid it little heed as he strode to Broc's chamber.

Camdyn pounded on the door. When Broc didn't answer it immediately, Camdyn pounded on it again.

"All right!" Broc shouted. "I'm coming."

The door swung open and Camdyn said, "I need you to look for Saffron again."

Broc signed wearily and shook his head. "Camdyn, I've tried. Numerous times. I can no' find her, Deirdre, or Declan."

"I've got to find her."

"And I can help," said a voice to Camdyn's left.

He and Broc turned to find Laria watching him.

"Come," Laria said, and started for the stairs that led down to the great hall.

"She's your best chance," Broc said.

Camdyn gave a curt nod and hastened to follow Laria. Hope flared in his chest. It was like a beacon in the darkest of nights, and Camdyn knew all too well how crushing it would be if that hope failed.

But he wouldn't think about that now. He focused on Saffron, on the love growing in his heart. He had to find her. He would find her.

And he would bring her back to the castle.

Saffron could see Deirdre's hair lashing at her back in a kind of out-of-body experience. She could see the anger in Deirdre's face as Saffron gave no response. She could see Declan's glee at her blood spilling down her back. Could see her naked self hanging by her wrists.

"They won't stop," the ancients said, their collective voices speaking as one. *"They will end up killing you."*

Saffron wasn't ready to die. She had thought she would be protected with the ancients. Even now the drums and chanting were calling her to them.

"You are needed to defeat Deirdre."

That gave Saffron pause. She had thought it was only Laria that needed to be awakened to end Deirdre. What else didn't she know?

"It doesn't matter. You must wake. You cannot fight Deirdre if you are dead."

Still Saffron hesitated. She knew she wasn't strong enough to withstand whatever Declan and Deirdre had planned for her.

"You are. Your love for Camdyn will give you that strength."

Saffron's mind was suddenly filled with images of Camdyn. Her heart ached for what could have been. "He isn't mine."

"It is your love for him that will give you strength."

Saffron had hoped the ancients would tell her that Camdyn was hers, that regardless of what she had seen in her vision, they would be together.

She should have known better.

With one more look at her bare back where Declan had ripped off her shirt, Saffron saw the crisscrossing of cuts and knew she was going to be in tremendous pain.

But she would do it. For Camdyn. Because she knew how desperately he and the other Warriors wanted Deirdre killed.

Saffron just hoped she survived so she could find a way to kill Declan. Even as the thought went through her mind she knew she wouldn't.

Declan would never let her go. Never.

Saffron listened to the chanting once more and let the magic fill her. When the magic was nearly bursting from her body, she allowed herself to withdraw from the drums and the chanting.

She kept her eyes closed as she came back to herself. She

fisted her hands, biting back a scream as pain flooded her body. Her back felt as if it were on fire, and every breath she took only made the agony flourish.

When it felt as if she were drowning in the pain, her magic welled up and soothed her. Saffron concentrated on her magic, putting all her focus on it. Until she could breathe normally once more.

She opened her eyes to find herself staring at Malcolm. The Warrior's maroon eyes flared for a second. It was so quick she would have missed it had she not been looking at his stony face.

"I wondered how long it would take you to join us," Declan said as he caressed a finger down her cheek. "I was hoping Deirdre wouldna have to cut you to pieces, but I was willing to let her try."

Saffron cut her eyes to Declan and spat in his face. "Do whatever it is you have to do. Blind me, kill me. Whatever. But I'll never help you."

"You should know never to say never," Deirdre said, her voice low and filled with laughter.

Saffron lifted her chin. She'd never been so afraid in her life, but she refused to allow them to see it. They would use it against her. And even though they would most likely win in the end, she intended to fight them every step of the way.

She just hoped it would be enough. Her magic wasn't that strong, and she hadn't been able to hold off Declan's magic. There was no doubt in her mind she would lose against both Declan and Deirdre.

But maybe she could hold them off long enough for Camdyn and the others to get there. If only she knew how to break their blocking spell for just a short while. Maybe then Broc would be able to locate her.

"No one will find you unless we want them to," Deirdre said as she stroked Saffron's hair.

Declan leaned close and eyed her bare breasts. "I told you that you would always be mine. Did you think I was jesting?"

"You may win against the MacLeods this time, but in the

end, they'll defeat both of you. No amount of spells, no amount of black magic, will save you from death," Saffron said.

Deirdre grabbed a handful of her hair and jerked Saffron's head back. "They will kill you along with us, because you'll be one of us."

Dread filled Saffron's stomach until she thought she was going to be sick. The pain she had held off surged again. She closed her eyes to fight it off.

And then she felt Declan's and Deirdre's magic surrounding her, swallowing her. Overpowering her.

CHAPTER
FORTY-THREE

"The ancients have Saffron," Laria's voice rang out in the great hall.

Camdyn blinked and looked around him to see if anyone understood what Laria was talking about. "Explain yourself."

Laria smiled at him. "She withdrew to the chanting, Camdyn. It was her defense against Declan and Deirdre. While the ancients want to protect her, Declan isn't going to give up. In his quest to dominate Saffron, he'll end up killing her."

Camdyn got to his feet with a roar.

It was Ramsey and Galen on either side of him that held him in check.

"Camdyn, we need to hear this in order to save Saffron," Dani said.

Ian's grip tightened on Camdyn's shoulder. All Camdyn wanted to do was rip someone apart. He wanted to deal out death, to see blood and hear screams of terror, his fury was so great.

But for Saffron he reined in his god and took his seat once more.

"The ancients are convincing Saffron to leave their safety and fight against Deirdre and Declan," Laria continued.

Gwynn fidgeted with her fingers and asked, "Can she? Does Saffron hold enough magic to fight them both off?"

Camdyn knew the answer before Laria slowly shook her head. There were few Druids who had enough magic to fend off two powerful *droughs* like Declan and Deirdre.

"Saffron is taking the magic of the ancients in now. I'm hoping that will be enough to break through Declan's blocking spell so that Broc can find her," Laria said.

Without being asked, Broc closed his eyes. Camdyn watched his friend across the table, silently begging that Laria was correct and Broc would be able to find her. Even if it was just a moment, it would be enough for them to locate her and possibly rescue her.

"I have her!" Broc shouted as his eyes flew open. "Wait . . . I lost her again."

Laria blew out a breath. "As I assumed."

Camdyn slammed his fist on the table, rattling the glasses. "Where is she?" he demanded of Broc.

A muscle in Broc's jaw jumped. "She's in Declan's dungeon again."

Camdyn squeezed his eyes closed. The one place Saffron was so terrified of that nightmares had plagued her. Camdyn released a deep breath and looked around him. "I'll go after her."

"Wait," Laria cautioned.

Fallon narrowed his eyes on Laria. "Why? We know where Saffron is."

"Along with Declan's mercs and their X90 bullets," Gwynn added with a glance to Logan.

Logan frowned. "Declan's is no' the place to attack. His magic is too strong there."

"I willna wait!" Camdyn bellowed.

Ramsey said, "But you must. If we want to extract Saffron on the first try, we must be smart about it."

"I agree with Ramsey," Hayden said.

One by one they all agreed. Camdyn sank his claws into the table. Every fiber of his being wanted to dash off to rescue Saffron immediately, but his mind told him the others were right. He needed to go about it carefully.

Finally, he gave a quick nod of his head.

"Good," Fallon said as he rose. "Since we know they're at Declan's, I'm going to head there now and see what they are about."

"Not without me you aren't," Larena said as she stood and took his hand.

Camdyn watched them share that secret, loving smile and felt his heart split open at what he was missing with Saffron.

"Trust Laria. We'll find Saffron," Ramsey whispered.

Camdyn removed his claws one by one from the wood. "Last time he took her sight. What do you think Declan will do to her this time?"

Saffron looked at herself in the mirror and hated what she saw. She was dressed in tight jeans and what was nothing more than a corset.

Of course it was Declan who had chosen her clothes.

"Amazing," Declan said as he walked into the room and whistled.

Saffron looked at him in the mirror and wanted to use her nails to slash his eyes out. But no matter what she wanted to do, or begged her body to do, it was Declan and Deirdre who controlled her.

But they couldn't control her mind.

She let them think they did, but even that small charade had its price. Saffron wasn't sure how much longer she could hold up the pretense.

Every minute she expected one of them to realize she was faking it. Saffron didn't think she could survive another blast of their combined *drough* magic.

Just thinking about it made her want to retch.

"It's almost time," Declan said as he used his finger to move her hair from her shoulder so it fell with the rest down her back.

Saffron merely looked at him. Their control over her body was nearly absolute. They told her where to move and what to do. She couldn't even speak. They had taken that away from her as well. She liked to think it was because they feared what spells she might use.

"Come," Declan said, as he held out his hand and turned to the door.

Saffron tried to resist, but her body obeyed without hesitation. She turned and placed her hand in his. Saffron was screaming inside her mind, calling Declan the worst kinds of names, but none of it mattered.

She was theirs, and as frightening as that was, not knowing what they had planned for her kept her stomach tied in knots.

All she could hope for was that it didn't involve those at MacLeod Castle. Even when she knew in her heart that it did.

There was no way she could stand there and do something to harm them. She'd never forgive herself. There had to be some way to break this spell Deirdre and Declan had cast on her.

Saffron walked beside Declan as they descended the stairs and reached the front door where Robbie and Malcolm stood on either side of double doors.

"I've news on your other inquiry," Robbie said.

Declan released her hand. "And what would that be?"

"We've narrowed it down to the northwest. We'll soon have a town to give you."

"And another of my runaways will be back where they belong," Declan said with a smile.

Deirdre appeared at the top of the stairs then, clad in black skintight leather, and made her way down. "Declan, you picked those horrid clothes for Saffron, didn't you?"

"Of course. I do know what looks good on women."

Deirdre rolled her eyes. "Nay. You like to think you know what looks good on women."

"You liked the leather enough that you still wear it."

Deirdre's smile was cold and malicious. "I wear it because it suits me, not because you chose it."

"You can no' lie to me."

"Watch me."

In the next instant Declan had Deirdre up against the wall kissing her. Saffron swallowed the bile that rose in her throat. She recalled all too well the vision she'd had of Deirdre, her stomach large with child, standing over a dead Declan.

Had they already shared a bed? Did the child already grow within Deirdre?

Saffron lowered her gaze to find black combat boots in front of her. She could do nothing as Robbie's finger traced the swell of her breasts, the desire evident in his gaze.

"You're going to be mine," he whispered. "I'll make you scream by the time I'm done with you."

Saffron was inwardly shaking her head back and forth, trying her damnedest to raise a hand and slap Robbie. But without permission she was nothing more than a mannequin who breathed.

Robbie's finger slid between her breasts as he rubbed his arousal against her. Suddenly, he let out a bellow as Malcolm bent his hand backward until the bone was about to break.

"Is this how you take women?" Malcolm demanded. "They have to be under a spell where they can no' refuse you in order for you to relieve yourself?"

"You're about to break my hand," Robbie cried as he fell to his knees.

Saffron watched as Malcolm held Robbie's shoulder and bent the wrist back another fraction. Malcolm's Warrior eyes were narrowed into slits as he glared at Robbie.

"I think these two really hate each other," Deirdre said.

"Stop him now, Deirdre," Declan demanded.

Deirdre raised a white brow. "Or what?"

"You need me," Declan reminded her. "If you still want my aid, call off your Warrior."

Deirdre rolled her eyes and sighed. "Malcolm, release Robbie."

Saffron was surprised Malcolm didn't instantly obey. There was a moment where she could see how he debated breaking Robbie's wrist anyway, but then he inhaled a deep breath. Malcolm let go of Robbie's hand and shifted his gaze to her.

She wanted to tell him thank you, to let him know she

was glad he stopped Robbie, even if it wasn't because of her but because of his hatred for the mercenary.

Malcolm turned on his heel and opened the door. Saffron watched him walk out into the sun toward the helicopter waiting for them.

"It's time," Deirdre said.

Declan motioned for Saffron to follow. She was in the helicopter and buckled by the time Declan had the blades moving.

Saffron found herself in the middle with Robbie on one side and Malcolm climbing in the other. Saffron noticed how Malcolm stiffened and touched his face with his fingers.

He didn't say a word as he took his seat and shut the door right before they took off.

Camdyn watched the helicopter rise into the sky and then take off. It had taken some doing, but he'd managed to talk Fallon into bringing him along. But now he wished he hadn't.

To see Saffron walk to that helicopter as if she wanted to be there, dressed in . . . something that certainly wasn't her style left his mind reeling.

"Doona believe all you see," Fallon cautioned him. "Deirdre has her tricks."

"You saw her, Fallon. She wasna even fighting them."

Fallon blew out a breath. "We doona know what they've done to her. You need to remember that. And—"

"I know," Camdyn said. "That even if we do get Saffron back she may never be the person she was before."

Fallon put a hand on his shoulder and squeezed. "Deirdre forced Isla to become *drough*. I wouldna be surprised to learn she did it again."

Camdyn nodded. "How are you holding up?"

Fallon refused to meet his gaze. "Larena is a strong Warrior. Her power to be invisible will give us an advantage, as well as helping us learn what they've done to Saffron."

"I wouldna have been able to let my wife go with them."

"Sometimes you have to trust that they can keep themselves safe."

Camdyn, his gaze still on the helicopter, wondered if Fallon believed his own words. Despite his assurance, Camdyn knew Fallon was anything but all right.

Without alerting him, Fallon jumped them back to the castle.

"Did it work?" Lucan asked when they appeared in the great hall.

Fallon nodded. "Larena's plan was carried out flawlessly. She is with them now. They've taken a helicopter."

Broc smiled as he looked at Fallon. "No' even *drough* magic will keep them from blocking Larena from me."

Camdyn's impatience grew as Broc touched Fallon's torc and closed his eyes. Larena wore a matching armband that bound them. It was powerful magic that could not be covered. And something Deirdre knew nothing about.

"They're headed to the Ring of Brodgar," Broc said.

Camdyn looked at Fallon. "We go now."

CHAPTER
FORTY-FOUR

Charon put his Mercedes in park and sighed. With both hands on the wheel he looked out over the vast expanse of the Orkney isle. Even without his enhanced vision he still would have been able to see the massive stones of the Ring of Brodgar rising from the earth.

There was a knock on his window. Charon turned his head to find Phelan bent over, a brow raised in question. Charon gave a shake of his head and opened the door.

"Having second thoughts?" Phelan asked as he backed away so Charon could climb out.

"Nay." Charon closed the door and inhaled the brisk winter air.

"Why did you want to come back here?"

Charon shrugged. "There just seemed something off about Deirdre leaving so suddenly. She had half of the Mac-Leod Druids trapped belowground and her wyrran were keeping the Warriors who had gotten out busy."

"So?"

"So, there was another Druid here."

Phelan crossed his arms over his chest and scowled. "A *mie*?"

"Nay. A *drough* with almost as much power as Deirdre."

"So why didna the bugger help Deirdre?"

"That is the question, is it no'?" Charon asked as he started walking toward the stones.

Phelan easily caught up with him. "What do you know that you are no' telling me?"

"Nothing."

"I doona believe you."

Charon halted and turned his head to look at the Warrior. "You doona trust anyone, do you?"

"Do you?" Phelan asked in answer.

Charon smiled and shook his head. "Nay."

"So what's the problem?"

Charon chuckled and started walking again. He didn't want to like Phelan, but he did. It still boggled his mind to know Phelan had been kept in Cairn Toul since he was a small lad. No wonder he hated Druids. He'd seen the worst side of them.

And while Charon agreed with much of Phelan's feelings on the matter of Druids, even Charon knew there was a line drawn between the Druids.

Marcail had known he was spying on Quinn, Ian, Duncan, and Arran. She had known Deirdre was using something against him.

"How do you tell the difference between *mie* and *drough* magic?" Phelan asked.

"A *mie*'s magic feels pure and bright while a *drough*'s black magic feels heavy and suffocating." Charon glanced at Phelan and the thoughtful look on his face. "You've felt *mie* magic, have you no'?"

Phelan nodded. "Many centuries ago I helped a winged Warrior and a Druid escape Deirdre."

"That would be Broc. He spied against Deirdre, earning her trust and helping the MacLeods gather information. Broc is still alive, and I would bet my entire fortune that the Druid you helped is with the MacLeods. Why did you help them if you hated Druids so?"

"It was the Warrior. The way he stood against Deirdre. He knew he was going to die and he didna care."

"Had you no' helped him, I've no doubt Deirdre would have gotten her vengeance on him."

"Aye," he said thoughtfully. "So this other *drough*'s magic you felt, did it feel like Deirdre's?"

"Similar. Verra similar," Charon said as they reached the ring of stones. "Do you feel the magic here?"

"I think even a mortal would feel the magic of this place."

"The stones were once used for ceremonial purposes by the ancient Druids."

Charon stopped and looked to the sky. A heartbeat later Phelan turned in the same direction.

"A helicopter," Phelan said.

"And *drough* magic."

"They're still a ways out."

Charon stiffened as he felt magic stir behind him. He turned and spotted Ian as well as Quinn walking toward him. Druids stood in a group watching. "Phelan, you're about to meet the MacLeods."

Camdyn and Hayden were behind Ian and Quinn as they walked to the other two Warriors. Isla wanted to go, but Hayden had refused.

Camdyn had heard talk of both Phelan and Charon, and he was surprised to find them here. Especially together.

"Charon," Ian said, and held out his arm.

Charon didn't hesitate to clasp Ian's forearm. "Ian."

"I hate to sound unwelcoming, but what are the both of you doing here?" Quinn asked.

Charon looked at each of them before he said, "By happenstance, but since all of you are here and I suspect the helicopter on its way holds Deirdre, I think there's going to be another battle."

"Another?" Camdyn repeated.

Phelan took a step closer. "That's what he said."

Camdyn narrowed his gaze on Phelan with his long dark hair and gray-blue eyes. "That's a problem for me if either of you were here for the first battle and didna bother to help."

"Why would we?" Phelan demanded with a sneer.

Camdyn got in his face until their noses were inches apart. "Isla may want to bring you into the fold, but I'm telling you right now if you doona help us today, I'll make you pay."

"Camdyn, easy," Hayden said as he put a hand between them and pushed them apart.

Charon ran a hand down his face and started to turn away. But Camdyn knew the more Warriors they had the better their chances of succeeding.

"We need your help. Please," Camdyn added. "I need your help."

It was Quinn who put a comforting hand on his shoulder a moment before he turned to Charon. "Deirdre is no' our only enemy. There is another *drough*."

"Declan," Camdyn ground out.

Phelan looked at Charon. "You said there were two."

Ian rubbed his jaw. "How did you know of Declan, Charon?"

"I didna," Charon answered. "I felt a second *drough* here during the first battle. But I never saw him."

"Holy hell," Quinn said and rubbed the back of his neck.

Camdyn was fast losing control of his fury. "He was here. The bastard was here."

"And we're going to end it all today," Hayden said.

"I say we begin by bringing the chopper down," Phelan said with a smile.

Quinn's nostrils flared. "You do that and you kill my brother's wife. She's on that helicopter."

Charon frowned. "Fallon's wife?"

Quinn nodded.

Phelan rolled his eyes. "I'd like to be included in this conversation."

"Her name is Larena," Camdyn answered. "She's a female Warrior."

Phelan's cocky attitude changed instantly. "What's her power?"

"Invisibility," Ian answered.

Camdyn looked at the sky. "They'll be here soon. We can no' be out in the open."

Charon held out his arm to Camdyn. They clasped forearms, but Charon didn't release him. "Who is she?"

Camdyn didn't pretend not to know what he meant. "Her name is Saffron. She's a Seer. Declan held her prisoner for three years."

"We rescued her," Hayden said.

"And Declan captured her again."

Charon's hand squeezed his arm before he released him. "Looks like we need to get her back once more."

The four of them as well as Charon and Phelan walked back to the others. Introductions were given and Camdyn noticed how uncomfortable Phelan was around the Druids. He spoke to them, however, all except for Isla.

She pretended like she didn't care, but Camdyn saw the way she turned to Hayden for comfort. Camdyn wanted to be there to offer Saffron comfort. He wanted to hold her, to cherish her.

To love her.

He closed his eyes as the sound of the helicopter drew closer.

"Hide," Fallon bellowed.

Camdyn hunkered down behind one of the mighty pillars as he kept his gaze on the helicopter. Saffron would emerge soon. He'd do anything to get her free of Declan, even sacrifice his own life if that's what it took.

He would not allow her to be trapped in that world.

Saffron looked at the Ring of Brodgar and recalled the last time she had been there. So much had changed in her life that day. It seemed eons ago when in fact it had been days.

She had faced her ultimate fear, found magic she hadn't believed existed inside her, and opened herself up to Camdyn.

Camdyn.

God, how she missed him.

The helicopter began its descent from the sky. Robbie put

his hand on her thigh and slowly moved it up her legs until he was nearly at her sex.

"I already warned you about touching her," Malcolm said in a deep, gravelly voice.

Robbie winked at her. "Doona worry, love. The beast willna be around all the time. We can have our fun when he's gone."

Saffron closed her eyes and turned her gaze away from him. All too soon they had landed in the Orkneys. Declan shut off the engine, and they all climbed out of the helicopter.

"I want everyone set up before I alert my sister that we're here," Deirdre said.

Saffron's heart jumped in her chest when she heard the screech of a wyrran as dozens of them came rushing toward Deirdre. After a few moments where Deirdre spoke to them, the wyrran fanned out over the peninsula.

Saffron looked to one of the pillars and remembered how it had felt to be joined with the Druids among such magic. And to have Camdyn there keeping watch over her.

A pair of dark eyes suddenly met hers. Saffron inwardly smiled as she locked gazes with Camdyn. She wanted to run to the safety of his arms.

"Saffron, come here," Declan ordered.

She fought the order, grappling with the spell. For a few precious moments she actually got the upper hand and was able to keep from moving. But the spell quickly overpowered her.

Saffron turned and walked toward Declan—away from Camdyn. With each step, her heart broke. Her chance to break the spell and help the others had come and gone. She had failed them and herself.

Deirdre stopped in midstride and turned to Declan. "It appears as if I needn't contact Laria. She's already here."

A figure moved from behind one of the stones, her long blond hair braided and lying over her shoulder. "That's right, sister. You didn't really think you would be able to stay hidden from us forever, did you?"

"I didn't need forever. I just needed a few days."

Laria rubbed her hands together. "Shall we begin, then?"

"Not quite yet," Deirdre said, and wrapped her fingers around Saffron's arm. She jerked Saffron next to her. "I believe you know Saffron. She has joined me."

"Then she'll die along with the rest of you."

Saffron wanted to cry when she heard Camdyn's bellow, but the tears wouldn't come.

Deirdre gave her a vicious yank as another spell fell from her lips. The world began to spin faster and faster with each word, and there was nothing Saffron could do to stop the vision.

"Tell me your vision," Deirdre whispered.

Saffron couldn't stop the images that filled her mind, nor her voice that put them to words.

CHAPTER
FORTY-FIVE

Camdyn watched Saffron carefully. She stood beside Deirdre, but something wasn't right. He didn't know what it was, only that Saffron wasn't herself.

As soon as Deirdre grabbed her, Camdyn was on his feet ready to do whatever it took to get Saffron away from Deirdre.

"Careful," Charon said, and moved in front of Camdyn.

"Get. Out of. My. Way."

Charon shook his head. "If I do you'll only succeed in getting yourself killed instead of rescuing that pretty Druid."

"Listen to him," Ian cautioned.

Camdyn filled his lungs with air and listened to his friends. "I'll get Saffron away from Declan."

Camdyn's attention jerked back to Saffron when he felt a wave of Deirdre's magic. Camdyn saw Saffron's face go blank and her eyes stare off into the sky. He didn't need to see her eyes to know they had gone milky white and were swirling.

Somehow, someway Deirdre was making Saffron have a vision.

"Tell them!" Deirdre shouted to Saffron.

"A Warrior will betray you, tipping the scales of balance."

Camdyn put a hand on his chest as the ache grew. It hurt

to see Saffron in their clutches, to know they had done something to change the woman he had fallen in love with.

"No," Gwynn said from behind Camdyn, her accent thick with emotion. "I don't believe any of y'all would do that."

Camdyn's gaze swung to Phelan who stood glaring at Deirdre with such hatred. Phelan's head swiveled until he met Camdyn's eyes.

"If you believe I'll be the one to side with Deirdre, you've got it all wrong, mate."

Camdyn then turned to Charon.

Charon snorted. "Automatically you all turn to me."

"Nay," Ian said. "It's just that you have no' helped us in the past."

"Because of this," Charon said, "I knew you all would doubt my loyalty, I just didna think it would be so soon."

"It's no' any Warrior at the castle," Camdyn said. "You two were here even before us."

Phelan chuckled, his skin turning gold as his claws lengthened from his fingers. When he looked at Camdyn again, gold eyes stared at him. "We could tell you the story, but I doona believe we have time for that."

"I agree," Charon said and released his god so that his skin turned copper.

Ian nudged Camdyn. Camdyn turned to find the other Warriors had released their gods. Sculel was ready for battle, demanding it. With barely a thought Camdyn's god surged free.

Power rippled through Camdyn. That was his woman in danger, his woman who was being used. Declan would pay for all he had done to Saffron.

Deirdre's laughter filled the peninsula. "Did you hear that? One of the infamous Warriors of MacLeod Castle will betray you!"

Fallon moved from behind a stone with Lucan and Quinn moving to either side of him. The brothers stood together, their skin black from their god.

"I know my men. They willna betray me," Fallon replied.

"Enough," Laria said. "Deirdre, this fight is between you and me, but if you want to make it more, I'll comply."

Deirdre sneered at her sister and shoved Saffron away from her. "Always so polite, Laria. Tell me, how did you hide your magic from me when we were children?"

Laria's answer was a sly smile. "It doesn't really matter now."

Camdyn felt Laria's magic build a second before she released a blast toward Deirdre. And just like that, the battle began.

Wyrran came running toward them screeching their fury. Camdyn glanced over to see several Warriors surrounding the Druids who stood behind Laria adding their magic to hers.

Camdyn let out a roar and raced to meet two wyrran. He held out his claws and sliced their heads off as he ran past them.

He saw Larena's iridescent skin as she impaled a mercenary through the heart right before she turned invisible again.

Camdyn growled when a wyrran jumped on his back and its claws sank into his skin. He elbowed the small beast in the face and smiled when he heard teeth crack.

"Maybe now you can actually close your lips over those nasty teeth," he yelled.

Camdyn reached behind him and grabbed the wyrran. He flipped the creature over his head, which caused the wyrran's claws to rip viciously from his back. He reared back his hand and decapitated the wyrran.

With each kill, with the blood on his hands and coating the earth, Camdyn's god smiled with glee. For the first time since he had gotten control of his god, Camdyn gave him free rein. He didn't care how many he had to kill as long as he got to Saffron.

Camdyn glanced up to see Saffron standing beside Declan, but her eyes were on him. Several mercs surrounded Declan and Saffron and began to open fire on the Warriors.

Camdyn barely had time to grab the dead wyrran and

hold it in front of his body. But it afforded him enough time to dive out of the way.

When he came to his feet, he took hold of Phelan and pulled him to the ground as X90 bullets rushed past them.

Phelan lifted his head and looked around. "Thanks, mate."

"Stay alert. Those bullets have *drough* blood in them."

"Bloody hell," Phelan muttered as he was off again.

Camdyn glanced around him to see Logan on one knee, his hands over his head and Gwynn desperately calling his name. Laria had warned them that Deirdre would try something, and it looked like she wasn't wrong.

He searched the others until he found Isla with Hayden beside her. By the way she swayed on her feet, her gaze locked with Deirdre's, something was going on between them.

But Camdyn knew both Logan and Isla would be all right as long as Gwynn and Hayden were there. So instead of helping his friends, he turned back to the battle.

Camdyn jumped to his feet and faced six wyrran. He smiled at them, ready for more death. He had sliced one's head off, and had taken the heart of another when the bullet slammed into his left side.

His leg gave out and he fell to his knee. Despite the fire now burning through his blood, Camdyn was able to kill three more wyrran.

And then the second bullet punctured his right shoulder.

Camdyn roared, the world beginning to spin. He braced his left hand on the ground and tried to slash at the sixth wyrran who was circling him.

The wyrran cut five gashes down his back. Before Camdyn could react, the wyrran had done it twice more. Pain from the *drough* blood filled every portion of his body, blinding him with agony.

Camdyn tried to stand, tried to use his claws, but the *drough* blood was sapping his strength. So much so that his wounds weren't healing as rapidly as they had before.

And then the wyrran collapsed on the ground, blood pooling from a hole in its chest where its heart had been.

"Get up," said Larena's voice near him.

Camdyn couldn't see her since she was invisible, but he felt her hands on his arm trying to get him to his feet. It would be so easy to lie down and let the *drough* blood in his veins have him.

But there was Saffron.

It took two tries, but Camdyn got on his feet. "Go," he told Larena. "Take out the mercenaries."

"My pleasure."

Camdyn knew he didn't have long before the *drough* blood killed him. He had to do something to help free Saffron, and it didn't look like he'd be fighting his way to her side now.

He pulled up the power of his god and focused it on the ground. The earth began to rumble. And then a wave rippled beneath the ground, starting at Camdyn's feet and aiming for Declan and his mercenaries.

Camdyn had just enough power to make sure Saffron was thrown free a moment before the earth opened up and swallowed Declan and the remaining two mercenaries.

Saffron couldn't take her eyes off Camdyn. She had seen him get shot. Twice. She knew he was in pain, but still he fought Declan.

She'd known as soon as the earth began to rumble that Camdyn was using his power. To her shock, he cast her out of the way.

Saffron hoped the fall would kill Declan, but if it had, his magic was still in place and controlling her. She tried to lift an arm, tried to call out to Camdyn. But the spell wouldn't release its hold.

There was no way she was going to have magic hold her when Camdyn was risking his life to save her. There had to be something she could do.

Then she recalled the words the ancients had told her. That her love for Camdyn would help her.

Saffron reached inside her and took hold of the love she had for Camdyn. Flashes filled her mind of the precious times they had spent together. His smile, his voice, his kisses.

She let them fill her until she was bursting with her love for him.

Her fingers curled into a fist. Hope sprang up in her chest, and she continued to let her love fill her. To her surprise, her magic welled up as well. It pushed against the spell like a battering ram. And with every heartbeat Saffron found she was gradually gaining back control over her body.

But would it be in time?

She saw the MacLeod brothers fighting side by side in deadly precision. Hayden, Ian, and Galen kept the Druids safe while Ramsey, Charon, Arran, Phelan, and Broc continued to battle the wyrran. Only Logan and Isla seemed to be in discomfort.

That's when she recalled Laria's warning to them. It didn't matter that Laria had been right, what mattered was everyone getting away with their lives intact.

Saffron noticed dead mercenaries lying all around her, but she hadn't seen any Warriors get close enough to kill one.

"Saffron?"

She jerked as she heard Larena's voice but couldn't see her. How could she have forgotten that Larena was able to turn invisible thanks to the goddess inside her?

"Can you hear me?"

Saffron managed to part her lips, but no words came.

A hand touched hers and Larena said, "If you can hear me, squeeze my fingers."

Saffron eagerly did as requested.

"Good. I rode in the helicopter, so I know there is a spell upon you. Can you break it?"

Saffron gave a light squeeze that she hoped told Larena she was trying.

"Stay safe. I'm going to get Camdyn so he can carry you out of here."

Saffron tried to squeeze again, but Larena was already gone. All she could do now was continue to beat against the spell and use the love within her to free herself.

* * *

Malcolm stood off to the side and watched the carnage the other Warriors were doling out. It was quite a sight to see the colored skin of the Warriors and how easily and savagely they killed.

And how ferociously they protected their women.

Malcolm's gaze found the deep brown skin of Camdyn. The Warrior's wounds weren't healing, and the blood that flowed freely from the wound in his shoulder and side told Malcolm the X90 bullets had been used.

He turned and found Saffron, still under Deirdre and Declan's spell and unable to move.

He'd heard her prophecy, but unlike the others, he knew none of the Warriors from the castle would betray them. It wasn't until Saffron's words that Malcolm knew what he had to do.

Laria's magic might be strong, but even with the Druids adding their magic to hers, it wasn't besting Deirdre. At least Declan and Robbie were no longer able to help Deirdre.

That just left one person who could help turn the tables and give the advantage to the MacLeods.

Malcolm walked up behind Deirdre. He met Fallon's gaze, and with a roar, he plunged his claws into Deirdre's back.

CHAPTER
FORTY-SIX

Saffron couldn't take her eyes off Malcolm. With his claws sunk deep in Deirdre's back, Deirdre screamed and tried to dislodge him as well as keep her magic strong as she battled Laria.

This was the time for Saffron to break the spell. This was the time for her to finally win over Declan.

She was able to move her arms now, and was beginning to move her legs. If only she could walk to Camdyn. He was still making his way toward her.

On either side of him was a gold-skinned Warrior and a bronze Warrior. She had no idea who they were, but it was enough that they were helping him fight the wyrran.

Saffron wanted to shout for joy when she was able to slide one of her feet forward. It wouldn't be long now before she would break the spell for good.

The agony was unbearable every time Camdyn tried to take a breath. But he wouldn't give up. His gaze was trained on Saffron even as he beheaded a wyrran.

When he faltered, he was surprised to find Charon and Phelan on either side of him. Camdyn tried to thank them, but all his concentration was focused on staying upright.

"You look like shit," Phelan said.

Camdyn grunted and peeled back his lips as the fire in

his veins burned hotter. He could feel his body begin to slow down, and not even his god could save him now.

He was going to die, of that he was certain. But if he could save Saffron he would be happy.

"Can you use your power again?" Charon asked.

Camdyn halted. As weak as he was he couldn't walk and use his power at the same time. "Will. Try," he bit out.

The ground beneath his feet began to shake, but it was as weak as he. Still, it might be enough to kill some of the wyrran.

Camdyn opened the earth to swallow dozens of wyrran. Their shrieks were cut off mid-sound when he closed the hole.

"Fuck me," Phelan said. "That's impressive."

There was a wave of *mie* magic that mushroomed out from Laria and the other Druids. Camdyn turned and found Ramsey now stood beside Laria.

The magic grew richer, stronger, and entirely more potent when Ramsey joined his magic with Laria's. It still boggled Camdyn's mind that Ramsey was part Druid as well as a Warrior.

Wyrran suddenly swarmed the Warriors protecting the Druids, and without a second thought Phelan and Charon joined the others in defending the Druids.

Camdyn wanted to help them, but he'd never make it. He was closer to Saffron anyway. With renewed vigor, he lifted a foot and started toward her.

The *mie* magic that surrounded him was so powerful he knew it was the only thing slowing the *drough* blood inside him. He'd taken half a dozen steps when Deirdre let out a frustrated, angry scream.

Camdyn watched as Laria and Ramsey's magic pushed Deirdre backward. Malcolm, it seemed, had betrayed Deirdre. He clawed her back again and again, cutting her hair each time.

Being attacked from the front as well as from the rear without Declan and his mercenaries to aid her was taking its toll on Deirdre.

Camdyn smiled. He'd waited a long time for the bitch to die. He'd wanted to be a part of it, but now the only person he cared about was Saffron.

When he looked back at Saffron it was to find she had taken a step toward him. It was as if she couldn't move. As if a spell had been put on her.

Camdyn fisted his hands and made his legs and feet get moving again. He was about ten steps from her when the magic swelled again, just before there was a loud boom.

He glanced over to find Deirdre was lying on the ground with Malcolm standing over her, but no one was cheering. That's when Camdyn saw tears roll down Saffron's face.

A look at the others showed there was another body on the ground as well. Sonya knelt beside Laria to try and heal her, but it wasn't working. None of them had realized it could very well cost Laria her life to end Deirdre's.

Relief swept through Camdyn that Deirdre had finally been vanquished, though he hated that Laria had lost her life in the process.

Now, he just needed to hold Saffron in his arms one last time. He managed to take two more steps before his legs gave out on him.

With the *mie* magic no longer filling the air, the *drough* blood had nothing to slow it.

"Camdyn!" Saffron yelled.

It took a considerable amount of effort to lift his gaze to Saffron. She had taken another step toward him, but it wasn't going to be soon enough.

Saffron's heart wrenched in her chest when she saw Camdyn fall to his knees. His god had faded, and his skin was pasty. He'd left a thick trail of blood on his way to her.

She had nearly gotten past the spell when he'd fallen. And now that she could see the life draining from him, her love pushed through the last of the spell. She couldn't allow him to die without holding him.

Instantly she could feel the difference in her body. She

started toward him when a hand grabbed her from behind, wrapping around her neck.

"You didna really think you could get away from me?" Declan whispered in her ear. "I told you, Saffron, you're mine."

"No," she said through clenched teeth.

"The Warrior is dying. You seem concerned. Does he mean something to you?"

"Leave her be," Camdyn ground out as his skin began to turn the deep, dark brown of his god.

Declan laughed. "What can you do, Warrior? My bullets are verra inventive, are they no'? Is it as painful as I've heard to have *drough* blood in you?"

Time slowed as Saffron heard Camdyn roar as he launched himself at Declan, his claws out and ready to kill. Camdyn grabbed Declan and spun him away from her.

The force sent Saffron tumbling to the ground. She didn't take her eyes off Camdyn though. He landed them so that he had a knee on Declan's chest, pinning him down.

Camdyn lifted his arm back, his claws out.

"No!" Saffron screamed as Robbie rose up behind Camdyn and fired the rifle. Camdyn jerked from the impact of the bullet and lifted his eyes to Saffron as he fell to the side.

Robbie helped Declan to his feet, and when he reached for her, Saffron let out a blast of magic so strong Declan and Robbie both went flying backward.

Saffron ignored them as she rushed to kneel beside Camdyn. Tears fell freely down her face when she caressed his face. The sight of her magnificent Warrior fading before her eyes was too much.

"Doona cry," Camdyn whispered.

She sniffed and bent to kiss him as the sound of the helicopter blades began to fill the air. "You'll be all right."

"Nay. It's too late."

"Don't say that. Please don't say that."

He took her hand in his and tried to smile. "I'm sorry for no' being in your bed when you woke."

"Shh. It doesn't matter," she said.

"But it does. I was afraid of the feelings you stirred within me. Feelings I swore I'd never feel again."

Saffron blinked through her tears and rested her forehead on his. The sound of the chopper grew distant as it rose in the air and flew away. "You can't die on me. I had a vision of you, Camdyn. You were laughing, and you had a child. A son."

He squeezed her hand. "I love you, Saffron Fletcher."

The sound of footsteps running toward them made Saffron glance up. She spotted Sonya and called for the Druid to hurry. When Saffron looked back at Camdyn his eyes were closed and his breathing had diminished to almost nothing.

"No," Saffron said. "No. He can't die."

Dani wrapped an arm around her and held her as Sonya's healing magic enveloped Camdyn.

"I'm going to need Warrior blood," Sonya called.

It was Phelan who held out his arm. "Take mine."

Saffron watched with bated breath as they turned Camdyn this way and that so Sonya's magic could pull the awful *drough* bullets from his body.

Phelan cut his arm with one of his golden claws and the blood flowed into Camdyn's wounds.

"I'm going to need more," Sonya said.

Isla shook her head. "Nay. Phelan's blood is . . . special."

With just a small amount of Phelan's blood in each wound Saffron could see them already healing. She rose up on her knees and kissed Phelan on the cheek.

"Thank you. From the bottom of my heart, thank you."

Phelan blinked, seeming to be taken aback by her show of affection.

"Saffron," Dani called, her voice filled with horror. "Oh, my God. Your back."

Saffron had forgotten her back and what Deirdre had done to her. It had been easy because Deirdre's magic had concealed the wounds and taken away the pain.

Now that Saffron had remembered, she could feel the wounds had opened and blood was pouring down her back and into the sleeveless corset she wore. The pain of her back and the frigid temperatures didn't matter though now that Camdyn would live.

Phelan stuck his arm out in front of Saffron's mouth. "Drink. It will heal you."

She recoiled. "You want me to drink your blood?"

"Just a small taste. You'll heal faster by ingesting it than if I put it on your wounds."

Saffron lifted her gaze to Isla who gave her a smile and an encouraging nod. Saffron waited for Phelan to cut his arm again, and then she leaned forward and licked up a bead of blood that ran down his arm.

Immediately she could feel her body healing. "How?" she asked him.

Phelan shrugged and stepped away from her to stand beside Charon.

Saffron forgot all about Phelan as Camdyn groaned and opened his eyes. Saffron smiled through her tears and moved aside a lock of his midnight hair that had fallen in his face.

"Saffron?" Camdyn said.

"Phelan's blood is apparently very powerful. He healed you after Sonya got the bullets out."

Camdyn hadn't expected to live. He'd felt the life drain out of him, had known he was leaving all he knew and loved behind. He hadn't wanted to, but not even his god could save him.

He climbed to his feet, and after helping Saffron up he held out his arm to Phelan. As they clasped forearms Camdyn said, "I owe you a debt."

"Nay," Phelan said and released his arm.

Camdyn helped Sonya to her feet. "Thank you."

Sonya gave a short laugh. "I did nothing. It was all Phelan."

"He healed Saffron as well," Dani said.

Camdyn's gaze jerked back to Saffron. "What is Dani talking about?"

Saffron shrugged as someone draped a coat around her shoulders. "Nothing."

"Deirdre flayed her back," said a male voice in the back of the crowd.

Everyone parted until Malcolm could be seen. No one said a word as they looked at him, the scars Deirdre's Warriors had given him visible once more now that Deirdre was dead.

Malcolm gave a nod to Saffron. "You can tell Camdyn yourself now."

"I will," she said with a smile and slid her hand into Camdyn's.

Camdyn saw Deirdre's body as well as Laria's. "So they both died?"

"Laria was Deirdre's twin," Ramsey said. "In Laria's effort to kill Deirdre, it took her life since they are connected."

Ian nodded solemnly. "Twins are connected in ways that people doona understand."

There was a pause as everyone's mind went to Duncan, Ian's twin, who was killed by Deirdre's order but by Malcolm's hand.

"I'll never be able to make up for that," Malcolm said.

Ian released a deep breath. "You helped kill Deirdre. That's certainly a good start."

"It's time to celebrate Deirdre's demise," Logan said as he rubbed his hands together.

Camdyn looked down at Saffron and caressed the line of her jaw.

"You didn't stop coming for me," she said.

"I told you I'd always protect you."

"I didn't lie, Camdyn. I did have that vision of you with your son. I don't have visions about my future."

He pulled her against him and gave her a light kiss. He wanted her to forget about that vision for right now. Right now, he wanted her to know how much he loved her. "Did you hear me? I love you."

She laughed and wrapped her arms around him. "And I love you."

"Then that's all that matters. I fought what was between us, and I was a fool. I know what I feel, and I know you are the other half of me." He paused and swallowed. His future depended on her. "I need you, Saffron. With me. Always. Without you—"

She kissed him, stopping his words. Her amazing magic swirled around him, uniting them and strengthening their love. "I could never resist you, my Warrior. I'm yours. I've always been yours."

"Just what I needed to hear."

EPILOGUE

MacLeod Castle
Later that day . . .

Camdyn had a new take on life now that he had been given a second chance. He put away the hurt of the past and looked to the woman who had opened his eyes to the world around him.

He laughed more in a few hours than he had in centuries. He even danced. It had surprised Saffron when he pulled her out onto the floor, but her laughter as they danced around the great hall had been worth it.

But more than anything he had Saffron. He didn't care about her vision she'd had of him and his son. Whatever the future held was not something he could change. He would face it, however painful it was, because her love gave him that strength.

Added to their joy was the call she'd received on her mobile from her attorney stating the judge had halted all proceeds of Elise's claim of Saffron's demise. Elise, however, was another matter they'd have to take care of soon.

Camdyn wasn't looking forward to meeting the woman, but regardless, she was Saffron's mother.

Saffron touched his arm and whispered, "I need to sit down."

Camdyn took in her pale, waxy complexion and immediately brought her to the table where she sank onto the bench. "Sonya," he called.

"I'm fine," Saffron argued as she laid her head on her arms on the table. "I'm just a little nauseous."

Sonya hurried to them. "What is it?"

"Saffron. She's no' feeling well."

"It's just everything I've been through," Saffron said.

Camdyn didn't need to prod Sonya because the Druid already had her hands raised over Saffron and her healing magic flowing. A few moments later Sonya lowered her arms and slowly looked at Camdyn with wide eyes.

His gut clenched. After surviving death and Saffron living through her time with Declan and Deirdre, he couldn't imagine her ill. "What is it?"

"She's carrying your child."

Saffron jerked so abruptly she almost fell off the bench. Camdyn steadied her, as dumbstruck as she.

"But I was taking the potion you and the others make monthly to keep all of us from getting pregnant," Saffron said.

Sonya laughed and shrugged her shoulders as she rose to her feet. "What will be, will be. No magic can stop that."

Camdyn sat beside Saffron as they looked at each other. Then a slow smile pulled at his lips. "My son, perhaps?"

"But . . . I never have visions of my future."

"There's a first time for everything. You said yourself your magic increased after being in the labyrinth."

Saffron blinked, an excited smile forming. "I don't think I've ever been happier."

Camdyn agreed with her, and knew there was something else he needed. "There's only one more thing that can complete this day."

"What's that?"

"Be my wife."

Her eyes filled with tears before she threw her arms around him. "Yes. God, yes!"

"We're going to have another wedding," Hayden bellowed near them.

Camdyn and Saffron shared a laugh and several kisses as the great hall erupted in cheers.

Malcolm smiled as he watched Camdyn and Saffron celebrate their love. He felt the tug of scarred skin on his cheek and the smile faded. He was able to move his right arm, but only because of the power of his god. With Deirdre gone, her magic was as well, which meant the scars she'd hidden for him were once more visible to the world.

He hadn't peered into a mirror yet, but he didn't need to. He knew exactly what the scars looked like. But his scars were nothing. One of the world's greatest evils was gone.

It felt good to defeat Deirdre and return to MacLeod Castle.

But he couldn't stay.

As much as he wanted to call the castle home, he couldn't. The things he had done for Deirdre were too horrific. He needed to atone for those things before he would feel comfortable in the castle again, and he wasn't sure if eternity was long enough to make up for his sins.

"You're leaving, aren't you?" Larena asked as she approached.

Malcolm nodded. "I was going to say farewell this time."

"Sure," she said dejectedly.

He tried to ignore her sad smile. "I'll return. One day."

"You're welcome to stay. You belong here, Malcolm."

He opened the door and looked out at the clouds hovering in the sky, signaling another snowstorm. "I doona know where I belong."

"You're family. Remember that," she said, and kissed his cheek.

Malcolm wrapped his arms around her and hugged her fiercely. "Thank you for no' giving up on me."

"Never," she whispered.

Malcolm lifted his gaze to find Fallon staring at them. Malcolm inclined his head to Fallon who returned the gesture. With a sigh, Malcolm pulled away from Larena.

"Be careful out there," Larena said.

Malcolm forced a half smile for her sake. "I'm a Warrior. You should worry about everyone else."

He walked out of the castle before he changed his mind and stayed. He'd already decided where he was headed first. Declan's mansion. The bastard needed to die.

Phelan sighed as Isla stood in front of him. He'd ignored her up until then, but the Druid wouldn't be disregarded.

"Thank you for helping us, especially for what you did for Camdyn and Saffron."

He shrugged and lifted the mug of ale to his lips. "It's nothing."

"I hope you and Charon decide to stay," Isla said, her ice blue eyes hopeful as she watched him.

Phelan lifted a shoulder in a shrug. "I did what I came to do."

"There is still Declan to defeat."

"As long as the bastard stays away from me, I doona have a problem with him."

Isla rolled her eyes. "Don't be a fool. Declan isn't done. He has a plan, and all we can hope for is to kill him before he carries it out."

Phelan stood and set aside his mug. "Good luck with that."

"Don't you want your god bound?"

He halted in his tracks and slowly turned to face her. "You have that spell?"

"No, but we're searching for it. Laria gave us a clue to where it might be. Now that Deirdre is dead, we can search for it."

For several moments he regarded her before he said, "I like being immortal."

"Can you forgive me for what I did to you?" Isla asked before he could walk away.

Phelan didn't bother to look at her as he shook his head. "You took me away from my family when I was just four years old. I doona even remember them or even where I came from. What do you think?"

"You're from the northern Highlands near Oykel Bridge, Phelan. You had two older siblings and three younger brothers."

It was more than he'd ever had before, and he wouldn't beg for more. Phelan strode from the castle toward his motorcycle. A trip to the north was in order.

Declan sat on the chair and held the mirror up to watch as David stitched the gashes the Warrior had given him when he'd yanked Declan away from Saffron.

He still couldn't believe Saffron had bested him. She was supposed to have been under a spell, but it appeared the Seer was more powerful than he'd realized.

But more upsetting than losing Saffron was discovering Deirdre was well and truly dead. The MacLeods had beaten her with the help of Laria.

Deirdre was supposed to have been his. They were supposed to have ruled the world together. The MacLeods with their Warriors and Druids would pay for what they had taken from him.

"Declan," Robbie said as he walked into Declan's bedroom. "We found her."

Declan finally had something to smile about. "Tara thought she could stay hidden from me. I told her she'd be back."

"Shall I go for her?"

"No," Declan said with a shake of his head. "I'll go for her. She willna be able to refuse me. Prepare the car."

Robbie hesitated and Declan narrowed his gaze. "What?"

"I think it would be better if I recruited more men first. All of them died during the battle."

Declan slammed his fist on his leg and glared at the doctor when he stuck Declan with the needle. "I'll give you two days to round up some men."

"Two days," Robbie repeated, and left the room.

Declan drummed his fingers on his leg. He knew he'd been lucky to leave Orkney with his life. Saffron could have done much more damage had she not been so concerned with that Warrior.

With the spells he'd put around the house there was no way anyone from MacLeod Castle was going to get in. And once he had Tara they wouldn't be able to get away from him fast enough.

Read on for a look ahead to

MIDNIGHT'S WARRIOR

The next Dark Warrior novel,
coming in December from
Donna Grant and St. Martin's Paperbacks!

Dunnoth Tower
Northern Scotland

Tara tapped her toe beneath her desk as she discreetly listened to her iPod in one ear. She quite enjoyed her job as a booking agent, tour guide, bookkeeper, and anything else they needed at the castle.

She hadn't thought of where she would go when she left Edinburgh after that disastrous run-in with the Warriors and Druids. She'd driven and driven and driven until the road had led her to the sea and Dunnoth Tower.

Tara had stopped at the medieval castle to eat and stretch her legs. She'd been instantly taken with the structure and took the tour of it. To her surprise there had been a position open, and she'd applied. She'd started work that very day.

It had only been a few weeks, but she was thoroughly enjoying her time at Dunnoth, which she hadn't expected after teaching. Yet she found the quiet and peace of the castle and the North Sea helped to settle the turmoil inside her.

It also helped that the owners were pleasant, her coworkers friendly, and the tourists so eager to learn about the castle that they weren't much of a problem to handle.

Although tourism in the middle of January in the far north of Scotland wasn't much of anything to talk about.

Most tourists were at the ski resorts, but come summer, the castle was going to be very busy.

Tara looked forward to it. For now, she was reading over the accounting books to make sure everything was in order, and booking the castle for the summer.

A door opened to her left and in walked the newest castle employee. Tara's mouth had dropped open the first time she saw the tall, black-headed hunk with the amazing gray eyes that seemed to see right into her soul.

That had been the day before. And now she found herself staring at him again as he walked across the entryway and began to work on the electrical outlet that had shorted out months ago.

Though this time she did manage to keep her mouth closed and not make a complete fool of herself.

He filled out his navy short-sleeve tee to perfection with his thick shoulders and muscular arms. Yesterday evening they'd been hit with a rain and snow mix, and he'd been caught in it. When he'd come rushing into the castle with his shirt plastered to his abs, she'd been able to count each and every muscle in that washboard stomach of his.

Having seen that made her wish she could see him without his shirt on to get a good glimpse of that tanned skin and ripped body.

Tara smiled. She'd always been a sucker for a man who knew how to take care of himself. But with Ramsey it wasn't just his body. It was his long, black hair that hung past his shoulders with just a hint of a wave to the shiny locks. He kept it pulled away from his face in a ponytail, but she longed to see him with it all down.

Then there was his face. She sighed. What a face it was. Sculpted jaw with just a small shadow of whiskers, square chin, strong nose, and a high forehead with black brows slashed over his eyes. His lips were full and wide, and he had eyelashes so thick, so black that any woman would be envious of them. His steel-gray eyes held a hint of laughter in them, as if he knew far more than anyone around him, and he wasn't going to share.

"Good morn," Ramsey said in his deep baritone voice.

A shiver raced over Tara's skin every time he spoke, like her body was dialed into his husky voice. "Morning, Ramsey."

"What are you listening to?" he asked. He stopped at the wall and bent to open his toolbox and pulled out a couple of tools.

Tara blinked. "Huh?"

Ramsey glanced at her and smiled. "Your music, lass. What are you listening to?"

"Ah . . . Rihanna," she answered, still baffled that he had known she had her iPod on. She had turned it down low enough so that no one would hear, and the cords to her earplugs were hidden by her hair.

Tara's heart began to pound as her mind raced. Had the Warriors found her again? She scooted her rolling chair back, prepared to grab her purse and keys and run.

Until she spotted the white cord against her black sweater.

She looked at Ramsey to find him staring at her. After a moment, he shrugged and turned his back to her.

Tara released a long sigh and put her elbow on the desk before she dropped her head into her hand. She was so paranoid. She hated living her life this way, but for her, there wasn't another way.

Because she was a Druid. And not just any Druid.

She was a dangerous one.

Tara squeezed her eyes closed and thought over the past ten years of her life. It wasn't that she'd had a good or bad childhood. It had been average, just like her grades in school.

Hell, *she* had been average. Average height, average looks, average clothes, average everything.

She had known since she was a small child that she had magic. It ran strong through her family, which never worried her. That is, until the day of her eighteenth birthday, when she learned far more about the Druids than she had ever been told before.

Her family had lied to her all those years before, telling her that all Druids were the same. Not only were there two different kinds of Druids—*mies*, the good Druids, and *droughs*, the ones who dabbled in black magic and gave their souls to the Devil—but her family were all *droughs*.

That wasn't what bothered her. What made her begin to run was that they wanted her to become *drough* as well. They demanded she give her soul to Satan, condemning her to Hell when she died.

For some odd, inexplicable reason, that didn't bother anyone in her family. Just her. And they didn't understand her. Not that they ever had before.

Tara hadn't wanted anything extraordinary out of life. She had just wanted a life. A husband who loved her, children surrounding her, and a house filled with lots of laughter.

Instead, she couldn't stay anywhere too long before she had to leave again. Already she had spent ten years in Scotland, which was most likely ten years too long. She should have gone somewhere else when she ran away from her family, but she had always loved Scotland too much to leave.

However, she knew this was her last stop in her beloved land. She was going to have to leave. And it saddened her.

It was just five days until her birthday. She had always thought by the time she reached twenty-eight she'd have at least two children.

Instead, she was alone.

She didn't even allow herself to make friends, because friends asked questions and became curious about her past. And she hated lying. So she kept to herself.

There had been one time she'd made the mistake of thinking someone was a friend. But Declan Wallace had been anything but.

To this day she didn't know how he had found her in that pub in Aberdeen, but his good looks, charm, and silver tongue did the trick for a scared, confused eighteen-year-old who had run away from home.

Tara should have known what kind of man he was, but she blamed her emotional state for overlooking it. She had stayed at his mansion for a month before she'd learned he was a Druid.

When he didn't push her to undergo the ceremony to become *drough*, she worked with him on strengthening her magic for several more months. Tara had been careful about how much she used her magic. No one, least of all her, had understood why her magic was so out of control.

But Declan had pressed her to use more of it, to learn to control it. He hadn't understood her reluctance, and she hadn't told him. Nothing had worked, yet he hadn't been upset. He seemed to enjoy the fact that her magic was all over the place. If her emotions were high, she could blow up a light bulb without even trying.

Then one night, she hadn't been able to sleep and she'd ventured downstairs to get something to eat when she'd overheard Declan's plans for her.

Once again she was on the run.

She knew eventually she would be caught. Would it be by her family? The Warriors after her? Or Declan? Which would it be that ended her life? Would they come in the middle of the night, or in the light of day? Did it even matter anymore?

"Tara?"

She jerked at the feel of Ramsey's hand on her arm. "Yes?" she asked as she tugged the bud out of her ear.

"Are you all right?" His brow was knitted, his gray eyes full of concern.

"Yes," she lied.

He raised a thick black brow and flattened his lips. "I doona believe you're telling me the truth, but I willna press you."

The heat of his body seared her skin through her sweater where his hand was, but it didn't hurt. What it did was cause her blood to heat and made her think of leaning close and pressing her lips against his.

She cleared her throat and looked away from his hypnotic eyes. "I'm fine. Really," she said and plastered on a smile as she glanced at him.

He released her and stepped back. Instantly she missed his nearness, his touch, and his heat. How he could walk around in a short-sleeve tee in this frigid January weather where snow was several feet thick she didn't know. But she wished she could do the same.

"How long have you been at Dunnoth Tower?" he asked as he once more knelt in front of the outlet on the opposite wall.

She hated when people asked her questions, but for some reason she wanted to answer Ramsey's. Which wasn't a good sign for her at all. "A few weeks."

He pulled the outlet from the wall and inspected it before he twisted a few wires. "Hmm," he responded.

"What brought you here?" She licked her lips, refusing to wonder what made her ask her own question. She never did this. It made it appear as if she were interested when she needed to keep her distance.

But there was something so alluring, so fascinating about Ramsey that she couldn't help herself.

"Chance, maybe." He shrugged and tightened a wire. "Who knows? How about you?"

"I was driving and the road took me here."

He looked up and met her gaze. "Definitely chance on your part."

She grinned as she leaned her forearms on her desk. She had no idea what had come over her asking and answering questions. And she had even left her answer open so Ramsey could ask something else.

But he didn't.

The fact he didn't gave her the insane urge to inquire about something else. Thankfully, the phone rang, saving her from making an utter fool of herself.

Tara kept glancing at Ramsey as she looked at the calendar for booking a company conference. She grew agitated at the woman on the other end of the line because Ramsey was finishing up with the outlet and she was still on the phone.

And then Ramsey closed his toolbox and stood. He gave her a smile and walked away.

Tara sighed. "I beg your pardon, ma'am. I didn't hear that last bit. Could you repeat?"

As she wrote down the dates in the calendar and calculated the deposit, Tara told herself now wasn't the time to find a man she was interested in.

The problem was there was never a good time for her to get involved with anyone. . . .